KITH
AND
KIN
ANDRÉ
KAMINSKI

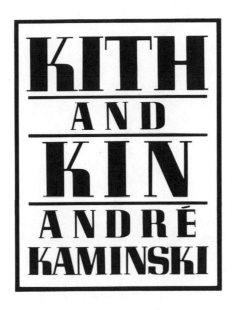

KITH AND KIN
ANDRÉ KAMINSKI

TRANSLATED BY
HARRY ZOHN

FROMM INTERNATIONAL
PUBLISHING CORPORATION

NEW YORK

Designed by Kingsley Parker

Printed in the United States of America

First U.S. Edition

Library of Congress Cataloging-in-Publication Data

Kaminski, André, 1923–
  Kith and kin.

  Translation of: Nächstes Jahr in Jerusalem.
  I. Title.
PT2671.A446N3313   1988   833'.914   88–305
ISBN 0–88064–104–5

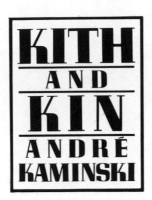

KITH
AND
KIN
ANDRÉ
KAMINSKI

1

~~~

MY UNCLE HENNER ROSENBACH WAS ONE, A PSYCHO-path and two, the most magnificent liar of the Austro-Hungarian dual monarchy. In theory he was my great-uncle, but I doubt this, for he resembled me incomparably more than did his brother Leo, who is supposed to have been my grandfather. In any case, Uncle Henner was a descendant of the famous rabbi Shloime Rosenbach, who wrote his treatises in the Bukovina three hundred years ago and on whose gravestone appears the following maxim: "Truth is the most precious of all possessions, and should be used sparingly and with restraint." My family has always tried to live by this motto. For generations we made pilgrimages to Czernowitz every year on Yom Kippur, that holy day, to pray for the soul of our great ancestor. When Czernowitz came to be behind the Iron Curtain, this custom ended, but the old scholar's descendants were consoled by the fact that his epigram became the maxim of the international communist system from the Elbe River to the coast of the Sea of Japan.

Time and again people have asked me what my Uncle Henner's profession was. To this I respond with an embarrassed cough, "You know, he was—how shall I put it?—a dreamer." I know that this is not a satisfactory answer. Dreaming is not exactly a profession and does not earn one a living, but then Uncle Henner is not living any more. He died sixty years ago, utterly destitute and ostracized by his family, even by my closest relatives, who were and are

1

not a whit better than he. Nevertheless, I must explain how he earned a living. He was a *shnorrer,* and among us Jews this amounts to an occupation and is in any case a source of income. He called himself an inventor, which is not entirely untrue. You see, he lived off his inventions, but in all those years he invented only one thing, and opinions differ even about that. He invented color photography. Unceasingly, nonstop.

Both Uncle Henner and his brother Leo, supposedly my grandfather, dedicated their lives to the true-to-life depiction of reality on photosensitive material—at that time, glass plates. I assume that this was no accident. My family has always had a troubled relationship to facts. The reflection of objects gives us greater pleasure than the objects themselves. Nothing fascinates us more than a successful illusion. If, however, my grandfather confined himself to reproducing the forms of the Almighty, Uncle Henner endeavored to imitate the colors as well, with such perfection that no one was supposed to recognize the distinction between semblance and reality. His goal was the duplication of the world, total schizophrenia through the creation of a secondary reality that could be preserved, retouched, or, if necessary, destroyed at will.

Thus the Rosenbach brothers lived and died for photography, that peculiar black art somewhere between optics, chemistry, and painting that the fateful magician Louis Daguerre had devised in the 1830s. They were practitioners of black art in the truest sense of the term, and Uncle Henner attempted to enrich the black component of that craft with the hundred nuances of the spectrum. But I don't want to get ahead of the events, and so I shall begin my account . . .

Leo Rosenbach, the person who is said to have been my grandfather, came to Stanislav in order to get married. He was already over forty and still a bachelor, though he could look back upon a successful career. For twenty years he had lived in Munich as the court photographer of Ludwig II of Bavaria. He knew—at least from afar—the pleasures of life, which he had been able to admire countless times through the lens of his camera. Strange that despite this he was still wandering through life without a wife. Why did my grandfather-to-be leave Munich, a city so full of joie de vivre, to seek his fortune in the sleepy provinces? This was attributed to his nature. Despite his excessive shyness, he is said to have had a tendency toward bluntness and calling a spade a spade. Princess von Fürstenberg, whose figure left a lot to be desired, is supposed to have complained that Leo Rosenbach had made an unflattering portrait of her. The king sent for the court photographer and asked what he had to say to the noblewoman's complaint. My grandfather made a deep bow and declared that the portrait was a perfect likeness of the lady. If she did not like it, she should argue with her procreators and not with him. His Majesty could not suppress a little smirk, but that day Leo Rosenbach's career at the Munich court came to an end. He had to pack his bags and be on his way—to the land of his ancestors.

At the Stanislav railroad station my grandfather's fate was decided, and consequently mine as well. As providence would have it, a porter named Simche Pilnik took charge of Leo Rosenbach's baggage to transport it to the Hotel Bristol, which was located on Jagiellonska Street and was reputed to offer the most luxurious accommodations in town. On the way it turned out that Simche Pilnik was not only a baggage handler but also a so-called *shadchen*, a matchmaker, who took advantage of his main occupation to obtain clients for his sideline.

It was a wet, cold April day, and the city was drowning in slush. Cheerless windows gaped from crumbling facades. Behind these windows sleepy citizens were stretching and yawning. The streets stank of urine and the cheap booze the Poles call *bimber*. Horse-drawn carriages rumbled past, spraying slush to all sides. The pedestrians muttered im-

3

precations, turned up their collars, and slipped into dark archways. After only a few steps Leo Rosenbach sensed that this place would bring him no luck. He told Simche Pilnik to turn around and take his luggage back to the station. The porter stopped for a moment, then went up to the stranger and whispered something in his ear. Ten minutes later my grandfather signed the hotel register as Leo Rosenbach, Royal Court Photographer from Munich. He was given the most elegant room, which was usually reserved only for prominent people. That evening everyone in Stanislav knew that a celebrity had arrived.

The following Thursday Leo Rosenbach called on the matchmaking porter and had a conversation with him that was to have decisive consequences. Simche Pilnik produced a dozen photos of extremely well-built ladies, casually mentioning each one's dowry. With a theatrical gesture he threw one picture after another on the table, like a card-player showing his trumps. My grandfather seemed bored. At each succeeding photo he emitted a grunt indicating that he had seen better out in the world. The twelfth picture caused him to jump: "Who is that?" The *shadchen* wrinkled his nose and said disdainfully, "The daughter of a tanner's assistant. Not bad-looking, but she doesn't have anything." Leo Rosenbach rose from his chair and said emphatically, "Mr. Pilnik, she's the only one for me!"

That Sunday in early spring the sun shone, and the court photographer paid a formal call on the tanner's assistant. Here I must explain that Leo was small, almost dwarflike. For that reason he was wearing calfskin shoes with buckles and high heels, yellowish brown striped flannel pants, a tight-fitting velvet jacket, and a big top hat. This made him appear somewhat taller, but it did not make his figure less ludicrous. Leo Rosenbach was downhearted as he walked through the streets of the outlying workers' district in which the Wertheimers inhabited a miserable hovel. The gorgeous Jana, whom Simche Pilnik had called "not bad-looking," stood impatiently behind a lace curtain

4

and peered out at the bend of the road, for the mysterious suitor would soon emerge around it. She knew no more about him than her parents did. All she knew was that he was a celebrity, the court photographer from Munich who occupied the most elegant suite of the Hotel Bristol, and that he intended to marry her. Today he would ask for her hand in marriage, this Prince Charming who was said to have turned pale at the sight of her photo and to have exclaimed, "Mr. Pilnik, she's the only one for me!" She imagined him to be like Tamino in *The Magic Flute*, and since she was not only beautiful but overemotional, she expected a demigod, Michelangelo's David.

There is a Jewish saying that every disappointment is the compound interest of a self-deception. When I say that Jana Wertheimer was disappointed, I am not telling the whole truth. She was not disappointed; she was absolutely furious, to put it mildly—disgusted and outraged because they were imposing "something like that" upon her. She caught sight of the gussied-up Lilliputian—"pet terrier" is what she called him—as he walked gingerly up to their house and pulled the bell—cautiously, as if he wanted to apologize for having come at all and for being presumptuous enough to call on his highness, the tanner's assistant. The girl was seized with disgust and unspeakable rage at her parents, who had sent for this "microorganism." What had happened to her Prince Charming, her Tamino, her marble David? Her dreams shattered, Jana took flight. She did not know where, but come what may, she was determined not to meet this "runt." She screamed that she would die if he kissed her hand, let alone her mouth. Jana lost her head, and, even though it is true, no one will believe what happened next. She ran out into the back yard, which was surrounded on all sides by a palisade. She was trapped and could not escape her destiny. In the yard there was only a plum tree with a gnarled trunk and empty branches. With death-defying courage the girl climbed up that tree, and when she could not go any higher, clung to a branch as though she were drowning. Suddenly the gate to the back yard opened and old Wertheimer came panting up, mold-green with rage and incapable of uttering a sensible sentence. "Jana, you're breaking my neck. You're throwing shame in my face. My hand's gonna grow out of my grave, and I'll bust a gut if you don't come down."

"Let it bust. I don't want to live any more."

Aaron Wertheimer rumpled his sparse hair and shrieked, "The court photographer has come from Munich. That's three times as far as Berdichev, and he served the king of Bavaria. But you're sitting on a tree without shoes, in the middle of winter, freezing your feet off."

"Let them freeze off. I don't care."

Now the tanner's assistant lost his head completely. "He comes from Munich special for you, but you make a *shmuck* out of your father, because he's only a filthy workingman and has red hands because he isn't a lawyer but a piece of cow dung that's got to toil from early till late so the young lady can play the piano and read Latin books. I'm having a stroke."

"Go ahead and have one. I'm staying where I am."

That was too much. He ran back into the house and returned clutching an ax. Cursing and wheezing, he began to whack away at the tree trunk. He hoped the tree would come crashing down with his daughter and bury him. At that point a dwarf came running up, determined to alter the course of events. It was the court photographer, who rushed at the raving father and demanded that he stop immediately. "Madness is no argument, Mr. Wertheimer. This won't get you anywhere."

The tanner's assistant had not expected this. He was so dumbfounded that he put the ax down and wiped the sweat from his forehead in perplexity. Leo Rosenbach took three silver pipes out of his pocket and skillfully put them together. He pursed his lips, pressed them tenderly against the mouthpiece, and began to improvise a doleful melody. It sounded so delicate and exotic that suddenly a voice came from the tree.

6

"God, how beautiful this is! Who composed it?"

The dwarf looked up, saw the princess of his dreams for the first time, and whispered what he had whispered that evening at Simche Pilnik's. "She's the only one for me!"

She was, in point of fact, a hundred times more charming than in the picture that the *shadchen* had shown him, even though her eyes were still flashing with rage. Her black hair curled over her neck and her shoulders like a tangle of angry adders. Around the corners of her mouth flitted a barely perceptible smile. Leo Rosenbach answered more gently than ever before—or afterward, "This melody wasn't composed by anyone. It is a dewdrop that fell from heaven. By the way, I am your husband-to-be and have brought you your bridal present."

"What bridal present?"

"Climb down, Miss Wertheimer! I can't give it to you up there!"

The miracle happened, the only miracle in my grandfather's life. Jana came down from the tree and struck a royal pose in front of the "microorganism." "You claim to be my husband-to-be. That's strange. I didn't even know I was engaged."

Leo Rosenbach took a black case from his vest pocket and opened it. In it lay a pearl necklace of shimmering beauty. Jana could not believe her eyes. She touched the necklace with her fingertips, took it out carefully, and put it around her neck. Old Wertheimer, who did not understand any of this, stood next to her and screamed, "Jana, are you *meshugge*?"

"Yes."

"And?"

"I'm going to marry him."

"Do you like him?"

"No, but I'll marry him anyway."

The wedding was as dreary as most weddings. This one was even drearier, because the Wertheimers were among the liberals: neither a candle for the Good Lord nor a pitchfork for the Devil. They were somewhere in between, or more precisely, nowhere. They regarded themselves as enlightened, but they were not happy. Leo Rosenbach was of the same type. He knew neither Hebrew nor Yiddish (at least that is what he claimed), spoke German with a pronounced Bavarian accent, dabbed himself with French perfume, and wore English suits. In his circle people loudly declared their faith in the exact sciences and dabbled in physics and biology. They thought they had a deep insight into the world because they had memorized a few formulas. Of course there was no such thing as miracles; these were ridiculed. Whenever something incomprehensible happened, they were amused and shook their heads. Yet they behaved in an extremely unscientific way; they raved, raged, and tore their shirts over some stupid nonsense. They did not cease to be Jews, but less out of loyalty to tradition than out of fear of death. They made fun of the rabbi, but recognized his authority in nonmaterial matters. A passport to the beyond could be useful sooner or later. That is why the wedding was celebrated according to the Jewish ritual.

Mr. Kobryner, the chief rabbi of Stanislav, was scheduled to give the address. Simche Pilnik took care of the practical details, especially the seating arrangements. He was the only one who knew how much property each one had, and thus whether he had to be seated up front or in back. The main problem, however, was visual. How should the bride and the groom be placed so as to keep people from noticing that dainty Jana was taller than Leo Rosenbach, her prominent court photographer from Munich? After all, they were going to be photographed as a permanent record for future generations. Simche Pilnik came up with a solution. He had a carpenter build a throne from which the bridegroom could tower over the entire wedding party from a majestic height.

A Hasidic orchestra played jolly tunes, and everyone waited for the speech of the chief rabbi, who had joined the celebration even though Aaron Wertheimer was only an uncultured tanner's assistant. But he had a daughter, the incomparable Jana, and no Jew in Galicia would have missed the opportunity to see the sparkling girl from up close. Besides, here was a chance to gape at a man who knew the king of Bavaria, the famous Ludwig II, the world-renowned patron of the arts and personal friend of Richard Wagner. For years Leo Rosenbach had been on intimate terms with him, so to speak.

In short, the chief rabbi accepted the invitation, and delivered a sermon on the mystery of the photograph as a symbol of eternal life: "Dear members of the wedding party, the Scripture says that thou shalt not make any graven images for thyself. That is why there are people who regard photography as a sin. They are mistaken. You see, the commandment has a deeper meaning: Thou shalt not make a false—I emphasize *false*—image for thyself. Thou shalt not poach on God's preserves! He knows what he is doing, and he does it well. The commandment concerns painting, and particularly bad painting, such as is being done in Paris and in Vienna today. The Almighty wanted to warn us against all the daubers and scratchers who in their presumption try to alter Creation. *They* are what the Holy Writ refers to, not the true-to-nature depiction of God's work. Maimonides taught that a mirror is without sin, and the blasphemy begins only with the distortion of reality, for it is written that thou shalt not bear false witness. Thou shalt not lie! A mirror does not lie. It only reproduces what it sees. It is the same with photography. What is beautiful is beautiful; what is ugly remains ugly. Photography praises God's perfection. It lends permanence to what shall endure. It preserves what deserves to exist beyond death. Who would keep our bridegroom, the honorable Mr. Rosenbach, from capturing for all time on a glass plate the incomparable harmoniousness and the unique splendor of his young bride Jana from the house of Wertheimer? Is it not the real duty and obligation of a human being to praise

God's miraculous work? Is it not the expression of true love to depict the beloved object in its bloom? Is there anyone in this hall who knows a better way of glorifying the youth of this Jewish girl than by means of this photographic apparatus?"

"I do, chief rabbi. I know a far better way . . ."

Someone must have gone crazy. No one had ever before dared to interrupt the chief rabbi of Stanislav. True, he had asked a question, but surely not with the intention of receiving an answer. But now someone stood up who had evidently come from nowhere, a stranger, an uninvited person whose existence Simche Pilnik had not even been aware of, and this nonperson had the *chutzpa* to take the floor. "Yes, indeed, chief rabbi. In a matter of weeks I shall produce a machine, the prismatograph, that will capture the budding youth of this young woman a thousand times more perfectly than Leo Rosenbach is able to do. To Leo Rosenbach the lips of this girl are black; to me they are red. To Leo Rosenbach the pearls of her necklace are gray; to me they are as rosy as the dawn. Leo Rosenbach too is poaching on the Creator's preserve, for he botches—yes, ladies and gentlemen—*botches* God's work and reduces the numberless colors of reality to black, gray, and white . . ."

An angry mutter ran through the wedding party. Old Wertheimer went up to the troublemaker and was about to throw him out unceremoniously when the court photographer raised his hand soothingly and said in a conciliatory tone, "Leave this person in peace, Mr. Wertheimer. He is my brother and doesn't know what he is doing."

That was the climax of a celebration that the participants would probably have forgotten if crazy Henner had not put on his act. After Leo's noble words he rose from his chair and went up to the newlyweds' table, where he put on another show. He fell on his knees in front of Jana, seized her hand, and gave her a long and zestful kiss on her fingertips. Jana gladly acquiesced, for she really liked her brother-in-law. He matched her fantasy image of

Tamino from *The Magic Flute,* and was the exact opposite of the man she had married. When Henner rose to his feet again, she looked deep into his eyes and asked him, blushing slightly, "You want to invent color photography, Mr. Rosenbach? I think that's splendid, and am looking forward to it. When will it be ready?"

"You can call me Henner, my pretty child. We are related now and have many things to do together, don't we?"

That was typical of Henner. He skirted the question about the timetable of his invention with an answer that was to plunge Jana into lifelong confusion.

After the wedding day Uncle Henner stayed with his brother, who had acquired a house on Mickiewicz Street and fixed up a studio in it. This house was roomy, and yet it was too small for its three inhabitants. Everything in it was conceived in such a way that the three persons moving about in it were bound to appear too tall, almost majestic. Miniature furniture stood about, tiny tables and fragile armchairs covered with yellow and sky-blue silk. On the walls hung dainty paintings by minor Austrian masters. The living room was dominated by a grandfather clock with golden ornamentation that tinkled out a minuet on the hour. On the four-poster in the upstairs bedroom lay silver-embroidered cushions in the shape and size of gingerbread hearts. This was the doll's house that Leo had built for his princess and that Henner had chosen as a temporary refuge. He swore up and down that he would vacate his room in a month at most, but for the time being it was impossible for him to live in his own house. "Leo, my wife is a cocotte. No more and no less."

"Sarah is an artist, but she is not patient enough to endure your eccentricities."

"If I tell you she is a cocotte, I know what I'm talking about."

"Sarah is supersensitive. Her life belongs to music. That's why she can't live with you."

"The other way round, Leo; *I* can't live with *her*. She flirts with her students. She flirts with all the bohemians in Galicia, and in my absence she has men come to the house."

"You're just imagining this, Henner. You have a morbid imagination!"

"And besides, she bangs away at the piano relentlessly. Wagner from morning till night—and she knows that I can't stand Wagner. Then there's my son Nathan. He is a wunderkind, sure, but for hours on end he fiddles away on Paganini études—the racket is enough to drive you out of the house. I can't complete my invention under such conditions. Impossible. I'm on the verge. It's a matter of weeks, perhaps just days; then the prismatograph will be functional and we'll be rolling in money. Believe me, Jana! My idea dwarfs anything ever devised by science. I went to see Lumière in Lyon, the greatest Frenchman working in this field, and showed him my sketches. The man put his arms around me and kissed me on both cheeks. With tears in his eyes he offered me ten million gold francs— in cash. But the man is crazy. I'm not about to sell the greatest invention of the century for a handout of ten million! That's why I went to New Jersey to see Thomas Edison, the light-bulb king of America. Do you know what he told me? That compared to him I was a giant and that he was going to invest fifteen million gold dollars in my prismatograph. I turned down this offer too, because I don't need any partners. I want to be the only star on the firmament, like Napoleon in world history. In a few weeks you'll be rid of me, and retroactively I shall pay you so much rent that you won't be able to count the money. Ten thousand crowns a day! Three hundred thousand crowns a month! Not because you deserve it, but because I am fond of you—especially *you*, my bird of paradise. In thirty days I shall leave this house forever, and you will breathe a sigh of relief."

"Oh, but Henner," responded Jana, who had been listening to her brother-in-law open-mouthed, "I really don't want to be rid of you. On the contrary, I want you to stay. Forever. Because you have such big eyes, with a fire that warms me."

I do not know how close the relationship between Henner Rosenbach and the incomparable Jana really was. All I know is that the inventor did not vacate his room and was still there nine months later. Under these circumstances the marriage between Leo and his young wife could not really flourish. On the other hand, Jana sprouted breadthwise. She was in her eighth month and resembled a big, full, shiny drop of resin hanging from a tree and ready to burst. She was expecting the child that many years later was to become my mother. Whether her lawfully wedded husband was my grandfather is open to doubt. The only certain thing is that on All Soul's Day 1891, color photography had still not been invented, and Leo Rosenbach, the royal court photographer, made another of his sarcastic remarks: "Mankind continues to wait for the prismatograph. But my brother is sitting in my house, scratching his behind and courting my wife."

To which brilliant Henner responded that color photography was already a reality—in his head—but that one silly little ingredient for the developing solution was still lacking: pure spring water from the Bistshitza. But since a thick ice crust was covering the river, they would have to wait until spring. Whereupon Jana remarked with an angry sidelong glance at Leo, "Mankind doesn't need to wait any longer. I shall get the water."

On the next morning the city was covered with crystalline hoarfrost. People ran through the streets wrapped in furs, and those who could stayed home. Jana went to see Boychuk, the carter behind St. Mary's Church, and asked him whether he could take her to the Bistshitza in his sled.

"I can all right, *prosze pani,* but I don't know if I want to."

"And what do I have to do to make you want to, *panie* Boychuk?"

"To the river it's fifteen miles, *prosze pani,* and back it's another fifteen miles. It's wicked cold, and that costs money."

"How much, *panie* Boychuk?"

"Twenty kreuzer a mile, *prosze pani,* and for Jews it's thirty."

"Why the difference?" asked Jana indignantly.

"On account of the Lord Jesus, *prosze pani.* And besides, you are in the family way."

"Have you been drinking, *panie* Boychuk?"

"If you don't like it, *prosze pani,* you can walk . . ."

Shortly thereafter the carter hitched two nags to his sled, put a pickax in the coachman's box, cracked his whip, and drove off through the outlying districts in the direction of the plain. Jana sat in back, her sable hat pulled over her face, making her almost invisible. A biting wind whistled over the fields, the frozen snow crunched under the runners, and Boychuk drove his team of horses through gloomy frozen birch groves and past isolated farms. The sun was in its zenith, melancholy and yellow, when they finally reached the river. Jana got out and asked the carter to chop a hole in the ice. Boychuk did not move. He merely threw the pickax in the snow and grumbled, "I'll wait here, *prosze pani.* You know better what you need."

"But I can't do it, *panie* Boychuk."

"Then we'll drive back and get help. Twenty kreuzer a mile."

Jana bit her lip. She took the ax and stalked out on the ice. Doggedly and bursting with rage, she set to work. The old man had lit his pipe, and in front of him burned a fire at which he warmed his hands. Jana chopped away at the white crust. The hole grew larger, and when the sun was already over the horizon, water spurted out at last. Now Jana took a bucket from the sled, then another one, and said, "I beg of you, *panie* Boychuk, help me!"

"I'll drive to the next village and get a farmhand. Two crowns extra."

Tears ran down Jana's face. Bravely she scooped the water from the river and wedged the containers into the sled. No one knows what happened after that, but two days later Jana awakened in her bed. Next to her whimpered a child that had turned blue. Dr. Lichtenbaum predicted it would not live more than three days, but in defiance of all the laws of medicine it survived, and was named Malva. This name is neither Jewish nor Catholic; no one understands why the wretched little creature was given it. Perhaps it was named after the so-called Malva neglecta, the mallow that grows on walls and rubble heaps and is generally regarded as a weed. However that may be, the child weathered the critical days and grew up to be an enchanting creature. But this is really not what I wanted to talk about. I was going to tell about the water that the overwrought Jana had gotten from the Bistshitza in order to prove to her small-minded husband that her brother-in-law was a genius and that she did not hesitate to stake everything to help bring an epoch-making idea to fruition. This almost did her in, and little Malva along with her, and still for the time being color photography did not materialize.

Henner Rosenbach sat by the bed of the convalescent and explained his failure: "But I told you *pure spring water,* silly girl. From the source to Lipa, where you chopped a hole in the ice, it's two hundred miles. On the way the river picks up dirt, mud, and filth. It soon stops being water. Am I expected to implement the invention of the century with excrement? I know with what devotion you champion my interests, but that was utterly senseless and, if you'll pardon the expression, crackbrained. Either you go to the source or you stay home. Such flights of fancy are touching, but utterly useless for science . . ."

At this point Leo entered and heard his brother call Jana an eccentric person. Livid with rage, he screamed in a thin voice that Henner had been a parasite in his house for nine long months and that if he did not clear out immediately, he would have the police put him out in the street. Jana turned pale and replied, "If your brother leaves this house, I'll leave with him. You can do what you like. Get another wife, if you can find one, but I won't have an inspired inventor thrown out just because you are envious of him."

"How do you know that this inventor is inspired? So far he is nothing but a con man who hasn't invented a thing. A windbag, that's what he is, an incorrigible blatherskite. That's all."

"You take that back, Leo, and apologize to him!"

"I'll do nothing of the sort."

"Take it back, otherwise you've seen the last of me."

"I'm not taking back anything. Henner, get out of here!"

After Leo had said that, Jana rose from her sickbed. She was wearing a diaphanous chemise through which one could see her marble body, and she looked more beautiful than ever. It was a stormy December morning, but the barefoot Jana ran down the stairs. There was no doubt that she was going to rush out to the street in that get-up. She was bound to catch her death of cold, and Leo knew that he could not restrain her. He ran after her and flung himself at her feet, crying. Wringing his hands, he implored her not to leave, saying that he took it all back. Henner could stay if he wanted to; after all, he was his brother. "And you, Jana, don't you do anything foolish! I adore you."

Leo Rosenbach played for money and hoped for a miracle, but he wasn't a gambler. Gamblers have class; Leo didn't. Gamblers stake everything, and win from time to time; Leo staked very little and lost all the time—with one exception: the first time he sat down at a roulette table. His brother stood behind him and whispered that he should bet on all the prime numbers. Leo did so, and won a fortune. From that day on he was beholden to his brother and could no longer throw him out of the house. Henner had helped him collect ninety-eight thousand crowns. That was his first and last success; after that there were only

16

losses. In his first twelve years of marriage Leo gambled away all his possessions—the ninety-eight thousand crowns, his income, and his Munich savings. All he had left was Henner, a drain on his assets. That person had a secret trick, a system, something supernatural that opened all doors to him. Leo had no system, though he would have liked to have one. He yearned for some order, but he wasn't able to find it. He did not believe in God and laughed at the rabbi and the synagogue, but he felt that there had to be some meaning, some hidden idea in things. If there wasn't, one might as well hang oneself. Perhaps it was the world spirit at the end of every road, perhaps it was something else. Daily life was so dismal that one needed a system to so much as breathe.

Leo's relationship with Jana was one endless humiliation. He possessed her, as they say; he called her his own. He slept with her and probably fathered a child, but it certainly wasn't love. Jana was brutally honest. Sometimes he asked her whether he meant anything to her, and then she was apt to reply, "No, Leo, you don't mean anything to me. Hand me that scissors on the chest." How could a man bear this without a system? Behind this torment there had to be some promise—but what? Leo had to track it down; then everything would change, good fortune would come in the door, and possibly love as well. If he were a rich man—so he speculated—if he could give his wife gold and precious stones, he would mean something to her. Maybe, but maybe not. His brother was penniless and had never given Jana anything but his attention. He was a fourflusher, a crook, a nobody. He swindled his way through the family and bummed cigarettes from strangers, but Jana adored him. What's more, she came right out with it and said emphatically that Henner was her great love and gave meaning to her existence. Even Malva was already his slave. She had become a young lady, and was convinced that Henner was going to marry her some day. All this was unbearable to Leo; he remained a stranger in his own house. He spent the major part of the day in his studio, which was frequented by the elite of Stanislav coming to have their pictures taken. The women played up to him in hopes of being preserved for posterity as flatteringly as possible. He was the undisputed master of the art of photography, but his success left him cold. He had no eyes for other women; all he saw was the capricious creature who had fled from him up a plum tree, the heartless Aphrodite about whom he had said, "She's the only one for me," and who from the very beginning had declared that she didn't like him. And so it happened that he spent fewer and fewer evenings at home and more and more at Glovatsky's, where the rich Jews sat at their accustomed marble tables and played for high stakes over coffee and cake. The conversations usually revolved about one subject.

"It's too risky for me here, Loewenthal. I'm off to America."

"And I'm raising two hundred, Dr. Lichtenbaum. What do you mean, risky?"

"That I like to dance, but not on a volcano."

"In Austria there are no volcanoes, gentlemen. Here we are as safe as in the safe of a bank."

"But Kishinev is just a short distance away. Just across the border. Those of our people who survived will flee to the other end of the world."

"Are you in this game, Wassermann, or aren't you?"

"Australia is the only safe place, Magierkovitch. Here they're going to exterminate us like flies."

"I'm raising three hundred, Loewenthal. They're blaming us for all the catastrophes in the world—for a bankruptcy in Port Arthur and a general strike in St. Petersburg."

"You're an alarmist, Wassermann. We're in Austria, not Russia."

"I'm raising five hundred, Dr. Lichtenbaum, and I bet that the czar and the emperor will come to an agreement. *We*, gentlemen, will be the victims."

"I'm raising seven hundred, Loewenthal. Let's see what

you have. Right now the emperor is still calling us his dear Jews."

"Right now, Wassermann, but what is he going to say later? That is the big . . . Look who's coming! Our court photographer."

"Greetings and salutations, gentlemen. May one join your game?"

"Theoretically one may, but practically one may not, for one owes us eleven thousand crowns."

"But . . ."

"No buts, Rosenbach. We told you yesterday that you've got to pay up. At times like these one pays one's debts or gets out."

"What times, doctor? Has something happened?"

"He asks if something has happened. The Russians are losing the war against Japan. The rabble is rising against the czar, and they're making *us* the scapegoats."

"In Austria?"

"In all of Europe. If we want to go on living, we have to emigrate."

"I don't believe it, doctor."

"But *I* do, Mr. Rosenbach, and that's why we are insisting that you pay up."

"Then give me a chance," said Leo, with supplication in his voice. "Let me win, just this once, and I'll pay up immediately."

"We've been giving you a chance for fourteen years, you turkey. You used to be a man of honor, but you've kept losing for years. What kind of a person keeps losing?"

"That's what I'm asking myself," replied Leo, and rushed out of the room.

Really and truly, he thought, what kind of a person am I, always losing? My wife despises me; my daughter hardly knows me; my studio is about to be repossessed; solid citizens point their fingers at me; in card games I'm a loser; I am drowning in debts. What tree shall I hang myself from?

"From none, Leo. A few more days, and we'll be rolling in money. A few more days, and color photography will be a reality. I swear it by our parents' honor."

"Don't swear, Henner! Your invention has been a reality for fourteen years. For fourteen years you've been promising us big money, and what have we got? Nothing but *tsuris* and a bagful of fleas."

"I'm telling you the truth, Leo. All I need is a gem. Not quartz or halite, but a gem with twenty-four facets that breaks light down into the colors of the spectrum: red, green, and the other hues of the great scale. Give me a diamond, and we'll be rich."

"They're murdering the Jews, Henner. In Kishinev, Lodz, Berdichev. They're burning us alive. Our people are being ruined, and you need a diamond. Oy, Henner, my *meshugge* brother! Don't you know what's going on in the world?"

2

IT IS SAID THAT MOST REVOLUTIONS TAKE PLACE IN BAD weather, when it is cold and wet and discontent drips from the roofs. The Bloody Sunday of St. Petersburg, for instance, took place in late January 1905 in the coldest winter of the century, when the weather was so severe that people's tongues froze to their palates. Under the leadership of the false priest Georgi Gapon a mass deputation of approximately thirty thousand down-and-outers approached the czar's palace in order to hand a petition to the Emperor of all the Russias. Having no use for petitions and deputations, the czar had his soldiers fire into the crowd. More than a thousand people bit the dust, or, more accurately, the snow. What followed was a chain reaction of historic earthquakes that have not ceased to convulse our planet to this day. The rage of the people blazed heavenward, the temperature sank to thirty-nine degrees below zero, and the revolution spread like the bubonic plague. A few days after the massacre of St. Petersburg, Warsaw was aflame; later the fire spread to Lodz, and finally all over Russian Poland.

Among the Warsaw insurgents were the sons of a certain Yankel Kaminski, who had for years managed to keep out of the troubles of the times. He was fond of schnapps and women even though he was married and the father of sixteen children. His business was flourishing as never before, and if his dining room curtains had not disappeared on that memorable third of February, he would hardly have noticed that Warsaw had been turned upside down. Shortly before breakfast Fela, the hysterical cook, rushed through the house making an infernal racket. "Holy Mary, Mother of God! The world is coming to an end, and the Day of Judgment . . ."

Upstairs a door opened. Yankel Kaminski appeared in the semi-darkness with a wool cap on his head and rubbed his sleepy eyes. "Dammit. What's going on, *do jasnej cholery?* Why are you screaming like that?"

"The world is breaking into a thousand pieces, *panie* Kaminski . . ."

The patriarch looked sternly at the clock on the wall and then at the cook, who was wringing her hands. "It is half past seven, Fela, and you've already been drinking. So tell me already what's going on!"

"The shape's gone, *panie kochany.*"

"What shape? I don't understand a word you're saying, and you reek of *bimber.*"

"The red shape's gone. Gone from the window with the yellow binges."

"You mean the red drape with the yellow fringes. How'd that happen?"

" 'Cause the world's going to pot, *panie* Kaminski. The Russkies are coming . . ."

"Whaddaya mean, they're coming? They're here already. Been here for a hundred years."

"But now we're gonna make them kaput; that's what people say . . ."

It was a bitterly cold morning. The streets were icy and the fog crept through the rows of houses. A company of Cossacks came riding from the citadel to the Vistula, and from there through the Mostova up to the cathedral. Yankel Kaminski stood by his curtainless window, looked out, and shook his head. What do these people want? Why this excitement? Everything is all right. Or isn't it? Maybe I'm too old, he thought, to understand this. Shots rang out in the distance, but Yankel had no idea for whom they were meant.

In the old city barricades were being erected out of stones, iron bedsteads, and battered baby carriages. At the Pivna eleven fellows put up a red flag on the newly built protective rampart. The oldest among them was twenty-four; the name of the youngest, who was fourteen, was Hersh, though his brothers called him Hershele. Bullets whizzed through the air and projectiles struck their targets. Smashed bricks flew off the roofs, but Hershele did not stop chuckling to himself: "Our silk drape on the barricades of the proletarian revolution! *Mazel tov*, gentlemen! Our old man will go out of his mind when he finds out!"

The streets were empty. Now the trampling of horses' hoofs could be heard, and the Cossacks appeared in Castle Square. They were scarcely fifty steps away from the eleven lads when a shot came whizzing over the pavement. A direct hit tore the curtain, and Hershele intoned the *Czerwony Sztandar*, the Song of the Red Flag. He sang in a booming voice but very ardently, and his brothers bellowed along with him as though they wanted to drown out the fear that was constricting their throats—and, one might say, not without reason, for that very day they appeared before the magistrate.

Barefoot and with shaved heads, they stood chained together in the detention room of the Warsaw citadel. Peevishly plucking gray hairs from his moustache and looking at himself suspiciously in a tilting mirror, the Russian police captain asked them the usual questions. At the opposite end of the room, also in chains, stood a few dozen factory workers as well as a group of adolescent secondary-school students. The magistrate was careful not to speak to the captives directly. He addressed his questions to his assistant, who was dully staring at the picture of the czar that hung resplendent on the wall. "What are the names of these fine gentlemen?"

"Beg to report, captain, the gentlemen all have the same name."

The officer now turned the mirror toward the wall and concentrated on his fingernails. "Same name, same shame. But Siberia will knock some sense into them; that I personally guarantee."

"Yes, captain. In Siberia they will come to their senses and bear the following names: Ber Kaminski, born 1881. Shloime Kaminski, born 1882. Yitzhak Kaminski, born 1883. Mordechai Kaminski, born 1884. Moishe Kaminski, born 1885. Adam Kaminski, born 1886. Lazik Kaminski, born 1887. Benzion Kaminski, born 1888. Menahem Kaminski, born 1889. Aaron Kaminski, born 1890. Hersh Kaminski, born 1891."

The magistrate ran his eyes over the eleven Jewish louts. They were all healthy and vigorous. He plucked another hair from his moustache and growled angrily, "We need people for our lead mines. A lot of people, especially those with fire in their bellies." He went up to the oldest Kaminski and asked his assistant, "The father of this Jewish pig— what is he?"

"Another Jewish pig, captain."

"Sure, but what does he do?"

"Business."

"That's what they all do, these worms. Does he have money?"

"Like sand by the river, captain."

"And his sons?"

"I'll have to ask them, captain." He turned to the oldest and asked him, "So what are you doing, all of you?"

"At present we are doing a revolution. In peacetime we are students and do not wish to be called Jewish pigs. We are Poles . . ."

"So you are Poles," said the officer, lashing the impertinent Ber's head with his whip. Then he screamed, "There are no Poles, you Jewish pig! We have wiped you off the map! Russians is what you are, *panjemasz*, though you really don't deserve to live in Russia."

"No, captain," responded Shloime, the second oldest.

"What do you mean no," panted the officer.

"We really don't deserve to live in Russia, for Warsaw is in Poland."

An approving murmur went through the room, and the captain felt that he had to do something, so he menacingly swung his whip and roared, "Warsaw is in Poland, you say? I really didn't know that. But I do know where Siberia is. You see, Siberia is in Russia, *panjemasz*, and now you'll pull down your pants, otherwise you'll be castrated."

"No, captain, my hands are bound."

"In Siberia you will learn whether Warsaw is in Russia or not." With that he lashed Shloime's back with his whip. "Do you know now where Warsaw lies?"

"No, captain, Warsaw doesn't lie, it stands." This was said by the youngest, the fourteen-year-old Hershele, who had watched his brother being tortured and was now grinning at the captain. The officer could not believe what he heard. For the first time in his life he began to doubt his methods and gasped, "How dare you, you circumcised pig? Don't you have any respect?"

"No, captain."

"Can't you say yes?"

"No, captain."

"What *can* you do, then?"

"Sing, captain."

Hershele's hands were in chains, and so he was unable to defend himself when the whip lashed his neck, but his voice that blared out the Song of the Red Flag was clear as crystal. Now the captain lost his composure completely. Blindly he lashed away at the eleven brothers and ranted, "In Verkhoyansk you're going to sing till your vocal cords freeze and your balls crunch between your legs, till you croak—and the sooner, the better. Got that?"

No answer.

"I asked if you got that."

It was quite still in the interrogation room. "Answer me, or I'll tear your guts out!"

At that point at the other end of the room many throats intoned a song: "For our purple flag is red from proletarian blood."

The captain had intended to divide them—here the Poles, there the Jews—but he had achieved the opposite. All of them were now singing the same song.

The Vistula was frozen and a thick fog hung over the pavement. On a glassy February morning Yankel Kaminski ascended the granite staircase to the iron gate of the citadel, which was guarded by twelve heavily armed men. Next to the gate was a wooden shack for visitors. Yankel deposited his passport with the soldier on duty at the window and told him that General Kalugin was expecting him. This impressed the soldier; the gate opened, and a Cossack major appeared. He clicked his heels, motioned to Yankel to follow him, and led him past the drill yard to the inner fortress. There they walked through endless corridors, up steep staircases, and past hundreds of doors. Occasionally the major stopped and gave brief explanations. "This is where the anarchists are imprisoned. Most of them are doing life . . ."

Yankel remained unmoved, as though he had not been listening. In front of him an iron grille was raised and they walked over a steel bridge. "This is the beginning of the north wing. It's for the Reds, also called Siberiaks. They're sent away above the Arctic circle, and very few people come back from there . . ."

Yankel understood the allusion. He stubbornly remained silent, however, and followed the officer to iron bars that fenced off a gloomy inner yard. Through the bars one could see a crude pinewood gallows. "This is the last stop. This department functions only once a day. At six in the morning, when the cock crows. It's directly under the general of our army post."

"That so?" said Yankel, as though he were not really interested in this information.

"Yes. Directly under General Kalugin. He is a charming man who listens to reason. As far as I know, only every tenth man is strung up. How many sons do you have?"

Yankel did not respond. The major led him through a lighted corridor, and was pleased to note that the patriarch was trembling. They arrived at the door of the almighty general. The major repeated, "I asked you how many sons you have."

"Eleven, major," replied Yankel, taking off his fur cap.

The general moistened his index finger and turned over a file sheet. He did not look at the file, however, but through the two men who had entered. Now he stared at a spider that was descending on its web. The dignitary thought of the proverb according to which a spider in the morrow brings sorrow, and he turned pale. Then he said softly, almost in a whisper, as if in an effort not to tempt fate, "What's the name of the Jew?"

"Kaminski. First name of Yankel."

"Lives where?"

"Three Mostowa Street, Warsaw."

"It says here that he has eleven sons."

"And five daughters, if you please."

"I hear that his sons are paying us a visit," said the general, and turning to the Cossack major, he asked wearily, "That is correct, isn't it, or am I mistaken?"

"Yes, general. All eleven with room and board."

Kalugin smiled gently and said, "No one has any complaints here. What does the Jew think?"

"I think," replied Yankel cautiously, "that your hospitality is a great honor for us. Still, I would be pleased to take those fellows along with me."

"I can understand that. Major, you are dismissed."

"Yes, general," said the officer and disappeared from the scene. Kalugin put a pistol on the table in front of him and motioned to Yankel to come closer. "My hospitality is an honor for you. Very well, but the hotel bill hasn't been paid yet."

27

Yankel understood what the fatherly, godlike general was driving at. He took a checkbook out of his breast pocket and asked in a businesslike way, "What do we owe you, Mr. Commandant?"

"The present temperature in Central Siberia is some fifty degrees below zero."

Yankel suspected the worst and smiled coolly. "A land of unlimited possibilities. Russia's future is in Siberia."

The general understood the allusion and replied sharply, "Two thirds of the survivors come down with scurvy."

Yankel offered the general a cigarette, took matches out of his coat pocket, and gave the almighty man a light. "How much, commandant?"

"Ten thousand apiece, Mr. Kaminski. That makes one hundred ten thousand rubles for the whole kit and caboodle."

Yankel's voice broke. "Did I hear you right, general?"

"Not a kopek less, *panie* Kaminski." The governor licked his index finger again, turned over a file leaf, and said with his eyes closed, "Those fellows haven't been sentenced yet. What I am reading here looks like life terms. If all goes well . . ."

"And if it doesn't, commandant?"

"I hope the Jew gets my drift."

"So you said fifty thousand?"

"Now there is a revolution. That's why we're giving more severe punishments."

"Sixty thousand is a huge sum of money."

"We must scare people off, otherwise this sort of thing will spread."

"For God's sake, where will I get seventy thousand rubles from?"

"If the prosecutor demands the death sentence, I'm powerless."

"And if he doesn't?"

Kalugin closed the folder and got up. "A hundred thousand rubles, Mr. Kaminski, and you can take them with you."

"All eleven of them?"

The general yawned into his hand. "I said the whole kit and caboodle."

Slowly and grimly Yankel Kaminski wrote out a check for a hundred thousand rubles. As he handed Kalugin the check, he sighed, "Wish I had eleven daughters!"

Three droshkies were waiting outside the eastern wall of the citadel. Three coachmen sat on their boxes; they were freezing in their shaggy fur coats, and icicles were hanging from their beards. They puffed on their pipes and did not stir when twelve men came down the stairs single file. Yankel Kaminski was followed by his sons. Hershele, the youngest, brought up the rear looking cheerful, as though he had come straight from Paris. The fog had lifted, the Vistula gleamed, the birch branches at its banks were covered with glistening gold powder, and one could feel patches of hope lying over the city. Yet the old man was furious—in fact, boiling with rage. Silently he pushed the boys into the coaches and ordered the coachmen to drive off. The procession started moving. No one dared to speak. A terrible storm was brewing. The droshkies rumbled along the river over railroad ties and potholes to the Castle Bridge. From there they went uphill toward the old city and reached their destination, Three Mostowa Street. But the eleven boys knew that the catastrophe was still to come. Yankel was the first to leap off the footboard, and paid the fare. Then he unlocked the door, clattered up the stairs, and called to his wife, "Noemi, come to the dining room! It's starting!"

The stage on which the following event took place was ten meters long and six meters wide. The only props were a long oak table and eighteen chairs. By the bare window the mother stood and wept. At the table, behind their accustomed seats, the eleven heroes awaited further developments. In front of the mirror, like a two-headed hellhound, stood the lord and master of the house. Menacingly he drew his belt from his trouser loops and began the monologue that he spoke for his wife's rather than his sons' benefit. "This riffraff is supposed to be my children, Noemi? These are *your* children. They have nothing to do with *me* . . ."

"These are *your* children, Yankel. All of them as *meshugge* as their *tata*. Immoderate and imprudent."

"If they were *my* children, they wouldn't bankrupt my firm."

"They don't like this world, Yankele. They want to improve it. Is that a crime?"

"Worse than a crime, Noemi. It's bad business, and Yankel Kaminski has to sweat for it. They tear the last drapes off my windows. A hundred thousand rubles I pay this *gonif* of a general, may he drop dead, so he wouldn't chop them up on the guillotine. Ber, pull down your pants and lay down on the table!"

"I'm twenty-four, father!"

"And I'm sixty, you *putz*, and I know what I'm doing. Pull down your pants and lay on the table, belly down."

Ber bowed to his fate and obeyed. The eleven sons knew that it was possible to bargain with the general, but not with the patriarch. Yankel gave Ber ten lashes, and meted out the same to all the others. At each blow he found different words to give vent to his anger: "A hundred thousand rubles for a shitty ideal. For socialism, for Karl Marx, for the working class, for women's emancipation, for Negro liberation! Shloime, take your hands out of your pockets! For all this I'm supposed to pay my hard-earned money? An old Jew toils away. Lay straight, Moishe. My whole life long from morning till evening so my sons should learn something. So they should be more educated than their father, and what do they do? Instead of going to school they go out in the street. On your belly, I said, Menahem. Make a row and bother decent people . . ."

Yankel caught his breath for a moment. Then he went up to his wife and wheezed, "What kinds of monsters did you give birth to, Noemi? Eleven bandits who get their kicks out of playing world history at their parents' expense!

30

They're gonna pay for their stupidity! There's no revolution in Warsaw no more. I can't afford it . . ."

He wiped the sweat from his forehead and continued flogging his sons.

World history has no imagination. It repeats itself. Granted, there are minor variations, but basically it is always the same. In October 1905 there occurred for the second time what had already transpired in January. As she did every morning, hectic Fela came wheezing up into the dining room with the breakfast dishes and a steaming coffeepot, but when she entered, she turned green as a cucumber and dropped her load. The noise of breaking dishes was followed by heartrending screams. Noemi came running up, behind her came Yankel, and finally their five daughters. Fela launched into one of her hysterical fits. "Holy Mother of Czenstochowa, stand by us, the heaven is bursting."

Noemi fetched a broom and handed it to the cook. "Not heaven, Fela, but my china. What's the matter now?"

"In January we attired a new tablecloth . . ."

"Acquired," corrected Yankel. "Speak Polish, then you won't make any mistakes!"

". . . bought a new tablecloth, *yak Boga kocham,* so help me, when the river was frozen, in Wokulski's store, I remember exactly, on Targowa Street, over in Praga, and we slid over the ice on foot."

"She's been drinking again, the slut. What's happening?" Yankel began to suspect the worst.

"What's happening," shrieked the cook, "is that it's fall now and the leaves are already whirling from the trees. I look at the table, *yak Boga kocham,* but what do my blue eyes see?"

"Come to the point, Fela, or I'll throw you out the window. What do your blue eyes see?"

"The new tablecloth. Of red silk. From Wokulski's on Targowa Street. It's gone. Disappeared."

"And where are my sons?"

31

"Gone and disappeared, *panie* Kaminski. Taken off. Their doors are open and their rooms are empty."

On Castle Square there was shooting again. Cossacks drove a crowd into Pivna Street and blood flowed on the pavement. From the buildings bricks were hurled down at the Russians and household goods were dropped from the roofs—chamberpots, brass kettles, and wagon wheels. A red silk flag was raised on the roof of a solid citizen's house; the Kaminski guard was in action again. The tablecloth fluttered in the autumn wind. The lad who had raised it was scarcely fifteen years old, and a worker's cap covered his shaved head. He had a shrill voice and roared with infectious enthusiasm, "Proletarians of all countries, unite!"

On that October morning they were not uniting. The élan of the February days had dissipated. The crowd had become smaller and more timid. Fear dominated the city. For the second time Hersh and his ten brothers were arrested and taken to the citadel. They were given cell 13 right next to the "last stop" behind the dark fence. From the skylight one could see the gallows, whether by accident or design can no longer be determined. It was probably a ruse intended to soften up Yankel Kaminski, to prepare him to make a second payment of a hundred thousand rubles.

Kalugin had made inquiries. In those dark days of the Japanese war, Yankel's firm was more prosperous than ever. In 1905, when the first revolution afflicted the country, Yankel's sales tripled, for he manufactured material for uniforms. The more vehemently the Japanese stormed the czarist bastions and the more fearlessly the people demanded their rights, the more indispensable the army became and the more Yankel's business flourished. If old Kaminski had been able to see beyond his boozer's nose, he would have supported his sons' revolutionary activity, for it benefited his business. But that would have been asking too much of a sexagenarian patriarch. He was a shrewd little man, and a big businessman in little. He had performed the feat of producing textiles without raw materials, as it were, making a fortune on rags, bags, remnants, and cast-off clothes. He specialized in buying the uniforms of fallen soldiers at cut-rate prices and reducing them to wool fibers, from which he wove new material for uniforms. He made the greatest profit, however, from his preference for women, whose emancipation he ceaselessly championed. As a matter of principle he employed only women, proclaiming publicly that women were better, cheaper, and more industrious workers than men. Besides, he said, the young ones among them were ready to supplement their income with all sorts of favors, and that was nothing to be sneezed at either.

On that October afternoon the patriarch was sitting in his office, supervising through a window the automatic looms at which several hundred girls were working. Fascinatedly he gazed at the flywheels and weft reels, the lug straps, heald shaft guiding spools, and warp beams that rattled through the hall in wild syncopation. He did not or would not notice that two men had entered on what appeared to be urgent business. One of them, Chaim Lewin, was Yankel's chief clerk and right-hand man; the other, Sokolow, wore the epaulets of a high-ranking police officer. Lewin stopped at the doorway, waiting to be recognized by his boss. He cleared his throat several times, but this did not attract Yankel's attention. Lewin then said in an imploring voice, "We have the pleasure, or rather the rare honor, of greeting among us Timofei Sokolow, an officer of the local police . . ." But his voice faded, for Yankel was staring down into the hall from which a steady din rose. He did not even stir when Lewin roared in his ear, "He has been sent by His Excellency General Kalugin personally. Do you hear me, *panie* Kaminski? The strong man of Warsaw has detailed him . . ."

The patriarch took a bottle from the table, poured himself a glass, and gulped it down without offering any to the Russian. In Poland that is a snub, but in Russia it is a provocation, and the powerful policeman grabbed Yankel by the collar and hissed, "I assume that you are the Jew Kaminski. Yes or no?"

"Let go of me!"

"I asked if you are the Jew Kaminski. I represent General Kalugin, and am not in the mood for jokes."

"I'm not in the mood for joking either. Let go of me, or you won't be a police officer much longer."

That mysterious threat might mean anything. Since Sokolow had no idea what was behind it, he took his hand off Yankel's neck, but noticed that the patriarch was still stolidly staring out the window. Now he changed his strategy and said in a somewhat more conciliatory voice, "I am sorry to have to inform you that your sons Ber, Shloime, Yitzhak, Mordechai, Moishe, Adam, Lazik, Benzion, Menahem, Aaron, and Hersh are behind bars at the Warsaw citadel . . ."

Yankel reached for the bottle and again poured himself a drink without offering any to the two men.

Lewin thought that Yankel had never been so insufferable, and sought to reduce the tension somehow. "Won't you sit down, lieutenant?"

Sokolow remained standing and continued his intimidating speech in a dry voice. "Your sons are charged with one, undermining the authority of the state; two, offering armed resistance to the Russian army; three, spreading revolutionary propaganda at secondary schools and institutions of higher learning; and four, stubborn disobedience of the third degree . . ."

Lewin was beside himself. Wishing to be helpful, he pulled out a cigarette case and invited the officer to help himself. The latter ignored him and continued in a menacing drawl, "The persons named on this document—Ber, Shloime, Yitzhak, Mordechai, Moishe, Adam, Lazik, Benzion, Menahem, Aaron, and Hersh—have been sentenced to eighteen years of forced labor in the lead mines of the extreme north . . ."

Yankel gulped down a third glass, pinched his lips, and began to walk up and down as the officer continued, "However, the father of the eleven delinquents is free to make an appeal to His Excellency, General Kalugin."

Yankel stopped and said in a barely audible voice, "Give Kalugin regards from the Jew Kaminski and tell him that he doesn't know what he's talking about."

"Watch out, you *durak!* We've sent people older than you to Siberia!"

"You take back the *durak,* and if one of us goes to Siberia, it certainly won't be *me.* So tell your commandant that he doesn't know what he's talking about—because I have no sons. I haven't had any and I won't have any."

"I warn you for the last time, *panie* Kaminski. According to the civil register, you have eleven sons."

"And according to Yankel Kaminski, I have none. Good day, lieutenant!" So saying the patriarch looked out the window again and considered the conversation closed. The policeman was speechless. Such a thing had never happened to him before. Dumbfounded, he turned toward the exit, followed by Chaim Lewin, who once again was at his wits' end.

3

IN MY FAMILY THERE IS A SECRET. A BLACK SPOT IN THE chronicle. A sore point that no one discusses. Something strange evidently happened there. The eleven do-gooders who in December 1905 were put on a cattle car at the East Station in Warsaw never arrived at their destination. Wearing the striped garb of prisoners and chained together, they traversed all of Russia from west to east. Normally they should have arrived at the lead mines of Verkhoyansk some time in the early summer of 1906. But this did not happen, for otherwise I would have had no father and my father no son, and this history would never have been written. Improbable though this may sound, the cattle car with the eleven brothers got lost. Just like that. Like a needle in a haystack.

Nine hundred kilometers east of Novosibirsk lies the railroad junction Atchimsk. There some of the cars were uncoupled and rerouted to the line going to Abalakova. The uncoupling went according to schedule and so did the rerouting, but after it was done a cattle car was missing. However, at Irkutsk a fresh team of trainmen alighted from a carriage. They were all much younger than the others, and the majority wore glasses, which is rather rare among railroad employees. On the journey of almost ten thousand kilometers through the lichen steppe, the tundra woods, and finally the endless wasteland of the taiga something had happened that was never mentioned by any member of my family on my father's side. We will never know how it happened. Today it can no longer be determined whether it happened with or without the cooperation of comrades, or whether force or money was used. It surely could not have been accomplished without some kind of pressure. After all, two members of the military police and nine men of the Trans-Siberian Railroad disappeared; they were stripped of their uniforms, and then they dissolved into thin air. In their place eleven Bolsheviks in Russian uniforms traveled to Vladivostok, and no one seemed to be surprised. You may say that it sounds like a detective novel. Yes, but this detective story is true—evidenced by the fact that the eleven sons of Yankel Kaminski arrived at the coast of the Sea of Japan unharmed and full of joie de vivre, and began a new chapter of their lives.

4

⌁⌁⌁

ON JULY 12, 1906, MALVA ROSENBACH, NOW ALMOST
fifteen years old, sat in her room and looked in the
mirror. The window was open. A mild breeze came in from
the garden and sweet fragrances beguiled the senses of the
lovely girl. It was an ordinary day, and yet Malva felt a
strange unrest within herself, a vague feeling that somewhere her fate was being decided, and that a boat was
moving toward her. She opened her diary, which was
bound in velvet, and put her thoughts on paper:

> I know that he exists, but I wonder where he is now.
> Not in Stanislav; that I know for sure. There is nothing
> for him here, and if there were, he would not be the
> bird of paradise of my nights. He is a Hercules, a demi-
> god of white alabaster. He rides on the waves of world
> history, but I don't even know what he looks like. Perhaps
> he looks like Uncle Henner. With violet eyes that bubble
> and whirl like moist mussels at the bottom of the sea. I
> would like him to resemble that raving inventor. Why
> can't it be Uncle Henner? It makes me cry. He is three
> times my age. And three times as good-looking. He
> doesn't even look at me. He sees only himself, and pos-
> sibly my mother. To him I am a child. Well, he has no
> idea that I have been a woman for a long time. A hot
> blossom with sweet honey in its calyx. But there is another
> man, and he will see me. Immediately. At first sight. He
> should be full of longing. He should seek the impossible.
> I shall never love a man who has both feet on the ground,

as the saying goes. Liebermann boasts of having both feet on the ground, but he is a cipher. A stuffed, puffed-up cipher. He wants to drum it into me that life is the art of the possible. Such an idiot! This very combination of words makes me raving mad: the art of the possible. If it's art, it can't be possible. And what is possible is not art. Only a faded Latin teacher can claim such nonsense. And his name is Liebermann. What a laugh! Such an old fogy wants to teach me what art is. His very name is an absurdity: neither *Liebe* nor *Mann*. He is a neuter. Neither fish nor flesh. And stuck to the earth. My Napoleon flies through the air. He looks for me on the arrows of the wind rose. He yearns for the comet in the dusky eastern sky. I don't know him. I don't know what his name is, but I don't doubt for a moment that he loathes the laws of nature, for they are too confining for him. Mathematics is a torture. For him as for me. A straitjacket of the imagination. A cage with round figures in it. Where are there round figures in the world? At the very beginning there is a lie: two times two is four. Why not threepointnine or fourpointone? Two times two people. All totally different. Not even twins are like each other. What are four people? Three hangmen and a philosopher. Are these four people? Four islands maybe. Four riddles. I loathe numbers. Only the innumerable is true. The immeasurable. I love Uncle Henner because he is beyond numbers. Because he plays for high stakes and always loses. He is a stake. A flaming fire that flickers toward its goal and will never reach it. You unique Henner. Why are you my relative and not my lover?

On that uneventful twelfth of July 1906 three strange things happened that were to have weighty consequences for the fate of the blossoming Malva. Ten thousand kilometers east of Stanislav eleven brothers who were disguised as trainmen left the Trans-Siberian express and ventured on the most daring escapade of their lives. Fifteen thousand kilometers west of Stanislav, in the green hell of French Guyana, a prison guard entered the cell of the convict

Alfred Dreyfus and informed him that the Court of Cassation in Paris had set aside the verdict of the court-martial of Rennes, that the captain, who had been sentenced as a German spy, was rehabilitated and raised to the rank of major in the French army. In Stanislav Leo Rosenbach brought home a man named Baltyr, who was not Jewish but who emanated a magic that no one could resist—not even the royal court photographer, who had always vowed that he would not fall victim to any fascination. Baltyr was a Russian refugee who had participated in revolutionary plots and had been sentenced to death the previous December. On the eve of his execution a mysterious woman had managed to smuggle him out of the notorious fortress of Petropavlovsk and get him to Austria through the Ukrainian swamps.

On that day in July Baltyr appeared in my grandfather's studio. He frankly admitted that he was an anarchist being pursued by the czarist Ochrana Guard and that he had to hide out somewhere. He said that since he was a trained photographer by profession he could, if Leo Rosenbach had no objections, stay with us for awhile and make himself useful. My grandfather was anything but a friend of violent activities. He was the most loyal Jew in the Austro-Hungarian dual monarchy. When Leo heard the word "anarchist," a chill ran down his spine, but Baltyr's declaration that the Russian barbarians had sentenced him to the gallows sufficed to win his sympathy. Besides, Baltyr was an uncommonly charming man. He was blond, with prominent cheekbones, deep eyes that seemed to be flashing constantly, and a melancholy smile. Leo was not the only person who liked him; everybody did, and the family received him like a brother. That evening Malva made the following entry in her diary:

> He has a deep voice. I number him among the family
> of the string instruments. A viola, I would say. He sang
> us a Russian song, and I got goosebumps. I felt that he

was singing the truth. I understood next to nothing, but it became clear to all of us that he believes in something. Our family does not believe in anything. Uncle Henner is the only one who believes—in himself, to be sure—and they laugh at him. This Baltyr we are taking seriously. Probably because he has been sentenced to death. And because we know that his persecutors are wild beasts. I wonder what he believes in. He says he is an anarchist and wants to abolish the state. Does that make sense? If he stakes his life on it, it has to make sense. If one is ready to die for a cause, it must be a just one. A mysterious woman is said to have liberated him. She is supposed to be a daredevil. Of course she's one. Wonder whether I would have the courage to risk my life. I don't know. For Baltyr I probably would. He is so delicate and so vulnerable that one would like to stroke him all the time. Soft and velvety as a string instrument. For him I would sacrifice myself. Actually not for him, but for his cause. For the songs he sings, which I know to be true. Strange. To me Baltyr is not a man but more of a brother. And Uncle Henner is to me not an uncle but a man.

It was Baltyr who had brought the news of Dreyfus's rehabilitation. He was as excited as if the event concerned him personally, as if he were a twin of the French staff officer.

"How come you feel so concerned?" asked Uncle Henner scornfully. "You don't even know him."

"You don't know him either," responded Baltyr, "but you cried when you learned about it."

"That's not the same thing. Dreyfus is a Jew, and so am I. His rehabilitation is mine too."

"And mine, though I am not a Jew. The scoundrels who sent him to Devil's Island are the same scoundrels that sent me to Petropavlovsk."

"There's a difference," said Leo, joining the conversation. "Dreyfus was innocent."

"That's what I reproach him with, my dear Mr. Rosenbach. No one has the right to be innocent. Our innocence is going to wreck the world."

"This is no joking matter to me, Mr. Baltyr. In my house we are for law and order. I too would condemn Dreyfus if he had really betrayed military secrets."

"*I* wouldn't. On the contrary. Revealing military secrets serves peace. State secrets lead to war. If there weren't any left, there would be no more genocide. Believe me . . ."

"You're going too far, my dear guest," shouted Leo. "You are justifying high treason. This I cannot and will not tolerate."

"I'm not justifying a thing. It's simply that I loathe any kind of obedience. Obedience runs counter to individual self-determination. Dreyfus is a bourgeois. An officer from the ruling class. A puppet of the banks and heavy industry. If he is ordered to attack Germany or England or Italy, he will obey and mow down thousands of people who have never done anything to him. He is innocent. He is not a traitor, and that is his crime."

"And what about you, Baltyr?" suddenly asked Jana, who had been listening in silence. "Are you a traitor?"

"Yes," replied the Russian, smiling. "According to the Russian criminal code I am one, and I'm proud of it. I am always ready to rebel against the authorities, against the czar, the government, and the military. I am even prepared to fight against my own people if they let themselves be misled by charlatans. When the howling mob runs through the streets of Kishinev or Bialystok and massacres the Jews, I shall be a traitor. I shall rise up against the people who speak my language and belong to my stock. Unfortunately Dreyfus did not do this, and therefore he is innocent."

"So why are you pleased," asked Henner in a mocking falsetto voice, "that he has been rehabilitated?"

"Not for his sake, Mr. Henner. For the sake of the rulers of France who had to suffer a defeat. They were trying to weld the people together with the aid of anti-Semitism. They wanted to whip up a nationalistic frenzy so that they might attack Germany and Austria at the next opportunity. This they failed to do. It is a signal for the whole world that people cannot trust the ruling classes, and the world understood. That's what I am pleased about."

An unfathomable enmity smoldered between Baltyr and Henner. They were too similar in their view of life. One was an anarchist, the other an inventor. Both longed for the overcoming of gravity, for the impossible, as Malva liked to say. Both also suspected that they would hardly live to see the fulfillment of their dreams. Perhaps they were jealous of each other, for both Jana and her daughter Malva began to compare the two men, and, whether consciously or unconsciously, the men actually vied for the hearts of the two women.

On November 24, 1906, Malva wrote in her diary:

I'm having my fifteenth birthday. Up to now I have been a child, or at least I have been treated as one. Something seems to have changed there. Around five in the afternoon, when it was already dark in the house, Henner took me aside. He looked at me for a long time, as though he were looking through my clothes at my bare skin, and to my astonishment it felt awfully good. Tingly and intoxicating, like cool champagne. It made me quite drunk, and he reached for my hand and kissed the palm. Then something happened that I can hardly describe. Something quite new that I can only compare to fireworks. My blood grew boiling hot. It surged from my neck and hips, my breasts and thighs toward my center. I felt an earthquake in my whole body, a crisis that shook me, a raging fever that rose higher and higher. My throat tightened up and my hips became cramped. I clenched my jaws, my heart stopped, and then I burst apart. My soul flew in the air, and a cascade of voluptuousness flowed through my flesh. Henner was still standing in front of me and kissing the palm of my hand. With the tip of his tongue he tickled my skin between the thumb and the index finger. I got quite weak in the knees and knew that I was about to fall—into his arms, for which I have always longed. That's probably what he wanted, for he came so close to me that I could hear his heart beating. At that point a shrill voice came through the stairwell: "Malva, where are you?" I hate mama for her tactlessness. Where are you? That meant: What mischief are you up to now? She resents me because I am young and she is old. She is jealous because Henner is starting to notice me. No. I'm going too far. She isn't old at all. She is as beautiful as a peacock. All men turn to look at her when she passes them. And Henner hasn't been the cock of her walk for a long time . . . Now it's Baltyr. She is in love with Baltyr, I'm convinced of that, but I can't understand it. All right, Baltyr is a *mentsh*. A *mentsh* through and through, but Henner . . . How shall I put it? He's a man, a knight, a Prince Charming. I know, of course, that Baltyr is better. Papa would say "more valuable." After all, he has risked his life. For freedom. For his ideas of self-determination. He's not a Jew, but he would be prepared to die for us because we are persecuted. Because we are despised. He is selfless to the nth degree. Henner isn't. On the contrary. He thinks only of himself. He pays attention to me to make mama jealous. Yet he doesn't care about mama. He is just annoyed that she is now crazy about this Baltyr. Henner is a perfect example of an egotist . . . He isn't searching for color photography but for glory, and yet I'm sure that he is going to succeed with his invention. Papa thinks he is a good-for-nothing and a cheat. But I'm convinced that Henner will triumph. He wants mankind to cheer him. He wants to be loved and idolized. He is selfish and inconsiderate. Such people reach their goal. Oh Henner! Why do I love you so much?

The showdown between Henner and Baltyr could no longer be avoided. It took place on the first of May 1907, and ended in a draw. Jana, Malva, and the two rivals sat at the breakfast table and discussed the rally that was supposed to start at eleven o'clock at the square next to the railroad station. Henner spread honey on his bread and said with a contemptuous sidelong glance at the Russian, "I assume you'll be there."

"Of course. Why do you ask?"

"Because you feel so comfortable in a herd. Or don't you?"

"I'd like to know why you are asking me that."

"I'm just surprised that a person can be so stubborn. For twenty years now you've been tilting at capitalist windmills, but nothing comes of it."

"And you, Mr. Henner, have been inventing color photography for the past sixteen years, so I've been told, but you are no more successful than I am."

"I'm one step away from triumph, Mr. Baltyr, which is more than can say about yourself."

"Don't be so conceited," said Jana, joining the conversation. "Mr. Baltyr risked his life for his idea. He was sentenced to death, and yet he goes on fighting, whether he wins or loses."

"I'm not blaming you for not reaching your goal, Mr. Henner. It's simply hard for me to understand why you are sitting around not doing anything. Inactivity is the beginning of the end."

"You take that back, Mr. Baltyr!"

"I've known you for almost a year now. Can you claim that during this period you have so much as lifted a finger for your idée fixe?"

"Take back this drivel!" screamed Henner, grabbing the bread knife from the table and menacingly approaching his rival. "I'm about to lift a finger for my fixed idea. I'm going to destroy you, you Russian barbarian."

"You are insulting my guest, Henner," cried Jana indignantly. "He may be a Russian barbarian, but he is standing up for us Jews, something that you don't seem to appreciate. Shame on you, you bigmouth!"

"I'll kill him!"

"Because he is telling you the truth." With these words Jana wrested the knife away from her raving brother-in-law.

"He isn't telling the truth," sobbed Henner, suddenly quite small, his whole body trembling. "This very summer, when the corn is ripe, I'll buy you a golden carriage with four Arab stallions."

"We don't need a carriage, Henner, and certainly not horses."

"Oh, but you do, Jana. Your husband is bankrupt, in case you haven't heard. He is up to his ears in debt. Already, in the early morning, he is sitting in the café and gambling away his coat buttons. Soon the bill collectors will be here and throw you out of this house—but Henner Rosenbach will rescue you. My invention isn't an idée fixe. It is as good as ready."

"What do you mean, as good as ready, Henner? It's been fifteen years since I got that water for you. From the frozen Bistshitza. And now?"

"We will eat golden pheasant, you doubting Thomas. And we'll send to Paris for the wine."

"As good as ready, you swear. One step away from triumph. What are you still lacking?"

"The dot over the *i*, the *kropka*, Jana." Henner still had tears in his eyes, but now he began to beam and his voice became soft as silk. "I'm lacking only a trifle, for white light is an illusion. There is no white light. It is composed of red, blue, and yellow. Just look at the light shining through the window. It lies."

"Mr. Henner, are you trying to imply that we are color-blind?"

"Of coure you are color-blind, you pitiful philistine. To you the world is only black or white. Good or bad. Beautiful or ugly. You have gray filters in front of your eyes, Mr. Baltyr, but I shall make you see. I shall break white light down into its components, but for that . . ."—he stared at Jana as if he wanted to hypnotize her—" . . . I need . . ."

46

"What, Henner? A prism?"

"I am supposed to dissolve the mendacious white light into its colorful components, into the fragrant colors of nature, and you bring me a prism? A pitiful piece of glass. We need a diamond, Jana. A genuine sparkling diamond."

"With what money, you simpleton?"

"He's not a simpleton, mama," exclaimed Malva, who was sitting there and gazing at Henner adoringly, "he is a genius. He has stayed young, in contrast to you, mama, and all of you."

"Thanks for the compliment, Malva, but I am asking a sober and realistic question: Where is my brother-in-law going to get the money to acquire his diamond?"

"I don't know, but I swear by everything that is dear to me. By my son, by my family . . ."

"You have ruined them. They have nothing to eat."

"Are you of so little faith that you have to doubt all the time? Don't you see that my cause is going to triumph?"

"So is mine, Mr. Rosenbach," replied Baltyr with a weary smile. "My cause is bound to triumph. It is the will of the laws of history, though I don't know when. I am not worrying about it, because I have no intention of putting golden pheasant or choice wines from Paris on anyone's table. Good-bye for now. The rally starts in an hour . . ." With these words he rose and walked to the door. Malva called out to him, "Please wait! I'm coming with you."

May 1, 1907. This can't be true. It's incredible. They've arrested Baltyr. Right in the middle of the square at the railroad station. I can imagine why. He probably planted the bomb that was supposed to blow up Stolypin. The mass murderer of St. Petersburg. The prime minister of all punitive expeditions and pogroms. He ought to pay for his bloody deeds, but the plot failed. Now it's not Stolypin who is in for it, but Baltyr. When he was being arrested, he whispered to me, "The beast will die anyway. I'm counting on you." Then they took him away. What could I have done? Today nothing, but wait till tomorrow. I have vowed to continue on his path, for he is counting on me. What will happen if they extradite him? He will be hanged, that much is clear. And if they hang him, I'll have to avenge him. He is counting on me. I have no idea how one goes about taking revenge, but I'll think of something. "The beast will die anyway," he said. He said it so ardently, as though he were giving me an assignment. Now I have a goal. I don't love Henner but Baltyr. Henner is a wreck. Handsome and seductive, but a wreck. Like papa, who sits in the café and gambles his life away. They are all gambling their days away and getting old. Tonight he came home and cried. I asked him what had happened, and whether he was crying on account of Baltyr. Then he said, sobbing, and this is typical of my family: "I'm crying for myself, because I'm bankrupt. Let Baltyr cry for himself!" Then Henner put his arms around him and swore by the God of the Jews— Henner, of all people, who doesn't believe in anything but himself—he swore that next Sunday he would present his invention to the world, the prismatograph which is a reality at last. Papa believed him. Out of sheer despair. *I* don't believe him. This morning he said again that the only thing he lacked was a diamond, but where is he going to get one? He wants to give us carriages and Arab stallions. He is a fool. I really believe that my heart now beats only for Baltyr. He is counting on me. That is an obligation.

It was a warm day in May. Jana flitted through the crowds in the inner city. Elegantly dressed as always, she had a particularly chic hat on. From time to time she looked behind her suspiciously, as though she feared being observed. When she was certain that no one was following her, she disappeared in a dark arcade and entered the jewelry store of Leonidas Kornetzky, who was known as a playboy and ladies' man. Kornetzky was sitting behind his counter, reading a Polish newspaper. When he saw Jana enter, he got up and bowed respectfully. "What can I do for you?"

"I have a request, you might say, but it is strictly confidential."

"The more confidential, charming lady, the more desirable," whispered Kornetzky, and kissed Jana's hand.

"Could you, under the seal of secrecy . . ."

"*Je suis la discretion même, piekna pani.*"

"I would like to have a pearl necklace appraised, Mr. Kornetzky."

She took a black case out of her handbag, opened it hesitantly, and asked, "Do you attach importance . . ."

"That depends on a few little things, fair lady."

"Then I shall go to someone else," replied Jana defiantly and prepared to put the necklace back in the case. "You don't seem particularly interested."

"I'm very interested," said Kornetzky, picking up the necklace and running it carefully through his fingers. "I would just have to know who this jewelry belongs to . . ."

"It belongs to me," replied Jana, blushing. "It's a bridal gift from my husband, but certain circumstances make me entertain the idea of offering it for sale—but of course, only at a good price. What is your estimate . . ."

"Seeing that it's you, *laskawa pani,* I would say, more or less and not making any binding offer, approximately three thousand crowns."

"And that diamond in your glass case—is it for sale?"

"A wonderful specimen from Central Africa. A flawless yukunkun. Three thousand five hundred crowns, and that's a special price for charming ladies. A unique stone with a brilliant sparkle. Colorless and clear as water. On your neck, *laskawa pani,* or between your breasts it would be regal in the true sense of the word."

Jana took the necklace out of Kornetzky's hands and put it back in the case. "We are not striking a bargain, *panie* Kornetzky. Either you swap your diamond for my necklace, an even exchange, or we shall not do business."

"If you could come by again this evening, we could discuss the matter leisurely. Over a glass of liqueur, *vous com-*

prenez, and by candlelight, if you don't mind. Surely you understand that a rich man and a charming lady always agree on terms."

"How do you mean that, *panie* Kornetzky?"

"You're not a child any more, madam . . ."

"At what time?"

"After business hours," said Kornetzky with a sly, happy smile.

Things happened in rapid succession. The terrible first of June came. On St. Erasmus Day—that is, twenty-four hours later—Leo's property was to be repossessed. He was going to lose not only his furniture but his house as well. Weariness and dejection paralyzed the family. Malva sat in her room all morning and scribbled in her diary.

> Now the time has come. I no longer have a choice. For thirty days I have had no news from Baltyr. He may be dead. But that doesn't matter. To me he is more alive than ever. I love him, and he is counting on me. He gave me an assignment, and I have to complete that assignment. "The beast will die anyway," he said. I now have to see to it that this happens. I shall learn how to handle explosives and not be afraid. The worst thing is fear. Why are we girls always taught to be fearful rather than ruthless? I want to become ruthless and hard as granite. Tomorrow we shall be thrown out of the house. That's fine. Now I have to act, like it or not. Property makes one soft, says Baltyr, and he is right. Henner swears that he is going to help us. It is enough to make you cry. This clown, of all people, who is himself beyond help. He swears by the life of his son that this time he is ready. Yet all of us know that he doesn't give a hoot for the life of his son, and lets him go to rack and ruin. He says that everything is different now that he finally has the diamond he lacked all these years. At six this evening, so he claims, a new era will dawn—year one after the invention of color photography. Poor uncle is hallucinat-

ing. He has feverish fantasies, but we believe him. Why do we? He must have hypnotized us. We surrender to his charm and adore him. We cling to his lies because he is our last shred of hope. He swears to mama, "Tomorrow we'll be rich. I shall show you what I am capable of. We shall send for my wife and my beloved Nathan. For sixteen years everyone has thought I'm crazy. Now I want you to be present when it happens. All of you. I want you to be proud of me, for I am the founder of a new era. We shall have millions. We shall drown in gold. We shall throw the repossessors out. The whole world will be at our feet." This is how he fibs, and we watch his lips and hang on his every word. I must admit that he has enchanting lips. He looks like a demigod. He is our only hope, though we know for sure that he is a cheat and have no idea how he obtained his diamond. Maybe he stole it. I suppose he would be capable of stealing, but he is hardly a common thief. He has too much class for that. At worst he is a con man. A brilliant crook who gets roast pigeons to fly into his mouth and women into his arms. And yet I'd like to know where the diamond came from. They say that such a jewel costs a few thousand crowns. How did Henner get that money? We can't pay for our bread and the milkman gives our house a wide berth, but my uncle gets himself a yukunkun. Say what you will, this man is a phenomenon. A veritable magician. Right in the ocean of our misery he finds a few thousand crowns and declares that he is going to save us. Perhaps he is a practitioner of the black arts. We shall see what he is. He will lead us around by the nose for the hundredth time, but we go on hoping. Tonight at six!

The elite of Stanislav had shown up. All wanted to be present and watch Henner Rosenbach inaugurate the new age: the Jews from Café Glovatsky as well as the doctors and lawyers whom Leo owed money. Elegant Magierkovitch in his white tuxedo. Wassermann the millionaire in his black dress suit. Bald-headed Loewenthal with his silver cane and yellow gloves. The chief rabbi and Simche Pilnik, the matchmaker who had once engineered everything. Even Henner's hapless wife Sarah had come with their son Nathan, who was already eighteen and so handsome that all those present fell silent when he entered the studio. So that was Henner's son, who was known to be a gifted violinist, a prodigy with snow-white skin and melancholy eyes. And that was the delicate woman whom Henner had pursued with his jealousy until she finally threw him out of the house.

The studio was twice the size of the house in which the Rosenbachs lived. Against the walls, which were decorated with silk tapestries, stood elegant armchairs. On a flower-bedecked table were gleaming silver platters with mounds of open-faced sandwiches. Malva wore a tight-fitting dress of pink brocade. She went from guest to guest, made small talk, and offered delicacies that had been specially ordered from Lvov: lobster with mayonnaise, salmon with capers, turkey in caviar sauce. Jana offered cold drinks: Tokay, vodka, various kinds of schnapps, and exquisite liqueurs. Leo stood in a corner with his camera, which was mounted on a heavy tripod. Over the camera hung the obligatory black cloth. In his hand he held a cup with magnesium powder, the device used in those days for flash photography. He pulled his watch out of his pocket and noted that it was five minutes before six. A few more minutes and the die would be cast. The only person who was missing was Henner.

Leo felt that he ought to address a few words to those assembled, so he cleared his throat and, his voice fluctuating between soprano and baritone, spoke, presumptuously and pointedly. "My honored guests, you can be proud to have the unique opportunity to witness a historic event. It will be a source of pride for you that you will be able to say some day, *I was there.*"

The hero of the evening had still not arrived, however, and those present took this as a bad omen, but this did not disconcert Leo. "You were not there, ladies and gentlemen, when Galileo discovered the moons of Jupiter with his telescope. Nor did you watch James Watt set the first steam engine in motion. None of us were able to gape at the Lilienthal brothers when they were overcoming gravity and sailing through the firmament free as birds. But in a few moments"—Leo pulled out his watch again and sorrowfully looked at the dial—"you will experience my brother Henner Rosenbach developing the first color photograph in world history."

"God willing," clucked the always skeptical Mr. Wassermann, "but most of the time he isn't willing."

Scornful laughter shook the room, and suddenly Leo's voice turned suppliant. "I beg you for just a little bit of good will, ladies and gentlemen, for a speck of patience. Give the inventor a chance before you taunt him."

"We'll give him a chance," boomed Magierkovitch, "but unfortunately he isn't here."

"Surprise, surprise," said a voice from the corridor. "I'm here and shall prove to you that God is on my side. For he helps those who trust in him."

Henner entered with a black case in his hand and a top hat on his head—from top to toe a fakir, who arrogantly bestowed a brief glance on the guests, then said, "I shall show you something that may astonish you . . ." With a magician's gesture he pulled a diamond from his handkerchief, held it up, and let it gleam in the light of the chandelier. "God gave me this jewel, and with his help the impossible becomes possible."

"Are you trying to tell us that the diamond came from above?" cried the bald-headed Mr. Loewenthal. "From the Almighty himself?"

"Not from the Almighty himself, dear friend, but through the good offices of a person who is devoted to me and whose name I shall not reveal."

"So there are high-carat jewels in this house," cried Wassermann, "but they owe us thousands of crowns."

"You will soon be proud to be our creditor, you unimaginative person."

"Hoo ha."

"You'll beg us on your knees to be allowed to invest even more money with us."

"I said hoo ha. Show us your invention, and we'll talk."

"Permit me to retire to my laboratory now. I see that my son Nathan has brought his violin along. He will play for you in the meantime. Sarah, his mother, who is a success in every way, will accompany him on the piano. Until later."

With these words Henner disappeared in the darkroom and locked it from the inside. The prodigy took out his instrument, informed the guests that he was going to play Arcangelo Corelli's *Follia*, and tuned his violin. Suddenly the sonorous voice of the chief rabbi was heard. "It is written in the Scriptures that the dead are to be mourned for seven days. Fools, however, should be mourned for all the days of our lives!"

From the laboratory came the voice of the sorcerer, who made an unexpected response to Mr. Kobryner. "The Scriptures also say: 'Why are ye fearful, o ye of little faith?' "

The chief rabbi responded in an angry voice, "Have a care, Mr. Henner. That is not from the Old Testament but from the New Testament." To which the inventor replied, "A testament is a testament. The newer, the better."

That ended the skirmish, and Henner turned out the light in his laboratory, which set the scene for the great moment.

Everyone was dead quiet as Nathan played the famous theme and variations. The fair Sarah sat at the piano, and as she accompanied her son she glanced suspiciously from the music to the door to the darkroom. She did not know whether she should be hopeful or doubtful. Again and again she hit false notes, but except for the melancholy cherub no one seemed to notice. The guests' attention was not directed at art but at science, or rather, business. Sarah

54

could have played anything she pleased and no one would have cared.

At sixteen minutes past six Nathan finished his concert and the relieved listeners applauded, for finally they were permitted to talk again. Now it had to happen. Leo Rosenbach had disappeared under the black cloth. Any moment now the door would open and the fakir would appear, holding in his hand the first color photo of all time. He would bow and speak words of wisdom. The festive party would jump from their chairs. To see. With their own eyes. He, Leo, the brother of the genius, would ignite the magnesium powder and press the release. The document of the century. Unfortunately only in black and white, but it would prove that an epoch-making event had taken place in the Rosenbach house. A picture for posterity. For the history books of coming generations.

As we have already said, among those present was Dr. Loewenthal, a man-about-town who was sitting right next to the piano. He turned to Sarah and said in a stage whisper, "You know me as a gynecologist, madam. I know little about men, but this inventor is a psychiatric case."

"To say the least, doctor. You see, he is my husband . . ."

"That can't be!"

"Used to be my husband. It's been almost sixteen years. Do you know him personally?"

"I have observed him. Just now, when he introduced himself. It remains a mystery to me how such beautiful women get such men."

"A lot of people think he is a genius."

"I think he is completely crazy. This man is, to put it mildly, a menace to society."

After Loewenthal had made this remark, Leo called out from under his cloth, "Henner, how much longer shall we wait?" The sorcerer called back, "Exactly one minute more."

Leo removed the black cloth from his head, looked at his watch, and proclaimed solemnly, "Fifty seconds more,

55

my esteemed friends. You will never forget this date. Remember: June first, six o'clock and nineteen minutes Central European time, in the Galician garrison town of Stanislav, in the reign of Emperor Franz Joseph of Austria. In a minute we shall find out, Dr. Loewenthal, who is *meshugge* and who isn't . . ." Leo took the release in one hand and the magnesium powder in the other. "When the door to this darkroom opens, a new era will begin. What I shall photograph in a few moments is an unexampled sensation. Please look at the doorknob! Fifteen seconds, five . . . Attention!"

Now it was so still one could hear people breathing. The suspense became unbearable, but nothing was happening yet. Leo was so nervous that the sweat dripped from his nose. "Henner, are you ready? Answer yes or no!" Henner did not answer, but Wassermann could be heard whispering to Sarah, "Nu, what did I tell you?"

"I'm a bit nervous," replied the woman, who was white as chalk. "I can't remember what you told me."

"Then I'll repeat it for you, madam. I said hoo ha. No more and no less." This was the high point of the evening. His face red as a beet, Leo hurled himself at the tail-coated Wassermann, intending to choke him. At the last moment, however, he stopped in his tracks and instead rushed to the door of his lab, where he began to scream in a wild voice, "Open up, Henner, otherwise I'll beat in the door!"

For the second time there was no answer. At that point tear-choked sobbing could be heard in the background. It was Jana, who, strangely enough, had scarcely been in evidence that evening. "He's done something to himself, the unfortunate man. Nobody wants to believe in him. You are all heartless and small-minded. You have murdered him, I feel it, and especially you, Leo. Out of envy—because *he* is great and *you* are small."

That was the last straw. Leo drummed on the door with both fists and screamed, "For the last time, Henner! I will count to three, and then there will be a misfortune!"

Again there was no answer.

"I've had enough now, Henner! One ... two ... and ..." At the count of three he forced the door open with his left shoulder. It broke into pieces and Leo stumbled into the darkroom, panting, snorting, and gasping for air. He looked around, but no one was there. The room was empty. The window was open, and in front of it was a stool. Not a trace of Henner.

After a moment of consternation Simche Pilnik started talking. For almost twenty years he had been planning to take revenge because Henner had ruined Leo's wedding for him. Now he saw an opportunity, and he said with biting sarcasm, "Congratulations, Mr. Court Photographer! It's a historic moment for our garrison town. The inventor has evaporated like smoke from a pan. And he took along the diamond that was worth three thousand crowns. More or less. God alone knows who gave it to him ..."

Jana proudly walked up to the *shadchen* and hissed at him like a furious cat, "*I* did, Mr. Pilnik. Does that answer your question?"

Leo felt as if he were choking and screamed, "*You?* And who did *you* get it from?"

"That's none of your business. Good night!"

Jana left the studio, and Magierkovitch said derisively, "Take our picture anyway, Mr. Rosenbach! Perhaps there'll be a photo for the history books after all. You see, it's a classic."

Sarah said sarcastically, "A picture for the history books, ladies and gentlemen. The only question is what caption we shall put with it ..."

Loewenthal rose from his armchair and put his hat on. As he walked to the door, he mumbled, "What we shall put with it, madam? We'll write 'Diddled dupes at putrid party.'" With these words he left the studio.

June 1, 1908. Tomorrow we shall be dispossessed. Today was a lot of fun. Uncle Henner hoodwinked the whole town. I think it's fantastic. They all came, though they did not believe him. But if they didn't believe him, why did they come? Perhaps simply because they are spiteful scoundrels. They wanted to see a person being ruined by his imagination. They are totally without imagination themselves. They see only what is visible, and are scared of the invisible. They repeat and listen to the old chestnuts for the hundredth time. They speak platitudes and stick to old attitudes. New things seem ugly or hateful to them. New paintings, new music, and new poetry make them uncomfortable—more than that, they fill them with loathing. They loathe everything that comes into being. They hate young people because they are themselves old as the hills. They were born with moss on their heads. The only person who had hopes for last night was my papa. But his hope was a selfish one. He had no other choice. After all, his life was at stake. It was a matter of survival, for he is up to his neck in debt. Tomorrow the men will come and take all our possessions away. Under such circumstances it is easy to hope. If he only knew how little I care about all this! What *I* have in mind requires neither gold nor gems. Only courage, and courage is something that can be learned. Baltyr smiled when they handcuffed him. Baltyr has no fear, because he has no property. Because he needs nothing and has nothing to lose. Tomorrow the men are coming . . . Strange. One couldn't say, "Tomorrow the women are coming." Women don't come to take anything; they come to give. Now we know that it was mama who obtained the diamond. I suspected that she had a finger in the pie, because she loves Henner. She doesn't deny that. Why shouldn't she love him? But I feel that her love isn't pure. Just as papa's hope wasn't pure. She wants something from Henner. His body, I suppose. I'm not saying that this is bad. But *I* am different. I love Baltyr and want nothing from him. It would be hopeless, anyway. We have no news of him. He is probably dead. I love Baltyr for his courage. Because he is unselfish. That is the highest form of imagination. To risk your life and ask nothing in return. He stakes his person and loses. A gambler in the truest sense of the word . . . I feel sorry for papa. No one ever talks about him. He knows that in order to get the diamond, mama . . . But papa would never ask. He isn't strong enough for that . . . *I* would ask point-blank where the money came from. In what way she procured it, and whether she strayed from the straight and narrow. But *he* isn't allowed to say anything. He has to be glad if he is tolerated in his own house, which tomorrow will no longer be his house. How does he come to love her so much? What does he get in return? Nothing. She doesn't even see him. For her he simply doesn't exist. Though he toils for her. Though when he has money he brings her presents. Mama doesn't even thank him. She can't say thank you. She thinks it's all right for him to lie at her feet like a dog. That's terrible. I've got to get away from here. Otherwise I'll become just like the rest. Tomorrow mama is going to Radauti. To beg for help. From straitlaced Uncle David, who despises us. They say that he is a usurer, but he is still permitted to despise us. Because he has money and we don't. He can have whatever he wants and whenever he wants it. He doesn't even need to smile. People are afraid of him and do his bidding. With the exception of my mama. She isn't afraid, and even claims that she will "crack" him. That's a nice expression, isn't it? She said she was going to return with ten thousand crowns, and that would save us. They'll leave us the house and we'll be able to stay here. Yet I want to get away from here . . . I'd like to know how she's going to crack him. She probably has a method by which she also "procured" the diamond. Another such word. Procure. Crack. She has a trick, I'm sure of that, but what is it? She has never revealed it. Such things aren't talked about here. Too bad, but I shall find out. It can't be that hard . . . I know it from Liebermann, my Latin teacher. He plays the learned professor, but when I look into his eyes, he blushes and his nostrils quiver. Then I know that I could do whatever I want with him. He adores me with his ox-eyes. His hands get moist and he smells like wet remnants. Cracking him would be a cinch, whatever "cracking" might mean. He would chop one of his hands off to have me. What does it mean to "have someone"? I think two people undress in front of each other and then they kiss; men are supposed to take the initiative in that. No one has tried this with me yet. Why is that so? I wouldn't let Liebermann do it, that's for sure. I'd belt him one. But with someone I like, why not? Henner, for example. But he's gone now. Or his son, that unreal Nathan. He's gone too. Vanished from the face of the earth, like his father. He looks like an angel, and angels can fly. If he caressed me, my breasts or thighs, I would swoon with delight. He flew off with his fiddle. Fluttered after his father, and together they're over the hills and far away. Tomorrow everything will be decided. Mama is going to Radauti to "crack" the old bloodsucker. She also called it "softening him up," and so he can't be that hard. Maybe he has a heart in his chest after all. Who knows. Perhaps it involves not his heart, but other organs. But they keep quiet about that too. If mama gets the money, we'll stay. If she doesn't, we'll be out in the street. Being out in the street at last is my most ardent hope. Then I'll do what Henner and Nathan have done: disappear. Toward the East. Through the swamps and the woods. Always toward the sunrise. I'm coming, Baltyr. Whether you are dead or alive. You are counting on me. When they took you away, you smiled . . .

5

VLADIVOSTOK IS A CANCER. TO BE SURE, IT WAS NOT founded until 1860, but by the beginning of the new century it had grown into the most important seaport of eastern Russia. It developed into a supply center for the entire Pacific Coast, and it is no accident that its name means "ruler of the East." The St. Petersburg government turned the metropolis into a fortified naval base. The city also became the home port of a big whaling and sealing fleet. Factories and whole industries sprang up in the harbor area. Shipyards, rolling mills, and blast furnaces were built. Finally, it was to its location as the terminus of the Trans-Siberian Railroad that the city owed both its power and its impressive ugliness.

As I have already related, the eleven sons of Yankel Kaminski arrived in Vladivostok on July 12, 1906. At the railroad station, which was corroded by salt and disfigured by coal dust, they bought a newspaper. In it they read the news of Dreyfus's rehabilitation, his promotion to the rank of major, and his release from his dungeon on Devil's Island. There it was, in black and white: "released from the dungeon on Devil's Island." So there were no prisons from which it was impossible to escape. This was tremendous news. That the impossible became possible and that the eleven cloud-movers managed to escape from the peoples' prison of the czar was in no small measure due to this information. Ber, the oldest, turned to his brothers and said, "The law of gravity is suspended, comrades. Apples no longer fall from the tree to the ground, but from the ground to the tree. What was sauce for the French goose is sauce for the Russian gander. Justice is indivisible. It prevailed in one place and will prevail everywhere if we want it to. It depends on us and on no one else. We shall fly up to the stars, and I ask you, Do you wish to fly along?"

All of them answered, "We want to fly along."

"Let anyone who harbors doubts, speak up now! Tomorrow it will be too late . . ."

And when no one spoke up, he said, "Let us make a vow, then: Forward with Dreyfus to the New World!" They all repeated, "Forward with Dreyfus to the New World!"

As we have already said, the eleven boys were disguised as railroad men. Nothing made them conspicuous, though their wire-rimmed glasses were a bit unusual. But thank God, they were far to the east, and there people had seen more unusual sights than that. To understand the further course of events, you must know that in those days all lower-ranking employees wore the same uniform. That made it difficult to distinguish, say, a ticket collector from a customs inspector or some other official of the Russian imperial administration. Hence no one was surprised when on that summer day eleven men appeared in the harbor and said that they had to inspect the cargo of the *Abraham Lincoln*, an American freighter carrying furs that was about to sail for western Alaska. It was shortly after eleven, and the sun was approaching the zenith. No one bothered the alleged customs officials as they went on board, where they were greeted by a Captain Fairchild and taken to the hold via the afterdeck. Everything went pleasantly and smoothly until an explosive charge suddenly went off a scant hundred meters from the crow's nest. The freighter was shaken to its foundations and the eleven comrades as well as the captain were knocked off their feet. This caused indescribable confusion on the freighter and in the surrounding harbor area. The crew of the *Abraham Lincoln* rushed ashore. Everyone wanted to see what was going on and how the catastrophe had happened. The jetty was crowded with curiosity-seekers shouting in a veritable babel of tongues. Everyone gesticulated, everyone had his theory about the cause of the misfortune. The captain was the only one who kept his composure. He got up, adjusted his cap, and said good-bye to the eleven officials, telling them to please go ahead with their work.

It soon turned out that neither the furry nor the human cargo had been damaged. People were astonished, but they gradually returned to their boats and no one thought of inquiring where the eleven customs inspectors were. They had been forgotten in the excitement. Twenty minutes later the ship's sirens wailed and the freighter put out to sea. Nobody knew that there were eleven stowaways on board, including one Moishe Kaminski, until recently a student of chemistry.

The eleven escapees sat in a daze among mountains of boxes containing furs. They now had time to reflect on their fate and on the dangers they might encounter on the voyage across the Bering Sea. Menahem was as pessimistic as ever. "They are looking for us. Our Wanted poster hangs in all the Russian ports. If a storm breaks out anywhere between Sakhalin and Kamchatka, God help us! Then this damned American ship is going to put in at Tilichiki or Anadyr, policemen will come aboard, and our adventure will be over . . ."

"Nothing is over," grumbled Mordechai, who was as strong as an ox. "We are in the majority. We dressed up as trainmen, and we can put on sailors' garb too. Didn't everything go smoothly in Irkutsk? With my bare hands I . . ."

"Oh, spare me your bare hands!" replied Ber. "Irkutsk was our original sin. Brawn instead of brain. We ought to be ashamed of ourselves. We are no better than our enemies."

"What were we supposed to do?" said the second oldest brother scornfully. "Dance with them or what?"

"Not dance but talk. As one human being to another. But we are too primitive to do that."

"You want to talk with Russian policemen? With professional killers, with our mortal enemies? If we don't destroy them, they'll destroy us . . ."

Shloime got more and more excited. His rivalry with his oldest brother welled up and he incited the others. "They are going to drown us in the floods of the Sea of Okhotsk. All that will be left of us will be a pitiful police report. Somebody has pushed us into a trap. This somebody is called Ber. My oldest brother Ber, who wants us to believe that we'll get out of here if we start a nice conversation with our hangmen. One human being to another—till they make chopped liver out of us . . ."

Ber smiled a superior smile. "Dreyfus was deeper in the muck than we are, and he got out alive. The trap that Shloime is afraid of is steaming straight toward Alaska. Alaska belongs to the United States of America. There we shall be free and begin a new life. Or should we have stayed? Pursued by a thousand stoolpigeons, only to wind up in Verkhoyansk after all?"

"We'll starve before we arrive. We don't have anything to eat."

"Then we'll simply raid the kitchen."

"So they notice that we're here and turn us over to the authorities?"

"American sailors? Twenty-four-karat proletarians who are on our side! I bet there are comrades among them."

"How are you going to identify them? By a litmus test?"

Lazik had not spoken a single word; he had been lying on his back, apparently daydreaming. Suddenly he snapped his fingers and said jubilantly, "I'll lure them here."

"Who?"

"The comrades, of coure."

"How are you going to do that?"

64

"Wait and see."

Lazik was a latter-day Orpheus. Women ran after him, and so did men, for he enchanted them all. He played all sorts of musical instruments and was a master imitator of animal sounds. That evening, after the sailors had retired to their cabins, sweet chirping came rippling over the 'tween deck. Anyone who listened closely could make out that some encoded signal was being warbled, a secret code that could be deciphered only by those who knew the revolutionary hymn called the *Internationale*: "Peoples, listen to the signals. Forward to the last battle!" And on that freighter with a cargo of furs there were people who listened to the signals. Two sailors heard the call of the Pied Piper and understood it instantly. They climbed down to the cargo area and found the stowaways, who from then on were protected and no longer had anything to fear.

Three weeks later the *Ketchikan Tribune,* a provincial paper and Alaska's only daily, carried a headline that was reprinted by the entire yellow press of the New World: "Men Under Czarist Death Sentence Escape to America." The story read as follows:

In mysterious fashion eleven revolutionaries from Russia—that is, from Warsaw—who have been sentenced to death managed to board the *Abraham Lincoln* unnoticed and, proceeding from Vladivostok through the Bering Strait, to reach the American mainland. Such a daring feat would never have succeeded without the complicity of like-minded Americans. This should serve as a warning to our authorities and shipping lines. The eleven revolutionaries have no papers, but they claim to be brothers and make a relatively civilized impression, though they have neither washed nor shaved in a month. Our chief reporter Bob Ferguson was able to interview the fugitives and asked them this logical question: What actually prompts you to sacrifice your lives to the destruction of our civilization? To this question he received a number of answers, which we shall print in their entirety.

Ber Kaminski, 24, medium size, compact build, with leadership qualities: "If anyone is destroying civilization, it is not us but the Great Powers, which subjugate entire continents, exterminate peoples, and prepare wars that, if we don't do anything about it, will lead to the end of mankind."

Shloime Kaminski, 23, wears glasses, extremely near-sighted, self-righteous and sarcastic: "Today's industrial society is based on free competition—that is, the crushing of the weaker by the stronger. But since the weaker are in the majority, they will one day smash and destroy the existing civilization."

Yitzhak Kaminski, 22, wears glasses, yellowish skin, a wag who inclines to cynicism: "The civilization you have in mind is obviously the struggle of all against all. Completely in the spirit of Satan, who teaches us to despise our neighbor as ourselves. This fight will go on, God willing, until mankind eradicates itself."

Mordechai Kaminski, 21, heavy-set, large-boned physique, small eyes: "I am not in the habit of talking much. I am a man of action, and share the opinion of my brothers."

Moishe Kaminski, 20, keen-witted intellectual type: "You needn't fear that we shall destroy your civilization by force. It will be wrecked without us. By its own contradictions. By the conflict between the small group of all-powerful capitalists and the millions of debased proletarians."

Adam Kaminski, 19, realistic and sensible, young manager type: "What I can't stand is bad business. Bad businesses must be liquidated, and the quicker the better. What people call civilization today is nothing but a sinking ship."

Lazik Kaminski, 18, the most delicate of the eleven brothers, an impractical artistic type: "Of course I am a revolutionary. Because I despise this world. I want to change it—not in a destructive frenzy, but in self-defense. You see, we are Jews. For 2000 years we have been beaten, tortured, massacred. For two millennia we have been chased from place to place, from country to country, and if anyone holds his head high, it is chopped off. This is what I am rebelling against, and I shall do so to my last breath."

Benzion Kaminski, 17, markedly Jewish features, bad-tempered neurasthenic: "What are you talking about? The civilization of the czar? Of the Prussian empire? Of the sultan of Constantinople? If you had spent even one day at the Warsaw citadel, you too would risk your life for the destruction of this civilization."

Menahem Kaminski, 16, fanatic eyes, prophetic gestures: "Everything is born amidst convulsions and spasms. All modern states are products of civil wars and revolutions. The United States of America, for example. Or France. Or Great Britain. A smart Jew—you probably don't know him, his name is Karl Marx—wrote that all history to date is the story of class struggles. He might have added that future history will also be the story of class struggles. Wait ten years, and there will no longer be a czar in Russia, there will be no Kaiser in Germany, and not even the name of the Turkish sultan will be left."

Aaron Kaminski, 15, practical and likable, could be a worker or a craftsman: "It always depends on your point of view. You speak with horror of the destruction of the old. I, however, speak with delight about the construction of the new. You can reproach me with felling a tree in order to make a table. Is the table worse than the tree? Not as far as I am concerned. To me it is a higher form of tree. A synthesis between nature and intellect. A product of the human faculty of invention."

Hersh Kaminski, 14, vivacious sprite, theatrical temperament: "Permit me a counterquestion: Do you think Christ would have been nailed to the cross if he had liked our civilization? After all, he wanted a better world, a different world, and that is why he had to die. If he came back today, he might not be crucified, but he surely would not be allowed to do anything."

Last night the eleven revolutionaries were discharged from the custody of the sheriff of Ketchikan. They left for New York, where they are alleged to have relatives. They also plan to try to obtain residence permits.

6

~~~~

For almost two years now Yankel Kaminski had had no word from his sons. As he used to say, that mattered to him no more than an empty bottle, for he did not have any sons. He said loud and clear that he never had had any and never would have any. If anyone started talking about those eleven fellows, he ordered him to change the subject. Not even Noemi, his wife, was allowed to broach the delicate subject. For nights on end she lay awake and wept. Yankel knew exactly how she felt, but he pretended not to notice anything. He could not sleep either. He suffered the torments of hell, but he did not say a word. A godless heathen is what he was. He was on the outs with God just as he was with his sons, but he had pangs of conscience. He had once gone to the synagogue, and if, contrary to his custom, he thought of death, he remembered long-forgotten words: "Do not fall into heartlessness, for it would consume your strength like a bull; it would eat up your leaves, destroy your fruits, and leave you like a dried-up tree." He, a dried-up tree? Ridiculous. He was small and rotund, but strong as an ox. Hotheaded and irascible when something did not go his way or annoyed him. He had all the women he wanted. He was known in every tavern, because he could drink till the small hours of the morning. He was the most popular jokester, known far and wide, but he was not loved. He knew this, and that is why he brooded for hours on end in his office without saying a word. He stared through the window into the machine room and chewed on his thoughts: No more than an empty bottle. They've cost me a hundred thousand rubles. They've ruined me. They make fun of their father. So who is the heartless one? Me? And what is heartlessness, anyway? That sort of thing isn't traded on the stock exchange. In Warsaw one has to be hard, or one is crushed. Yankel Kaminski won't let himself be crushed, least of all by his own sons. Another hundred thousand rubles? Am I a fool? If I'd sprung them from the citadel, a few days later they would have been locked up again. Now they are in Siberia. In Verkhoyansk, they say. No one has ever returned from there. You go into the lead mines, but you don't come out of the lead mines. Oy, Yankel Kaminski, what a life this is! A *shmeck* and a *shmuck* and *gehakte tsuris* . . .

There was a knock on the door, but Yankel heard nothing. Another knock made him look up. "Someone wants to disturb me, *do jasnej cholery*. Who's knocking?"

"It's me, the mailman."

"So don't make such noise, and come in! What's happening?"

"Nothing new, *panie* Kaminski. The Kaiser has landed in Morocco. There's war with the French."

"What have you got in your head? Sauerkraut?"

"When I told you three years ago that there was going to be war with Japan, you threw me out."

"I kicked you down the stairs. But not because you told me that there was going to be war."

"Why else?"

"Because I don't want to know what you tell me. Your voice makes me sick."

"Do you want me to leave, *panie* Kaminski?"

"First give me the letter and then get out of here."

"What letter, *prosze pana*? I have dozens of letters for you . . ."

"I don't want dozens of letters, just one. You know exactly which one I mean, but that's the very one you don't bring me, just to annoy me."

"Where is it supposed to be from, your letter?" The mailman pinched the corners of his mouth spitefully.

"From Siberia, you meathead. Why do you ask if you know?"

"I don't know anything. I didn't even know you were doing business in Siberia."

"I'm doing bad business in Siberia. Lousy business. And now go, and don't come back till you have the letter!"

That evening the old man went to Haskel Sonnenschajn's tavern and hit the bottle. A thick haze enveloped the place, and it smelled of *bimber* and tobacco. The habitual drinkers were sitting at the tables with black hats on their heads. Yankel Kaminski was the only one without a hat. He was so rich that he did not have to observe either commandments or prohibitions. People sat around and philosophized into their glasses, as they say. Hunchbacked Grabyk stood in front of the bar and plucked his balalaika. Yankel was in a foul mood and said darkly, "The *revolucja* is dead and buried because it means a deficit. It's bad business, a simple miscalculation, oy!"

Bony Pinkus replied, "As the Ukrainians say, the snake dies and a swan crawls out of its egg."

Yankel had his glass refilled and growled, "The swan's croaked too. Hope was a figment of the imagination. Progress is dead."

At that point Grabyk stopped his strumming and sighed. "The Germans have invented a light bulb that burns ten years without going out."

"Nu?"

"Anybody can screw a light in his lamp and read books all night."

"So?"

"A person gets smarter when he reads."

Now slit-eyed Schajchet looked up from his glass. "Smarter maybe, but discontented."

"Who says he should be contented?" asked Grabyk. "Is he supposed to wag his tail if he's hit in the face? On the contrary. He should be angry. He should defend himself, otherwise he isn't a man but a dog."

"You'll see: A swan will crawl out of the egg."

"And from the swan will crawl a fart, oy!"

Schajchet grimly shook his head: "Have a good trip to Siberia! There you'll go on gabbing. In the lead mines of Verkhoyansk there's room for all of you. There you'll read all night and be smart alecks all day. By the way, what do you hear from your sons, Yankel Kaminski?"

"I hear that you're a crablouse, and I'm going to step on you if you keep asking."

Sensing a brawl, Grabyk tried to calm them down. "As the *goyim* say, life is like a card game. One day you're in the carriage, the next you're under the wheels. Take this Dreyfus. First they make a spy out of him. They degrade him, send him to Devil's Island, sentence him as a Jewish traitor . . ."

"There's your light bulb."

". . . but ten years later they acquit him. They bring him back to France and promote him to major."

"And what do the *goyim* say? Beg your pardon, they say, we made a mistake."

"A swan does crawl out of the egg, but with clipped wings."

"Yankel Kaminski, I'd like to know what you hear from your sons."

"I don't know what nonsense you're talking, Mendel Schajchet. I have five daughters, and that's all. Before you marry one of them, I'll chop off both my legs, oy!"

"I'm not asking about your daughters but about your sons. Don't you think we know that you have them on your conscience, you old skinflint?"

"Shut your trap, Mendel Schajchet, or you'll be damn sorry."

"Do you know the story about the horsedealer from Kalisz? Everybody knows it. He traded his *mishpocheh*, all his kith and kin away to the devil. And what do you suppose he did with the proceeds?"

"I'm telling you for the last time: Keep quiet!"

"He went to the tavern, put the money on the table, and guzzled it all up . . ."

At this Yankel's patience snapped. He grabbed the bottle in front of him and beat Schajchet over the head with it. And what happened? A miracle. The bottle broke to bits but Schajchet was unhurt.

Old Sliteyes smiled coolly. "Yessir, Yankel Kaminski. He sold his *mishpocheh* and boozed the money away. Then he went home and dropped dead."

Everybody looked at Yankel, wondering what he was going to do. And what did he do? He put on his coat and called out, "Haskel Sonnenschajn, the bill!"

7

WHEN YANKEL KAMINSKI LEFT THE TAVERN, IT WAS 3:00 P.M. in the western hemisphere—in New York, for example. Anyone who went along Lexington Avenue or Third Avenue on the Lower East Side might imagine he was in Zhitomir or some other Jewish *shtetl* in Eastern Europe. The same textile stores, the same kosher restaurants, little carts with *kishkes* and bagels, dusty books and candied fruit. The same patriarchs who presided over the sidewalk with long beards and round hats. At a street corner musicians were playing. Next to them a fanatic made incendiary speeches, and in the background stood brownstone houses. One of these housed Jim Weissplatt's men's hairstyling salon. Only half of the thirty barber chairs were occupied, but the discussion was just as lively as at Sonnenschajn's in Warsaw or at Glovatzky's in Galicia: "Twenty times as many immigrants as last year. Boy, America is going to *plotz* from all these immigrants."

"Let it *plotz*. Things can only get better."

"What have you got against immigrants? You're one yourself. Everyone is an immigrant here. Only the Indians aren't, but even they aren't doing so good."

"The Indians and the niggers are our misfortune. They can neither read nor write. They don't pay taxes either, because they haven't got anything. The devil take them!"

"But they're healthy, while we're dying off from tuberculosis. Spelling don't make you rich in America."

"The devil take them, I said. They'll take any job for lousy pay, and if the unions decide to strike . . ."

"We don't need no unions or strikes, just order and a canal between the East Coast and the West Coast."

"And you think a canal can save us? I spit on the canal."

"Then you're spitting on Teddy Roosevelt, mister. Teddy Roosevelt's the best president the Jews ever had. With a parting or without one?"

"With, if you please, and a little brilliantine, but Teddy Roosevelt is too expensive for me. His election campaign cost us a million six hundred thousand dollars. We can't afford that. He may be good for the Jews, but what business does he have in Latin America?"

"Teddy Roosevelt said we have a sacred right, you understand, a sacred right to see that there's law and order there."

"And I, mister, have a sacred right to cut off one of your ears with my scissors."

"That's not the same thing, sir."

"It's exactly the same. 'Cause I've got a scissors and you got none. That's my sacred right, and you oughta be ashamed as a Jewish immigrant that's been beaten up in Lodz or Kishinev just a couple years ago, and now you yourself go to Latin America and beat up the Indios . . ."

As the barber was saying this, the door opened and eleven customers entered. At their unkempt appearance all those present fell silent. The branch manager, who had been devouring a Yiddish scandal sheet, rose from his chair and asked in a weary, oily voice, "A haircut or a shave?"

The leader of the lads answered for his brothers, "Neither nor, thank you."

"There isn't a third thing here, gentlemen. Good-bye."

"Then please give us the fourth thing."

"This is a barbershop, as you can see. The toilets are in the next block. Good-bye."

"We want to speak with the boss, mister. His name is Weissplatt."

"May I ask you to leave this shop."

"Call the boss at once! Are you deaf or what?"

"If I call anyone, it'll be the police. Get out of here immediately!"

"Is Jim Weissplatt the owner of this business or isn't he?"

"Jim Weissplatt is the owner of fifty-seven barbershops and some other enterprises. Clear out of here this instant!"

The manager pulled the alarm, which rang outside and attracted dozens of curious onlookers. "And now I'll have you thrown out!"

"Or the other way round, sir, because Jim Weissplatt is our uncle."

"And Teddy Roosevelt is my aunt. Do you take me for an idiot?"

"Yes!"

Under ordinary circumstances this would have marked the beginning of a brawl, but at that moment three policemen came rushing in.

By comparison with the Warsaw citadel, any other prison in the world is an amusement park, and the police station on Third Avenue even a nightclub. Under the liberal surveillance of two cops the Kaminski boys sat on an upholstered bench and with amused smiles listened to the conversation between their uncle and the police chief.

"We cannot fulfill your wish, Mr. Weissplatt."

"But they're the sons of my sister, who lives in Warsaw and is married to my brother-in-law Yankel Kaminski at Three Mostowa Street."

"The gentlemen have to leave the United States of America within forty-eight hours. That is my final word."

"If that's your final word, my nephews will be hanged. Escaping from exile is a capital crime."

"That doesn't concern me, mister. They don't have immigration permits, but still they're here. So they are breaking the law and will be deported. We are a constitutional country, Mr. Weissplatt."

At this point Hershele joined the conversation. "I have a question for you, chief."

"Someone without any papers has no right to ask any questions. What would you like to know, young man?"

"What's the name of that statue in New York harbor? I saw it for the first time and I don't know what it is."

"That's the Statue of Liberty. Everybody knows that . . ."

"Except you, chief."

"Without documents there's no freedom here, do you understand?"

"No, I don't understand," replied Uncle Weissplatt. "You want to send my nephews to their deaths. Why?"

"Because I'm an official. I do my duty, and that's all. But you are free to put up bail."

"In what amount?"

"Ten thousand dollars, and you can take them with you."

"Here's the money," sighed Weissplatt, writing out a check. Then he went to the door and turned around once more. "I hope it gives you heartburn like a rancid fish."

With that he was about to leave the police station, but the chief called him back. "And what are we going to do with those fellows?"

"Disinfect them, mister. At public expense!"

The eleven boys soon were the talk of the Lower East Side. In Jim Weissplatt's gentlemen's salon on Lexington Avenue they were the only topic of conversation. The branch manager told his astonished customers, "Eleven cowboys with glasses on their noses. That is unprecedented in world history. They stink like yellow jaundice and threaten to make kindling wood out of the shop."

"I've heard that the boss wants to fire you. Is that true?"

"Sure. 'Cause I did my duty and called the police."

"The paper says that you acted in self-defense."

"Of course in self-defense—what else? Eleven giants. Papers they don't have, they hang around, they don't talk, and then they say that Jim Weissplatt is their uncle. What does a person do in such a situation? So I pull the alarm. The alarm sounds, three cops come in, arrest the boys, and it turns out . . ."

". . . that Jim Weissplatt really is their uncle. That's what it says in the paper."

"And he had to cough up ten thousand bucks for the police chief in person. That isn't in the paper, but it's true nevertheless."

"Bail is bail, mister. You get it back, and no harm done."

"Jim Weissplatt forked over ten thousand dollars, but he never got a receipt. So the bail isn't bail but a tip. Sure, a tip for the police, and I'm supposed to pay for it. A dog's life with *tsores* galores . . ."

There is no arguing about taste, least of all Jim Weissplatt's, for his aesthetic norms were in conformity with those of about fifty million other Americans. With such majorities there are no arguments. Shall I carry on a hopeless struggle against that Indian silk carpet on which are embroidered two coconut palms and a sleeping lion and of which there are about twenty million copies, all of them machine-woven by the same factory in Singapore and imported by the same furniture wholesaler in Brooklyn? What shall I do about the life-sized china deer that used to stand in all dining rooms between Manhattan and San Francisco? Is there the slightest point in questioning the ungainly leather armchairs, twelve million of which Samuel Finkelstein threw on the market at two hundred dollars apiece? No, for the whole edition was sold out in three weeks, which is sufficient proof of the perfection of the above-mentioned furniture.

Uncle Weissplatt's apartment was an excellent example of American *haut goût*, for it contained scarcely anything that could not have been ordered from any reputable mail-order house. The long dining-room table with twenty-four chairs had been supplied by Lippmann & Ferber. The credenza and the matching glasses as well as the silverware and the elegant Wedgwood china were recognizable as an anniversary offer from Hajnotzky, the big department store on Washington Square. Even Sally Weissplatt, the third wife of the millionaire, tallied one hundred percent with the ideal of fifty million Americans. With the purring voice of an Angora cat and the dazzling smile of a mouthwash ad, she was the American dreamgirl. She had the perfect figure of a model and a face that was the spitting image of all the faces in the rotogravure sections of all the Sunday papers. She had moved in exactly six months after the demise of the second Mrs. Weissplatt, and assured anyone who asked that she had never been so happy in her whole life. She loved her husband as tenderly as she did her automobile, her private yacht, and the passbook of the Bank of Boston, which she always carried.

With a gracious gesture she invited the eleven young men to be seated, noticing that even the burly Mordechai was more appealing than her corpulent spouse, whom she had met through Maccabi, the elegant marriage bureau on Second Avenue. She felt instinctively that the visit of the eleven relatives might upset the comfortable equilibrium of the house. That is why she demonstrated her critical detachment to the boys by constantly munching candy and staring out the window while Uncle Weissplatt tried his best to give it to his nephews straight. "I'm not a philanthropist, boys. I've already paid ten thousand dollars for you, because you are the sons of my only sister Noemi, whom I love like my own wife. Don't get me wrong, Sally! You I love differently, and you know exactly how. But I want the money back, with the usual interest . . ."

"I hardly think," interjected Adam, "that our father is going to pay. He is mad at us, *broyges,* and will never forgive us."

"Your father? What has Yankel Kaminski got to do with your debts? Not a damn thing. You'll go to work here, and I'll get my money back."

"How much do you want to make on us?" asked the oldest brother with an amused undertone in his voice.

"Two hundred percent, boys, otherwise you'll be a clubfoot on my leg."

"And what if we refuse, Uncle Weissplatt?"

"You have no papers, boys. That's why you'll accept. What are you trained to do?"

"I'm a candidate for a doctorate in philosophy."

"Hoo ha. What else?"

"Yitzhak studied at the art academy."

"Hoo ha. Go on."

"Shloime is writing a dissertation on Roman law."

"Not enough to live on. Next."

"Mordechai is a teacher of physical education."

"Finally a *mentsh*. And?"

"Moishe is a student of chemistry."

"Not bad either. Go on."

"Adam is studying mathematics."

"A profession for *shnorrers*."

"Lazik attended the conservatory and is going to be a musician."

"A nightingale, if I understand you correctly. Sings all summer and starves in winter."

"Benzion is studying Assyrian grammar."

"How to be a millionaire."

"Menahem occupies himself with occult sciences."

"That's what we call a fakir in America. Let him become a magician and join the circus."

"Aaron is a watchmaker's apprentice."

"Thank God. A third *mentsh* in the family. And?"

"Hershele wants to become an actor, but he is still in school."

"Boys," groaned Jim Weissplatt, in his desperation stuffing a handful of peanuts in his mouth, "I am a lucky man. I have the most beautiful wife on the Lower East Side. I own more than fifty barbershops in New York and a dozen gambling casinos on the West Coast, but tomorrow morning I'll be flat broke if I finance you. We're not in Russia, dear boys, but in America. Here people have no time for Roman law and Assyrian grammar. Here you have to fight or you go under. Do you know what that means?"

"We were sent to Siberia because we fought."

"Fighting isn't enough, boys. You have to achieve something. What do you want to achieve in this world?"

"Justice for all, Uncle Weissplatt."

"And what else?"

"What do you mean, what else? Justice is the main thing."

"But you can't live on that."

"Perhaps we won't live on it. Perhaps we shall founder in the struggle, but one thing is certain: We shall either win or die."

"Are you sure?"

"Dead sure."

"And you won't give up at any price?"

"Not at any price."

"That's a deal," said the millionaire, with a crafty smile in the corners of his mouth. "I have a big business deal to propose to you."

"Go ahead and propose it, Uncle Weissplatt. We'll see."

"You are eleven healthy fellows. Am I right?"

"You are."

"You'll never give in. Is that correct?"

"Correct."

"Swell. I'll make a soccer team out of you. Under one condition."

"And what's that?"

"That you won't lose. Under any circumstances!"

8

~~~

MALVA WAS NOW EIGHTEEN, AND SOMETHING LIKE A magnetic North Pole toward which the compass needles of all captains on the high seas oscillated. "Our child is like flypaper," Leo used to say, "half of Stanislav sticks to her. We can't let her go out in the street alone; otherwise there'll be trouble." For this reason he accompanied the girl on all her outings, with the pride of an old dandy—he was now sixty years old—who takes his young mistress for a walk and arrogantly and sourly registers all the winks directed her way.

On that summer day he was sitting with his beautiful wife and his even more beautiful daughter in the outdoor café at the municipal park where a band was tooting its way through a medley of schmaltzy military tunes. The three Rosenbachs were addressing themselves to slices of raspberry cake decorated with whipped cream and washing them down with chilled chocolate. At one of the adjoining tables there was some high jinks. A dozen students, fraternity brothers adorned with dueling scars, were swaying in beery bliss and singing lustily:

> Count Radetzky, noble omen,
> Swore to sweep the emperor's foemen
> From deceitful Lombardy.
> In Verona he was hoping,
> But with more troops he was coping,
> And our hero could feel free.

Leo Rosenbach glowed with enthusiasm. When the musical patriotic demonstration was over, he got up and whispered to Jana, "I have to go and congratulate the gentlemen."

"For heaven's sake, don't!"

But Leo would not be detained. He walked up to the nearest student, took his hand, squeezed it devotedly, and said, full of servility, "I am proud that there are still men in Austria."

The student jumped up from his chair, saluted, and roared, "Long live our Emperor Franz Joseph!"

To which Leo responded just as snappily but less loudly, "You are a credit to our fatherland, gentlemen." He made a brief and respectful bow. "I have the honor to introduce myself: Leo Rosenbach."

After a pause that was a bit too long, the student replied, "But your German is excellent. We are honored as well."

Leo knew exactly what was meant by these words, but he responded with false humility, "Former court photographer of King Ludwig of Bavaria."

The fraternity brothers rose as one man, clinked their glasses, and thundered derisively, "Come, let us drink to Bavaria's king."

Leo made one last attempt to break through the wall of boisterous hostility and said, "It would be our pleasure, gentlemen, to grant the dashing elite of the empire a special discount on any kind of photographic work." Now the student standing next to him clicked his heels, and amidst the applause of his besotted fellow students delivered himself of these nasal remarks: "The dashing elite of the empire makes obeisance to your accent-free German, your business-minded offer, and especially the incomparable young lady who is sitting next to you and making our hearts beat faster. Three cheers for her!"

"This young lady is our daughter and the receptionist in our studio, which is located at Eleven Mickiewicz Street."

"Three cheers for the receptionist: Hip, hip, hooray!"

At that point the band started playing again. Jana was

boiling with rage. Her face bright red, she stood up and said loud enough for the students to hear, "Here it's too noisy for me in every respect. Hand me my parasol, Leo!"

The next morning Jana and Malva crossed the railroad bridge on their way to Dr. Daschynski, about whom various rumors were circulating. He lived in the attic of a six-story apartment house right behind the tracks. In his bachelor apartment he gave private lessons and held little meetings in the evening. The two women were excited and in high spirits, as though they were going to an illicit assignation. Jana kept using the shop windows as a mirror to adjust her hat or see whether her makeup was all right. Suddenly Malva asked, "What does he look like, mama? Like Henner or more like Baltyr?"

"The most important thing is that you don't breathe a word to papa. I beg of you!"

"The suspense is killing me. Is he short or tall? I really can't picture him."

"You'll see that he is a handsome man, but papa must not find out that we went to see him."

"I wonder why."

"Daschynski is a socialist. A leader of the party, and you know your father's views, don't you?"

"You say that he is a leader of the party, but all he became is a tutor."

"Because his ambition lies elsewhere."

"If he is so handsome, why isn't he married?"

"*I* am married, Malva. So what?"

"You are the most beautiful woman in the world, mama. I love you."

"I love you too, my child."

They climbed up the steep staircase. It smelled of middle-class apartments and floor polish. On the second floor was the apartment of a Professor Kwiatkowsky, Dean of the Medical School, and Jana whispered, "Daschynski also wanted to become a professor, but they turned him down. They said he was bad for young people."

"I would not have rejected him. I am fascinated by dangerous men. Aren't you?"

"I don't know, Malva. Papa isn't a dangerous man. And by the way, don't be so nosy!"

Finally they reached the sixth floor, the top. Malva curled her lips and said softly: "I'm disappointed, mama. I imagined him as a young god. But here it says 'classical philologist.' "

"I told you not to be so nosy." Jana pulled the bell.

The door opened. The two women faced a man who was anything but what Malva had imagined. He was about forty-five, neither short nor tall, but extremely compact, as though a minimal body contained a maximal human being. He was not handsome, was perhaps even homely, what with his prominent cheekbones and his pointed nose. His eyes sparkled and from them emanated an almost childlike trust. At his temples were tiny creases that indicated both friendliness and watchful reserve. A typical Pole, proud and impulsive. Yet from his features flashed that critical distrust that bespeaks detachment and authority. He gave the two ladies a searching look and smiled. "Mrs. and Miss Rosenbach, I presume. You wrote me. Which is the mother?"

Jana blushed and replied in confusion, "I know you, doctor, and admire you. That's why I took the liberty of paying you a visit. I hope you will want to teach my daughter."

"And I know *you*," replied Daschynski, leading his guests to his study. "I noticed you at one of our rallies."

"You attend rallies, mama?" said the surprised Malva, who was looking at the bookshelves with curiosity.

"It's not enough for me to be your father's housekeeper. You ought to understand that."

"And what do you tell him when he asks you questions? Do you tell fibs?"

"There are things one does," responded Jana with a

84

meaningful sidelong glance at Daschynski, "but keeps to oneself. One really needn't tell everything. One has one's private sphere that belongs to one alone, but I don't like to fib."

Malva embraced her beautiful mother and whispered in her ear, "Mama, I adore you."

Daschynski, who had observed this scene, lit his pipe and said, "The Athenians believed—please have a seat—that a citizen would rather hear seven sweet lies than one bitter truth. What do you think of that?"

After an embarrassed pause Jana replied, "I think the Athenians were clever people. But I have no use for sweet lies. I prefer to keep silent."

"And you, Miss Rosenbach?"

"My papa is a good person, but he doesn't know anything about the age we are living in."

"Do *you* know something about the age we are living in?"

"I'm eighteen, doctor, and my feet are firmly planted in the twentieth century."

"In that case I would like to know why you want to study Greek. And with *me*."

"In the first place, I don't *want* to, I *have* to in order to graduate from secondary school. You see, I want to study at the university—even if I am the first woman to attempt it. And in the second place, I've heard that you are a menace to young people. I'd like to be menaced by you."

Jana winced and whispered, "Don't act crazier than you are, Malva!"

"Greek is a dead language, mama. I want to live as long as I can."

Daschynski took a sepia-tinted photo from his desk and showed it to the girl. "I suppose this wouldn't really interest you."

"Why wouldn't it? I think it's wonderful. The Venus of Milo. It's in the Louvre. In Paris. Some day I'll go to Paris to see her."

"The sculptor who created her, Miss Rosenbach, has been

in his grave for more than two thousand years, and so has the girl who acted as his model."

"Are you trying to convert me, doctor?" replied Malva, who understood what the man was driving at.

"I simply wanted to say that sometimes the dead are more alive than the living."

"But this doesn't mean that I shall be delighted to study Greek vocabulary."

"If you are not, I would advise you to forget it. One can live without it."

Her daughter's nonchalance made Jana nervous, and she said, "But you wanted me to bring you here, didn't you?"

"To the socialist and tempter of the young, mama, not to the classical philologist. His grammar bores me. Or should I lie and say that it's fun?"

"Socialism and classical culture need not be mutually exclusive," replied Daschynski, emptying out his pipe and stuffing it again. "The demand for equality for all human beings originated in Athens."

"What good is it to me if it remains a demand and never becomes practice? Where is equality for the Jews, for example? We have been humiliated for thousands of years and nothing has changed."

"It's very simple: Because you let yourself be humiliated. Women are humiliated too. Workers are humiliated, and so are the have-nots of all countries—because they don't unite. Because they allow themselves to be divided, time and time again. If they were to band together, all the debased and the insulted, all the Jews and Negroes and Indians, all women and proletarians, then the demand would become reality."

"If you give me this in writing, I'll cram Greek vocabulary. But you can't."

"You want a printed guarantee, Miss Rosenbach? Like when you buy a cuckoo clock or a music box . . ."

Malva blushed to the roots of her hair and stammered, "I'm . . . I'm sorry. I . . . I believe you."

"So do I," added her mother. "I'd like to be present now and then. May I?"

"You are always welcome here," responded the man and looked deep in Jana's eyes.

October 1, 1909. I love mama even though she swipes all men from me. Yet she doesn't even try. As soon as she shows up, roast pigeons fly into her mouth. Even Daschynski, this man of mind, loses his mind when he sees her. I wonder what I have to study to be as successful as she. Not Greek vocabulary, that's for sure. This impresses no one, least of all that classical philologist. What kind of person is he? A typical Pole. Yet he's quite different. The Poles despise us and never miss an opportunity to humiliate us. Yet they look like drunken frogs. Daschynski doesn't humiliate anyone. One can't even imagine him humiliating anyone. Not even his mortal enemies, he said. He is really quite different. Baltyr believes in the solitary hero and the solitary revenge. A well-aimed shot, and Stolypin is dead. Daschynski laughs at such ideas. He regards the anarchists as silly fools. They shoot a bloodhound, but a hundred bloodhounds rush to take its place. He claims that what needs to be liquidated is not Stolypin but the whole morass of meanness. Maybe he's right. Actually, I like him. No, I don't. He disturbs me. Last night I dreamed about him. He was standing in an autumnal park. Colorful maple leaves were lying on the ground, and he was admiring a marble statue. I think it was the Venus of Milo. I was lying next to it, on a basalt tombstone, and I was crying. He carefully walked up to the statue and put his arms around her without noticing that I was there. He kissed the nipples of her breasts and whispered: "Sometimes the dead are more alive than the living." I didn't say anything. Hot tears were rolling down my cheeks, and I thought I wanted to die or become petrified. Then he would embrace me and press his lips on the buds of my body. My breasts aren't any less beautiful than those of the love goddess, but I'm too young for him. He doesn't even see that I'm a woman. Or does he? Sometimes, between two grammatical rules, he looks me over, and I have the feeling that his eyes are spraying gold dust. But I can't imagine that he really desires me. Not him. In the street men turn around and look at me. With oily eyes. They disgust me, and a chill runs down my spine. Or the customers in the studio. Their voices break when they tell me their boring things. Always the same. The same phrases that mean nothing and are only supposed to mask the fact that they lust after my body: "I kiss your hand, my highly esteemed young lady." Yet they don't esteem me at all, and if there's anything they'd like to kiss, it's certainly not my hand. All this is awfully repugnant to me, but still I'm full of longing and don't even know for what. I long for Henner, who has disappeared and whose whereabouts no one knows. I long for Baltyr, who has given me an assignment. He's gone too, and I sense that he is already lying in his grave: "Sometimes the dead are more alive than the living." Oh God, help me and give me the strength to believe in you!

The People's House was jam-packed, for the barometer of world politics indicated stormy weather. Hundreds of people stood in the lobby because they had not found a seat. Everyone wanted to hear what Daschynski was going to say at the rally about the latest events. When he mounted the rostrum, he received an enthusiastic reception. Two thousand people rose from their seats and sang the Song of the Red Flag. Then he began, in a piercing, inflammatory voice: "Fellow citizens and comrades . . ."

As Daschinsky said this, he caught sight of a delicate-looking woman in the first row who winked at him mysteriously. Therefore he corrected himself and said, "Ladies and gentlemen, my fellow citizens, my comrades, female and male. There is bad news in the papers. We are facing terrible things. But this does not mean that we are afraid. On the contrary. The more hopeless the situation of the masters, the more promising the situation of the servants.

The crowned heads can no longer rule as they wish. The peoples are beginning to assert themselves. The nameless are knocking on the gates of the palaces. The have-nots are demanding their rights, and the monarchs are beginning to tremble. The German Kaiser recently dissolved the constitutionally elected Reichstag because the socialists denied him credits for armaments. The czar of Russia disbanded the democratically elected imperial duma because the delegates of the people wanted to give land to the starving peasants and bread to the emaciated workers. And what is his colleague in Vienna doing? You know who I am talking about, but I am not allowed to utter his illustrious name, for this would be lese majesty, and nothing is further from my mind than to insult our dear majesty . . ."

At this point derisive laughter broke out in the hall, but the tribune continued unswervingly. "The colleague in Vienna fears the disintegration of his empire because his peoples have for some time desired self-government. He badly needs a frenzy of patriotic fervor as well as a scapegoat for the discontent of the masses. He has found one. Yesterday he invaded two Slavic states, Bosnia and Herzegovina. Now the stage is set. Things will start happening now, because Russia pretends to be the protector of all Slavs, and it is going to declare war on us. Not on us, of course, for we are Slavs ourselves. But we are Austrians at the same time, and so he will declare war on us anyway. As you know, Russia is allied with France and with England, which is why sooner or later we shall be at war with the whole world. As Poles we love the French. As Austrians we must learn to hate them. As Poles we admire England. As Austrians we must despise it. Rejoice, Polish comrades! Congratulate yourselves on your fatherland, for the fatherland of the southern Poles is called Austria. The fatherland of the northern Poles is called Germany. The fatherland of the eastern Poles is called Russia. That is what we learned in school, so it must be true. For more than a hundred years we have been ruled by three Great Powers. If the three emperors are at one another's throats, we shall be forced to shoot our Polish brothers. Isn't that wonderful? The Polish problem will solve itself. The Poles will exterminate one another, and the three majesties in Vienna, Berlin, and St. Petersburg will remain as the victors. Isn't that what you want, ladies and gentlemen, my comrades? Yes or no?"

The whole hall rose as one man. As from one throat came a thunderous cry of thousands: "*Nie, nigdy, niech zyje Polska!* Long live Poland!"

"So you do not want it? You want neither the ruin of our homeland nor the destruction of this world by the Great Powers?"

More thunder: "*Nie, nigdy, niech zyje Polska!*"

"Are you ready, then, to support the decision of the socialist international—that is, to use any means to prevent the word war that threatens?"

"Any means, we swear it. Long live Poland!"

"And if we cannot do that, to use the conflicts among the Great Powers to overthrow the prevailing capitalistic order, and build for all eternity a world with social justice . . ."

As the speaker was saying this, the woman in the front row rose from her seat and cried in a passionate voice, "I am ready, comrades. You can count on me!"

Now a storm of applause broke out in the hall. All were on their feet and intoned the *Internationale*, but a few inconspicuous gentlemen had an eye on Jana and signaled each other to keep a closer watch on the beautiful woman.

Daschynski now came to the apotheosis of his speech. Modestly waving the applause aside, he declared, "The war of the monarchs would be the last war to shake our planet. It would be the beginning of an era of peace. Out of the ruins of the last war, my comrades, our fatherland would be reborn, our beloved Polish homeland . . ."

He was not allowed to go on. All present, women and

men, stood on their seats and intoned the national anthem: *"Jeszcze Polska nie zginęla póki my zyjemy . . ."* Poland is not lost yet, for we shall go on fighting . . .

It was pouring. A solitary pair was slowly strolling through the dimly lit streets. They did not seem to notice that a veritable flood was coming down on the city. They had opened a huge umbrella, and under its protection they walked through the night. "What are you doing at my rallies, Mrs. Rosenbach?"

"Call me Jana!"

"A cherry blossom like you has no business among us."

"I may be a cherry blossom, but that is the very reason why all this moves me."

"So you don't come only . . . on account of me?"

"Oh yes, on account of you. Because you are smart and have a lot to say."

"I say a lot because I know little. I talk about beautiful dreams."

"I know. You dream of things that do not exist, that do not exist as yet. That will exist some day when we are no more. This is what I find fascinating beyond all measure."

"I also dream of things that already exist. I suppose this will disappoint you . . ."

"For instance?"

"Now, under this umbrella, I am dreaming of your mouth. But one should not speak of such dreams."

"Do you think so?"

"Not at public rallies, anyway. The comrades would be against it."

"I am a comrade, and I would be for it."

Daschynski stopped under a gaslight and stared at Jana. Suddenly he noticed that he had stepped into a puddle and was standing in water up to his ankles. He smiled and said, "Ladies and gentlemen, my comrades, we are sinking into the morass, and more than ever it is important to face facts. How do you like my speech?"

"Go on, we'll see!"

"And these eyes confuse me greatly, for they are as mysterious as the night, and honey-colored stars sparkle in them . . . Shall I talk about your eyelashes too?"

"It's *your* speech, not mine. But why talk about my eyelashes?"

"All right, then I'll talk about your hands. In these times, ladies and gentlemen, my comrades, we must link hands"—Daschynski took Jana's hands, carefully removed her gloves, and kissed her fingertips—"for those hands smell like forest violets . . . or is it forget-me-nots?"

"I don't know what's what, doctor, but my hands are ice-cold."

"Warmer days will come, my brothers and sisters. The sun will shine. Our hearts will run over, and so will our mouths. I am now talking about your mouth and your lips, Jana."

"Not here, please."

"Then come to my place. To my apartment!"

"Another time, if you please!"

"Why not today?"

"Next Thursday, if all goes well."

"And if it doesn't, Jana? Who knows whether we shall see each other again."

"Then give me a pledge. Something that I have to return to you."

"Here is my amulet. A memento of my mother."

The Balitzki brothers were twins of noble lineage and a simple-minded nature. One was named Gustav, the other August. Since birth they had appeared as doubles; they resembled each other like a person's two buttocks. Both Gustav and August were conspicuous by their unsurpassable lack of humor. It goes without saying that they wore the same suits, socks, shoes, and hats. Furthermore, they always got up together, sat down at the same moment, and blew their noses simultaneously. They coughed, sneezed, and hiccupped together. When a joke was told—which, understandably enough, rarely happened in their presence—it took them exactly the same time to understand it. They were obviously a miracle of nature, and since they played a fateful role in the life of my family, I am telling a bit more about them than is really necessary. Oh yes, Gustav Balitzki had the idiotic habit of starting sentences and not finishing them. August, for his part, began where his brother got stuck.

One fateful November day the twins came to Leo's studio and wished to be photographed. Like two freshly spruced-up guards they clicked their heels and rattled off a formulaic greeting that was directed exclusively at fair Malva and, as usual, came in two parts: "Highly esteemed young lady . . ." ". . . accept this expression of our great respect."

The two gentlemen briefly caught their breath and rattled on, "It is our pleasure and unparalleled privilege . . ." ". . . to pay the homage that is due to your beauty."

While the two blockheads were frozen in a deep bow, Malva said, twisting her mouth into a malicious smile, "How do the gentlemen wish to be photographed? Together, separately, or one for two?"

"It depends, you one and only lady . . ."

". . . on which variant would be the greatest bargain."

"One for two, of course."

"But we are twins," protested Gustav, and August added, ". . . which is why we have only been photographed together since our birth. Thus we wish to be snapped together at a flat rate."

"Fine, gentlemen, but then we'll do a half-length portrait. That's logical, isn't it?"

The Balitzki brothers wrinkled their brows and tried to think of some clever repartee. Then Gustav blurted, "It may be logical, but your papa had the unspeakable kindness . . ."

". . . to offer a special discount to the elite of the nation."

"Do the gentlemen belong to the elite of the nation?"

was Malva's impertinent response. "Do you have a document that says so?"

The twins clicked their heels again and replied in soldierly fashion, "Gustav Balitzki . . ."

"August Balitzki."

"The third-oldest noble family of Galicia . . ."

"And law students at the University of Lvov . . ."

". . . as well as members of the dueling fraternity Habsburgia . . ."

". . . Hip hip, hooray! Hip hip, hooray! Hip, hip, hooray!"

Fortunately Malva was so young, her skin was so lily-white, and her lips so raspberry-red that she could afford to remain unimpressed. "I beg the third-oldest noble family of Galicia to be seated on the couch and not look so stupid. Otherwise you'll say afterward that it's my papa's fault or that the photo is blurred."

At this point Leo, who had come into the studio, intervened. He came to the aid of the twins, for he felt that Malva had gone too far and was detrimental to his business. Therefore he apologized with the humility of a hereditary vassal and said in a conciliatory tone of voice, "The child isn't even nineteen, illustrious gentlemen. She has no idea whom she is dealing with."

"I know it exactly," responded Malva. "I am dealing with the elite of the nation. Three cheers, four cheers, five cheers."

"Now you keep your mouth shut at last, Malva, and get out of here!"

The students were of a different opinion, and replied in their usual two-part harmony, "The presence of this charming person . . ."

". . . is the real reason why we came here, Mr. Rosenbach."

Not knowing what to reply to that, Leo thought he ought to acquaint the honored customers with the backdrops. "Here you see the rolls with backgrounds that can be pulled down on strings as desired. They are the work of the well-known stage designer Slavomir Schantzer from Cracow, who also furnished the entire studio. Here, for example, you see Schönbrunn Castle. This is the Acropolis, there you see the Colosseum, and finally here is the Cheops pyramid with an excellent likeness of a caravan of camels. In front of which backdrop would the gentlemen like to be photographed?"

"In front of none of them," replied Gustav drily, and August finished his sentence, "For we desire something military."

"Perhaps a horse, gentlemen?"

"We'd prefer a cannon, Mr. Court Photographer."

"I'm sorry, but I don't have any cannon in stock."

"Then bring us a uniform—that is, two . . ."

". . . one for me and one for my twin brother."

Leo smiled obligingly and ordered his daughter to look through the costume wardrobe and bring two uniform coats, "identical, if possible!"

November 21. In three days I'll be nineteen. Another year and I shall be officially considered an adult. Actually, I have been one for a long time, but people continue to regard me as a child. I understand and see through everything, but no one will take me seriously. Papa treats me with condescension and an indulgent smile that I find terribly degrading. In reality he idolizes me, but he won't admit that I am an island. A separate world in the ocean of mankind. Today two soap bubbles came to the studio. Two absolute nobodies from a distinguished house. Twins who get their kicks only from being confused with each other. They are proud that people can't tell them apart. Isn't that typical? The real meaning of life ought to be to mature to individuality. But no. They long for the opposite. Those fellows courted me. That was delicious. Papa was quite befuddled by an illusion. "Do you know what this means?" he said. "The Balitzki gentlemen are interested in little you." A dear idiot. An old jackass who thinks I am little. My little finger is more interesting than these two ciphers put together. Members of a dueling fraternity with fencing scars over their mouths and noses. Candidates for degrees in jurisprudence. That's good for a horselaugh. Only their scars let you guess who is Gustav and who is August. Otherwise they are as alike as two liver dumplings. They talk constantly, but their words are hollow nuts on a dead branch. Papa is under an illusion if he thinks they are interested in little me. Incidentally, if I am anything at all, then I am a big me. I am a differentiated organic compound of all elements of the periodic system. A kaleidoscope of all hues of the spectrum. To these gentlemen, however, I am a parakeet that can be caught and locked in a cage. They would like to penetrate my sphere. Stab me with their sting until I lie there, or more precisely, they lay me without resistance. But they are terribly mistaken. They won't have me, even though my name is Rosenbach and theirs Balitzki. Papa admires them because they are members of the third-best family. Because they are university students. When papa says "university," his eyes grow moist. He wants *me* to study at the university too. Doesn't matter in what department. I am simply supposed to rise. To the upper levels of society. He is a poor devil. He didn't manage to do it. He was thrown out, the way all Jews are thrown out sooner or later. He experienced on his own body the impermanence of titles, dignities, property, rank, and honor. He often sighs, "Knowledge is the only thing no one can take away from you," and that is why I am supposed to study. Climb as high as possible. Papa confuses higher with better and assures me he only wants what is best for me. Yet he does everything wrong. Today, for example. Those two creatures left the house and he called me to the dressing table. In his hand was a clothes hanger, and on it were the two uniforms. He took one of them, held it up to me, and whispered solemnly, "Put it on, my child. I'd like to see how you look in it." I thought it was silly and said this coat had nothing to do with the university. The Balitzkis wear it for their duels and drinking parties, but under it they are nothing but common ordinary protozoa. Then papa said I should do as he told me, and I

96

went along with the masquerade. I put the uniform on and stepped in front of the mirror. It was pitiful. I looked like a costumed ape. I was so ashamed I wished the earth would swallow me up, but papa was delirious. Malva Rosenbach with a saber, a tassel, and a golden hilt. "My daughter is going to register at the university as the first female student. They'll be astonished, my child. Come closer, my angel! This is how I must photograph you. Exactly like this. As a member of the Habsburgia . . ." I let him do what he wanted even though it disgusted me. He wanted half a dozen poses. From the right and from the left. From close up and from a distance. With the saber and without it. "Yes, now it's fine . . ." Truth to tell, it wasn't fine at all but downright ludicrous.

With this last remark, however, Malva was off base. It was no laughing matter; on the contrary. Leo's delivery man, senile Mr. Serotzki—called Sclerotzki, because he was so forgetful he mixed everything up—made a mistake that was to prove disastrous for the Rosenbachs. On the shipping shelf the photos for the distinguished gentlemen Gustav and August were on the left and the half-dozen photos of the enchanting Malva Rosenbach as a fraternity brother, complete with saber, silk sash, and cap, were on the right. By mistake Serotzki wrapped up the wrong pictures and took them to the Balitzkis' house. What happened next was a comedy of errors, or more precisely, a melodrama with a tragic ending. The following morning the door to the studio opened and the twins rushed in. One of them held a yellow envelope in his hand, the other one six half-length photos. "Words fail us, Mr. Court Photographer . . ."

". . . to express our indignation."

"We protest against this blasphemy . . ."

". . . and demand that our money be returned."

Leo turned white and his eyes widened in horror. He stammered, "Is something not . . . I mean, entirely in accordance with your wishes?"

"One might say so, you miserable dirty slob . . ."

". . . because those photos are a provocation. You see, we are Austrians and Catholics."

Leo was crushed. This was a low blow against which he was defenseless. "You would be the first customers, gentlemen, with cause to complain about my work."

"Who says complain? You will have to answer for your dreck."

Trying to justify himself, Leo began to mount a helpless counterattack. "I am extremely surprised, gentlemen. Your conduct offends me."

"Ha, the Jew feels offended. Yet it is we . . ."

". . . who have been offended."

With these words August Balitzki threw the corpus delicti on the floor. Six photographs of Malva Rosenbach were spread out in front of Leo. The court photographer's face reddened. "I beg of you . . . Try to understand . . . I implore you to forgive me, most illustrious gentlemen. This is an unpleasant misunderstanding, if I may call it that."

"No, you may not. This is far more than an unpleasant misunderstanding . . ."

". . . this means insulting our fraternity and spitting on our fatherland."

The perspiration was now streaming down Leo's forehead. He had no idea how to arouse compassion in his customers, and whispered softly, "My dear Messieurs Balitzki, isn't it possible . . ."

"We are not your dear Messieurs Balitzki. Watch your language!"

"Won't you understand that a mistake has been made here which I myself cannot . . . cannot explain."

Now the indignant Gustav bent down, picked up one of the photographs, held it between his thumb and index finger as though he were touching a contaminated object, and screamed, "Is that your daughter, yes or no?"

"But I've tried to explain . . ."

"There's nothing to explain. In Austria it is forbidden . . ."

"... strictly forbidden for female persons to wear our colors."

"But that was only a joke, gentlemen. In the privacy of my studio."

"We won't stand for such jokes ..."

"... and beg to inform you that the Habsburgia is not prepared to swallow such an affront, Mr. Rosenbach."

"Besides we must inform you ..."

"... that we have detailed information on the double life of your wife, Comrade Rosenbach."

Leo turned white and stammered, "A double life is out of the question, and ..."

"Your wife has been seen at a subversive rally. Our security service knows everything. I assume you realize what this means."

"My family is one hundred percent behind our emperor, gentlemen. Your accusation is extremely defamatory."

"What you permit your wife to do is even more defamatory. It is an offense against the honor of our fatherland, and you have to answer for that. In Stanislav you are finished."

Leo sat down and laid his hand over his wildly pounding heart. "What are you asking of me, gentlemen?"

"If you mean your lousy money, you can keep it."

"Please tell me what I am supposed to do!"

"There are only two possibilities, Mr. Rosenbach. Either you name your seconds and fight a duel with us ..."

"... or you get out of this city. We'll give you three days."

If Jews change their place of residence, they have their reasons, and compelling ones, for in theory they display a stability that is almost religious in nature. It is true that they are a nomadic people, and are said to roam the earth restlessly. This is a well-known cliché, but it has little to do with the hereditary substance of the Jews. If they move from one place to another, it is because they are hunted, because people always make things too hot for them where they are. That is, on the one hand, their historical misfortune, and on the other, their fateful opportunity, whether they want it or not. They are obliged to compare. They get a front view and a rear view of the world—first from the perspective of the hopeful arrival and then from that of the disappointed departure. They do not have time to get accustomed to anything, to become intellectually sluggish. They are always in flight. They are forced to measure and weigh things comparatively. Concepts and ideas, too, have no opportunity to congeal and rigidify. Again and again they must be questioned, for what was right in one place may be wrong in another. What seemed good yesterday is bad today. Our peregrinations force us to reflect, our flight makes us shrewd. Take a good look at us! We have a special way of wagging our head, and by this we express that one can say both yes and no to a problem. We use our hands to talk, variously turning our palms up and down. As we do so, we raise our eyebrows, as though we wanted to say that it is bad this way and not good another way.

I said that we are of an almost religious stability. By this I meant that movement is our way and rest our goal. Perhaps you know that at parting we express this hopeful wish to each other: "Next year in Jerusalem!" This is our way of begging the Almighty for an end to our painful journey, for the conclusion of our flight, and for arrival in the safe harbor of motionlessness.

It was an icy December day. It had snowed during the night, and Stanislav, usually a dirty gray, had put on an ermine coat. The coachman sat on his box and sucked on his pipe, which the cold had long since extinguished. Packed in tight on the wagon were the entire household effects of the Rosenbachs. Next to the coachman sat Jana, Malva, and Leo, who held a wooden tripod squeezed between his legs. On it a camera was mounted. The court photographer grimly clenched his jaw. "If only I had stayed in Munich that time," he muttered through his teeth. "What business does a sensible person have in Stanislav?"

"That's what *I* have always thought," commented Jana unmercifully. "If you had stayed in Munich, you wouldn't have married me. But there they had no use for you either."

Malva seemed to ignore her mother's malice and rejoined, "I hate this godforsaken place with a passion, but on Friday we'll be in Vienna, and by Saturday I will have forgotten everything."

"You were born here, Malva," replied Jana sadly, "and so was I."

The carriage rumbled over the railroad bridge and past Daschynski's house. Jana furtively looked up to the sixth floor and sighed, "I leave a lot behind in this town."

"Tracks in the snow," mocked the unsuspecting Leo, "and even they will disappear when there is a thaw."

Jana kept silent and gave her husband a poisonous look out of the corner of her eye. Malva felt the tension between her parents and tried to cheer her father up a bit. "Do you see the balcony up there? The one with the green glasswork on the rusty bars?"

"You can have it."

"That's where Daschynski, my Greek teacher, lives."

"You can have him too."

"I had an appointment with him at nine. Now he's waiting and doesn't even know that we're leaving."

"Let him wait some more, the jackass."

"How can you say a thing like that?" hissed Jana. "You don't even know him."

"I know this town and its inhabitants. Bandits, all of them."

"Is Vienna any better, papa?"

"A city of millions, my child. Mozart lived there, and Schubert."

"You always talk about the dead. I'm interested in the living, papa. Who lives there, anyway?"

"The leading lights of the monarchy. Everyone with any standing and reputation. And first and foremost, of course, our emperor."

Jana made a derisive face, rummaged in her handbag, and said snidely, "I assume that His Majesty will be at the railroad station to welcome us. With a brass band and the successor to the throne in person."

"He is the only head of state in the world who holds a protective hand over us. My dear Jews—that's what he calls us."

"I feel honored, Leo. And I imagine that if you incur debts again playing cards, he will pay them."

"We will start a new life in Vienna; you know that."

"I know, Leo, but you've started so many new lives."

"Why are you suddenly so fainthearted, mama?" asked Malva, who had noticed the tears in Jana's eyes.

"Me fainthearted? Who was the one who ran away? Certainly not I. Who was afraid of that academic riffraff?"

"Should I have fought a duel with them?" responded Leo, subdued. "You would have liked that. If they chopped up my face. If they killed me because I photographed my daughter in their rags. Do you think I'm crazy? They would have drawn and quartered me, those bloodhounds, and what would have happened then? Who would feed my family?"

Jana was still turning her handbag inside out. Finally she found what she was looking for. It was the amulet that Daschynski had given her as a pledge. She frantically squeezed it in her fist and sobbed silently, scarcely listening to Leo's continued self-justification. "Do you think I'm a brawler? I'm supposed to fight a duel for my honor? Look for seconds? Get a weapon? You can have this honor. My honor isn't theirs, and vice versa. Riffraff, these refined people. These best, second-best, and third-best families. They are common thieves. Am I right?"

"Of course you're right, papa, but you're also late. Until yesterday you kissed the asses of these soap bubbles. Now you realize that your world was composed of illusions."

"What was I supposed to do, for God's sake?"

"Stay and fight," said Jana, blowing her nose and drying her tears. "Not with a saber, of course. There are other weapons."

At that point the coachman knocked out his pipe and growled: "You're at the railroad station, *prosze Pajnstwa.* Get out, please!"

9

JIM WEISSPLATT HAD DECIDED TO MAKE THE ELEVEN KA-
minski boys the champion soccer team of America. His
competitors laughed up their sleeves and said he was crazy.
His friends shook their heads in incomprehension and
wondered what had happened to him. His employees
beamed and gloated, but they were prudent enough to refrain from any commentary. As for his young wife, she
threw up her hands and wailed, "You'll do us in, James.
If you keep carrying on like this, I'll kill myself."

Jim, however, didn't let himself be deflected from his
scheme; he knew what he was doing. He had read the Bible,
though he didn't have much use for religion. He went to
the synagogue only once a year, and cursed like a Cossack.
He couldn't even say the prayers properly, but he liked
the Bible. "A sensational book," he would say, "a bestseller
from which you can learn something for life, for in the
Scriptures it is written that we were a people of champions
and crushed the most powerful enemies as long as we were
convinced of the rightness of our cause."

"What cause?" people would ask him, and he would reply, "It don't matter *what* cause, but it's gotta be a cause!"

To be quite certain, Jim Weissplatt paid a call on Mr.
Goldbloom. This was unusual, to say the least, for Mr.
Goldbloom was the Fourteenth Street rabbi and a man famous for his intolerance toward the lukewarm and the
semi-kosher, as he called them. And Jim Weissplatt wasn't
even semi-kosher but a heathen, a sinner before the Lord
who ate ham when he felt like it and did not give a hoot

for the ritual laws. Nevertheless, he went to see the rabbi and asked him whether it was good business to found a Jewish soccer team and what the holy man thought of the idea. The holy man, who smelled publicity for his business, was astonishingly accommodating. He looked right through Weissplatt, rubbed his right nostril with his index finger, and averred that he was thinking hard. "Number one, it's a bad business, because you could lose money. Number two, it's a good business because you might make money. The *goyim,* may God punish them, think we're strong in the head but weak in the feet. That's why they will underestimate our muscle and calculate that they can mow us down with their little fingers. That is a chance, Mr. Weissplatt. We can make them kaput—both with our head and our feet. What did Samson from the tribe of Dan accomplish? He tore apart a lion who was ten times as strong as him. And little David looked like a little *shmuck,* but he took the fortress Zion. He beat the Moabites, pulverized the Syrians, and killed Goliath, who mocked him and was twice as strong as him. Or take Deborah, a frail woman. She went to war against the Canaanites, who had nine hundred steel carriages and such a tremendous army that the sky was black from their spears, but she won because she was serving a good cause . . ."

"Get down to brass tacks, Mr. Goldbloom! What will be with my nephews?"

"Your nephews are going to win if they serve a good cause, but . . ."

"But what?" asked Weissplatt uncertainly.

"But they're going to lose if they are such damn sinners as you. They'll lay on the soccer field like horse manure if they become such idolaters as their uncle, if they pray to Mammon and to Baal . . ."

"They pray neither to Mammon nor to Baal but to the proletarian revolution. They don't want wealth but poverty. They believe in socialism and that all people are equal on earth and in heaven. Is that a good cause or a bad one?"

"If they believe, it's a good cause; if they know, it's a bad

105

one. A man must believe in the impossible, and that raises him up to our Lord. A man only knows what he sees, what he has, what he can touch, the miserable everyday filth, and that's what pulls him down the drain. You say they believe in poverty, in the victory of the weak over the strong, of good over evil, like Samson and David and Deborah. They don't care about rewards, but fight like the Jews in the Holy Writ. They bravely wage a hopeless struggle. That is good. They will win."

"And what if their opponents also believe? If they fight an even more hopeless fight than my boys? What will happen then?"

"Then the others will win, Mr. Weissplatt; and now go home, you lost soul. I'm busy . . ."

"Okay," Weissplatt responded. "I'll start the soccer team. My nephews are completely *meshugge*, the greatest dreamers between Alaska and Brazil. I'll make a lot of money on them, and that's the main thing."

Uri Taubenschlag was the most expensive trainer in New York and thus, by American reasoning, also the best. He owned a gym at Gramercy Park where he trained the sports elite of the United States or, more accurately, drained it, for he mercilessly drove his charges to high achievements. The best-known athletes had passed through his hands: James Rector, Olympic silver medalist in the hundred-meter dash; Martin Sheridan, gold medalist in discus-throwing, Greco-Roman style; George Dole, world champion in freestyle wrestling; Harry Porter, Olympic high-jump champion. In short, there was no foilsman, swimmer, or hurdle racer who had not earned his spurs at Gramercy Park. Uri Taubenschlag called his school the Manhattan Academy of Athletics, and that very name was a guarantee of quality. Jim Weissplatt called on him and asked how much Uri would ask to train his eleven nephews to be master soccer players. Taubenschlag replied that he wanted no cash but a share of the gate.

"The gate?" asked Weissplatt. "How do you know that they're going to win?"

"Because my pupils always win, for one thing. And for another, because you are known as a skinflint. You wouldn't invest any money in those boys if you had the slightest doubt."

"All right. I offer you ten percent."

"Go to my competition, Mr. Weissplatt!"

"Twelve percent, but you are driving a hard bargain."

"Hire O'Brien. He costs less than I do."

"Fifteen, but that's my final offer."

"Fifty, Mr. Weissplatt, and not an iota less!"

Weissplatt signed the contract, for he had no choice. He was so impressed by the profit margin that Taubenschlag had wangled out of him that now he too believed the Kaminski boys would win.

Exactly a year later Jim Weissplatt appeared in the gym at Gramercy Park and was overwhelmed. In twelve months these eggheads had been turned into muscle men. This impressed him no end, for he was an American and believed in primitive physical virtues. There they were, his nephews, working out on the long horse and the parallel bars, on the horizontal bar and the rope, on the wall bars and the window ladder. There was Hershele, hard as rock, about to perform a somersault. Ber, bursting with strength, was doing a forward dive across the springboard. The delicate Benzion had turned into a weight lifter, and the hairsplitting Shloime had become a Herculean boxer who kept pummeling a punching bag. The uncle's eyes were shining as he said, "Those boys are first-class, Mr. Taubenschlag."

"They will be in a year."

"I'll take them along. They're okay, as far as I'm concerned."

"In twelve months at the earliest."

"I already paid you a hundred seventy thousand dollars, sir. I rented an apartment for the boys, up in the Bronx. They'll eat at Woolf's Restaurant on Fifth Ave. They'll need a doctor, a dentist. They have to play in three months, otherwise I'll be broke."

"In twelve months, I said. Not a day earlier."

"In three, and if necessary, change your method!"

"My method is world-famous."

"For *goyim,* Mr. Taubenschlag, but not for Jim Weissplatt's nephews. My boys are crackerjack. Having them work out isn't enough."

"What, then? Shall I say prayers with them?"

"You should motivate them. Understand?"

"No."

"If you motivate the boys, they'll win their first game in three months and be in the quarter-finals in six."

"And how would you do that, Mr. Weissplatt?"

"I'm not an athlete, Mr. Taubenschlag, but I would explain to them that they're not playing soccer but engaging in a class struggle. I would prove to them that their opponents are hatching an imperialist plot or something. I would tell them that the others are reactionary pigs and that what is at stake is not the cup but world revolution."

"And I'm supposed to tell them all this for a profit margin of fifty percent? Such nonsense would cost an additional five points."

"Two points, Mr. Taubenschlag, and do what I ask! I'll give you three months."

A great deal happened in 1908. Paul Ehrlich produced the famous Salvarsan, the first chemotherapeutic remedy for syphilis. Frederick Cook became the first man to reach the North Pole. Rockefeller donated half a billion dollars for the promotion of science, Weissplatt signed a supplementary contract covering the political motivation of America's first Jewish soccer team, and Yankel Kaminski went to the theater for the first time in his life. I say this as if it were perfectly natural, and yet it marked a break in the family history, a total break that one would not even want to mention—a turning away from Jehovah, as it were, for theater is blasphemy. That isn't in the Holy Writ, but it is a blasphemy nonetheless. Theater is an imitative art and therefore a sin, because it attempts to imitate the Cretor, or even worse, to correct him. Any rabbi will explain to you that playacting is presumption, that it is not proper to poke one's nose into the Almighty's business or to show him what his world ought to be like. Every Jew senses this and need not talk or reflect about it. We don't have to be shown that actors are a dubious lot. We know it, and that's enough. This was self-evident to Yankel too, though he had never bothered to investigate the matter or form an opinion about it. He simply felt in his guts that nothing serious could take place on the stage, or at least nothing useful—and what isn't useful displeases providence. Oy!

10

I T CANNOT BE CLAIMED THAT UNTIL THAT VISIT TO THE theater Yankel's life had been of great usefulness. His carryings-on in the taverns or with girls of easy virtue were neither useful nor pleasing in the eyes of God. But this he did not worry about. Even though he did not know theater people, he despised them as mountebanks, buffoons, and prestidigitators. They were superfluous to society and suited neither his philosophy nor his taste. He was an old heretic. All sins tempted him and exerted a wild fascination on him. He laughed at the commandments and seldom went to the synagogue. Nevertheless, he regarded visits to the theater as unseemly, and for sixty years had managed to give a wide berth to everything that was in any way connected with the stage.

This time he went anyway, and for the trivial reason that a girl was appearing there who was said to be "the most enchanting actress of all time." This was an exaggeration, of course, like everything connected with show business. Incidentally, I must add that all the members of my family are said to have been of a theatrical nature and characterized by an incurable inclination to overdo things. To tell you the truth, I don't see anything so bad in that. On the contrary. Exaggeration tends to bring out the substance and penetrate into the heart of things. Isn't literature a form of exaggeration too? Or painting? Thus, when people claimed that this blue-veined orchid was the most enchanting actress of all time, all they meant to say was that she was simply incomparable and emanated an extraordinary fascination. That is true, and does not represent a falsification of facts. Not at all. She was a phenomenon, no one questioned that. She had emerald green eyes, fiery red hair, and a voice that rippled through the night yearningly, like the call of a blackbird in May. The newspapers outdid one another in superlatives, saying that she did not imitate life but created a new dimension of it, that she lifted every role into the realm of the supernatural and mystical, that she seemed to be burned by the words that flashed from her mouth like fire, that she aroused a sweet disquiet and a feverish restlessness in the people who listened to her, and so on and so forth. All Warsaw was talking about her, though only relatively few people had an opportunity to admire her. Her name was Rahel Feigenbaum, and she had no competitor as the hit of the season.

With the exception of the VIP boxes, all seats had been sold out for months. For the patriarch this in itself was sufficient reason to go. If there are no more tickets, so he reasoned, Yankel Kaminski must demonstrate that he can get some. There is nothing that Yankel Kaminski cannot get. "A box seat, you say? All right, let it be a box seat. How much? A hundred rubles? Since when does a theater ticket cost a hundred rubles? What? Weizmann paid a hundred and thirty? Then give me a ticket for a hundred and forty. It can be more too, but tell me what they are playing. *Romeo and Juliet?* Not the faintest idea. Never heard of it. Don't know him or her. You want to know my name? Why do you need my name? Oh. Then send the ticket to my office, but discreetly, if I may ask. Yes, to Yankel Kaminski, Fourteen Freta Street."

The Teatr Warschawski was located on Nowy Swiat and was one of the most elegant buildings in the center of the city. Both the facade with its high baroque windows and the shimmering black marble columns emanated dignity and nobility of taste. One stepped into the foyer, a circular hall with mirrors, as Yankel Kaminski and by the time one left one's coat in the checkroom one had become a human being. A fireworks of fragrances wafted toward one when one ascended the staircase. It smelled of jasmine and almond blossoms, violets, roses, and women with plunging necklines. Resplendent on slim granite pedestals were the statues of impressive-looking men whose very names inspired respect: Aristophanes, Aeschylus, Shakespeare, Molière, Pushkin. These were strange names, known neither at the stock exchange nor in the municipal trade register. It simply was impossible to remain a barbarian in such surroundings, and the old man assumed a posture that surprised even him. He bought a program, and when he finally took his seat in the box, he began, against his better judgment, to leaf through it . . .

Thus began that memorable evening which had the most incredible consequences for my family. When the curtain rose at the stroke of eight, Yankel thought he was on another planet. The actors moved with a wonderful grace, as though they were weightless. They did not speak, but declaimed with artful majesty. Words fluttered through the hall like exotic birds that seemed familiar to Yankel Kaminski but would never, not in a million years, have passed the lips of a man like him:

> O Romeo, Romeo! wherefore art thou Romeo?
> Deny thy father and refuse thy name;
> Or, if thou wilt not, be but sworn my love,
> And I'll no longer be a Capulet.

The patriarch shook his head disapprovingly. He bent over the side balustrade and accosted a lady sitting in the neighboring box. "I don't know what she wants. Change her name or what?"

"Psst!"

"She said Capulet, but I thought her name was Juliet. A nice name."

"Quiet, *prosze pana!* This is a theater."

"I want to know whether her name is Juliet."

People around him hissed angrily, and Yankel preferred to hide his face behind opera glasses.

> 'Tis but thy name that is my enemy.
> Thou art thyself, though not a Montague . . .
> So Romeo would, were he not Romeo called,
> Retain that dear perfection which he owes
> Without that title. Romeo, doff thy name;
> And for thy name, which is no part of thee,
> Take all myself.

This was beyond Yankel's comprehension. Either you've got a name or you haven't. Her name is Juliet, but she calls herself Capulet and wants to change her name. His name is Romeo, but he is supposed to be called something else. All because they are in love. What's the meaning of all that talk? The old man felt like leaving the theater. But he stayed after all. Those people are drunk, he growled. Nobody talks like that. What are they trying to do with that stammering? Perhaps they have something in mind, but *I* don't understand them. Yet what they're saying sounds good. It drips into your ears like honey, but their speech is so stilted. Why can't they say what they mean simply? Maybe they could if they wanted to, but they sense that one can't express it with simple words. Maybe their hearts are so full that everyday language no longer is enough. The Holy Writ isn't written in everyday words either. Perhaps it would be better if it were more ordinary. Then I would understand it. I wonder whether my heart ever was full. One single time, I think. When my youngest, Hershele, was born, may God protect him. That was the blackest night of my life. I thought Noemi wouldn't make it, and the little one either. Noemi was lying in her bed and staring at the ceiling with black eyes. The child had gray scales all over his body and whimpered. I remember it exactly. I said,

"Noemi, stay a few more years, don't leave me alone!" And Noemi answered in a broken voice, "What for?"

These terrible words killed me. "What for?" I ran to the window and tried to open it wide. I wanted to see the river behind the house and the clouds over the city. I wanted to scream but couldn't. My voice died in my throat, and I allowed myself to fill up. For three days and three nights. When I awoke from my intoxication, Noemi was sitting in an easy chair. Motionless. Only her hands were moving, because she was knitting. Tiny little gloves. And then I knew that Hershele was alive. That they were both alive. Then I ran to the window for the second time and wanted to scream like a madman, this time out of happiness, but again I couldn't. My voice failed me for the second time, and in my temples those horrible words were pounding: "What for?" Suddenly I knew what she had meant. I never kissed her. Sixteen children I had squirted into her body, but we never caressed each other. What for? She doesn't even love me. Nor does she have any reason to love me. What for, why, how come? This theater is splitting my head apart.

> Thou knowest the mask of night is on my face:
> Else would a maiden blush bepaint my cheek
> For that which thou hast heard me speak tonight . . .
> Dost thou love me? . . . O gentle Romeo,
> If thou dost love, pronounce it faithfully.

She never asked me if I loved her. She doesn't want to know. If she had spoken a single word, I would be a different person. I am a stopped-up spring. Petrified and old. My sons I have cast out. My wife doesn't speak to me, and soon my last hour will strike, but I don't want to go yet. I frittered my spring away, and now I have to catch up. Oh, dear God. I am your prodigal son. Do not cast me out!

Yankel Kaminski listened to the words of the nightingale and felt an ardent desire to take her in his arms. He thought she was speaking to him. He was all alone in his hundred-and-forty-ruble box, right above her. He was sure she was looking at him. That had never happened to him before. She was caressing his heart and insinuating herself into his soul. She shook him out of his sexagenarian semi-somnolence. He rose from his seat and left the box on tiptoe, softly so as not to annoy her. Out in the corridor sat a sleepy usher. Yankel pressed twenty rubles into his hand. "Bring me twenty roses!"

"What color, baron?"

"Red, yellow, or white; it doesn't matter, but please hurry!"

He had never before said "please," but today he was speaking with the tongue of angels, and to an ordinary usher who stank of *bimber* and disinfectant. When he returned to his seat, he felt twenty years younger. Something had changed. From today on he belonged to this house with the splendid mirror foyer, with the fragrances and the bird of paradise that was twittering and enticing.

> . . . Come, Romeo; come, thou day in night,
> For thou wilt lie upon the wings of night
> Whiter than new snow upon a raven's back.
> Come, gentle night; come, loving, black-browed night;
> Give me my Romeo; and, when he shall die,
> Take him and cut him out in little stars,
> And he will make the face of heaven so fine
> That all the world will be in love with night . . .

Nobody spoke like that, this he was sure of. But what of it? Juliet spoke like that, and that was enough. There really was no Juliet. Her name was Rahel Feigenbaum. She was a girl of flesh and blood and could not talk like that. She had to pay the rent, go shopping, speak to the baker and the milkman. The old blockhead considered that a consolation. Such sentences are possible only on stage, not in life. She was no angel, thank God, but a woman, and a woman can be had. He wanted to have her, just as he wanted to have everything that aroused his senses. He had to have her. At that moment the door to the box opened and the usher entered with the roses—just when the play was almost at an end and the Prince was speaking the final words:

> A glooming peace this morning with it brings.
> The sun for sorrow will not show his head.
> Go home, to have more talk of these sad things,
> Some shall be pardoned, and some punished;
> For never was a story of more woe
> Than this of Juliet and her Romeo.

The curtain descended. The two lovers were dead. A pall of gloom hung over the auditorium. The spectators' hearts stopped. No one dared to move, and all thought they were dreaming when the damask curtain parted and the supernatural girl stepped forward to take a bow. A thousand spectators rose from their seats, and a storm broke loose. A refreshing downpour after stifling heat. A miracle had happened. Juliet had risen from the dead. She smiled at the crowd, which was giving her a wild ovation. The patriarch was swept along by the hurricane and clapped like crazy, though he did not know at whom his enthusiasm was directed—at the dead Juliet, the living Rahel, or himself, a man who had on that evening caught a glimpse of a better world. He applauded till the last moment and a bit longer. The audience was already streaming out of the hall when the actress appeared in front of the curtain for the very last time, brought there by the magic of the impetuous Yankel, who now plucked up his courage and threw the bouquet in front of the girl's feet. She looked up at the box in astonishment, whereupon he called out to her, "Each rose is a drop from my heart!"

From that evening on Yankel sat in the same box night after night. Dozens of times he experienced the death of the immortal couple, and each time he let himself be intoxicated anew by the magic of the theater. I do not wish to claim that a conversion had taken place. He was too hard-boiled and callous for that. He was still the same barbarian—or nearly the same—who drank in dives and chased women. In his own house he was a tyrant. He sat in the office in his factory and watched the female workers with the keen eyes of a slave driver. He continued to disown his sons, and was still convinced that he was a fixed star in the sky and could have everything his heart desired. For all practical purposes the box overlooking the stage on the left now belonged to him, for he had rented it for the rest of the season. Every night when the incomparable one stepped forward he threw roses onto the stage, and in doing so he had long since stopped paying homage to her art exclusively. His desires had become palpable: He already desired her body and her lily-white skin. He was now dreaming of her lips, her neck, and her breasts. He had decided to conquer this woman, and whatever he got into his head had to become reality sooner or later.

Nevertheless, he was afraid. Until recently he had never stopped to think that he was old, that he was going to die some day, and that there might be limits for him. Rahel now reminded him of that. This was the new and unusual thing about the story. Up to now he had been in the habit of reporting to his schnapps buddies about the women he had had and the ones he was going to have. Now he wrapped himself in silence and became mysterious, which indicated how smitten he was. He was in love. His head ached with painful desire, but—as had never happened before—he lacked the courage to accost the girl. Of course, after every performance he threw his roses on the stage. After every performance he shouted compliments at the actress, concealing the true dimensions of his feelings behind the noisy publicity of his appearances. Surely he could not be taken seriously while he was offering his compliments in front of a thousand people. Everyone thought he was an old crackpot with a big mouth and no teeth in it. They were wrong. He still had all his teeth, and could bite with them. He cracked nuts between his jaws. He was as strong as a bear. And there he was, standing at the balustrade of his box, waving his fur hat, and crying things like "I am longing for you, you peach blossom" or "I kiss your eyelashes, my pretty child" or, on another evening, "You should live and be well with raisins and almonds." When the people in the next box hissed that he should behave himself, he roared even more loudly, "You should live to be a hundred, with drums beating and trumpets sounding!"

Thus it went all winter and into early spring. Yankel had become the talk of the town. A tabloid even ran a cartoon of him. Already there were some people who went to the theater only to watch the old coot carry on. In the beginning people were amused; it made a change in the monotonous theatrical fare of those years. But gradually the whole business became an annoyance. Initially there were witty remarks, then people began to complain, and in the end the wave of indignation carried jarring overtones. "A typical Jew," people began saying, "lascivious and loutish. What business does he have in this theater?" No one seemed to notice that Rahel was also a Jew, for she was too flowerlike and too young. The discomfort began only when Yankel's rapture became transformed into importunity.

One day in March the patriarch felt the irresistible urge to end his platonic relationship and make a frontal assault. The ice on the banks of the Vistula was cracking, a mild breeze blew over the city, a pale moon blinked through the clouds, and Yankel knew that it was a matter of now or never. His heart all aflutter, he went to the theater. Grimly clenching his jaws he walked up the staircase. That evening he made the greatest stir in months. You see, this time he refrained from throwing roses on the stage. Nor did he shout at the actress, and people shook their heads over this. Sour disappointment spread through the auditorium, and many thought the performance was probably not as good as usual. Rahel felt a wrench, for she had become accustomed to the demonstrations of the eccentric millionaire. What was the matter? Had her acting deteriorated, or had she lost her magic? She was sure of one thing: The evening was down the drain. She returned to her dressing room in a foul mood and peevishly looked in the mirror. She didn't like what she saw. Ill-humoredly she took off her costume and removed her make-up. She felt insipid and common. "I was a flop," she said to Rychlitzowa, her old dresser, who was standing next to her and taking off her wig.

"You weren't a flop, my child, but raspberry with whipped cream."

"I look like an old cheese. I can't stand myself tonight."

"God is my witness that you look like a cherry in July."

"What are you flattering me for? I know myself whether I was good or not. Today I was a washout, and people noticed it."

"People, people! You know as well as I do there's a full moon tonight and the whole world is in a crazy mood. You are quite cracked yourself."

"I had only eight curtain calls. Yesterday there were nine."

"Put something on, Rahel. You'll catch cold."

At that moment the door was flung open and a man rushed in who was obviously out of his mind. In his buttonhole was a carnation and around his neck he wore a silk scarf. There was a gold watch in his breast pocket. His fingers were clasped around an exquisite leather case, and he bowed as deeply as his gout permitted. "I am an old Jew, and have the honor to idolize you body and soul."

"What do you think you are doing, sir?"

"My name is Yankel Kaminski. My teeth are chattering and I am shaking like a seal. I've been sending you roses for five months."

"This is a dressing room, *prosze pana,* and you will have noticed that I am insufficiently dressed."

"Sufficiently or insufficiently, you have bewitched me and I think of you day and night."

"I have no intention of receiving anyone, sir. Get out of here!"

"These diamonds, Miss Feigenbaum, are genuine," whispered the patriarch, opening the case and pulling out a magnificent necklace, "as genuine as my pounding heart when the curtain goes up and you appear. As genuine as the water in the river and the stars in the sky and the sparks in your green eyes. I beg of you . . ."

"Show him the door, Rychlitzowa, this instant! I don't have any time to waste."

Now Yankel fell on his knees. He handed the girl the necklace and whispered, "Why are you so cruel, Miss Feigenbaum?"

"We don't know you, *prosze pana.* Get lost . . ."

"What got lost here is my heart and my mind. I've come to bring you this present. Next to you it is the most beautiful thing in this city . . ."

"I'm telling you for the last time. Go away, or I'll scream!"

"Accept my present and I'll go."

"Help!"

"I want to tell you . . ."

"Help!"

". . . that I'm dying from longing."

"I'll throw something at your head!"

At that point the door opened and Sokorski came into the dressing room. He didn't have a hair on his head, and was as bald and rosy as a newborn child. Drops of sweat ran down his nose. Sokorski was the administrator of the theater, the business manager, as he called himself, and he was used to untangling all kinds of knots. "Did you call, Miss Feigenbaum?"

The actress was shivering all over, for there was little heat in the dressing room, and she was so excited she

120

couldn't get a word out. Her dresser answered for her. "This bear was going to ravish us."

"With what, *prosze pani*," Yankel replied angrily, "with these diamonds?"

"With what else, you monster? At your age one ravishes any way one can!"

"Well? And did he succeed?" asked Sokorski, contemptuously looking down at the kneeling patriarch.

"Missed by a hair," replied Rychlitzowa. "Who can resist very long if diamonds are held in her face?"

"I thought so, *panie* Kaminski. We've had our eye on you for months. You are making a fool of yourself with your roses. You are the laughingstock of the whole town because of the way you carry on in our theater every night. You hang your feelings out on the clothesline. You roar your senile stupidities at the world. You annoy our audiences with your bad taste and, worst of all, you compromise a great artist by bursting into her dressing room and making her indecent propositions, though she is almost naked . . ."

"I told you that I long for her. Is that indecent, you baldie?" The panting Yankel rose from his embarrassing position.

"At your age it is obscene."

"I cried that I idolize her. Is that obscene?"

"In your situation it certainly is, because you are married. You have sixteen children, half of whom you have cast out. We know all about you, and I am asking you, Aren't you ashamed?"

"I'll squash you, you crablouse!"

"And I'll have you arrested, you dirty old man. Unauthorized persons are not permitted in the dressing room. It says so here in big letters."

"Unauthorized, you say? But I am authorized, and you are fired!"

"What's that nonsense? Are you completely off your rocker? Leave this building immediately or I'll call the police."

"We'll see about that, you nobody."

Yankel took an envelope out of his vest pocket, opened it ceremoniously, and pulled out a document that he slowly unfolded and waved under Sokorski's nose. "Since three o'clock this afternoon this theater has belonged to me. This means that I am the sole owner. I bought it for eighty thousand rubles in cash. Who is authorized here will be decided by me and no one else. Do you understand me now, you insect? I am the boss in this theater, on this stage, and in this dressing room. I begin to exercise my authority by saying that you are dismissed. I'm throwing you out."

The emerald eyes of the beautiful Rahel flashed and she said in a voice trembling with excitement, "If you dismiss Sokorski, you brute, I go too and you can close up shop. Without me this will be a museum and not a theater. Sokorski stays."

"Do you think so? Who is this clown, anyway?" asked Yankel, who was now choking up with jealousy. "Your fiancé or what?"

"He is my colleague. Do you know what that is? An employee who works for wages, just as I do. We are on the same side. And you on the other one."

Yankel didn't know what to reply. The girl was speaking the same language as his sons. He groped for words and then said conciliatingly, "As far as I'm concerned, he can stay, the lunatic, but under one condition."

"What condition?" asked the girl with a subtle smile, for she sensed that she had won the game.

"Under the condition that you won't be angry with me."

"What do you mean by angry?"

"You will accept this necklace and not look so stern."

"You've bought the theater, *panie* Kaminski? Did you think I was included?"

"I don't think anything. I am an old jackass, Miss Feigenbaum. I've fallen head over heels in love with you. Take these diamonds and throw them in the river! Give them to a beggar! Do whatever you want with them, but I implore you to take the pendant."

"All right, I'll take it, but leave this dressing room."

"May I come again?"

"You are the owner and may do anything. But you'll still have to knock."

"And will you smile?"

"If I feel like it, I shall smile. And now, get out!"

11

I F THERE WAS ANYONE WHO KNEW WHAT CAPITAL THE KA-
minski boys represented, it was the Olympic trainer Uri
Taubenschlag. He had worked on them for eighteen
months and knew each one of them as if he were his own
son. He extracted the utmost from that, and stimulated
their ambition to the limit. When he agreed to collect 52
percent of the receipts, he was already sure that the fellows
would win and that he would do a roaring business with
them. But since he was a shrewd Jew, he said that the boys
were still a long way from being a world-class team. "Those
fellows think too much, Mr. Weissplatt. That may be good
for politics, which I don't know much about, but for soccer
you need feet, you understand? This Ber is a philosopher,
a huge question mark that asks questions all the time. His
brother Shloime is a hairsplitter and a know-it-all. Yitzhak
is a comic and makes jokes when he's supposed to shoot
at the goal. Mordechai would be okay, a steamroller of a
boy, but he's fanatical to the point of imbecility. Moishe is
an inventor, Lazik is a poet with his head in the clouds.
Adam is sentimental and feels pity for his opponents. Benzion is a theoretician. Aaron has golden fingers but wooden
feet, and Hershele is not a sportsman but a cavalier."

"What's a cavalier, Mr. Taubenschlag?"

"Ask the *shiksas*, they know better than I do."

"I'll knock the *shiksas* out of him, I can guarantee you
that. But I wanna know if we're gonna win."

"What am I, a prophet, Mr. Weissplatt? All I can say is

that they've got too much up there and not enough down here."

"So tell me if we're gonna win. I'm a businessman, not a philanthropist."

"Maybe we'll win."

"You're getting fifty-two percent. For that you should give a clear answer."

"A clear answer costs more. I told you what I know."

"Listen to me, Mr. Taubenschlag! What they need now is a political motivation. Without that we're gonna lose."

"How do you do that, Mr. Weissplatt?"

"I'll explain to you."

Uri Taubenschlag was a technocrat of the old school. He was interested in his specialty and didn't care about anything else. He had never heard of political motivation. His pupils were above parties. They lifted weights, worked out on the horizontal bars, and made a scissors on the pommeled side horse, but they had never heard of the proletarian revolution. Why should they have? They were doing splendidly and ingesting eleven thousand calories every day. With the Kaminski boys it was different. Even worse; the exact opposite. However, since expectations were high that they were going to win, the Olympic trainer bowed to his destiny and made the following speech to them: "Tomorrow you're playing your first game—against the goddamn Gold Stars. I don't have to tell you who the Gold Stars are. They are financed by Ronny McCormick, and Ronny McCormick said pointblank in the Senate that he will no longer tolerate any Jews in the United States. He wants to drive us out with fire and sword because, so he says, we are subversive pigs. You are the first Jewish soccer team in America, and that's why you've got to win. You must show the old bastard that they can't throw us out, that we won't let them insult us. I wish you *mazel tov*, boys. Make mincemeat of him, the anti-Semite. But you're the first socialist team too. Next year we're going to elect a new president. In 1908 the workers' party got only 800,000 votes. Our candidate, Eugene Debs, wasn't known yet. The man who was elected was William Howard Taft, the imperialistic bloodhound. In 1912 Eugene Debs must get ten times as many votes. Eight million Americans shall vote for Socialism. But for that you'll have to win! Our victory will be the best publicity for our cause. In 1916, eight years from now, Eugene Debs will become president—if you play well. *L'chaim*, boys. For a socialist America!"

The Kaminski boys couldn't believe their eyes and ears. Their trainer was a comrade! It was the last thing in the world they had expected. That made everything appear in a different light. So they would have to try very hard to win. It was a sensation: Red Flag beat the Gold Stars five to four. Two of the five goals were scored by Hershele, whom no one would ever have believed capable of athletic prowess. How did he do it? Did he really believe that Taubenschlag meant what he said? After all, the Olympic trainer cared about money and nothing else. Even a blind man could see that, but Hershele was not blind, and that's why he didn't see anything. Hershele let himself be seduced. By Taubenschlag's shrewd words and . . .

You see, there was something else, but as the narrator who is telling all this from a great distance I would never have guessed it if I had not received a telephone call from a lady a short time ago. She was staying temporarily in a luxury hotel in Zurich and had found my number after many inquiries. Her name is Francesca Bertini, and I understand that around sixty years ago she was as famous as Sophia Loren is today. Our conversation lasted ten minutes and almost knocked my socks off.

"Have you ever heard of me, signore?"

"I can't remember. Can you give me a clue?"

"You are the son of a certain Hersh Kaminski, who used to be called Hershele. Is that correct?"

"It is and it isn't, signora. He Americanized his name and called himself Henry."

"That bastard. He Americanized himself. But to me he will always be Hershele, till the day I die. What made him think of Henry? That's a horrid name."

"Unfortunately there were times when Jews were reluctant to be identified as Jews. My father came from Russia, and there it was dangerous to be called Hershele."

"Don't talk nonsense! Your father didn't know what fear was. He was the bravest man I ever met. He had an ideal and was ready to die for it."

"His ideal was justice, not Judaism."

"That's one and the same thing, signore. Read the Bible and you'll know what I mean."

"Judaism is a disease, signora. An incurable malady that one cannot get rid of. This illness forces one to be cautious."

"Cautious—such a silly expression. He was a daredevil. He wasn't even afraid of *me*."

"Why should he have been afraid of you?"

"Because I was beautiful in those days. They said that I was the most beautiful woman in Italy."

"Where did he meet you, signora? Pardon my indiscreet question."

"He met me in New York. I emphasize: He met *me*, because he was impertinent and imprudent. It was in Brooklyn Stadium. I remember it as if it were yesterday. I was sitting in the VIP box, next to the mayor of New York, watching the first Jewish soccer team of America crush the Gold Stars."

"I'm very curious, signora. What had brought you to New York?"

"My first film, which was already an international success. I played Cordelia in *King Lear* and attended the American premiere as a guest of honor. New York treated me like a queen."

"But . . . how did he get to you? That couldn't have been easy."

"He scored two goals, signore. Sixty thousand spectators cheered him because he was the most delicate of all the players. He was as beautiful as a young tiger. You could see the little veins shimmering through his temples. He had amethyst eyes and a Pharaoh's mouth. To this day I'm yearning for his mouth . . ."

"And he simply accosted you?"

"Accosted isn't the word. He attacked me. I sat between the mayor and Baldassare Negroni, my director, who was guarding me like a watchdog. The victorious team was called up to accept the congratulations of the mayor. But your father ignored him; he rushed right up to me, kissed me so it almost took my breath away, and whispered in my ear, "Tonight at six, in the geometric center of the world!"

"And then?"

"I was sixteen and had never encountered such a crazy person. I didn't know what to say, and the only word I could get out was 'Why?' And the answer he gave was 'Because I love you, Cordelia. Because you tell the king the truth and suffer because of it.' "

"What happened next, signora? Did you keep the date?"

"Certainly, signore. Despite the mayor and the angry Negroni, who tried to lock me into my hotel room. He didn't manage to do that, and that is why I called you today."

"I don't understand . . ."

"I met him in the navel of the word, in the middle of Times Square, and I still love him. But because he is dead, I wanted to at least hear the voice of his son. You have a beautiful voice, signore, but his was even more beautiful."

"I'd like to ask you an indiscreet question. May I?"

"Go ahead and ask. I shall see whether I feel like answering it."

"How far did my father go? As far as I know, he was a go-getter."

"No, signore, he was not a go-getter. He was the most tender seducer I have ever met."

"He seduced you?"

"That very night. I have a daughter by him who is almost as perfect as he was. Your half-sister, by the way . . ."

"One last question, signora. Why didn't you two get married?"

"Because both of us were already married. He to the revolution, I to the movies. A pity . . ."

"I would like to see you, signora."

"God forbid, signore. I'm eighty-eight."

Permit me a digression, the meaning of which may not be discernible at first glance but which is of no small significance for everything that happened in the future.

A Scottish pharmacist named MacSnow, a man who was at once progressive and narrow-minded, formulated the astonishing cardinal rule about the quadratic growth of individual success—a rule that has not been disputed or questioned to this day. It states that the success of his or her plans strengthens a normal person both psychologically and physically and inspires him or her to strive for more and greater success. According to this theory, such lucky streaks proceed in geometric progression, and therefore they should in theory assume cosmic dimensions. But only theoretically, for homo sapiens is regarded as a faulty design and hence is incapable of reaching his potential. MacSnow believes that numerous impediments are active in man and that these keep him from reaching his goals and always fling him back into a failure mode. The Scottish pharmacist calls this fact "the immanent principle of self-impediment," and because of it with most people success proceeds not in geometric but at best in arithmetic progression—or not at all, which appears to be the usual case. True, there have been brilliant persons whose lives confirm MacSnow's cardinal rule, but even they repeatedly fell victim to immanent self-impediment at the end of their lives. Socrates wound up in prison, Jesus Christ on Golgotha, and Napoleon near Waterloo. There is no known case of a homo sapiens fully utilizing his chances. One day all die, thereby refuting the theorem of the incessant and quadratic growth of individual success, since in the final analysis death must be regarded as a failure.

But let us return to Hersh Kaminski. If he had really wanted to, he would have scored four goals in the next soccer game, eight in the one after that, and sixteen in the third—according to MacSnow and his geometric progression. Reality, however, did not follow the path of science. Reality is not ruled by theorems but by inertia, by the human, all-too-human principle of success refusal. Sure, Hershele kicked in a few more goals, but shrewd Mr. Taubenschlag's motivational speeches began to bounce off him. The real motivation was lacking: The most beautiful woman of Italy had returned to Naples and married her director, the jealous Baldassare Negroni, whom she did not love but declared to be the father of a baby that he had not fathered.

Nevertheless, the Kaminski boys continued to rush from one victory to another. This they owed not to their youngest brother but to the ever-aggressive Mordechai, who went into battle less with his head than with his feet. People began to notice the team, then to fear it, and finally the very mention of its name made them blanch in terror. Red Flag became the embodiment of Jewish perseverance and socialist aggressiveness. What the eleven brothers accomplished was not a rise to the stars but a vertical takeoff to them.

In April of that year Red Flag played against Chicago. The Jewish team won one to nothing, and made the quarterfinals of the American soccer championship. In late May they easily beat the famous Colombia team. The penultimate hurdle had been overcome, and Red Flag had qualified for the semifinals. The press had a field day. Weissplatt's team made headlines as far as the West Coast. The *San Francisco Post* spoke of a special kind of earthquake and an unprecedented triumphal march, and it called Mordechai the Goliath of American soccer. The *Saint Louis News* spoke of a human juggernaut that must have secret tricks at its disposal. From the four corners of the earth came offers of money and honors. Ber was even invited to become Professor of Athletic Sciences at the University of Durban. There was also a flood of offers of marriage. The granddaughter of a newspaper czar invited Hershele to visit her at her country home in New Hampshire and, if mutual feelings developed, to become her husband. The world-renowned film pioneer Edwin Porter made a full-length thriller about the eleven "Dreamboys from Russia," which had triumphal runs in all the big movie houses of America. The Kaminski boys shattered all the prejudices that had hitherto circulated about Jews and socialists. People had always claimed that the children of Israel were sickly and narrow-chested, but the Kaminski boys enjoyed unparalleled good health. It was and still is said that socialists are shirkers and weaklings. However, Jim Weissplatt's Brigade, as the yellow press called them, displayed tireless activity.

Those fellows had something, though no one in America could guess what it was. Or maybe someone could—one Dr. Sauerstein, an adjunct lecturer at Harvard University, who wrote articles so speculative that he was read only by snobs and outsiders. In one of his columns he wrote:

From all these experiences I conclude that in accordance with the laws of nature physical smallness is transformed into intellectual greatness. Not infrequently dwarfish size gives rise to a gigantic intellect. Napoleon Bonaparte, who is called The Great, suffered all his life because of his minuscule dimensions. Time and again the gnawing feeling of having drawn the short end of the stick and the sharp pain of frustration have given individuals the energy for tremendous achievements. The astonishing proportion of talent among Jews, homosexuals, and deviants of all kinds proves my claim. I have never had the honor of meeting the eleven Kaminski gentlemen personally. However, I permit myself the assumption that their unparalleled career on the soccer fields of this country is the fruit of innumerable degradations and insults. The fated path of persons who are cast out or stig-

131

matized leads either to social rebellion or to astonishing social rise. Jim Weissplatt's Brigade is a group of political and ethnic outcasts who had to flee from Russia under the foulest of conditions. The cup of their frustration runneth o'er, and I do not doubt for a moment that these men are going to win the final game.

On the ninth of September the boys were scheduled to play the decisive game. Jim Weissplatt had invested a fortune, and Uri Taubenschlag 412 days of intensive training. The eleven fellows imagined that the outcome of this game was going to decide the fate of the Jews in America, and possibly also the reputation of socialism in the entire world. When Uncle Jim appeared in the locker room, the noise of sixty thousand spectators was already flooding in. The hands of the chronometer pointed at 2:50 P.M. The atmosphere was aquiver with tension. Red Flag was close to a triumph, but at that historic moment MacSnow's secondary law exploded. Five minutes before the opening whistle Hershele quite unexpectedly turned to old Weissplatt and asked, "What's in that letter?"

"In what letter, boys?"

"You know what we mean. The letter from Warsaw."

"Oh, the letter from Warsaw. Nothing important. After the game you can read it."

"Not after the game, now. The first letter from home in years, and you say nothing important is in it."

"It's a surprise, boys. First you win the final game against those sons of bitches from Philadelphia and then, when all America is cheering you, when you are the big champions . . ."

"You're lying, Uncle Weissplatt. One moment you say 'nothing important' and a few seconds later it's 'a surprise.' Who is the letter from?"

"From my sister—that is, your mother—in other words, nothing special. What's important now is those bandits on the Philadelphia team, the avant-garde of the American plutocracy."

"You're part of that yourself, Uncle Jim. Don't give us any cock-and-bull stories! We want the letter."

"After the final game, I said, and what I say goes. Who told you that there's a letter, anyway?"

"We have comrades on every street corner. At the post office too."

"Do you know what this is? Nonobservance of the secrecy of the mails. Punishable by two months to two years in the House of Correction."

"We want the letter!"

"Sixty thousand Americans are sitting out there and waiting."

"Let them *plotz*. We won't play till you show us the letter."

"I won't be blackmailed. Can't you hear them calling for you?"

"None of us are going to play!"

"The people are screaming themselves hoarse. You've got to start."

"We're not moving a finger."

Weissplatt was boiling with rage. He bit his fingernails, then changed his tune. "And what if it's bad news? What then?"

"Then we want to know what it is."

"Will you play anyway?"

"Show us the letter without any conditions!"

"You don't have any right to it. The letter is addressed to me. Here's the address, in black and white: Jim Weissplatt, East Seventy-fourth Street, and so on. People are making a racket because you're not coming out. They've bought tickets and they're not getting anything for their money. Are you going to make chopped liver of me after all I've done for you?"

"Not chopped liver, but we're on strike."

"It's five past three. Are you going to play or aren't you?"

"Show us the letter and we'll see."

"Okay, I warned you."

Hershele picked up the letter, skimmed it, and turned pale. Then he began to read in a dry voice: "My dear brother, for the first time in my life I'm sending you a letter, though it isn't easy for me. Well, here's the whole truth. My poor Yankel, with whom I have sixteen children, has gone over the edge and suddenly lost his mind. He fell in love with an actress who's forty years younger than him. He's been gone for a week. All the men are gone. What's a *yiddishe mama* going to do without . . ." Hersh couldn't go on, for his voice died in his throat. Outside a tornado was raging. The crowd was whistling and shouting, and the whirlwind that was tearing through the stadium made the walls shake. At that point the door opened and Uri Taubenschlag rushed in, his face white as chalk and his features distorted. "One more minute and you'll be disqualified."

"We've already lost."

"Are you going to play or aren't you?"

"If we have to, we'll play. But we don't have a chance . . ."

"You owe us a fortune. If you don't play, we're ruined. And so are you."

"Okay, we'll play."

Outside the team was greeted with a storm of enthusiasm. No one had a premonition of what was going to happen. Weissplatt looked at the Olympic trainer with glassy eyes and moaned, "Mr. Taubenschlag, what will I do if we lose?"

"One bankruptcy more, one bankruptcy less don't matter, Mr. Weissplatt."

"What'll I pay my debts with?"

"Send the bill to Warsaw. There you've got a brother-in-law who's a millionaire."

"He's a millionaire all right, but he's not my brother-in-law anymore!"

The eleven Kaminski boys knew quite well that their father was a drunkard, that he never actually sobered up from his rounds of the taverns. They were not surprised at this, because they regarded alcoholism as an attribute of capitalism in its decline. Since Yankel was a capitalist, it was logical for him to indulge in schnapps. They had heard about his sexual excesses too, about the girls of easy virtue with whom he associated, and the dubious assignations that he used to have in broad daylight. This was even less of a surprise to them, for they regarded moral turpitude as the vermiform appendix of a decaying society. Hence his dissolute life mirrored the decline of the middle class, and his sons were under no illusions about their progenitor. On the contrary. After all, he had disowned them. He had permitted them to be sent to the lead mines of Verkhoyansk. They believed him to be capable of anything, and nothing could surprise them. Yet there was one thing that surpassed their revolutionary imagination: Their father had fallen in love. This was unimaginable and also impermissible, for Yankel was a married man. This they did not verbalize, for their theories of free love and abolition of the bourgeois family were sacred to them. Hence they camouflaged their prejudices with pseudo-progressive subtleties. For example, they claimed that their father was leading a hypocritical double life and that he had a wife and a lover at the same time—which was actually beyond good and evil, provided one had the courage to admit it. Of course he was too cowardly—so the boys said—to get a divorce. In public Yankel played the role of the stern paterfamilias and the faultless patriarch, but secretly he kept a mistress, a concubine who could be bought and was forty years his junior.

Money will buy anything, scolded his sons, even an adolescent actress. Probably a tart who was not an artist at all but some floozie from the nearest cabaret. But he isn't even ashamed, the old voluptuary, the gray-haired Casanova with bags under his eyes and rust spots on his skin. Doesn't he know that the girl loathes him and deceives him with young men? And if she does not, what good can she be if she goes to bed with a Methuselah, a father of sixteen children? She is no older than his youngest son, and when he dies, she will inherit everything. That, of course, is her intention. That is all she wants. She is certainly good-looking; the old man is under her spell and will leave her everything. The five daughters will get nothing, not to speak of the eleven sons. He has fallen into her trap, and he is too stupid to see through her. Serves him right. All his life he has squeezed others dry; now he is getting his punishment. And besides, one does not father sixteen children and then leave them high and dry. He is abandoning our mother and his daughters. That's just like him, the old fop, this Neanderthal without scruples and conscience.

Yankel's sons were of above-average intelligence. Most of them had studied at the university, read scholarly books, and reflected on the meaning of life. They also had a pretty clear picture of the world that they wanted to build some day, but they lacked the faculty to imagine the psyche of their father. Was there such a thing? It was not demonstrable scientifically, and no researcher had ever managed to distill it. The anatomists had dissected numerous bodies, but they never found the seat of the soul. In the writings of Marx and Engels it was presented as a hormonal secretion of various glands, and this appeared to explain everything. Yankel's soul was the secretion of an inert mass of protoplasm, the byproduct of degenerated protein compounds. He behaved like a protozoan, a sinister paramecium without ethical restraints. He resembled a machine that instinctively moved toward everything that served its own metabolism: eating, drinking, and whoring. So this monster fell in love and prattled about feelings when his existence consisted of business deals and evil deeds. Surely this did not fit the psychogram of this brute, for in the first place, he had no right, and in the second place, if he had to do it he should do it with his wife, and that's that! No one asked whether Noemi Kaminska loved her husband. Noemi Kaminska was their mother, and thus above all doubt. They idolized her and spoke of her as of a saint.

While Yankel's sons mocked the bourgeois laws and the

religious commandments, they were really guardians of the letter and among the legions fighting for law and order. And they were a soccer team of God that did not pray to the Lord above but to the proletarian revolution. Eleven inexorable rabbis intent on the mission of fulfilling the sacred writings of Marx and Engels. In the course of their American exile their anger at their father had gradually abated. Their store of hatred was distributed among other bugaboos: President William Howard Taft, the military, the New York stock exchange and all the scoundrels who were haggling over the fate of mankind there. Until that letter came. As unexpected as a natural catastrophe, which cruelly reminded them that they had a father. If an elevenfold Yankel had been their opponent on the other side of the playing field, they would undoubtedly have crushed him, smashed him to pieces, and torn him limb from limb. But unfortunately what was out there was not their procreator but a well-organized team. They lacked the motivation to deal them a crushing defeat, and neither Jim Weissplatt nor Uri Taubenschlag could do anything about it.

The game was a debacle from beginning to end; sixty thousand soccer fans witnessed the end of a world. Roars of enthusiasm came from the expensive seats and a chorus of boos from the cheap ones, but there was no changing the result. MacSnow's secondary law about the immanent success refusal celebrated its latest triumph. In the locker room of Brooklyn Stadium Jim Weissplatt sat with his legs crossed on a dirty sink. He turned up his collar resignedly and groaned. Another ridiculous five minutes, and then the fiasco would be official. Uri Taubenschlag came in panting; he had watched the second half from the bleachers. He looked as if all his teeth had been extracted, and for a moment he was unable to utter a sound. Then he screamed like a man possessed, "Eight to nothing, Mr. Weissplatt! That's your nephews for you, sir. They've skinned our heads and our *tochis!*"

"What do you want, Mr. Taubenschlag?" replied the entrepreneur gloomily. "We gambled on justice and lost."

"Who gambled on justice? Did *I*? No, *you* did, because you are a dreamer . . . I am absolutely normal, sir. I can give you that in writing."

"You went along for the ride, my dear friend. If I'm hanged, you'll swing with me. I'll see to that."

"God has decided to chop off our balls. He is all-knowing, he knows what he's doing."

"He's giving us a sign, Mr. Taubenschlag. We're supposed to learn from experience that socialism is no business for *yiden*."

"And not for the *goyim* either. Eight to zip, Mr. Weissplatt. The boys and their *mishpocheh* should drop dead!"

As he was saying this, an infernal uproar rocked the stadium. Orgiastic screams came from the better seats and furious howls from the not so good ones. Two minutes before the final whistle the Philadelphia team had scored its ninth goal. Weissplatt whimpered, "Not eight but nine to nothing, you phenomenal Olympic trainer, God's gift to the playing fields. I'm going to string myself up this very day."

"Why today, Mr. Weissplatt? Why not two years ago? Then you would have spared me this day, on which I am losing my last hair. *There* is your motivation . . ."

"A fine idea, sir, and a shitty business."

"You wanted me to motivate those idiots. I listened to you and made speeches. I told those fellows political *shmontses*, a lot of junk. Everything just as you wanted it, and where did that get us? We're standing here like two idiots in front of a urinal."

"I blew half a million."

"Your fault, Mr. Weissplatt. Who showed the boys that letter, you or me?"

"The letter," snorted the uncle, vainly trying to light his pipe, "that letter is my goddamn private business and you shouldn't give a shit about it."

"Nine to nothing just because old Kaminski found a young *shiksa!*"

The chaos after the game was indescribable. The sirens were howling; people were raving and refusing to leave the stadium. The boys returned to the locker room exhausted and dirty, the opposite of their usual selves. Mordechai went up to Weissplatt and said in a flat voice, "Uncle Jim, we lost."

"It wasn't *you* who lost, but me. First you'll pay me back, and then I'll throw you out!"

As Weissplatt was speaking, the door burst open and a news vendor ran in and cried, "Stolypin assassinated. The czar's prime minister riddled by three bullets!"

Hershele rushed up to his uncle and cried jubilantly, "We've won! Russia is on the verge of a revolution!"

"And I'm on the verge of bankruptcy. You owe me five hundred thousand dollars, and you can have Russia."

Now Moishe joined the conversation. He didn't talk much, but when he did, he astonished everyone with his logic. "Uncle Weissplatt, you can do figures, can't you? So think about it: Socialism will come in a few years—perhaps a bit sooner, perhaps a bit later, but it'll come as surely as a solar eclipse."

"You said it, Moishe," moaned Weissplatt, "a solar eclipse!"

"Science is science, uncle. What must come will come. With astronomical punctuality. It can be calculated in advance. Centuries in advance, whether you like it or not."

"And what good does it do me, smartypants?"

"Nothing. On the contrary. You are going to lose your dollars, your business, your houses, and your factories. They'll nationalize your last penny away. You'll be left with nothing. So what are you crying about?"

"Before it comes, your solar eclipse, you'll pay me back my investment, otherwise I'll have you locked up or deported."

Now it was Hershele's turn. He grinned and said: "You don't have to deport me, Uncle Weissplatt. I'm leaving voluntarily."

"You'll stay here."

"I'll go."

"Where will you go without papers? To the Wild West as a cowboy? To Alaska as a gold-digger?"

"To Russia, as a center forward. That's where the final game for the gold cup of the future is taking place. I'm leaving tomorrow!"

12

·~·~·~·

THE FOURTEENTH OF SEPTEMBER 1911 IS A MEMORABLE
day in the annals of my family. In New York the Kaminski boys lost the final game against Philadelphia; in Kiev
one Dmitri Bogrow shot the czar's prime minister Piotr
Stolypin, the most hated man in Russia; and in Vienna the
express train from Galicia arrived, carrying, among others,
the Rosenbachs, who had come to start a new life in the
Austrian capital. On his shoulder Leo was carrying a heavy
wooden tripod; on it was an antediluvian camera that constituted the entire working capital of the family. On the
staircase in front of the East Station the court photographer
ordered his two women to stop and pose for him, for he
was anxious to capture the historic moment in a photo.
Since his youth Leo had been on the lookout for historic
moments—first in the service of Ludwig of Bavaria, then
as the partner of his crazy brother, and now as a free-lance
dreamer in front of Vienna's East Station. "Malva, my sweet
child, please take off your straw hat, because today I can't
stand to have a shadow on your face. Certainly not today.
And you, Jana, be good enough to lean on your parasol,
nice and easy. That's it. That's wonderful. Here we are in
the heart of the world. By the beautiful blue Danube. Our
dear emperor Franz Joseph lives and resides here, may
God keep him. Please breathe deeply and . . . smile!"

September 27, 1911. For days I have been having the
same dream. I walk through the streets, aimlessly and

141

in love. Suddenly it seems to me that I am being observed. By a mysterious man who gives me goosebumps. I try to call out to him, but each time his name escapes me. It's on the tip of my tongue, but it tumbles out of my memory. Then I remember it again, but my voice fails me. Yet I know exactly who it is. My immortal beloved. The confidence man by the grace of God who can flourish only in Vienna, where everything is illusion and a fata morgana. The streets glisten as though they were gilded. Sparkling tinsel is reflected in a thousand windows. No one is in a hurry, yet everyone is on the lookout for adventures and illusions. The women leave clouds of scent in their wake when they rustle past. The men turn around and gape at you as if you were an apparition. Everyone has time. Patches of longing hang over the roofs. This is where I shall meet him. I am convinced of that. My skin is tingling. I feel it in my fingertips when I stroll through the streets. I can see him behind bushes and hedges. I can hear him and feel him kiss the palm of my hand. The street singers gargle sentimental songs and tears come into my eyes. That sounds ridiculous, but it's true. I gape at the shopwindows on Kärntnerstrasse, the fantastic hats on Kohlmarkt, the magnificent dresses on the Graben, and I am certain that he is following me. Sweet bliss wafts toward me from the cafés: Waiter, a *mélange!* Or a capuccino! Or a mocha with cream! Here I taste a cheese-filled doughnut, there a yeast dumpling filled with plum jam, and someone is watching me. Perhaps I'm just imagining it. Maybe I'm looking for him rather than the other way around. But I know he's there, hiding out somewhere. In one of these incomparable buildings. Behind an alabaster table at Kugler's, Demel's, or Sacher's. I am so in love that I can't tell day from night anymore. I stroll over to the Prater, to the Ferris wheel, the "Watschenmann" (Mr. Slapmyface, a test of strength), the roller coaster. A little carriage rolls out of the tunnel of horrors. I could swear that he is in it. That's him—word of honor—and next to him is an angel with sad eyes. Henner, I cry, look at me! He turns around and looks at me. A total stranger who thinks I'm cracked. The whole world is at my feet because I'm twenty. Yesterday I went to Schönbrunn with papa. He showed me the temple of the love-crazed nymphs. In it were hundreds of parrots in silver cages, jabbering away. Their magnificent feathers were reflected in dull mirrors. Delicate frescoes smiled down on me, and those strange birds turned and mirrored themselves like ostentatious courtiers who bumped into me impudently. One of them implored me with velvety cooing to redeem him. He said he was my lover, the greatest inventor of all time whom destiny had transformed into a cockatoo. Oh my God! I'm twenty. I'm in Vienna. I'm in the city of cities whose charm lies in its superfluity. It shimmers with frivolity, dissolute depravity, and joie de vivre. I long for you, you heavenly good-for-nothing. And for the other one too. The man of granite. For the hundredth time I read the news item that is breaking my heart: "With a fake ticket the notorious anarchist Dimitri Bogrow gained admittance to a theatrical performance that was attended by the Russian prime minister Piotr Stolypin. Before the beginning of the show Bogrow attacked the dignitary and fired three shots at him. The seriously wounded Stolypin was taken to a nearby hospital where he died shortly thereafter. The murderer was apprehended, summarily sentenced to death, and executed at dawn on September 26." A notorious anarchist. That can only be Baltyr. Or is it someone else? Another man of granite? It was his mission in life to kill the bloodhound. He had tried it twice, but in vain. Both times suspects were arrested and executed by order of a court-martial. Which of them was Baltyr? We'll never know, for they all sail under false colors. They use different names—Dmitri, Pawel, Baltyr. They have dozens of cover names, but you are the best among them. You are my rock crystal. You are one of those men who are nailed to the cross and rise from the dead on the third day. Yesterday morning they shot you. Tomorrow you will rise and come for me. You will knock on my door and bid me follow you. You know that I will follow you without hesitation. But you don't belong here; you belong in an ash-gray city. Novgorod, for example, or Tsaritsyn—the very name sounds like a sigh. You'll tell me how you fired those shots. How they grabbed you and clapped you in chains. I shall learn what you shouted in their faces at the court-martial. They heard the truth from you. The great truth for which it is a pleasure to die. I love you, Baltyr. You flung your dream in their faces. You will tell me how they took you to the place of execution. What you were feeling at that moment. What and who you were thinking of. Perhaps of me or a spring day. Of lilies of the valley and red carnations. Oh Baltyr, come to me at last! I am impatiently waiting for you and your strong hands. I don't want to belong to anyone else. Only to you. You will take me. Under the linden trees, in the heath. You will kiss my eyes. At the river bank or up on the embankment. I will open up to you like a water lily. I shall kiss away all the pain you had to endure . . . But what will happen if you don't come down from the cross? If they have killed you forever? What then? Then I will wait for your opposite. The colorful good-for-nothing who has been inventing color photography for years and finally ran off with our diamond. Where can he be, the wonderful counterfeiter? Why doesn't he send any word? He has a bad conscience, the fool. He lives in the clouds, like Baltyr. He confuses his intoxication with reality and is ashamed of being crazy. If he only knew that we are all crazy. A *meshuggene mishpocheh*. How could we be mad at him? What right do we have? We forgave him long ago. Both mama and I. Now we are longing for his return. Now we would give God knows what to have him suddenly turn up in front of our house. I'm in love. I'm in Vienna. I'm twenty . . .

13

.~.~.~.

U NCLE HENNER HAD READ SOMEWHERE THAT ENGLAND
was the freest country on earth, and he believed it.
Since he was firmly convinced that people were maliciously
obstructing his activities as an inventor, that mankind was
bent on tripping him up and dozens of dogs in the manger
on thwarting his great idea, he had set out to seek his fortune in London. He had some money from the sale of the
disastrous diamond and had found a flat at 13 Skull Street.
There he shared with his son Nathan an attic room that
had to serve as a lab, a kitchen, a sitting room, and a bedroom. The only good thing about this humble dwelling
was its view. If you looked out from the skylight, you could
see the Thames, London Bridge, St. Paul's Cathedral, and
Parliament. Clay-colored and sluggish, the water rolled toward the sea, seeking its way to the wide world. Since the
hectic days in Stanislav the inventor had been on the skids.
His blue silk tuxedo had lost both its color and its shape.
His shirts had once been snow-white, but now it was hard
to tell whether or not Henner had anything on under his
vest. He still insisted on wearing neckties, but what he wore
around his neck resembled a dead rainworm. Henner was
a caricature of himself, but he was still able to fascinate
both women and men. Miss Popper, his landlady, particularly adored him and forgave him a great deal, even his
bad English, a language that he had not mastered even
after five years of exile in Great Britain. One afternoon
he enchanted her with a speech that dwarfed everything

up to that time: "In your house, Miss Popper, in the middle of this stony desert of Lambeth, an unexampled error will down . . ."

"An era will dawn, Mr. Rosenbach, and you haven't paid me your rent in three months."

"I wow to you by the bells of St. Paul's that you will get back a hundred folds what I awe you . . ."

"Not awe but owe, and I'd like to know when. How long do I have to wait, and why? You avoid me, and so does your son. I admit that he plays like an angel, but I can't live on that."

"Today you get what I owe here. In a few moments begins the new era, for I have finally founded what I have sought for years."

"Not founded but found. You have to express yourself more carefully, Mr. Rosenbach. English is the language of Shakespeare and deserves to be treated reverently . . ."

"These little grains of resin," whispered Henner excitedly as he shook a honey-colored powder on the table, "that is the chemical compote . . ."

"Compound, Mr. Rosenbach, if you please."

"The chemical compound that will shake the world. Believe me!"

"I believe everything you say, Mr. Rosenbach, though you certainly don't deserve it, sir."

"I shall melt it. I shall pour it, Miss Popper. Here in this rotten room."

"I'll pretend I didn't hear that. This room is anything but rotten. It is in London, and London is in Great Britain."

"And from this powder, which doesn't look like much, madam, will come before nightfall the color-sensitive substance which will bear my name forever . . ."

"I wish it for you, sir, with all my heart, and I pray to God for you to succeed. Your good fortune is mine too."

"You are my charming witness, Miss Popper. You will see. With your violent eyes . . ."

"Violet, sir," the landlady corrected him, blushing to the roots of her hair.

"With your violet eyes you will see how colorful contours dimly appear in a colorless emulsion: green, orange, violet—a true-to-nature reproduction of God's Creation."

"I believe in you, you sorcerer," whispered Miss Popper, putting her hand on Henner's shoulder. "The Bible says that the last shall be the first. Will you?"

"What?"

"Be my first one?"

"Of course, Miss Popper. We shall return to Austria in triumph . . ."

"Who, darling?"

"My son Nathan and I. The emperor will receive us. In Schönbrunn. And my brother Leo will forgive me, for I shall be reach, enormously reach."

"Not reach but rich, Mr. Rosenbach!"

"The richest man in England . . ."

Henner went up to the shutters and closed them. Then he took a gas burner from the cabinet, placed a test tube on it, filled it with the powder, and lit the flame. He poured water over the solution through a glass funnel and said unctuously, "I have sinned, dear lady, but the sins of the successful are forgiven. We are about to experience a historic moment. You are going to tell your children . . ."

"I have no children, Mr. Rosenbach."

". . . tell your children and children's children that you were there. That in addition to Henner and Nathan Rosenbach only you were looking on when it happened. Pay attention now, Miss Popper. The liquid begins to bubble. A reddish vapor rises up. Do you notice the soapy smell? Now we're ready. On your mark, get set . . ."

At that point a terrible explosion shook the attic, and part of the ceiling collapsed with a crash.

What remained of my great-uncle, his son Nathan, and the rapturous Miss Popper was taken to Scotland Yard in a police cruiser. The two foreigners were handcuffed to each other and the old maid sat in the front seat, sobbing quietly. The driver was an overweight constable who now and then panted a few sentences. Seated between him and Miss Popper was a police officer who was attempting to fathom the deeper implications of the explosion. "The three persons have burns, Mac. Their hair and eyebrows are singed. Their clothes are charred and largely destroyed. What does this mean, Mac? It means that something was blown up."

"Jolly good thinking, old chap."

"The two men speak a miserable English, Mac. This makes me conclude that they are bloody foreigners. Russian anarchists from Sidney Street, I suppose."

"Sure they're Russian anarchists, mate, but if I can trust my nose, they speak German."

"Then they're not Russians but goddamned Germans, Mac. Fucking socialists who provoked our railway strike."

"Righto, mate, but what's that faded flower of a lady doing with them? She's a local, you know."

"Probably, but right now she looks like a grilled sausage."

"Well said, old boy."

"And I've got a hypothesis, Mac. These people are Irish. Common Irish arsefuckers who are ruining our state."

"Splendid, old chap. They're Irishmen who speak German to make us think they're Russians . . ."

"And the old maid is a feminist, Mac. Those women have their finger in every pie. A few days ago these geese blew up the telephone cable. The main line, London to Glasgow. And who was cheering? The Irish, of course. And that is why," he said, flashing evil looks at the burned woman, "we shall string you up on the gallows, you Irish sow."

"I've been English for forty generations," sobbed the landlady, "since King Arthur and the Battle of Hastings. You'll regret you called me an Irish sow, sir."

No sooner had Miss Popper said this than she made a sudden quarter turn and gave the officer two boxes on the ear, which the man received without stirring. He probably felt that he had gone too far, and said apologetically, "Maybe the lady isn't an Irish sow, but those two individuals are Russian anarchists." Now Henner could stand it no longer. He straightened up as much as he could and said with the dignity of a professional diplomat, "I have the incomparable good fortune to be a subject of His Imperial Majesty Franz Joseph of Austria—but I suppose that his name means nothing to you . . ."

"Terrorists are executed, you foreign son of a bitch. And as for your emperor of Austria, we'll rip his balls off."

"Austria's response to this insult to her honor will be war. Gentlemen, prepare for the worst."

After two weeks of detention Henner and Nathan were brought before the judge. The courtroom was full of official personages in black robes. The prosecuting attorney was enthroned in a red chair; he was visibly bored and doodled on his sheaf of documents. The attorney for the defense stood next to him, grinned sarcastically, and waved a Bunsen burner into the air, while Miss Popper buried her head in her hands and cried. The defense attorney said with mock pathos, "Your Lordship, is that supposed to be a corpus delicti? This is a ludicrous trifle that will make you the laughingstock of the British empire . . ."

The prosecutor looked up from his papers as if he were awakening from a deep anesthesia and said sleepily, "This ludicrous trifle caused considerable damage—to the tune of seventeen thousand pounds sterling."

"So the prosecution is serious in asserting that with this toy my client prepared assaults endangering the state?"

"Yes, sir. A lady with no police record very nearly lost her life . . ."

"But Your Lordship, the facts prove, and the psychiatric opinion corroborates, that the defendant, Mr. Rosenbach, clearly has a screw loose. If you took him seriously, gentlemen, you would disqualify yourself as Englishmen and jurists!"

"My esteemed colleague, science teaches us that each of us has a screw loose. But that's no reason why we should blow up all of England . . ."

"Indubitably, Mr. Prosecutor, but my client certainly did

not blow up all of England. It would be advisable to keep our feet on the ground a bit. The police report even says, in black and white, that the defendant threatened us with a military intervention. However, we cannot charge him with that because up to now he has not begun military operations. We are, thank God, a constitutional state. We punish only crimes that have been committed. In seven hundred years we have not been in the habit of prosecuting someone because of mere intentions . . ."

"You are mistaken, my colleague. It is by no means a matter of mere intentions. Mr. Rosenbach has already begun the destruction of our island empire." With these words the prosecutor took from his pocket a small bottle with a golden yellow powder. Confident of victory, he waved the bottle back and forth over his desk. "Here is the disastrous substance, gentlemen of the jury, with which this foreigner has destroyed three stories of a London apartment house. And this is what the defense attorney calls a trifle!"

"Your Lordship, these are little grains of resin. Harmless products of nature that have light-sensitive qualities, and that is why they were in Mr. Rosenbach's possession. For decades the defendant has been searching for the magic formula for the realization of color photography. To his great sorrow he has not found it yet. Miss Popper, my client's landlady, will confirm that her tenant had only peaceful intentions. Am I right, Miss Popper?"

"I am the injured party, Your Honor, and really ought to incriminate the defendant, but I can say only good things about him. I adore this person; he is a genius."

"Does that mean you are in love with him, Miss Popper?"

"That means what it means, gentlemen of the jury," said the landlady, and burst into muffled sobs.

"If it means what it means, gentlemen of the jury, the testimony of this witness is without juridical value. Miss Popper would then be prejudiced, and I would be obliged to put the defendant on the stand."

"I am at your disposal, Your Honor."

"Are you aware, Mr. Rosenbach, that in the kingdom whose hospitality you have abused the possession of explosives is strictly prohibited?"

"Of course I know that, but I protest against the imprison that I have abused the hospitility of this country."

"Then you have deliberately committed a crime?"

"No, Your Honor."

"How so, Mr. Rosenbach?"

"Because I could not foresee that my substance was going to explode if it was heated."

"Why were you not able to foresee it, when you claim to be a scientist?"

"I never said I was a scientist, Your Honor. I am an inventor. That is a subtle deference, but a very important one . . ."

"There are always people who claim to be inventors. Some assure us they are Galileo; others claim to be Benjamin Franklin or Isaac Newton. As a rule, these persons are put into straitjackets and properly isolated. Do you know what I mean, Mr. Rosenbach?"

"I understand exactly what you mean, Your Honor, and that is why I desire to leave this country."

"I shall do my best to keep you from doing that, sir."

"And I shall do my best to turn my back on this country. Britain's greatness is a thing of the past. A free spirit can neither breathe nor think here."

"The defendant wishes to turn his back on our country, as he so graphically puts it. He wants to leave us after vainly trying to destroy us. Splendid. And where would he like to go, if I may ask?"

"To Rome, Your Honor."

"To be received there by the Pope, I presume," mocked the prosecutor, who was gradually catching on that he was dealing with a hardened psychopath.

"The Pope will feel honored to make my acquittance."

"No one here doubts this, Mr. Rosenbach. And I suppose you are going to try to burn down St. Peter's Church. Am I right?"

"I understand, Your Honor, that you are trying to be clever at my expense. But it is not my extension to burn down St. Peter's. I want to have myself baptized . . ."

This struck like lightning. A storm of astonished merriment swept through the courtroom. The prosecutor bent over the balustrade and whispered something to the defense attorney, so loudly that all were able to hear it: "Not one screw, colleague, but two!"

To which Henner replied in the calmest voice in the world, "I'm perfectly healthy, Mr. Prosecutor. As healthy as you, anyway, but I still need a baptismal certificate."

"For scientific purposes, I imagine."

"Because I am an inventor and because life trickles away like sand in an hourglass. As a Jew one loses half one's life . . ." Henner paused. His voice broke and his eyes grew moist.

"How does a Jew lose half his life, Mr. Rosenbach?"

"He has to cringe, Your Honor. Always hide his feelings so as not to attract intention. Pull in his head. Smile without interrupture so as not to be insulted."

"Psychiatry knows delusions that it calls paranoia. Such persons have the feeling that all of mankind is against them . . ."

"Exactly. That is my illness. All of mankind is against me!"

At that point Miss Popper rose from her seat and cried to Henner, "That isn't true. Not all of mankind. I'm *for* you. You Jews are the chosen people and you are the chosen man. God is shedding his grace on you!" She sobbed out these words and turning to the prosecutor said in a choked voice, "Don't you see that he is the Messiah? He is innocent, Mr. Prosecutor, and as pure as the source of the Jordan."

"You are standing up for him after he has pulverized your house?"

"He is a saint. *I* want to serve his sentence. But let *him* go!"

14

VIENNA, OCTOBER 10, 1911. THE WATER IS UP TO OUR necks. We are drowning in debts. Papa is not earning anything, because we don't have a studio. We haven't seen any money for a long time. Mama went to see Samuel Teichmann, the charming rabbi who lives next door. He sent us to the Jewish Community Council. They told her she had come to the wrong place and referred her to the Rothschild banking house. There she was given a cool reception. The chief clerk said a loan was conceivable, but the Jewish Community Council of Stanislav would have to certify that papa is credit-worthy. Papa credit-worthy! That's enough to make one weep, and mama did burst into tears, because she knew that no sensible person in Austria-Hungary would certify that our credit was good. That official misunderstood her. He thought all the red tape at the Rothschild banking house was driving her to despair, and in a much more obliging mood he advised her to call on the well-known Baron Gutmann. He is said to be famous for his generosity, and also to have a weakness for beautiful women, which in this case is not without significance. When mama kept on sobbing (she is a virtuoso at this), he wrote her a personal recommendation. Now we are deliberating whether mama should go or not. It is, of course, a great risk. In the meantime we have lost our credit in almost all the shops of Floridsdorf. This bothers *me*, because they always send me to buy on credit. Three bakeries near us—Trunka's, Gröger's, and Grünlich's—have threatened to turn our account over to a collection agency if we don't pay up by the end of the year. The same goes for Hawlitschek the butcher. Kralik the grocer has put a yellow list in his window that says the persons named on it will not be served until they pay their outstanding debts, and until then should stay away from the shop. Our name is second, and I am embarrassed to be seen in the street . . . We have never been so miserably off, but to tell the truth, *I* have never been more cheerful. I am in high spirits, and ask myself quite honestly whether there is any connection . . . Who knows. Perhaps poverty is a requisite for joie de vivre. Maybe I am unfeeling and disloyal, but my parents' financial worries leave me cold. Somehow we'll survive. I don't doubt this for a moment. In some ways it's even fun. Every day is a lottery for life. You wake up with the tingling question whether you'll still be on your feet in the evening. This makes life awfully suspenseful—in any case, more exciting than the existence of the rich, whose every day is a carbon copy of the next. In ten days I shall take my final exam in secondary school. I shall pass, though I have a threefold disadvantage. First of all, as a girl. Second, as the daughter of a down-and-out Jew. And third, on account of my convictions. I still stand up for Baltyr and Daschynski. My heart beats on the left and my blood is red. I have to make it. This I owe to my hero, who was strung up in Kiev. All my successes shall avenge him, and all my victories will be his victories. I love him beyond the grave and thereby prove the immortality of the soul. True, I'm weak in mathematics, but what shall I do? Numbers and I don't get along. All the pharisees who can do figures are stuck to the earth and don't know how blue the sky is. I shall put on my black silk dress. The one with the low neckline that papa says makes me look like an equestrienne in a circus. All right, I don't mind that. I shall look like an equestrienne and be successful. Incidentally, today I witnessed a miracle. By chance. I returned to our home on Freytaggasse, and when I entered the kitchen I saw the strangest spectacle of my life. My parents were kissing. Not a comradely kiss but a lovers' kiss. On the mouth. Like young lovers. I once watched the Lilienthal brothers rise in the air in a

154

flying machine. That was fantastic. I also saw Mrs. Tschauner's cinematograph on Nussdorferstrasse. That was even more fantastic. I've heard the voice of the immortal Patti on a gramophone. That was the height of the fantastic. But now my parents were exchanging caresses! Papa was holding mama in his arms and whispering passionate words in her ear. She let him do it, and cried. She moaned quite softly when he kissed her neck. She whimpered and made a deep sigh, as if a huge iceberg were melting in her chest. The two were so occupied with each other that they didn't even notice my presence. Mama carefully unbuttoned papa's shirt and stroked his shoulders. As she did this she sobbed tonelessly and clung to the unprepossessing little man. Several times she repeated words that I wouldn't have believed her capable of and that somehow rang false in her mouth: "My poor Leo. Why am I so heartless to you?" For a long time papa was unable to utter a word. He was overwhelmed by the warmth that was streaming toward him, but then his tongue was loosened and he whispered, "Oh Jana. It's all my fault. I'm not worthy of you. You are my only light, my shining star in the evening sky. I've stolen your youth. I forced you and took the air out of you because I'm selfish, small-minded, and lowspirited. My faintheartedness is choking you, my firebird."

"My poor Leo, why am I so mean to you?" "*I'm* the mean one. I've never been able to tell you how much I love you, because I'm afraid of you. I die with shame because I'm a dwarf. I'm a nobody. A sad sack. An eternal loser. You deserved a better man, Jana!"

"Why am I so heartless to you, my poor Leo?" "I dreamed of showering you with diamonds. I wanted to lay the most beautiful dresses at your feet. I wanted to travel to foreign cities with you and show you off. I wanted to call out for everyone to hear that you are my queen, that I worship you and am your miserable servant. All this I wanted, but where are we now? In Floridsdorf, a poor suburb of Vienna, and all the cupboards are bare . . ."

As papa was saying this, an ineffable misery seized him.

155

He threw himself on the floor in front of mama, kissed her feet, and howled like a wounded dog. I couldn't stand this. I was determined to put a stop to this degrading scene and cried, "Mama, papa, for heaven's sake, what's going on?"

This roused mama from her ecstasy. She looked around, caught sight of me, and said in the matter-of-fact voice of a postal clerk, "Today is Yom Kippur, Malva, the Day of Atonement or Reconciliation. Didn't you know that? This is a reconciliation between us." I remember asking my teacher of religion when I was eleven what Yom Kippur really meant. He said it was the tenth day of the seventh month, the one called Tishri. On this day the Jews obtain the Lord's pardon for all the sins they have committed. He said Yom Kippur was, so to speak, a day of wiping the slate clean. The rabbi went on talking about this and that, but I wasn't listening, because his words were so stilted and his voice sounded so pompous. I had to laugh—this I still distinctly remember—and was punished. I found all that just comical. People bury their anger for twenty-four hours, and the next morning it starts up again. They insult one another, wish one another all sorts of bad things, and trip one another up. They do wrong, but on the tenth day of Tishri they take a sponge, wipe the slate clean, and everything is all right again. We are a practical people. We preach the possible. Three hundred and sixty-five days of loving one's neighbor are too much. Such a thing surpasses the human limits. Either you love yourself or your neighbor. Both together is a fantasy. Christians are dreamers. They are under the compulsion of the obsessional idea "Love thy neighbor as thyself." This they can't do. That is why they always feel guilty and run to confession. Mea culpa, they cry, mea maxima culpa! They accuse themselves of sinning because they are human beings and not angels. Because they are unable to love their neighbor as themselves. We Jews are more honest. We besmirch one another and from time to time celebrate a reconciliation. For twenty-four hours. The day after next we are all back to our old ways. I don't believe in brotherly love.

To me it is too selfless to be true. It is a moral one-way street. If I must believe in something, let it be love. It is based on giving and taking. One doesn't owe anything to oneself, and everyone benefits. There is no love between mama and papa. At best a reconciliation. In their marriage there is no room for love, because papa only gives. He feels cheated because for twenty years he has gotten the short end of the stick. Hence this comedy of conciliation and my mother's question, "Leo, why am I so mean to you?" Papa ought to give her a thrashing for that. Instead he personifies Christian humility. He takes all the guilt upon himself and perpetuates his degradation by elevating mama to the status of a queen, the sole ruler over his humble self. That is not a condition; that is self-destruction, and no Yom Kippur can change that. *I* shall live differently. Either equality in giving and taking—or nothing at all. I want to be neither a servant nor a master. There is no happiness in inequality. That I am convinced of!

Since her arrival in Vienna Jana had suddenly begun to care about externals. She was now forty and more attractive than ever. Her sense of form and color had become more refined. She regularly visited the flea markets where she gathered up remnants from which she sewed stylish dresses. When she entered the baron's waiting room, one could have thought she was the wife of a dignitary. A rotund gentleman jumped up, looked her over with the air of a connoisseur, and said nasally, "Mrs. Rosenbach, unless I am mistaken."

"Are you Baron Gutmann?"

"I am his private secretary. My name is Oppenheim. May I show you into the salon?"

Jana handed the man her letter of recommendation and said with an angelic smile, "I had already given up all hope of being received by you . . ."

The private secretary cast a covetous glance at the beautiful supplicant, skimmed the letter, and asked Jana to have a seat. "It says here that you are from Galicia. What are you doing in this Gomorrah?"

"Unfortunately my husband was obliged to leave Stanislav."

"Financial difficulties, I assume."

"Harassment—because we are Jews."

"We are Jews too, Mrs. Rosenbach, but we can't complain."

"My husband was challenged to a duel."

"So?"

"He has a family to feed, Mr. Oppenheim."

"It means that he ran away, if I understand you correctly. All the way to Vienna. And Baron Gutmann is supposed to get him out of this jam."

"It isn't my husband's fault, I swear to you."

"And I can swear to you that it isn't Baron Gutmann's fault either."

Jana did not have the strength to be humiliated further. She got up, put on her gloves, and said in an altered voice, "I see that I have nothing to expect from you. Good-bye!"

Oppenheim seemed surprised, and now tried to keep the dainty woman from leaving. "Does he have an occupation, this—what's his name—Leo Rosenbach?"

"For years he was the court photographer of Ludwig II of Bavaria."

"Why didn't you say so right away, madam? This puts a different face on everything."

"If you were prepared to grant him a loan . . ."—at this point Jana deliberately used her charms and gave Oppenheim a meaningful wink—". . . no more than a few thousand crowns, then he would fix up an unrivaled studio here in Vienna. You would get your money back with interest and compound interest."

The private secretary also rose and stepped close to Jana. "Then you would be prepared, madam . . ."

"My name is Jana, Mr. Oppenheim."

"Then you would be prepared, Madame Jana, to guar-

158

antee personally and with your honor that we shall get our money back?"

"What do you mean by personally and with my honor?"

"Exactly what I said. You guarantee with your person and with your honor . . . And since you are a desirable woman, Madame Jana . . ."

"By what date would the debt have to be paid?"

"By December thirty-first of next year. That gives you fifteen months."

"Six thousand crowns, then. Payable by the end of 1914 . . ."

Oppenheim went to the safe, opened it expertly, and took out sixty hundred-crown bills. He counted them pedantically and laid them on the table one by one. "Fifty-eight, fifty-nine, sixty. For the time being I ask only one quid pro quo . . ."

Jana winced. The man disgusted her. She asked haughtily, "And what would that be?"

Oppenheim gave her an unctuous smile. "Your signature, you enchanting woman!"

Vienna, October 30, 1913. Eureka! I have my secondary-school diploma. Even though I am a woman. Though I prepared for the exams all by myself. Though we pray to the false god, as they say, and I hold subversive views. Teichmann congratulated me. In Hebrew, and I didn't understand a word. Then he added in German that I owe it only to my black silk dress. He also said mockingly that with such a low neckline *he* would have been successful too. I like Teichmann, but he's a rabbi and doesn't know what's what. He is tall and slim, has ivory skin and a thick beard, but as a person he is a fossil. Such people belong in a museum. He is constantly on the wing and goes from house to house, but the leopard cannot change his spots. He is incapable of learning, because all he ever does is teach. That is why teachers are so stupid. He says that a woman should not be a university student, for the intellect is a male privilege. I have already met many

159

men who do not make use of their privilege. Baltyr is an exception, of course. And Henner and Daschynski. If the intellect were a male privilege, the world would look different. Everything is still a male privilege, but I shall endeavor to change this. Politics is carried on by men, and so are wars. One of the questions on my exam was what literary hero deserved our greatest recognition. I answered that this hero was a heroine named Lysistrata, the beautiful Athenian woman who called a love strike in order to force the men to make peace with Sparta. The expert grinned and asked me whether I knew who wrote that absurd play. I said the play was not absurd but disturbingly timely, and the name of its author was Aristophanes. The professor smiled and said I certainly could not deny that Aristophanes was a man. No, I replied, I cannot dispute that, but it was no accident that Aristophanes chose a woman as the principal character in his play. A man would never have thought of doing what she did. And besides, Aristophanes had been brought into the world by a woman. A woman had washed his diapers, and without women mankind would be extinct long ago. I added that peace was more important to me than the entire age of Pericles. What good are the tiles of the Parthenon and the wisdom of a Plato to mankind if the men keep devising new feats to destroy all that? Now the expert's face beamed. "So you admit that not only wars are the work of men, but also the arts and sciences, literature and philosophy . . . ?" "Certainly," I replied, "but Praxiteles and Socrates, Phidias and Aristotle are the work of women. All of them are sons of mothers who taught them how to talk and think." The professor said he was giving me a top grade because I had an astonishing amount of knowledge, but he warned me, "Smart women are not lucky in love, Miss Rosenbach." To which I responded, "I know. Dumb women are greatly in demand, which proves how easily satisfied men are."

15

.~.~.~.

HERSHELE WAS NO LONGER HIMSELF. AT LEAST OUT-
wardly. As a political precaution and for reasons to
be discussed later he had shaved the last syllable from his
family name and now called himself Henry B. Kamin. He
had cut his wild mane short, and instead of wire-rimmed
glasses he wore neat horn-rimmed ones that made him look
like an American businessman. In the last few years he had
developed into a splendid young man. He had silky black
hair, turquoise blue eyes, and what were said to be irresistible lips. He did not need to talk a lot to captivate people.
It was enough for him to smile; then silver sparks flew
from his eyes and he won everyone's heart. Men and wom-
en equally wooed him for his favor.

Even the crew of the German deep-sea freighter *Kö-
nigsberg* sought his company. Outside the elements raged
and the waves beat over the railing; in the crew quarters
below they all sat around him, told stories, or played cards.
To them he was *zweemal so schnafte wie dufte,* a Berlin saying
that indicated that they thought he was sweller than swell
and grander than grand, and they associated with him as
though he were one of them. A man named Rottmeister
was the only one who kept his distance from him and did
not stop trying to worm secrets out of Hershele, alias Henry. "Why do you want to stop playing, buddy?"

"Give me the address and I'll keep playing till tomorrow
morning."

"Lost too much, eh?"

"I said we'll go on tomorrow."

"You look like a dandy, you talk like a dandy, but you act like a proletarian. I can't fathom that."

"Sorry about that. Good night."

"If you don't have any money, we'll play for your watch."

"Tomorrow morning, I said, and for money."

"Why not for the watch?"

"Because it's a gift. From my mother."

"Where does she live? In America?"

"In Russia. I'm going to bed now."

"But you've got an American name. Something fishy there."

"How do you know?"

"It's on your trunk."

"I have Russian papers, am a Pole, bear an American name, and am on my way to Austria. There are things like that. Anything else?"

"If I sponsor you, friend, I've got to know who you are."

"Now you know. If you don't like it, I'll help myself."

"How much do you want for the watch?"

"I told you it's not for sale."

"My border smuggler isn't for sale either. What do you need him for, anyway?"

"Because I've got to get over there. To Russia."

"Then buy yourself a ticket and go by train!"

"I can't."

"You're not kosher, eh?"

"If I'm caught, I'm finished. Give me the address!"

"How much?"

"A hundred marks."

"Not enough."

"Two hundred and not a penny more."

"And how do you know that I'm not an informer?"

"And what about you? What if your man gets me across the river and a Russian bull grabs me on the other side?"

"Let's see your watch, comrade."

"What do you want with my damn watch?"

"I'd like to know where it's from."

"From Switzerland. So?"

"They say that everything that comes from there is classy."

"Not everything."

"What *I* have in mind is very classy."

"What are you driving at?" asked Hershele, who had begun to see that he was being given the third degree.

"Do you know a Russian named Ulyanov?"

"No idea who you're talking about."

"Too bad," said Rottmeister. "He lives in Switzerland and pulls strings."

"You mean Lenin, fellow. But he's no longer in Switzerland; he's in Austria."

"Are you certain?"

"Dead certain. He lives in Poronin, not far from Cracow . . ."

Rottmeister got up, patted Hershele on the shoulder, and growled, "You passed, colleague. I'll give you the address of my border smuggler. And for you it's free."

"Take my watch. It's free, too. To remember Hersh Kaminski by. That's my real name."

"Listen good, Hersh Kaminski. Our man lives in Vienna. On Schlosshoferstrasse in the twenty-first district . . ."

16

ON THE SAME DAY ON WHICH THIS CONVERSATION TOOK place—somewhere between New York and Bremer-haven—Leo Rosenbach opened his new studio. It was located at Three Freytaggasse, in the back yard of a four-story apartment house, and was one of the strangest ed-ifices in the factory district that bore the flowery name Floridsdorf. The studio was in the shape of a rotunda with a glass dome that could be reached via a passageway of green marble. At the entrance door there was an impressive brass plate with this ornate inscription: "Leo Rosenbach, formerly court photographer in Munich. Portraits and photographic work of all kinds."

The dedication ceremony was in keeping with the modest circumstances. Only a small number of acquaintances had shown up—two distant aunts from Galicia, a couple of fe-male cousins, the landlord (with whom, understandably enough, they wanted to have good relations), and a sallow bachelor from the third floor named Samotny, which means "lonely." He wooed Jana without any chance of suc-cess and kept staring at her with moist eyes. Samuel Teich-mann was there as well and delivered the obligatory ad-dress, which people were to remember for a long time. "This studio, ladies and gentlemen, breeds and perpetuates human vanity and should really be called a stud-io. This will be a daily meeting place of female vainglory and male craving for recognition. In this place profit will be derived from self-righteousness and arrogance, but this need not mean that Leo Rosenbach's artistry is a transgression against the principles of our religion. Not at all, honored guests. It is worthwhile to record human arrogance, for sooner or later every presumption is punished. In a few years we shall look at our likeness and note with horror what is left of past glamor and faded splendor. Whether we desire it or not, wickedness and vice leave their marks on our features. Sins of commission and omission destroy our countenances. It is only when we compare today with yesterday and yesteryear that we grasp the dimensions of our disintegration. It appears paradoxical, but I must say it: Blessed be this place, for the pictures that will come into being here will admonish us to observe the Commandments and to be God-fearing and obedient men and women."

Leo Rosenbach was a superstitious person, though he regarded himself as open-minded and unprejudiced. He was convinced that his first customer would decide the future of his business. His name, his background, and his appearance were to be signs of a meaningful oracle. This is why the erstwhile court photographer awaited with feverish impatience the moment when the person chosen by fate would enter the rotunda. Leo had placed an advertisement in the *Neue Freie Presse* and had reason to hope that he would have the honor of serving customers of high rank.

On the morning of the third day the doorbell rang and Malva, who was serving as receptionist, unlocked the door. There he stood, the man sent by destiny: a cavalry captain with fresh dueling scars on his face, puffed-up and self-confident, with a monocle in his left eye. Nasally and charmingly he said to Malva, "I have the honor to introduce myself, madam. Joseph von Schischkowitz of the Eleventh Hussar Regiment. You will have noticed that I have a few wounds on my visage, and I should like to capture them for posterity, as the saying goes."

"That can be done, captain. Won't you come in and let

me have your coat? It appears that you have had an accident."

"A trifle, charming lady. One of those affairs of honor among men. With a tragic result . . ."

"But I have the impression that you are still alive."

"I am, as you correctly noted, but the other man had tough luck . . ."

At that moment the side door opened and Leo, who had observed the scene from the darkroom, stepped into the studio. With a cheerful smile he went up to the officer, bowed modestly, and said, "Honored sir, you shall bring us luck in our new studio."

"With the greatest pleasure, Mr. . . . What is your name? You are a court photographer, if I read aright."

"I used to be one. At the court of Ludwig II of Bavaria, if the name means anything to you. You will bring us a double blessing, captain. We have just opened our studio, and here in Vienna you are our first customer. Besides, you dueled bravely and came out of it alive . . ."

"If I understand you correctly, you wish to reward me. I bring you luck and you want to reciprocate . . ."

"That will be my joyous duty, captain. You will be photographed free of charge. That goes without saying."

"Then I shall ask you to photograph me twice. You said that I am bringing you a double blessing, and so I would like a left profile and a right one. And if possible, another photo next to the charming lady!"

"If you insist, all right," said Malva reluctantly, "but first I want to know whether the other man is still alive."

"What other man, charming lady?"

"The one who had tough luck, as you put it."

"He fought pretty well, as my facade shows. But unfortunately it got him!"

"And this you say without any emotion, captain?"

"For an Austrian officer, mademoiselle, life is the exception and death the rule. Fear we leave to our enemies."

"I regard fear as an expression of intelligence and heroism as nonsense."

What Malva was saying made the court photographer wince. He remembered their flight from Stanislav and feared, not without reason, that his daughter's forwardness would precipitate another catastrophe. Therefore he tried to be as diplomatic as possible. "Today's young people have only silly ideas in their heads, Herr von Schischkowitz, but there really is no point in all this talk. The best thing would be for you to sit in the easy chair and get ready for the photo." Leo endeavored to remove even the last false note and added obligingly, "Does our guest of honor have a particular wish?"

To this the captain responded, "Your guest of honor would like to invite the gracious young lady to the New Year's Eve ball, and he will pledge himself to bring her home safe and sound."

Leo replied submissively, "No one here has any doubt about that, captain. We are pleased about your kind offer, and can only say that the captain's wish is our command."

Malva's mood had grown worse and worse. She was no longer willing to participate in this spectacle and said crossly, "What do you mean, command, papa? I won't let anyone tell me who to dance into the New Year with."

Leo gasped for air and pretended to have misunderstood. "Surely you didn't say that you are going to decline the captain's invitation?"

"No, I didn't say that. All I said was that a hussar captain's wish is not my command and never will be."

"Then you accept, if I understand you correctly?"

"You misunderstand me, papa. I'm not accepting and I'm not declining. I will think it over."

December 12, 1913. God only knows what I'm letting myself in for. This person runs counter to all ideas I have had of men up to now. There is no denying that he is handsome, but he has absolutely no sense of humor and is a bore. He wears a uniform both outside and inside. The ideas he expresses can't even be repeated because they are so indescribably meager. I'm almost twenty-two and am now certain that one either thinks against the tide or not at all. He has decided on the latter. He is in a mess and feels comfortable in it. He asks no questions and says yes to the world. He avoids any obligation to consider anything new. May God forgive him his narrow-mindedness, but *I* won't forgive him. He repeats all the banalities that circulate in his regiment: For an Austrian officer—this he says without blushing—life is the exception and death the rule. Good God, how asinine can you get? What did he come into the world for? To serve the emperor—that's his reply. And why is he serving his emperor? Because that's the thing to do. Has the emperor chosen him? Of course not, but such questions are beyond his mental horizon. He obeys the instructions he is given. He is a tin soldier with which His Majesty plays war. And yet I am letting him take me out. Am I a tin soldier too? A queen on a chessboard that can be pushed around? For twenty-two years I have let my mind be my guide, but on December 31 they will take me to the slaughterhouse and butcher me. That's tradition. I'm going to dance with him, and he will regard that as carte blanche to paw me. Not out of love or tenderness, but because he has to demonstrate his masculinity. The dashing hussar will bag a Jewish girl and boast about it. Why did I agree? Because he is handsome—a dashing fellow, papa calls him—and wears a uniform. I ought to know that with a uniform goes a saber, and with a saber one murders human beings. As simple as that. Then they say he had tough luck, and that finishes the matter. His very tone of voice makes me sick. He does not ask, he commands. Papa wants to photograph him for free, but that's not enough for him. He wants to have three photos—one with the charming young lady next to him—and of course everything gratis, because that's the proper way. You take without asking. After all, your name is von Schischkowitz and you are a member of the master race. What does he have in common with a Baltyr? With a Henner? With a Daschynski? The genitals, and that's all. But sometimes I ask myself whether these are really unimportant. Especially at night,

168

when I am lying in bed alone. When I feel that I am a woman and long for a man. Not for a person, to be honest. No. For a man of flesh and blood who could fulfill me. Who will penetrate my body and take me. Do I want that or don't I? This captain would slit me open and make me a woman. Or a slave. How should I behave? Should I surrender to lust or to reason? Be careful, Malva! Don't let them get you! Think of Lysistrata! We women have a secret weapon that makes us strong: Refusal.

One day after this entry something happened that was decisive for the course of this family history. It was a cold winter morning, and a pale sun broke through the snow clouds that had gathered over the capital. Cautious optimism reigned at the Rosenbach home. For several days the first customers had been dribbling into the studio. The first receipts gave rise to the hope that the lean years were coming to an end. Jana and Malva were busy baking goodies for Christmas and Hanukkah. Since the family prayed neither to Christ nor to Moses—did not pray at all, in fact—both festivals were celebrated, and as secularly as the temper of the times demanded. The sweet odor of cinnamon and sugar wafted into the apartment from the kitchen. On the table were raisins, roasted almonds, and candied fruit. Jana spread thick red currant jam on a cake. Malva put round wafers on a pastry board and caramelized sugar with grated nuts and stiff egg whites. She placed lumps the size of a pigeon's egg on the wafers and pressed a hazelnut on top of each lump. At that point the doorbell rang and Malva hurried out to see who it might be. She opened the door and froze in her tracks. In the hall stood an extraordinarily handsome man, a cross between the Eros of Piccadilly and Rodin's Thinker. He was around twenty-five years old and seemed to Malva like an apparition from the beyond. Neither the girl nor the man was able to utter a word. The two stared at each other speechless and overwhelmed. After a short eternity Malva stammered, "What do you want?"

The archangel answered in a velvety voice, "Nothing. Nothing at all. I've completely forgotten what I wanted."

"But you rang our bell . . . Who are you?"

"Are you afraid of me?"

"Yes," replied the girl, blushing.

"You needn't be afraid. I'm just—how shall I put it—a cloud in pants."

Now Malva was really perplexed. She stared at him, this necromancer whom she would have liked to clasp in her arms, but she controlled herself and only whispered, "I assume you've come about the room."

"About the room. Exactly. I've come because of the room, and now for other reasons as well . . . You see, I saw the notice on your door and thought . . ." He looked deep in her eyes and his voice broke. "I've forgotten what I thought."

"Then say something else!"

"I thought that I definitely had to ring this bell because otherwise I'd drop dead. I don't really believe in destiny, but . . ."

Malva felt that if she stayed in the hall with this fellow any longer she would do something foolish. So she called into the apartment, "Someone's here, mama, who is interested in the attic room."

"In what?" Jana called back.

The girl ran into the kitchen and whispered excitedly, "Go and look, mama! An Adonis is out there."

"What are you talking about, Malva? Have you gone crazy?"

"He is not of this world. I swear it. Go out there and see for yourself."

"Calm down, Malva! Speak in sensible sentences! Is he old or young or what?"

"He is a cloud in pants. These are his own words."

"I hope to God he won't bring a storm," murmured Jana. She rinsed her hands, looked briefly in the mirror, and went out to see the phenomenon with her own eyes. She froze, just as her daughter had done. She didn't know what to say, so she wrapped herself in matter-of-factness and asked coolly, "Have you come about the room?"

"I'm going to live here, yes. May I introduce myself. My name is Kamin, Henry B. Kamin from New York. I arrived today . . ."

"Very pleased to meet you, Mr. Kamin," replied Jana, who now had an opportunity to take a closer look at the man. Silver sprayed from his eyes and a strange stream of curiosity and high spirits pulsated in him. Jana had to smile at him, and she inquired, "What brings you to Vienna, if I may ask?"

"I am a medical student, and you might say that I'm passing through."

"If you're not planning to stay, why do you want to rent my room?" asked Jana a bit gruffly. "And where are you bound for?"

"We'll discuss my problems later," replied Hershele with a mysterious smile, "but now I shall ask you to show me the room."

Jana closed the front door behind her and took her guest up to the attic. When they had arrived there, she opened the door and said with some embarrassment, "There isn't much to show, Mr. Kamin, if that's your real name. It's more of a lumber room than a bedroom, and I'm afraid you won't like it here."

The Adonis entered and sat down on the bed while Jana remained in the doorway. He did not pay any particular attention to the room but lit a cigarette instead and said, "You'll have to permit me to decide for myself whether or not I like this lumber room, as you call it. I'll take this room, and immediately. It's exactly what I've been looking for. But what makes you doubt my name? Do you want me to show you my documents?"

The blood rushed to Jana's head and she answered in confusion, "I'm sorry if I offended you, but sometimes people like you have to—how shall I say it?—camouflage

171

themselves. Besides, you speak with a Slavic accent, and so I thought . . ."

"Do you take me for a counterfeiter, Mrs. Rosenbach, or for a man who doesn't pay his bills?"

"Call me Jana. I know that you're not a cheat. On the contrary . . ."

"What, then?" asked Hersh, whose eyes were now spraying crystal dust.

"I have the feeling that you are disguising yourself."

"And you trust me anyway?"

"Perhaps for that very reason. I'm on the side of those who are persecuted."

"In that case I shall undisguise myself. My real name is Hersh Kaminski—my brothers call me Hershele—and I intend to return to Russia. More precisely, to Warsaw, but illegally."

"I thought it was something like that. How long are you planning to stay?"

"That isn't up to me, but it will be decided soon. In any case, I feel comfortable in this house . . ."

Jana was fascinated. She sensed that this person would be no ordinary lodger. His words bespoke a familiarity and intimacy, an inner relationship, that reminded her of the time she went to see Daschynski with Malva. Hershele belonged to the same clan. He spoke with controlled assurance, insistently and softly, like someone who was certain of living for the right cause. Jana had a presentiment that destiny had sent this man here. Adjusting a crooked mirror on the wall, she glanced at herself before saying in Polish, "*Bardzo niechetnie,* I am reluctant to do it. I hate to give up this little room, *panie* Kaminski, for it's been something like a refuge for me."

"I won't cause you any problems, *pani* Janko. During the day I'll be at the university, and at other times I'll be meeting with my people."

"I'm renting the room only because I am under material pressure. It isn't easy for me, but because I like you . . ."

172

"I saved some money overseas," said the student with a boyish smile. "I'd like to help you out . . ."

"Thank you kindly," replied Jana, blushing, "but it will be enough if you pay your rent every month."

"Did you say you were under pressure?"

"My honor is at stake . . . but I'll manage somehow."

"I shall give you an advance, all right? A twelve months' advance. Please accept it!"

He tried to hand Jana a bundle of banknotes, but she was frightened and refused it. Her eyes grew moist and she said softly, "We weren't always this hard up. What are you doing here among us? This house is ugly and cold. Why do you want to be a lodger here, of all places? Anyone can see what environment you come from. This isn't the right place for you. It's embarrassing for me . . ."

"I'm going to live here, *pani* Janeczko. For a variety of reasons. For example, on account of your eyes."

"My . . . ?"

"We have the eyes of outcasts. Rage and tenderness blaze in our hearts. We are an army of dreamers. That is why we recognize one another. Everywhere. Even in the dark. There is passion in our voices and fire in our souls . . ."

"How strangely you talk, *panie* Kaminski. You practice alchemy with glittering words. Like those itinerant preachers that claim they are improving our world."

"Is that reprehensible?"

"I'd like to know where you're headed. What is it you want?"

Hershele smiled craftily. "I want to pay the rent. For the room. And, as I've said, a year in advance."

"You can't do that."

"I can do much more."

"In the first place, you don't even know whether I'll let you have this room."

"And in the second place?"

"How much I'm asking for it."

"I know everything, Frau Jana. I can read eyes."

"Try it!" said Jana coquettishly.

"Do you really want to know?"

"Certainly."

"You too must camouflage yourself. And your daughter."

"That is an insinuation."

"You are practicing the same alchemy as I."

"What makes you think so?"

"Your eyes, as I've already said. The alchemy of the pupils. I know that you are part of us. Both of you . . ."

While Hershele was speaking, Jana pulled out her necklace with the amulet that Daschynski had given her as a pledge. She opened it up, and there was a flashing golden sun against a purple background. "It is good, Mr. Kaminski, that we met. Accidents are shooting stars that plunge from the sky."

There he was, the demigod. The cloud in pants that had unexpectedly floated into the house and was spraying crystal dust from his eyes. Hershele took Jana's hand, kissed it, and whispered, "I ask for your discretion, Comrade Rosenbach. They are looking for me." With these words he put the bundle of banknotes—six hundred crowns—on the washstand and went to the door, saying, "You haven't told me whether you want me and for how much. But I shall live here. Whether you like it or not."

December 31, 1913, was an unpleasant winter day. An icy east wind blew through the streets, and part of the Danube was already frozen—a bad omen. Several hundred thousand Viennese prepared to bid an ordinary year goodbye. No one could suspect that this was the last New Year's Eve of the old era. If anyone had known what the New Year was going to bring and what times were in the offing, he would have engraved every moment of that fateful day on his memory. Instead, families, especially the women, spent the afternoon foretelling the future for one another, and for this they dug the strangest items out of their cupboards. Some sought truth in multicolored tarot cards and ivory dice; others searched for it in oriental dream books and all sorts of magic paraphernalia. Among the Jews it was a custom to open the Torah and to interpret the first word on a right-hand page chosen at random. The Rosenbachs were sitting in their comfortably heated living room, amusing themselves by melting tin figures. They poured the boiling mass into cold water, and the resulting formations were placed on a porcelain platter and subjected to an imaginative interpretation. Malva, who had the most to expect from the future, opened the seance by immediately pouring a small monstrosity that bore a slight resemblance to a five-pronged sphere; its five prongs were unequal in length but all pointed in the same direction. After a prolonged discussion they agreed that it might be a star, but no one was really satisfied with this interpretation. So Jana proposed that to make sure they should consult the Torah, and this appeared to be the most sensible solution. Leo was asked to take this otherwise rarely used book from the shelf and open it while rattling off a brief blessing. The result was astonishing. The first word on the right-hand page was *yad*, which means hand. Hence the five-pronged sphere was obviously a hand, and the only thing they had to find out was its significance. Jana, who had always played the role of a woman with the gift of extrasensory perception, covered her eyes with her ten fingers and whispered a prophecy that probably was more in keeping with her desires than with a magical inspiration: "I see a hand that is groping for you, Malva. A person will come and ask for your hand in marriage. Your hands will touch and become intertwined. He will put his hand on the Holy Writ and speak the vow of fidelity. He will pick up a pen and initial a document. Then he will stroke your hair—with the same hand—and show you the path you must follow . . ."

The Rosenbachs boasted of being above all forms of superstition. They smiled at the prevailing practices of the black art and disparaged them as remnants of the Middle Ages. Their religion too was always practiced with irony, and on the rare occasions when Leo attempted to read from the Torah he did so with the comical gargling voice of a eunuch, a performance received with sneers and giggles. On that afternoon of New Year's Eve everything was quite different. It had begun to snow and the cozy feeling of being in a warm stable pervaded the apartment. To be sure, the fortune-telling of Jana, who was usually so levelheaded, conflicted with the principles of modern thought, but she was astonishingly convincing and confused those present. Leo said he could smell a wedding in the air, and the only question was who the chosen man might be. Malva was irritated. Unwilling to let herself be pushed any farther by this dubious game, she suddenly declared in a humorless voice, "He wants to show me the path I must follow? Let him watch out, for I won't let anyone force any path on me either with a hand or with anything else."

So saying she seized the five-pronged sphere and threw it on the floor, where it smashed to smithereens. An embarrassed silence ensued. The thread of the conversation had been broken. Jana cleared the tin figures from the table. The fragile cozy atmosphere had evaporated, but Leo did not seem to be aware of the tension crackling in the air and asked naively, "When is he supposed to come, our hussar cavalier?"

He did not doubt for a moment that his wife's prophecy could refer only to the hand of the splendid Herr von Schischkowitz. Jana responded with an ambiguous smile, "Between eight and nine, Leo, but I'd be surprised if he were the chosen one."

"Well, who else?" asked the court photographer suspiciously, but he received no answer.

Malva had had enough. She was determined to end the speculation and declared coldly, "What do you mean by 'our hussar cavalier'? If you want to get married, then get married, but please leave me out of it!"

Leo wrinkled his brow and asked peevishly, "What are you brewing up here, my dears? Are decisions being made in my house from which I am excluded?"

"Certainly, papa," responded Malva icily. "As far as my private affairs are concerned, I am the only one who decides, and I'll thank you kindly not to interfere."

At the stroke of eight he pulled the bell with military punctuality and the impatience of an imperial-royal guards officer. Leo was in seventh heaven. So these fellows could be relied upon. A man of his word. Just as Herr von Schischkowitz had promised, he had arrived to take Malva to the New Year's Eve ball. He looked like a dummy in a shopwindow or a field marshal in a picturebook. Even Jana was impressed. Everything about him gleamed—the decorations and epaulets, the buttons on his jacket, his boots, even his reptilian eyes. Malva was flattered but by no means fascinated. This person, she thought, would be good to be seen with, but she could scarcely fall into his arms or swoon on his shoulder. He had the staring mud-green eyes of a frog and generally reminded her of an aquatic animal. Good-looking and cold, almost a bit slimy to the touch, like an eel. If you listened closely, his name sounded watery as well: Schisch-ko-witz. He made a deep bow, but behind his humility there were flickers of downright smugness. He dripped with admiration, and when he put his fully extended hand on his temple, he seemed to be saluting an imperial highness. His manners were so impeccable that Leo struggled for words to give expression to his gratitude. When finally the captain helped Malva into her fur coat, Leo's paternal pride exploded and he whispered in a quaking voice, "We feel ennobled."

The 1913 Baedeker mentions the officers' casino on Schottenring because of its incomparable ballroom and gives it two stars. It says that the edifice, which was erected during the reign of Empress Maria Theresia, is notable for its architectural grace and a waltz ensemble that was founded in 1834 by the famous Joseph Lanner and brought to full brilliance by him. In point of fact, there is no denying that even in 1913 said string ensemble offered the ultimate in musical saccharine and schmaltz. As early as nine o'clock or so there was a New Year's Eve atmosphere that could at any moment turn into boisterous abandon. Joseph von Schischkowitz had reserved a table on which his name was resplendent in ornate letters. Underneath it said: "Accompanied by Miss M.R." Malva said it was strange that only her initials were there when the full names of the ladies at the adjoining tables were given. The hussar captain replied charmingly, "That is a misunderstanding, esteemed lady. I shall take care of the matter right away."

Malva remained standing while Schischkowitz rushed out to correct the error. In her pink velvet dress and her gilded tiara she was like an unreal Esmeralda and a blue-veined orchid. A young blade immediately came up to her, made a deep bow, and murmured, "The New Year begins in three hours, madam. Count Ferenc von Karoly begs to inquire whether he may dance into it with you."

"Tell the count," replied Malva drily, "that I am not alone."

With these words she turned and paid no further attention to the supplicant, but he did not give up. He made a second bow and said much more obtrusively than before, "I definitely cannot give him this message, cruel lady, for . . ."

At that moment the band started playing and the last words of the unsuccessful lad were swallowed up by the honeyed cascades of the music. Joseph von Schischkowitz returned with a sour smile and casually motioned to Malva to follow him to the dance floor. Both were excellent dancers, which some people acknowledged enviously and others appreciatively. Soon more and more couples stepped aside in order to admire the dashing hussar and his mysterious companion. A circle formed around the two, and when the

178

last measures had died away, the spectators gave the pair an ovation. The unlucky supplicant approached the breathless girl and said in such a loud voice that everyone could hear it, "You are here the uncontested queen of the night, madam, but I still can't inform Count Ferenc von Karoly that you have an escort." Malva smiled condescendingly, for this man was beginning to get on her nerves, and she responded, "Then he's had tough luck and will never know . . ."

"He has already found out, for I myself am Count Ferenc von Karoly. And who are you, merciless lady?"

"My name is Rosenbach. No more and no less."

What followed now cannot be described as silence. It was a thunderous speechlessness that vibrated in the room like the flash of a bullet and found no outlet. A Jewish slut was exhibiting herself in the eagle's eyrie of the blue-blooded officers' casino, the most exquisite in Austria, and had the nerve to pronounce her miserable name, which they had sought to hide shamefacedly behind her mere initials. Then the storm erupted. The insulted count felt that he had to react now if the entire dual monarchy were not to collapse under the impudence of an unnameable woman. His face became dark red, his temples began to throb, and Ferenc von Karoly shot his most powerful bullets as he snorted, "Now the scales are falling from my eyes, Miss Rosenbach . . ."

"What do you mean, you importunate person?"

"That we had good reasons for reducing your name to its initials, and to my mind, even that was not enough."

Malva blanched. She turned to her escort and asked him to obtain satisfaction for her immediately. He whispered in her ear that she should not cause a scandal, if possible. Now Malva had definitely had enough, and she declared that she would have to obtain satisfaction herself. She went up to the count and slapped his face several times. Von Karoly did not bat an eyelash but took a card from his wallet, held it under the nose of the astounded von

Schischkowitz and said, nasally and arrogantly, "Either you give this Jew shrew the air or we shall fight a duel."

The hussar captain chose a solution that was in keeping with his watery nature. He took Malva by the arm, walked her to the checkroom, and said with a slippery smile, "Follow me, Miss Malva! We are going to leave this place."

Whereupon Malva replied loudly enough for even the slapped von Karoly to hear, "Why didn't you give this lout a whipping, Mr. Joseph? Surely that would have been your duty as an officer and a gentleman. Or am I mistaken?"

"Of course you are mistaken, Miss Malva. You see, I'm only a captain, but he is a major. We have our military hierarchy in Austria."

Vienna, January 9, 1914

Dear Ber, dear brothers,

I am in Vienna. Two steps from the Russian border, so to speak. I can see the other side. I listen for some signal from there, but none comes. Almost none, to be precise. I know that things are bubbling in the czarist empire, but they've been doing that for decades. Theoretically the volcano ought to have erupted long ago, but the concrete news that reaches me here is disappointing. Yesterday I spoke with Radek. He is even more near-sighted than before, and his lips are even thinner. He sounds as self-righteous and cold as ever. Our conversation disquieted and discouraged me. Before it I was determined to go across the big wall in a few days. Now I am quite uncertain, and that's why I am writing you. You must advise me what I should do. Radek said that the czarist empire was a time bomb that could explode at any moment, and thus it was impermissible to hang around in Austria and study folderol, by which he meant medicine. He knew all about our escape to America and said the party regarded us as deserters. I replied that Lenin too had fled from exile, and more than once. Radek screamed that if I compared myself to Lenin I was a presumptuous idiot. Lenin, he said, was our leader, a

180

giant, the brains of the movement, but we were a ridiculous soccer team who shit in our pants at the decisive moment. He knows all about us, and seems very well informed in general. He threw it up to me that I had fallen for a pretty face and that this was making me neglect my revolutionary duties. How does he know about that? Not even the girl knows, because up to now I have had neither the time nor the courage to tell her. I admit that Radek is a big shot in the party, but I can't stand him. He has an arrogant tone that is justified neither by his knowledge nor his political past. His speech is as wooden as an editorial, devoid of joy and passion. Everything he says seems logical and fits the way a key fits into a lock, but somehow he is off base. I could hardly reply to him, because I could not think of anything to say in response to his hair-splitting formal logic. So I asked him what the party expected me to do. That was the last thing in the world I should have asked, for it meant that I was recognizing his authority and conceding him the right to give me instructions. Which he did. He demanded that I leave for Warsaw right away (and I quote him verbatim) in order to remove the question marks over our name. This took my breath away. Nor could I think of a response when he lectured me that I would have to prove, by doing disciplined work on small projects, that I could be trusted even though we had deserted and cleared out without the consent of the comrades. He said I should leave Vienna by the end of the month and report to the appropriate Polish comrades. That was an order, and that's all he had to say.

I am now asking you, my dear brothers, what you think of this. Who is this Radek anyway? He tells everybody he is a friend of Lenin's, but the opposite may also be the case, for the most embarrassing rumors are in circulation about his person. In any event, I don't see what gives him the right to run my life. He isn't in Warsaw either, but in the golden West and plays gray eminence. How can he speak in the name of the party, this braggart? Did he consult it? Did someone appoint him? Who elected him anyway? As far as I know, he doesn't have a man-

181

date from anyone. Nevertheless, he does not hesitate to give me orders. But I am determined to listen to my conscience. Or are you of a different opinion? I want to finish my studies and go to Warsaw as a qualified physician. I am not cut out to be a professional revolutionary. That's why I have to have some training to be useful to our cause. You may say that I am guided by convenience, that I enjoy being in Vienna, and that all the rest of it is just an excuse. To this I can only reply that this city really is an Eldorado, the most comfortable and at the same time the most dissolute place on the globe. The amount of sparkling licentiousness, charming depravity, and decaying frippery is beyond belief. Vienna is a rotten swamp, but I certainly don't intend to become bogged down in it. On the contrary. The repugnant things repel me and strengthen my revolutionary consciousness. My convictions are stronger than ever. It is true that I have fallen in love, though not with a pretty face, as Radek put it, but with the most wonderful girl in the world. Is that treason? As I already told you, I haven't even declared my love yet, nor do I know what her reaction might be, but that isn't important here. I've got to have her. Come what may. Dead or alive! Not at the expense of my revolutionary obligations, of course. Either she participates or I'll forget her. If you can prove to me that my place is in Poland, I shall leave immediately and she will come with me. I don't doubt for a moment that she will come along. I've seen her only once. In the stairwell of her apartment house. But I know that she will be my wife and go to the ends of the earth with me. Otherwise my life would be meaningless. Write me soon! I feel that important events are impending.

Hershele

17

~·~·~·

IMPORTANT EVENTS WERE IMPENDING FOR ALL PEOPLE ON this planet. Including Uncle Henner, who up to now had lived past world history. In those days, you see, he was approaching the Eternal City. He had already forgotten that he had blown up a London apartment house and broken an English lady's heart. As I've already stated a number of times, he was a dreamer, if not a con man or a common crook. That's what we all are, in one way or another. He, however, became the blot on the family escutcheon, for he was now on his way to be baptized. You don't do that, even if you've got a noose around your neck. To stick to the truth, we are anything but God-fearing; yes, we are a clan of lightweights, and it's purely accidental that we belong to the Chosen People, but that's no reason to become an apostate. Granted, we don't believe in divine providence. We keep blaspheming, cursing, and sinning, but we don't change our colors. Under no circumstances. Our relationship to the Commandments is elastic. We eat pork without batting an eyelash, but we're not renegades. Once a year we go to the synagogue, not to the church of the *goyim*, who have been trying to exterminate us for two thousand years. Henner was the only one who did that, and that's why we cast him out, to use my grandfather's locution.

My grandfather exaggerates, of course. In our family everything is exaggerated. We scream and moan and wring our hands, we tear our shirts and bite our clenched fists, but that's all. We are extremists in our use of language, zealots of the tongue, but we haven't actually cast out anyone yet. The truth is that we turned our backs on Henner only temporarily—but even that is not quite true, for he continued to be our *meshugge* uncle, which among us Jews is something like a grim term of endearment. I suppose that people took it amiss that he had gone over to the competition without negotiating any substantial deal for himself. That was bad business, and no one, not even an angel, is forgiven bad business. They condemned Henner's lapse even as they hoped for an opportunity to make up with him. After all, he was Leo Rosenbach's blood brother, wayward Henner who had diddled and robbed us and held us up to public ridicule. But he was one of us, and that is the most important thing.

Henner, then, arrived in the Eternal City—barefoot, as dictated by his theatrical nature, and wearing ash-gray pilgrim's garb. Behind him Nathan, his silent son, schlepped himself along with a violin case under his arm and bleeding wounds on his feet. The appearance of these two was impressive and duly attracted the attention of passers-by. It was a radiant Palm Sunday. The Tiber River was glistening in the morning sun, magnolias were budding in the gardens, and the intoxicating fragrance of jasmine blossoms wafted through the streets. Henner and Nathan walked toward St. Peter's Square. As in a trance they hobbled past Castel Sant' Angelo and up to Via Crescenzia, where they suddenly heard a heavenly pealing of bells. Henner looked up rapturously, raised his hands, and cried in a tear-choked voice, "These are the bells of San Pietro, my son. Pick up your violin and play the *Ave Maria*. The God of Christendom shall hear us!"

Nathan put his violin case down on the ground. With his head bent to one side he tuned his instrument and then played more sweetly and with more tenderness than he had ever played before. He was no longer a wunderkind. He now coaxed tones from his violin that sounded as sophisticated and plaintive as a prayer. Soon a dense crowd gathered around the two pilgrims. Reverently the Italians listened to the cantilena, which, accompanied by the bells, swelled into a supernatural Sunday concert. The crowd was enthralled. The women especially stared at the young man who had such sad eyes and such marble-white hands. Suddenly, however, Nathan stopped playing. He put his violin down and tears ran down his cheeks. Surprised and uncomprehending the people stood in front of the weeping violinist. They didn't know what to do to make him go on playing. At that point Uncle Henner discreetly pointed at the violin case, and the people understood. The trick worked, as it had on the entire pilgrimage from England via France to Italy. Hundreds of small and big coins were tossed at Nathan's feet. There were even some gold coins among them, and Henner hastened to put them in his pocket. Now Nathan tucked the violin under his chin again and completed the *Ave Maria*. The crowd roared with enthusiasm, and with God in their hearts the two men went on their way again. It was nine-thirty in the morning when they reached their destination. Before them lay the square of squares and on their left was the Bank of the Holy Spirit, which is said to be the center of the Christian world.

Deeply moved, the prospective inventor of color photography and his son the virtuoso walked toward the main portal of St. Peter's Church. For them it was at long last the gate to the heavenly kingdom, the hope of their dismayed hearts. On both sides of the Porta Santa stood guards in colorful garb. They looked suspiciously at the visitors who were entering the church of churches in order to receive the grace of the Almighty. Henner walked up to one of these soldiers and said in a quaking voice, "You are Swiss, aren't you?"

"Keep moving, please!"

"I admire the Swiss because they live high up in the mountains, close to God."

"What does the gentleman wish?"

"To wash off my sins. Serve God and confess."

"If the gentleman wants to enter, he will first have to change his clothes."

"But I am a pilgrim. I come from England. Walked a thousand miles."

"Change your clothes, I said. I cannot let you enter like this."

"But in the Bible it says, 'Come unto me, all ye who labor and are heavy laden'!"

"Are you looking for something specific?"

"The Holy Father," replied Henner, and made a deep bow.

The soldier then saw what kind of pilgrim he was dealing with and responded, "The Holy Father, eh? He's been expecting you for a long time. His feet are already quite cold from waiting."

Henner ignored the irony of the Swiss and said proudly, "I'm sure he's heard of me. I am a divinely inspired inventor, and this is my son."

Now the guard became impatient and said, "Well, the Pope does not live here but over there. Only people who are decently dressed are admitted to this church. Now please move on!"

Henner tried another method and whispered, "Praised be Jesus Christ," to which the guard responded drily, "Forever and ever, amen."

Henner misunderstood these words too. He thought he was being permitted to enter, but the Swiss took him by the collar and said sternly, "I said not here but over there, and now get out of here!"

This marked the failure of Henner's first attempt to get himself baptized. Feeling miserable, the two men crossed St. Peter's Square in the opposite direction. Next to the fountain was a dealer who sold devotional articles, such as crosses made of wood, ivory, and silver. It dawned on Henner that he had forgotten the most important thing: He had to have a cross. A wooden cross, in keeping with a pilgrim's poverty, and one as big and heavy as the one borne by the Savior when he set out on his thorny path.

With this load on his shoulders Henner dragged himself to the portal that, so he thought, led to the chambers of the Holy Father. A man of gigantic build was just coming out of this portal, a priest over two meters tall who was wearing violet robes. Because of his dimensions Henner took him to be the head of Christianity. Unthinkingly Henner threw himself at the giant's feet, looked up to him rapturously, held his cross out to him, and cried, "A beggar flings himself at the feet of Your Holiness and begs you for your apostolic blessing."

To which the Goliath responded in a soft voice: "Vous faites erreur, mon fils, vous devez vous adresser à quelqu'un qui sait parler votre langue."

Henner did not doubt for an instant that the man standing before him was the Holy Father himself. He clasped the Pope's ankles and cried, "I am a son of sin, Your Holiness. Let me join the hosts of the Savior, and forgive me my origins!"

With these words he kissed the shoes of the priest with an ardor that ought to have softened stones, but the giant answered with cool detachment, *"Que Dieu vous pardonne, mon fils. Levez-vous de la poussière et n'avilissez pas ce lieu sacré! Vous êtes dans la ville éternelle!"*

With this he left, disappearing in the colorful crowd of St. Peter's Square. Henner, who did not understand French, did not notice, stayed on his knees, and answered, moved to tears, "I thank you, Holy Father. You have freed me from the shame of Israel. The taint of Abraham has been washed away. I am baptized. The grace of the Catholic God is bending over me and the work that I will complete."

Thankfully Henner pressed the newly bought cross to his heart, looked up, and noticed that the presumed Pope had disappeared. He had dissolved into thin air. A miracle had occurred, and from this Henner concluded that God had recognized him. Enchanted, he looked around, and beaming with happiness he cried, now with the fervor of a simon-pure Catholic, *"Laudeatur Jesus Christus! In saeculis saeculorum . . ."*

18

~~~~

B EFORE I REPORT ABOUT THE FURTHER ADVENTURES OF
my baptized uncle—and they are, to put it mildly, extraordinary—I must relate what happened in Vienna in
the meantime, for the house on Freytaggasse increasingly
became the central scene of the events concerning me and
my fate. In late March Henry B. Kamin received a letter
that was not to remain without consequences. It read as
follows:

New York, February 14

Dear Brother,
    I received your letter of January 8 and read it to our
brothers. What I am writing you is the result of many
hours of discussion. You asked us for advice. Here you
have it: We are astonished at your news that you have
fallen in love with the most wonderful girl in the world
but have had neither the time nor the courage to tell
her so. What is the matter with you, Hershele? You used
to be a famous center forward. What has happened? You
are afraid of a woman who, so you are convinced, will
follow you to the ends of the earth? Something is wrong
there. Or could it be that Vienna has already made you
so soft that you have become a coward? And what has
your courage got to do with lack of time? Are you trying
to tell us that you are studying medicine day and night?
If that were true, then Radek would be right and it would
be good for you to go to Warsaw. Medicine is no folderol—on the contrary—but it doesn't pay to become

stultified for its sake. There really is nothing in the world—not even the socialist revolution—that is worth losing your mind over. You write that you are torn and don't know whether to go over there or not. Why should you? You say that things are bubbling in Moscow and that theoretically the volcano ought to have erupted long ago. But as you yourself say, things have been bubbling in Russia for a hundred years, and everything is still status quo. With or without our help hardly anything has changed. As you put it, the news that is trickling in is disappointing. That's why we believe that no one needs you in Russia urgently enough for you to interrupt your studies. Radek orders you to return immediately in order to burnish our family's reputation again. The reputation of our family is none of his damn business. Radek is a notorious loudmouth. He is comfortable in the West, but he sends *you* to the front. Why you and not him? If things really start jumping in the czarist empire, then we'll come too. That's for sure. We have proved that we are ready to risk our lives for the party. When we defended our barricade at the Pivna nine years ago, Radek wasn't there, nor was he at the hand-to-hand fighting on Rynek or at the hail of bullets on Castle Square. In the citadel we met hundreds of revolutionaries, but Radek was conspicuous by his absence. We are here to live for the great cause and, as we have said, even die for it if necessary. But only if it is really necessary. Radek is a rabbit that likes to give commands in order to fill the blank pages of his biography. We don't need his orders.

We also discussed your need to have what you describe as the most wonderful girl in the world, dead or alive. On this score too we have decided to try to calm you down. If it is imperative that you have her, then it is better to have her alive. None of us can see why you should be so overcome with passion that you kill her. Be a sober Bolshevik and understand at last that our life is one big soccer championship. One time you win, another time you don't. In your particular case you should, in all probability, win. But you have to go out and play. He who stays home loses. Go to her and explain your position

189

to her. If possible, not with words but with deeds. What's the name of your wonder woman, anyway? It would be kind of you to enlighten us on this score some time. I embrace you in the name of all brothers!

Your Ber

While Henry was reading this letter up in his attic room, down on the ground floor Leo Rosenbach was opening a letter that was equally momentous but written in a much more snappy style. It read as follows:

Mr. Court Photographer,
The calamitous situation in which your charming daughter has put me obliges me to leave the capital of Austria on the fifteenth of next month and to take up quarters in the Hungarian city of Pozsony (Pressburg). The highest authorities suggested that I continue my career in the provinces, where social constraints are observed less rigorously than in Vienna. In this connection I desire, first of all, to enter the state of matrimony with Miss Rosenbach, and in view of my embarrassing situation and my fiery feelings, this brooks no postponement. Secondly, I intend to become united with the above-mentioned young lady through an official betrothal and to announce same in the official gazette of the City of Vienna. Thirdly, I shall permit myself to call upon you in your apartment this Saturday at 3:00 P.M. in order to ask formally for your daughter's hand in marriage in the presence of your family.
P.S. It is understood that prior to marrying the undersigned, Miss Rosenbach will have to convert to the Catholic faith.
With the expression of my deep respect, I remain

Joseph von Schischkowitz

Shortly after perusing this letter Leo read it aloud at the lunch table. When he had finished, Malva threw her soup plate at the wall and screamed that the hussar captain should go to the devil, he was reckoning without his host,

190

and she did not want to have anything further to do with him. Leo sorrowfully picked up the pieces and said that *he* was still the host and that no reckoning was going to be made without him. Consequently he was going to receive Herr von Schischkowitz in the manner he deemed proper. At that point Jana intervened and declared pointedly that she too had something to say in this house. She thought the officer had now gone too far and was scarcely acceptable any more as a son-in-law. The renunciation of the Mosaic faith was out of the question. Thank God, the times of the Inquisition were over. To ask for conversion to the Catholic faith was a presumption and would be unacceptable even if the emperor himself demanded it. Nowadays no one could force a woman who had come of age to give up her faith, and Leo should immediately write to the suitor that his visit was not welcome. What did that person think he was doing, continued the enraged Jana; first he behaved like a miserable toady, and then, a few months later, he hit them with an ultimatum as if nothing had happened. This man had forfeited any right to cross the threshold of the Rosenbach apartment. Period. Leo's rejoinder was that Jana was making a rash and emotional judgment. He simply could not afford to provoke an Austrian officer. He had already paid with all his possessions on a previous occasion for his daughter's incivility, and been forced to leave Stanislav in a hurry. Where should we turn, he asked sadly, if they drive us out of Vienna too? If Malva had not so recklessly slapped the count's face, things would never have got to such a pass. As Malva made her bed, so she must lie on it. The table talk had now reached the point where Malva's customary outburst was due. It did not materialize, however. She merely got up, haughty and pale, walked to the door, and turning toward Leo, said, "Let him come, papa! I know what I have to do . . ."

Vienna, March 5, 1914. This Saturday the die will be cast. My New Year's Eve cavalier is coming to see papa to ask for my hand in marriage. I'll be twenty-three soon and my hand already has some value as an antique. If I don't get married soon, I shall be left empty-handed, and that still is the most miserable thing that can happen to a woman. He is, as the phrase goes, a good catch. He receives his pay without doing anything for it. He is paid to look good, dress elegantly, and be a worthy representative of Austria. There is no doubt that he is doing that. He looks like a gypsy baron. He is a so-called dream man, and I would be ill advised to refuse him out of hand. To be honest, I am hurt that I did not hear from him after that New Year's Eve. I haven't heard from the other man either, though he lives in the same house, in our attic room. I fell in love with him at first sight. Why am I unlucky in love? Do men dislike me, or do I have an infirmity that I don't know about? The hussar behaved like a coward—but what right do I have to ask anyone to risk his life for me? He isn't a hero, that's all. Or perhaps he is one, but not for any old nonsense. It may be that he is saving himself. For more important occasions. For his fatherland, for example. But his tone gets on my nerves. These arrogant commands: "It is understood that Miss Rosenbach will have to convert to the Catholic faith." I don't *have* to do anything. Who does he think he is? If he adopts such a tone already, it will be a pretty mess when I am no longer "your charming daughter." No, I'll have none of that. And besides, I'm not so sure that I like him. Basically, he is a far cry from my ideal. He is neither a dreamer like Henner nor an idealistic activist like Baltyr, and certainly not a philosopher like Daschynski. My heart does not flutter when I think of him. Not in the least, to tell the truth. There is only one man who has really turned my head. He lives under the roof and keeps out of sight. Perhaps he is avoiding me, for we only looked into each other's eyes once. That time I thought I would drop dead. If he asked me whether I would climb Mount Everest with him, dive to the bottom of the sea with him, or walk through a tropical forest with him, I would say yes. A thousand times yes, but he isn't asking me. I suppose he hasn't noticed me. Or am I mistaken? Maybe he's waiting for a sign. In a few days it will be too late. Perhaps he is simply reserved and doesn't want to be too forward. Maybe he is shy, though he is more beautiful than a summer night. He described himself as a cloud in pants. Clouds are mute. Why doesn't he say something? The hussar is coming on Saturday with his ultimatum. This philistine with a carrot and a stick. He will tell me that he loves me, ask me to marry him, and then it will be all over. My history as an individual is coming to an end. Finis to my dreams, my whims and moods, my caprices and capers! I shall no longer have a choice. Oh, just one: between marrying Joseph von Schischkowitz and being an old maid on the shelf. If I consent, and I probably have no other choice, I shall be his spouse, or rather, his girl Friday, and spend the rest of my life in Brünn or Teplitz. Phooey! The very thought of it makes me sick. Why doesn't another man come? Why this vain dandy, of all people? Is my fate my own fault? Who knows? I do have innumerable admirers, but I show everyone the cold shoulder. None of them is good enough for me. None resembles the idols to whom I pray. That is why no one dares to woo me. They all give me a wide berth because they are afraid of being turned down. And what is the result of this? I am dying of loneliness and longing for a man. Perhaps I ought to take the first step—quickly, because I only have four days—but I lack the courage. In my genes are a hundred generations of patient, waiting, fading women. Thousands of years of dull passivity as the hallmark of womanly morality. It is all right for men to do anything they please. The more impudently they help themselves, the more they are admired. They take whatever they feel like. We, however, are permitted to cry, and that is all. That is our only right. I've had enough of it. I shall no longer participate, even if I am the first to end the tradition. I shall venture to take an atrocious action and write our lodger a letter. I shall shove it under his door. Perhaps something will happen, perhaps not. If worse comes to worst, there will be a scandal, but at least I shall have done something. The only question is how I shall express myself. Something like this: Dear Enigma, Unknown Person, Cloud in Pants. I am writing to inform you that I am facing an agonizing decision, one that I will hardly be able to evade. This Saturday an officer of the imperial guard will call on my father and officially ask for my hand in marriage in the presence of the entire family. As a consequence of this visit I shall more than likely become his wife, which fills me with disquiet. For these reasons as well as others I beg you to advise me, though we do not know each other. We have met on only one occasion, yet I pray to God that you will finally let me hear from you . . . Oh, but that isn't a letter; it's a declaration of love. I can't write anything like that. He would laugh at my helpless stammering. More than that—he would see through me and everything would be down the drain. But everything is down the drain in any case. Oh, what shall I do?

When Jews are at their wits' end they send for their relatives and feed them. The more hopeless the situation, the more is on the table. The more unpleasant the circumstances, the more numerous the guests. For March 7, 1914, Leo Rosenbach had invited the whole *mishpocheh.* Everyone who was in any way related to his family or his wife's family was invited by telegram.

In the morning the apartment on Freytaggasse began to fill with a colorful crowd of Jews of both sexes. Malva's cousins came; some of the female ones were already married. There appeared the wealthy Wertheimers from Cracow and Moritz Rosenbach, the well-known surgeon from Czernowitz. The poorer relations arrived on the noonday train from Eastern Galicia. There were the Feinstein brothers from Tarnopol and the Werfels from Brody, who were said to engage in shady business deals. By one o'clock more than thirty people had shown up, all bursting with curiosity. The invitation had been phrased mysteriously. A sensation was to be expected. Leo acted enigmatic and gave out only meager information. He said that at three o'clock a hussar captain would show up and ask for his

194

daughter's hand in marriage officially and in the presence of the entire family. Arrogant excitement gleamed in his eyes; it was obvious that today the court photographer would receive his great satisfaction. The blood of the Rosenbachs would be refined. A great day. Perhaps the greatest of Leo's life, though he did not feel too good in the stomach area. It was quite clear that something sensational was about to happen, but no one knew what.

He was there at the stroke of three. In his left hand he held a bouquet of twenty-five red roses. Saluting with his right hand, he bowed to Leo, whom he addressed from the beginning as "my highly esteemed father-in-law." An awkward pause ensued, because neither verbal nor written decisions had been made as yet and the principal, namely Malva, had not yet expressed herself on her good fortune. Herr von Schischkowitz displayed an arrogance that caused the temperature to fall dramatically. Even though the windows were open and sweet summery fragrances came into the apartment from the chestnut trees, frosty reserve reigned at the Rosenbachs'. Nearly fifty people stood stiffly along the walls and waited for someone to break the ice. Finally the Rosenkavalier pulled himself together and rattled off a few stilted greetings: "As a private person and officer of His Imperial Majesty, I have the pleasure of paying my respects to the esteemed gentlemen and ladies."

Leo answered with unmistakable sarcasm, "As you can see, the pleasure is all ours."

Continuing with his remarks, the hussar captain declared pompously, "These red roses I am bringing to the incomparable young lady who has ruined both my career and my heart with her wild temperament." With these words, which constituted both a compliment and a reproach, Herr von Schischkowitz went up to Malva, kissed her hand, handed her the bouquet, and continued to declaim. "I am, however, convinced that in your arms I shall be richly compensated for my damages, both military and sentimental, and that the Rosenbach family will be prepared to give its favorable consideration to the request I expressed in a letter . . ."

Leo bowed dutifully. He had understood what the officer was driving at, and said with a trace of displeasure in his voice, "You will, of course, have to be compensated for your damage, captain. We are in your debt and cannot rest until you have received satisfaction. But an injustice has been done to us as well, for my daughter was most obscenely insulted in your presence. With her conduct she defended both her own honor and the honor of the entire family. Therefore you must understand that we would not like to make any decisions that conflict with the desires of our child. We must also determine whether Malva is really willing to give up her traditional religion and embrace the Catholic faith. If she is, nothing will stand in the way of your wishes. If she is not, you would, of course, have to waive your conditions."

Herr von Schischkowitz blanched and his pupils dilated. This he had not expected from the little man. Actually, he had not expected anything, for in his circles people only looked upward. From those below obedience was expected, and nothing else. He had been sure that he was going to capture the Rosenbach bastion without a fight, especially because the commandant of the fortress was a timid Jew from Galicia. A nameless dwarf without rank and title who kowtowed with a smile and was used to obeying without any back talk. To his detriment the captain forgot that among us Jews there is a strategic reserve called a *mishpocheh*. This translates as "family," but it means a great deal more. The captain had no idea of the cohesiveness of Jewish clans when the honor of their sons or daughters is endangered. We are called a people of enviers, a wrangling pack who trip one another up, malicious schemers—which may be true in some instances, as it is of other people. However, if an enemy approaches and a danger threatens, then we multiply our energies. Like Gideon, who with three hundred loyal men destroyed a hundred thousand Midianites, we crush our adversaries with the little finger of our left hand. Not with cannons or grenades, but with the concentrated fury of the *mishpocheh*. Those who provoke us ought to know this. The hussar officer didn't know it, or didn't want to know it. Thus he underestimated the true relative strength and naively tried to tip the balance of fate in his favor, saying in a hoarse voice, "It cannot have escaped your attention, esteemed ladies and gentlemen, that I have made a few sacrifices for my passion, to which I had to refer earlier. One of the developments caused by the hot-blooded Miss Rosenbach is that I was transferred to the provinces, very much against my will—to Pressburg, if this geographical name means anything to you. Thus it would be only fair if you too made certain sacrifices."

That was a bit thick. Jana felt provoked, and responded, "You forget, captain, that my daughter did not invite *you* to the New Year's Eve ball, but the other way around. My daughter was your guest, and under your care."

This argument was irrefutable, and the hussar needed a moment to catch his breath and formulate a suitable answer. But then he said with self-righteous amiability, "It is, of course, correct that I asked your charming daughter to accompany me to the casino. But no one told her to slap the face of one of my higher-ranking colleagues in full view of the public there. You understand this, don't you?"

"That I cannot and will not understand," rejoined Malva, though she had resolved to avoid any arguments and let events take their course. "One of your higher-ranking colleagues had the unparalleled kindness to call me a Jew shrew, and no one was there to stand up for me. I emphasize: no one."

"I explained to you why I wasn't able to stand up for you, Miss Malva. Did you expect me to let myself be kicked out of the Austrian army because of an affair with a woman?"

Now Helli, the passionate cousin from Cracow, joined the conversation. She was only fifteen, but she already had

197

the Rosenbach theatrical sense and said with the dignity of a court actress, "I don't know my way around Vienna, but the house you're in is not a casino. If you regard your liaison with Malva as an 'affair with a woman,' you've come to the wrong place."

Uncle Moritz, the famous surgeon from Czernowitz and Leo's cousin, wrinkled his nose in disgust. He thought the dispute was embarrassing and declared, "In my job as a surgeon I must constantly make decisions. Any indecision can result in a fiasco. Hence I am an advocate of clear positions. Don't hesitate any longer! If it is to be yes, then say yes; if no, then no, but don't complain that you are making sacrifices. Everyone makes sacrifices; life is one big sacrifice . . ."

Old Werfel from Brody also had to add his two cents' worth, and said with a Yiddish inflection, "In any business ya gotta decide; in mine business too. By me the important thing isn't the life of my customers, it's the existence of mine firm. So I ask, plain and simple, if something pays or it don't pay. If you think that by us you're gettin' a raw deal, then take your roses and go to Pressburg!"

Now Herr von Schischkowitz sensed that he was facing a closed phalanx. All his plans were going up in smoke. He had to strike or his cause would be lost, and so he said in a piping voice, "I didn't come to lead the entire Rosenbach family to the altar. I'm interested in Miss Rosenbach and in no one else. My decision is a positive one, and I declare straight out that I am ready to take the marriage vows with her. It is, of course, possible to ask whether it is worthwhile to marry an officer who has been transferred for disciplinary reasons, or the daughter of a Jewish suburban photographer. I loathe such trivialities. I am guided solely by feelings of tender devotion and ardent passion."

Malva kept stubbornly silent. Jana answered in her stead, "As a prerequisite for the marriage you want my daughter to convert to the Catholic faith. Unless you withdraw this condition, we can consider neither a yes nor a no. Since our exodus from Egypt we have been praying to Jehovah, and we shall continue to do so, whether this suits you or not . . ."

"But it is unseemly, Mrs. Rosenbach, for an Austrian officer to get married anywhere but at a Catholic altar. This cannot be changed."

"Then get married, young man," replied Leo, who was beginning to find this dispute unbearable, "before the Catholic altar, if this cannot be changed, but without us!"

"Of course without *you*, Mr. Court Photographer," countered the officer, "but definitely not without Miss Rosenbach. After all, I still have at my disposal the requisite leverage for my demands . . ."

At that moment it happened. When the belligerent Herr von Schischkowitz was about to exert his remaining strength in an assault on the Rosenbach fortress, a person came climbing through the open window. Hidden by a curtain and unnoticed by the family he had been standing on the windowsill and observing the final scene of the battle of titans. His shirt was open and his hair disheveled. In his eyes shone an impetuous desire to cause a commotion. Right in the middle of the guard officer's threatening speech he let out an Indian war whoop and jumped off the windowsill into the living room.

The ladies were terrified and the gentlemen turned pale. The imperial hussar, however, hoped that this was the moment to polish his tarnished prestige again. Laying his hand on his saber, he asked with restored self-confidence, "Who is giving us the honor, you nameless boor?"

The intruder brushed his hair from his face and answered cheerfully, "Keep your tongue in check, sir, for otherwise I'll have to pulverize you."

The blood rose to the captain's head and he barked, "Who is this subhuman, Miss Malva?"

The stranger bowed and said: "This subhuman sublets from the Rosenbachs. I am from New York and my name is Kamin. I pay my rent regularly, and now I ask you: Who are *you*?"

The intruder's overseas background had so impressed

the *mishpocheh* that the officer was obliged to mount an all-out attack to prevent a definitive loss of face. "This nobody asks me who I am. I am an officer of the imperial guard and am about to throw you out the window through which you came in."

"You are welcome to try," responded the American, "but first tell me what you are doing here."

The captain loosened his saber in its scabbard, and his voice shook with anger. "I have come to make Miss Rosenbach my wife. But as for you, I advise you to get out, for the mere sight of you is an insult to my honor."

"You will not make Miss Rosenbach your wife, you silly boy. You can bet your boots on that."

"For the last time: Get out if you value your bones!"

"Don't come too close to me, sir. I care about hygiene!"

As he was saying this Hershele pulled a bunch of carrots from his pocket and handed them to Malva with a royal gesture. "Take these vegetables, you celestial phenomenon, as an expression of my boundless admiration."

That was too much. Herr von Schischkowitz lost his patience and roared in a breaking voice, "You are insulting a lady. Apologize this instant!"

To which Malva responded with a gentle smile, "Apologize? For what, captain? He has given me exceptional pleasure with his present. I have received hundreds of roses, but never any carrots."

"You call that a pleasure, Miss Malva? That is an insult I cannot tolerate!" With this he turned to his rival and spat, "I am challenging you to a duel, you bushman! Name your seconds!"

The American put on his glasses, squinted, approached within two steps of the hussar, and full of compassion asked, "Where did you get those pockmarks?"

"These are dueling scars, you cipher. Each of them is a monument to my combativeness. I repeat my challenge to a duel, and with weapons of cold steel."

Hershele grinned contemptuously. "I am honored by your invitation, bold warrior, but I decline."

"Just as I thought. You are a shit . . ."

With these words the hussar pulled his saber completely out of the scabbard and got into position. Hershele did not move but said with a disdainful shrug, "Surely you're not going to attack a defenseless civilian with your saber. Or is that the honor you spoke of?"

"Yes, indeed, that is it—the saber of an Austrian officer."

"Delighted, sir, but I am a socialist and frown on the use of force."

"Because you are a milksop."

"With one exception, though."

"Interesting," said the officer nasally, "and what would that be?"

"The weapon of the working class, sir. The fist."

So saying he crouched and floored the hussar with a right hook to the head. Once again the school of Uri Taubenschlag had demonstrated its great class, and Hershele bowed to his public: "*Shalom aleichem,* ladies and gentlemen! Don't let me disturb you!"

The American picked up the glorious Joseph von Schischkowitz, who had passed out on the floor between the credenza and the sofa, and gracefully carried him out to the hall. This ended the confrontation between the officer caste and the revolutionary proletariat in favor of the lower classes. The daring feat of the lodger was perceived by the assembled *mishpocheh* as a patriotic deed. The right hook to the captain's lower jaw was sweet revenge for the years of humiliation they had often had to endure without resisting. Sighs of relief, feverish applause, and finally a stormy ovation surged around the archangel from New York as he carried out the dandy who had dared to call Leo Rosenbach a "Jewish suburban photographer." The excitement was unexampled, the *mishpocheh* was in high spirits, and Jana was completely beside herself. She giggled and exulted, put brandy and choice liqueurs on the table, and invited the guests to celebrate the happy end of the comedy with some drinks. At that point the door opened and Hershele entered the room for the second time. He smiled with false modesty, but his eyes shone as if he had just slain a dragon. Quite casually he asked for some aluminum acetate, because he had inflicted some bruises on that swell fellow, as he called him. He said the boy was still unconscious and looked pitiful. He should be brought out of his coma, otherwise he would be late at the barracks, and under the circumstances he could hardly afford that.

With the aid of the famous surgeon from Czernowitz the hussar was bandaged and put into a fiacre. Looking the worse for wear, Joseph von Schischkowitz rolled toward his quarters in somewhat damaged condition. Leo Rosenbach, who had long since ceased to understand what was going on in his house, asked Hershele with whom he had the honor of speaking. While he was greatly indebted to his lodger, he did not know him. To which the archangel replied solemnly, "I am the red tomahawk from the Hudson River, the battle-ax of the humbled and insulted. I have crossed the great water in order to make the daughter of the snapshooting chieftain my squaw. Anyone who tries to stop me from doing this will be nailed to the stake and scalped. Ugh! I have spoken!"

Nothing like this had ever happened before, and the *mishpocheh* was, to put it mildly, dumbfounded. After all, they were a respectable family that accepted proposals of marriage either in due form or not at all. This man, however, was a typhoon, a terrible tornado, a Horseman of the Apocalypse who smashed all obstacles in his path. He had knocked out the hussar officer, restored the honor of the Rosenbachs, and put an honorable end to a humiliating situation. Well and good. But to climb in through the window coldbloodedly without announcing himself, knocking or ringing, and then to proclaim airily that he was going to take the daughter of the house for a wife was going too far. Before Leo had a chance to make a mistake, however, Jana got up from the table, clinked a champagne glass with her fork, and said, "Unless I am very much mistaken, you unpredictable whirlwind, you wish to become our son-in-law. You are the second man today to express such an intention. So please tell me what your desire is."

"I desire nothing and wish nothing. I am completely content and shall marry this girl."

"You seem to be quite sure of that, Mr. Kamin, but there is one very important question mark."

"There is no question mark. I want your daughter."

"And what if our daughter does not want *you?* What then?"

This caused the company at the table to fall silent. One could have heard a pin drop, and all eyes were on Malva, who had never been as beautiful as at that moment. She went up to Hershele and said, "I ought to slap your face, you red tomahawk, because you are so sure of yourself and so impudent. This is only the second time we've met, but you are already giving yourself airs and want to possess me. How do you know what *I* have in mind?"

"I know it because you wrote me, you peacock butterfly. I got your note today. An hour ago."

"It's true that I slipped a piece of paper under your door, but there was only one word on it."

At this the court photographer got hot under the collar and squawked, "You correspond with strange men, Malva? Behind your father's back, if I understand correctly, and without your mother's knowledge? What did that note say?"

"I'm of age, papa, and I write whoever I want and whatever I feel like."

"I want to hear what was on that slip of paper," shrieked Leo, absolutely furious.

"I can tell you, great chieftain," replied the American in Malva's stead. "There really was just one word on it: Help! Under it was the signature of the butterfly as well as the date and the hour."

"I did ask you for help, but that was all."

"That was not all. You see, I came and helped you."

"That is true too, but what gives you the right to imagine that you will have me?"

The American jumped up on the table. He shut his eyes mysteriously and, with his arms extended, whispered, "Me medicine man. Me know everything. Me see through peacock butterfly down to duodenum. Peacock butterfly in love like drunk monkey."

"Stop your foolishness," cried Malva, who was beginning to find the spectacle weird, "and come down from the table! We're not among Indians here!"

"Red Tomahawk rattle his bones and chatter with teeth. Red Tomahawk also in love like bear in heat."

"Come down immediately!"

"Why?" asked Hershele in a different voice. "Why should I come down, you wild rose?"

"Because I can't kiss you like that . . ."

19

.~.~.~.

ON JUNE 28, 1914, THE DESTINY OF MANKIND IN GENERAL and of Uncle Henner in particular was decided. You see, he and his son were hobbling toward the Austrian border, and he was determined to make his dreams come true at last. The two pilgrims looked unkempt. Unshaven, wrapped in rags, and perspiring, they climbed a hill, at the top of which a signpost indicated that their homeland was only four miles away. A feeling of uneasy joy seized the two men, whose only possessions were a cross, a violin, and an agonizing uncertainty about what was awaiting them at the border. Henner imagined an enthusiastic reception. Nathan was more soberheaded and feared complications, for they had once fled abroad with a stolen diamond. Years had passed since then, but who could be certain that the statute of limitations had expired yet? Henner looked trustingly heavenward and said that there had been a radical change in their situation. They had left as Jews accursed by God, and were returning as purified Christians blessed by the Pope. What was denied to the descendants of Abraham would be forgiven the children of Jesus, and they could face the future without fear. He was spouting this nonsense on the very day, and almost at the same moment, when the successor to the Austrian throne was felled by a Serbian bullet. Henner, however, did not concern himself with international politics but concluded his uplifting remarks with the following words: "Chin up, my son! This time we shall go to see the emperor himself. He will have to give us an audience, for we now pray to the same god as he. While you play for him, I shall explain the invention of the century to him. My color photography will give Austria a decisive advantage over its enemies. Our father in heaven will succor us."

It was a sultry summer day. In the distance the Isonzo River was winding its way through the valley. On its other bank lay their homeland with its green forests and lush meadows, though I must point out that on this side of the river the woods were no less green and the meadows no less lush. Here and there bloomed anemones and meadow sage, arnica and hawkweed. Sweet fragrances rose from the fields through which barbed wire entanglements and gray fortifications were scattered. No one could have believed that there was a gaping border here at which hecatombs of young men would soon die miserable deaths for their respective fatherlands. Unsuspectingly the two pilgrims hobbled over the Gradisca Bridge toward the ugliest customs house between Austria and Italy.

Like all such offices in the old world, this one stank of disinfectant and perspiration. Despite the noonday heat the windows were locked. Along the back wall long silk threads hung from the ceiling; on them were silver coins of various kinds. In front of a high-backed chair Major Pavlik, the commandant of the border station, stood and practiced the noble art of target shooting. His adjutant sat at the desk. A man not easily perturbed, he was working on yesterday's report despite the continuous noise. The major pulled the trigger; a silver ruble fell on the linoleum and Pavlik mumbled cheerfully, "Rush the Russians—long live Austria!"

The adjutant dreamily dipped his pen into the inkwell. Then he cleared his throat and asked, "What are they whispering about in the casino, major? Is there going to be war or isn't there?" Pavlik loaded his pistol again and severed a silk thread on which a French gold franc was gleaming. Pavlik beamed. "Wrench the French—if we're lucky, there'll be war."

The adjutant continued scratching out his report. Then he said abruptly, "But the Serbs are sneaky assholes."

The major held his pistol up to the light and peered into the barrel. "Which doesn't mean that they're bad shots. Say what you will about them, they can shoot."

The scribe seemed a bit perplexed that those subhumans were being praised by a professional and muttered softly, "They massacred our crown prince, those pigs. Now it's our turn. Serbia, we'll disturb ya!"

Pavlik fired a third time and a British pound rolled on the floor. He murmured grimly, "Every boom England's doom. But if we have tough luck, the Serbs will apologize and the war's down the drain again. We'll get moldy at this shitty station."

The adjutant now discovered a small hair on his pen and tried desperately to pick it off. As he was doing so, he philosophized gloomily, "If it don't start happening this time, it never will. Except if we think of something on this lousy river. The civilians in Vienna are praying for peace . . ."

Now Pavlik fired his fourth shot. For the fourth time he hit a thread, and a silver lira fell down. In the midst of the high jinks the door opened, a border official entered, clicked his heels, and bellowed, "Beg to report, major. This riffraff was nabbed at the checkpoint, and they're under suspicion because of their dress."

Pavlik didn't even seem to be listening. He pedantically took his pistol apart, brushed the gunpowder dust from the barrel, and inquired quite casually whether those arrested were from Belgrade. Henner never read newspapers and had no idea how tricky the question was. He replied, "We come from Rome, commandant. From the holy city on the Tiber."

"Such rabble doesn't come from Rome but from Belgrade."

"What have we done to deserve this abuse?"

"You know that as well as I do. Because the Serbs have murdered our successor to the throne."

207

"I'm terribly sorry that the successor to the throne has had an accident. But this is the first I've heard of it."

"You're sorry, eh? They slaughter our archduke, then they say they're sorry. But you'll pay for that, you goddam Serbs."

"Commandant, I wish to make a correction. I am not a Serb but a loyal subject of our head of state, Franz Joseph of Austria, may God keep and protect him for us!"

The major twisted his face in disgust, put his gun together again, and hissed, "You don't say! A loyal subject of our head of state—and you tramp across the border in your bare feet. What do you take us for?"

"I am a Christian pilgrim, major, and pray for the continued existence of our monarchy."

"A Christian pilgrim. That's good for a horselaugh. You're a Jew—even a blind man can see that. For starters, what's your name?"

"My name is Henner Rosenbach, and this is my son Nathan."

A sarcastic grin formed around the sharpshooter's mouth. "Of course, that's a horse of a different color. Your name is Henner Rosenbach and you're probably the archbishop of Galicia. You come straight from the Holy See, I suppose, and are bringing us a secret message . . ."

"Not straight, commandant, but I actually did see Pope Pius X, and he blessed this cross for me and baptized us."

Pavlik took a cartridge from his ammunition pouch and lovingly placed it in the magazine. Stubbornly looking past Henner, he continued his interrogation. "I imagine you don't have any occupation."

"I am an inventor, major. That is not an occupation but a vocation."

The commandant turned to his adjutant and jeered, "Write that down, sergeant. This is interesting. Henner Rosenbach. Pilgrim from Rome with the blessing of the Holy Father. Tramps barefoot and wants to . . . What does he actually want?"

"I have the intention of being received by the emperor, and as soon as possible."

That left Pavlik gasping for air. His eyes flickering with malicious mockery, he screamed, "So he has the intention of being received by the emperor. As soon as possible. That's great. Just the man we've been waiting for!"

"I have made an invention that is going to shake the world, and that is why I am asking the emperor for an audience."

"He wants to shake the world. That's just great. Turn the world upside down, in other words. An explosive invention, if I understand you correctly?"

"Extremely explosive, major."

"And the emperor is supposed to . . ."

". . . be given a demonstration, yes, commandant."

Pavlik now raised his gun threateningly and dictated the following text to his adjutant. "The prisoner speaks German without an accent, which is suspicious in itself, because Serbian agents in particular and foreign spies in general have an astonishing gift for languages and in that way manage to escape being detected by our intelligence. Only secret agents have such a perfect command of our language that we are tempted not to suspect them. Period. In addition, he admits that he is planning our emperor's assassination."

"I object, major. I did not say assassination but demonstration. A demonstration of my invention."

"I know better than you what you said and what you didn't say. You are a spy and will be court-martialed, something you'll regret. Period. And now get that rabble out of here. Take them away!"

20

～～～．

VIENNA, JULY 1, 1914. TODAY THE SECOND HALF OF my life begins. Since 3:55 P.M. I have been a woman. What I pictured indistinctly for ten years has now really happened, and in the strangest way imaginable. Boldly and impudently I climbed up to his attic room. I knew that papa was in St. Pölten on business and wouldn't be back until tomorrow. Mama is in Baden near Vienna for two weeks, taking the waters. I had thought up a pretext. Not a particularly clever one, but a pretext nevertheless. Since our heat wave has assumed devastating dimensions during the past few days, I decided to bring my dearest one a pitcher of lemonade. When I was outside his door, I asked him if he was thirsty. He answered with studied nonchalance that he couldn't hear me, and why didn't I come in. I did, but as I crossed the threshold the pitcher slipped out of my hand and broke to pieces . . . A German proverb says that broken dishes bring you luck, and they did bring me luck. Henry B. Kamin, that cloud in pants, the angel of my dreams, was lying on his bed naked and reading a fat book with which he quickly covered his face. I was so scared I couldn't make a sound. He, however, seemed to be in an excellent mood and asked me whether the sight of his nude nose had rendered me speechless. Normally I would have laughed at such a joke, but this time my sense of humor failed me. I didn't look at his nude nose, which he modestly kept covered, but at the peculiar piston that was beginning to stir between his thighs and grew out of his body like a mushroom. I was literally hypnotized. My propriety bade me run away, but my instinct told me to stay and taste the forbidden fruit. In my embarrassment I pretended that I had to pick up the pieces of the unfortunate pitcher, and this brought me quite close to my beloved. Henry was still hiding his face under his tome, and asked me whether I wasn't hot. This finally restored my speech and I answered—in a voice that must have rattled like an out-of-tune piano—that in this house the heat was utterly unbearable, up in the attic even more so than downstairs, and I supposed I ought to return to my apartment. Whereupon my idol said he would certainly understand if I took off my clothes as well. There was no reason to be ashamed; after all, he was naked too, and besides, the fat book on his face kept him from seeing anything. He had to promise not to look, and I stripped my clothes off, which made a sweet shudder run through my insides. When I asked him where I might sit to catch my breath for a moment—as I write all this down, I realize that I behaved like a complete idiot—he took my hand and carefully pulled me onto his bed. I write as if I had spent an enjoyable, or rather a quite ordinary, summer afternoon. In reality I was shaking from the roots of my hair to my toes. My thoughts were in a tangle, and the words died on my tongue, for I knew that it was bound to happen now. I definitely wanted it. At all costs, even if I had to die. I had yearned for that moment for years. I had dreamed of Henner, of Baltyr, and Daschynski, even of our rabbi, but I wanted to save myself for the chosen one, the true lover who would come to ignite the great fireworks in my body. I had read that defloration was a terrible torture, a degrading act of violence against a woman's self-determination. That is ridiculous humbug and a stupid lie. I did not cry; I laughed. So did he. At first he stroked my belly and my hips quite gently. Then he took a brush from his night table, dipped it in a little paint pot, and began to paint my body. He painted two funny birds on my two breasts, a giant sunflower around my navel, and finally a signpost on each of my thighs. On one of them he wrote: To Calypso's cave, 15 centimeters. On the other he wrote: To the Garden of Delights, 15 minutes. When I asked him why so long, he replied that this was all so tremendously enjoyable, one must not rush anything. I let him know that I did not have the patience to wait for half an eternity. Then he gave me a brush and invited me to paint *him*. Since I couldn't think of anything original, he suggested that I adorn his arrow with the colors of the French Revolution, and even though my hand was shaking, I tried it. In the process I had to touch that strange thing with my fingers, which produced the most wonderful excitement in me. It felt like a club of Hercules in a deciduous forest, like a cross between a silky blindworm and a prickly stalactite. I could hardly wait to be pierced by this weapon. Henry encouraged me to let his thorn slip quite gently and carefully into my chalice and kiss him on the mouth at the same time. I kissed his eyes and his neck. I felt a waterfall foaming through my loins. Bursts of fire shot through my spinal cord, and I screamed with delight and sweet pain, for after years of longing finally there was fulfillment. He pressed me to his body so that I almost fainted, and then I suddenly felt as though his soul were pouring into my body warmly and boisterously. That was the sixth day of Creation, the dawn of my life. By comparison everything up to that time had been only dalliance. Only today did I experience the true ideal. In the arms of the most tender and most handsome man on earth I experienced carnal delight. I love this human being more than anything, this madman with the tri-colored key of the French Revolution. It opened me, opened me up to the joys of bliss: *Vive le son du canon!*

21

~·~·~·

VILLACH IS A TOWN IN AN AUSTRIAN PROVINCE—A HICK
town, to put it mildly. It is located in Carinthia and is
known for its Gothic parish church, its thermal springs,
and the ugly fortress that for years was a bone of contention
between Germans and Slavs. Few of those who were imprisoned in the Villach fortress in those years ever returned
home. When Uncle Henner was sent there he is said to
have been asked which he preferred, the gallows or the
guillotine. To this he is said to have replied, "Neither one
nor the other, gentlemen, but if it has to be something,
then kindly kiss my ass."

From then on he was in a foul mood and refused to give
any more information. For days on end he stood in his cell
stiff as a poker. Through the barred window he stared
down at the courtyard where almost nothing worth mentioning ever happened—except for the changing of the
guard four times a day and sporadic executions. One fine
day in July something did happen, however. Henner noticed some feverish activity among the staff. Officers gave
marching orders, military music blared from all directions,
and commands rattled across the yard. Henner surmised
that the emperor had arrived to escort him personally to
Vienna. Around noon the door opened and a sergeant entered, roaring in a voice that broke hysterically, "Now
you're getting what you deserve, you Slavic skunks. We've
declared war on you. We'll rip your balls off. Not even a
crap can will be left of your kingdom. We'll shoot you down

213

like scared rabbits and make dumpling soup out of you, you bogus banknote, you leaning tower of Pisa, you Serbian spy. We'll hang you from the gutter, you crooked counterfeiter. Decks himself out with false feathers and tries to tell us Austrian idiots that he's one of us . . . You'll swing, you can bet your boots on that, and we . . ."

That was too much for Uncle Henner, who deigned to break his offended silence with the following words: "I have highly placed friends in Vienna. If one of us is going to swing, it's you!"

With this threat he hit the bull's-eye, for in the dual monarchy there was nothing more impressive than friends in high places. Therefore the sergeant replied in a somewhat more conciliatory vein, "We know all about that tribe. Agents, that's what you are. Agitators of the king of Serbia. A verminous bunch of terrorists and bomb throwers."

At this stream of vilification, the inventor suddenly opened his shirt and revealed the Habsburgian double eagle that he had once had tattooed on his chest in a moment of weakness. "And what is that, you lackey?"

"Our national emblem," replied the sergeant, automatically clicking his heels. "But the eagle is one thing and your clan is another. Who are your highly placed friends, anyway?"

"My blood brother is the court photographer of His Royal Majesty of Bavaria."

"If that's a lie, you'll be drawn and quartered."

"I will be in any case, you blockhead. That's why I can say whatever I like."

"And where does he live, this alleged court photographer?"

"Not in your district, you jackass. That would be too much of a slum for him."

"I'm asking you where he lives."

"In Vienna. Floridsdorf, Three Freytaggasse."

"Do you think he'll put up bail for you?"

"You've got to ask *him*, not me."

214

"And guarantee that what you said is true? Will he do that?"

"Maybe yes and maybe no. And if he doesn't vouch for me, you nameless nobody? What happens then?"

"Then you're going to be eliminated, understand? Hanged head down . . ."

22

I T'S HAIR-RAISING BUT TRUE. IN HIS OLD AGE MY MATERNAL grandfather became a war profiteer. All his life he had been a schlemiel. Most of the time he kicked over the traces and practiced the art of spending more than he took in. Or, more precisely, his wife practiced that art, regularly spending more than Leo earned. Since his wedding he had been dreaming of showering the incomparable Jana with presents and thus worming himself into her favor. Unfortunately he had never succeeded in doing so. But then came the memorable day on which emperor Franz Joseph declared war on his enemies and Franz Conrad von Hoetzendorf ordered the mobilization of the army. That was a moment of great change for the Rosenbachs as well. Hundreds of thousands had to go off to war and bid their dear ones adieu, so long lines formed in front of wedding license bureaus and photography studios. Some were rushing to get married before they were sent to foreign battlefields. Others had themselves captured in photographs because they felt that their road to war was a one-way street.

The Rosenbach studio was humming with activity. The stream of customers seemed endless. Floridsdorf was a proletarian district where the quota of fallen soldiers would probably be highest and the desire to leave an inexpensive keepsake was especially strong. As we know, the have-nots have always been the ones who get sent to the front line. The ruling classes have sufficient means at their disposal to keep their young people behind the lines. Thus the majority of those who had themselves captured for posterity by the court photographer were starvelings. My grandfather became the twenty-first district's wholesaler of keepsakes. He manufactured mementos for three crowns apiece and thirty crowns per dozen, and there was hardly a day on which he cleared less than a hundred crowns. Prosperity broke out on Freytaggasse, and along with the prosperity there were unexpected complications. On the morning of the very first day of the war Leo's waiting room was jampacked with soldiers who were having themselves photographed for the last time, usually in the presence of their mothers, girlfriends, or fiancées. Late that evening the exhausted Leo asked through the half-open door of his studio whether anyone was still there. There was—a scruffy sergeant and a trembling girl who clung to him and kept whimpering, "I'm expecting your child, Tony. If you die, I'll hang myself."

My grandfather was an imperial loyalist to the core, but such scenes broke his heart and made him conscience-stricken. But he masked his compassion by acting like a matter-of-fact official and rasped, "Your name, please."

"Anton Hawlitschek," replied the soldier, while the girl continued to bawl, "I'm having a baby, Tony. You can't die!"

Leo was close to tears himself, yet he asked coolly, "Address?"

"Twelve Am Spitz, a hundred steps from here."

"The son of the horse butcher, I presume?"

"Don't ask so many questions! I'm in a hurry."

"I imagine you're going to the front."

"Where else? Tomorrow morning, when you'll still be farting in your featherbed. Leaving at six. The young lady there, she's my bride, she'll come for the pictures."

The girl couldn't restrain herself anymore and began to sob uncontrollably, "If you don't come back, Tony, I'll jump out the window."

Leo turned away discreetly and called young Hawlitschek into the studio. "Your father can be proud, young man. He's giving our emperor a vigorous soldier. Take a seat, please, and smile!"

"I'm supposed to smile, Mr. Rosenbach? You are the ones who should smile; you're staying home, near the stove, where it's warm."

The embarrassed Leo crawled under the black cloth, where it was easier for him to deliver his platitudes. "God is punishing me for my sins, Mr. Hawlitschek. I have only one child, and unfortunately she is a daughter."

"Don't let that get you, Mr. Rosenbach! She'll have kids, and they'll die for a crappy cause."

"Do you think that our emperor is a crappy cause, young man?"

"Leave me alone with your emperor. He's no better than you, and makes a profit on the soldiers going to the slaughter."

Sensing that his talk was meeting with no response, Leo asked uncertainly whether today's young people were against Austria.

"Not against Austria, Mr. Photographer, but against the Jews. They put their dirty fingers on our cake and lick the butter off our rolls. When I go to the front, your daughter will be sitting in front of her mirror primping."

That made Leo's gorge rise, and he spat, "Maybe you don't feel like being photographed by my humble self?"

To this the sergeant responded with weary disdain, "By the time those pictures are ready, I'll be dead and buried!"

Leo realized that any further discussion was pointless, so he picked up the shutter release, declaring as he pressed it, "With your attitude, Herr Hawlitschek, we're not going to win the war."

Three days after the senile emperor Franz Joseph declared war on the king of Serbia, two days after the clamorous mobilization in Russia, and one day after the German ultimatum to France, a famous peacemonger was assassinated in Paris, the socialist leader Jean Jaurès. For years he had called on the proletarians of all countries to unite and prevent the outbreak of a world war by means of an international general strike. His prescription was simple. If it had been followed, our planet would look different today. But it was not, and Jaurès paid for it with his life. His voice was muted forever. The proletarians of all countries let themselves be led astray and preferred to act against their own interests. Like drunks they tottered through their respective fatherlands. They demanded war to the final victory. War against their brethren. War till the other side was exterminated. It became obvious that someone had made a mathematical error. Did not the theory of Marx and Engels, scientific socialism, teach that the working class of the five continents constituted an invisible force that would, at the outbreak of a war, turn its guns against its oppressors in order to seize control for good? Instead proletarians shot at proletarians and carried out the commands of the enemy of the working class. What had happened? How had this become possible?

Two lovers were sitting by the bank of the Danube Canal. The water was corpse-green and smelled of dead fish. White herons were circling in the sky. A freight train rattled over the bridge. In the distance there was the roar of the metropolis. Yellow clouds gathered over the Leopoldsberg. A storm was approaching, but the air was still calm and shimmered like silver dust. The man had his arm around the girl and gently stroked her hair. "It's terrible, Malva."
"What?"
"They've shot Jaurès. That's a signal."
"What kind of signal, Henry?"
"You may not want to admit it, but the catastrophe has begun. There will be a storm tide without parallel. All dams will collapse, but from the ashes of the war a new world will blossom . . ."

"You're beating about the bush, Henry, though I don't know which one."

"The working class of all countries is armed. Such an opportunity arises once every thousand years."

"You want to go to Russia. I feel it."

"There's been no comparable opportunity since the slave rebellions in ancient Rome."

"You want to leave me. Be honest!"

"Shall I stand aloof, Malva?"

"Yes, and love me."

"Could you believe in a man who pledges his life to a great cause and then runs away at the decisive moment?"

"Of course I could. Because I love you. Because I don't want to lose you. But *you* don't love *me*. You want to die a hero's death. For an abstract ideal, for a dubious flag to which you pray as to an idol. You aren't much better than those fatheads at the East Station who leave for the front bawling stupid songs."

"So I'm supposed to betray myelf?"

"Leaving me would be a betrayal—of you and of me. I don't give a hoot about your unique opportunities. Your unique opportunity is *me*."

"But I do love you. How can you doubt that? I long for your eyes, your lips, and the bud of your body, but please understand that I don't want to stop being a man. There are enough dwarfs in the world, hermaphrodites and cold-blooded animals that hide under lettuce leaves. They cringe, stick their heads in the ground, and feed on rain-worms. They quake and tremble for their lives. I despise them all. I have to do my duty now, otherwise I shall be ashamed to look at myself in the mirror. I've been swimming against the tide ever since I learned to think. I was fourteen when I took shots at the Cossacks. I was fearless when I went to the lead mines of Verkhoyansk. I stood under the gallows of the Warsaw citadel and wasn't afraid. And am I now supposed to surrender? At the moment when everything will be decided? When we shall either win or groan in chains for centuries? When every true human being is mounting the barricades in order to lead the masses into the last battle, the holy war against war? Now I am supposed to wrap myself in the blue cloak of a troubadour and croon sweet love songs? This I can't do . . ."

Malva realized that there was no point in arguing with Henry. Her bird of paradise wanted to fly off, and not even she could keep him from doing so. Tears ran down her face. Gently she detached herself from his embrace and rose from the grass. For a moment she hesitated. Then she rushed off, knowing that everything was over. That, at any rate, was what she believed.

She was wrong. She had no idea of the magic tricks with which men customarily embellish their occasional changes of course. Henry had decided long ago to choose the easier path, or let us say the more enjoyable one. His choice was between the abstract postulates of the party and the passionate kisses of a girl—and he did not hesitate for a moment. But he had a socialist conscience to which he owed tribute. Soon he would be twenty-five. Half his life had been spent on the barricades of the class struggle. He was proud of the red thread that ran through his years. He had a line that he pursued with steely determination. He had an ideal, and when Malva asked him to write something in her album, the best thing he could think of was a famous verse from Heine's *Germany: A Winter's Tale:*

> A new song and a better song,
> O friends, I'll write for you.
> Let's make on earth, right now,
> The heavenly kingdom come true.

Henry had no clear idea of what this heavenly kingdom was to be like. In any case, so he thought, it must be a fortress of humanitarianism. A bastion of mutual aid. A paradise of free and equal human beings that was worth living and perhaps even dying for. In this new world all the dreams of humanity would come true, and to turn one's back on these dreams would be treason. The perfect logic of the allegedly scientific socialism (and remember that Archimedes' principle can be used to prove the existence of ghosts) gave Henry the strength to endure the trials and tribulations of existence with a smile and to cross the ocean of life without the aid of a higher being. Now, however, he was facing the most difficult of all alternatives: revolution or love. A life for humanity or a life for "the most wonderful girl in the world."

Thus there raged in him the age-old conflict between mind and body, reason and madness, brains and balls. However, since Henry came from a family with unusually strong drives, the testicles passed the test, and the only problem was to justify his choice in a convincing manner, to turn the tables as craftily as possibly, and then pretend that his conscience was clear. When he saw Malva walking along the bank sobbing and showing no signs of having changed her mind even one bit, he jumped up and hurried after her. After he had caught up with her, he grabbed her by both shoulders and screamed, "You want to get rid of me!"

"*You* are the one who wants to get rid of *me!*" Malva answered hoarsely.

"So you don't want to live with me, Malva?"

"If you go to Russia, I want to die."

"Do you want me, yes or no?"

"If you stay here, yes."

"Then you don't see a provisional solution?"

Malva burst out in tears again. She couldn't utter a word, and Henry continued, now more gently, "Let me go! Just for a month, to take care of the most important matters. Or perhaps for three weeks, and then I'll be back . . ."

"In a lead coffin, I know. There is no provisional solution. Either you stay or I jump in the river. Immediately!"

Henry threw himself on the ground in front of her and clasped her, but Malva broke loose. She fled to the embankment and nimbly climbed over a rust-colored pipe that jutted into the river. Her hair was disheveled and she was breathing heavily. Another moment and she would jump. At that point the center forward lost what was left of his composure and roared, "I love you, you serpent. Come back!"

"Either you stay or it's adieu."

"You leave me no choice."

"Which means?"

"I stay. Will you marry me?"

"Swear that you'll stay!"

"I swear it. But tell me whether you want me."

"Of course, you idiot!"

Hershele alias Henry B. Kamin laid down his arms. At least so it seemed. In reality he had won. All along the line. He deserted from the ranks of the world revolution. He refrained from returning to gloomy Russia and stayed in Vienna. He obeyed his senses rather than the directives of the party, but he was able to say—to himself and posterity—that he had been the victim of extortion. This salved his conscience.

The world war that is called the first and is known not to have been the last was already in its fifth month. More than a hundred thousand mothers were already weeping for their sons. No end was in sight, and Leo Rosenbach's business was booming. He had become the happy owner of a bank account, which permitted him to rise to the class of the privileged and make transactions he had never even known to exist . . . He was sure that no power on earth could prevent him from repaying the pesky loan that he had received from Baron Gutmann the preceding year with the aid of his still-enchanting wife. But according to the proverb, man proposes and God disposes; proverbs are the deep sighs of much-tried mankind, and they are truer than one supposes. No one would have thought that on the same day when the Russians started their murderous offensive against Silesia and Pope Benedict promulgated his encyclical "Peace to the Nations," a policeman would show up in the hallway of my grandfather's house and inquire whether a certain Leo Rosenbach lived here. The person addressed blanched and felt a spasm in the region of his heart. "Sure, that's me. May I ask the lieutenant to come in and make himself comfortable?"

As was evident from his epaulets, the lieutenant was actually only a sergeant. Nevertheless, he felt flattered and let Leo show him into the living room, where he immediately began his interrogation. "Since when have you been living in this house, Mr. Rosenbach?"

Leo sensed that it was advisable to answer as truthfully as necessary and as imprecisely as possible. Therefore he replied, "Since moving to Vienna, lieutenant. May I offer you something? A slivovitz or a cognac? And won't you do us the honor of having a seat?"

The sergeant cared about detachment, and so he remained standing and cleared his throat meaningfully. "Hm, you once were, hm, domiciled elsewhere, or are we mistaken?"

Leo began to quake inwardly. He thought the guardian of law and order was referring to his unfortunate career in Stanislav, or perhaps to the high-born twins' challenge to a duel and his miserable flight from Galicia. What did that person want from him? Could a person not feel safe even in Vienna? After all, he was a wealthy man now, a member of good society noted for his loyalty to the state and his support of the monarchy. He replied uncertainly, "In point of fact, I was domiciled elsewhere, sergeant. For twenty years I resided at Neuschwanstein Castle and at the Munich court."

"With Ludwig II, it says here. Or are we mistaken?"

"You are not mistaken, sergeant. I used to be court photographer to His Royal Majesty, the incomparable patron of the arts and personal friend of Richard Wagner."

"We have been informed that you were on intimate terms with His Majesty."

"You might say so. But this great, this incomparable person is dead." Leo heaved a deep sigh, for he was still unable to guess what his inscrutable visitor was driving at. Then he added cautiously that the circumstances of the royal demise had still not been clarified and that the wildest speculations about it were in circulation, but that no credence should be given to them . . .

The sergeant became impatient and resolved to lead Leo back to the main line of the investigation. "Despite your Mosaic descent, Mr. Rosenbach, you are said to enjoy connections in high places, or are we mistaken?"

Leo did not know whether this was praise or censure, and so he replied noncommittally, "You really seem to know a lot about me, lieutenant."

"We know everything, Mr. Court Photographer. Every subject of our emperor is registered and under close observation." The conversation was making my grandfather more and more uncomfortable. "That's perfectly legitimate, lieutenant. Our life is becoming more and more dangerous. We are surrounded by enemies. The life or death of our monarchy is at stake. You share my opinion, Jana, don't you?"

Jana found her husband's servility repulsive and said proudly, "No, Leo, I don't share this opinion at all. If every subject is really closely observed and registered, if everyone in our country is under suspicion and accused of harboring subversive convictions, if the emperor has so little trust in his people, then woe to us! Then we cannot win this war."

The sergeant disliked Jana's thinking, even though he could not understand all of it. The woman was extremely attractive and quick-witted to boot, and this made him lose his balance. He thus thought it better to avoid a polemic and merely to ask whether Jana's maiden name was Wertheimer and whether she was from Stanislav. Probably fearing that she might smash more china, Leo replied for her that this was correct, and incidentally, it was his charming spouse's capricious custom always to say the opposite of what her husband said. The policeman looked Jana over disapprovingly and suspiciously and resolved to scrutinize her further remarks with increased vigilance. After an embarrassing pause he got to the real reason for his visit and asked with studied nonchalance, "There's supposed to be, hm, another brother. First name of Henner, or are we mistaken?"

Jana winced and Leo for a few seconds lost his voice. Then he said in embarrassment, as if some indecent subject were being discussed, "I do have a brother, if I may say so, and his name is Henner. But we have not seen each other in a long time, and we certainly don't regret this. I mean, I and my wife . . ."

"Speak for yourself, Leo! I'd give a fortune to know where he is now and how he is doing."

An ambiguous smile melted in the corners of the policeman's mouth as he bowed to Jana. "Then please give me your fortune, madam, because I can tell you that your brother-in-law lived in England for five years, was deported from there because of criminal acts, went to Italy via France, and today . . ."

Suspecting the worst, Leo interrupted the sergeant to state for the record that he no longer had anything to do with his brother, the failure. "I lost my brother, sergeant, under the most scandalous circumstances imaginable."

To which the policeman responded, "As far as your brother is concerned, all circumstances are scandalous. For example, he assures us he is an inventor . . ."

The blood rushed to Jana's head. She had had enough, and asked with undisguised ill humor, "What's so scandalous about someone being an inventor? Edison is an inventor, the Wright brothers are inventors, Marconi is an inventor. Without inventors we'd still be living in trees. Has it now become scandalous if a person tries to improve this world? Or do you think the world is so perfect that there is no room for improvement?"

The constable sensed false notes in Jana's speech for the defense, an undertone of an insubordination that he was not quite able to fathom. So he decided to ignite his bombshell before he had planned to and declared coldly, "Henner Rosenbach, alleged inventor from Stanislav in Galicia, also of Mosaic descent, is under strong suspicion of plotting an assassination, one directed against His Majesty Franz Joseph, the emperor of Austria. There is no doubt that the prisoner is acting under orders from the Serbian government. What do you say to that, madam?"

"I'll be brief, lieutenant. Anyone who asserts such a thing is a jackass."

Leo was dismayed—not at the accusation against his brother but at his wife's total lack of respect for a uniformed official—and cried, "Jana, you're crazy! You insult a police lieutenant, and through him the Austrian state, which is engaged in a life-and-death struggle. Apologize this instant!"

"I wouldn't dream of apologizing. I haven't insulted anyone, neither the policeman nor the Austrian state. All I'm saying is that anyone who accuses my brother-in-law of planning to assassinate the emperor, the heir to the throne, or anyone else is nothing but a low-down jackass. Henner may have every fault there is, but he is not an assassin. Are you saying the opposite, Leo?"

My grandfather needed a moment to reflect on his reply to the fair Jana. Finally he dropped down into an armchair, wiped the sweat from his nose, and whispered, "A terrorist he is not—as surely as we are brothers of the same flesh and blood. He may be a thief, a cheat, a con man, and a counterfeiter. But a terrorist? No!"

The sergeant had not played all his trump cards by a long shot. Now he launched his main attack. After downing the slivovitz the court photographer had poured for him, he said, "If you're convinced of your brother's innocence, you ought to be prepared to stand bail for him, shouldn't you?"

Leo looked desperately at Jana and replied, "Being convinced is one thing, lieutenant, and standing bail is another. Surely you understand this . . ."

Jana was aghast at her husband's small-mindedness, and shrieked, "Where is my brother-in-law? I want to know!"

At this the sergeant downed another glass of slivovitz and muttered, wiping his moustache, "Either you put up bail for him or he will be shot."

Leo was now trembling all over. His eyes imploring his wife for advice and help, he stammered, "Our biz, biz, business is, thank gaw, gaw, God, come, come, coming along fie, fie, fine. We have sir, sir, certain savings but by the end of the ye, ye, year . . ."

"No more gabbing, Leo!" cried Jana, her eyes flashing. "Make up your mind!"

"We have de, de, debts, my child. Our honor is at stake. You know what I'm talking about . . . And besides, we don't even know how high the bail would be."

The policeman seemed to like the schnapps. He poured down a third glass and answered, "You have a substantial sum in your bank account, Mr. Rosenbach—fourteen thousand crowns. As I told you, we know everything. So you put up fourteen thousand crowns, and that sum will be forfeited if our suspicion should turn out to be correct."

Jana answered in Leo's stead, "When do you need the money, lieutenant?"

"The execution of the judgment has been postponed till the middle of next week, madam."

Leo gripped the armrest of his chair. His heart pounded so hard that he was in danger of fainting. Almost inaudibly he murmured, "This will be the death of me."

Jana seemed unimpressed. She went up to Leo and said coldly, "If I understand you correctly, you want them to shoot him."

Leo was at the end of his strength. Tears streamed down his cheeks and he groaned, "I'm supposed to pay my debts. I'm supposed to marry off my daughter. I'm supposed to toil till I drop and . . ."

Jana interrupted him frostily. "Stop playacting, Leo! Here's a pen. Hurry up and write the check. We've survived worse things."

It was the thirtieth of December of the war year 1914. Noon of that day was the deadline for the repayment of the loan that Jana had been granted a year and a half previously. The condition had been the money or her honor. But since the money wasn't there—it had melted away because they had had to stand bail for Henner—the beautiful Mrs. Rosenbach found herself obliged to sacrifice her honor, and on that memorable day it was worth six thousand crowns.

Baron von Gutmann's stocky secretary was standing in front of the gilt-edged mirror on the wall of his office, twirling the tips of his moustache heavenward. He looked at himself morosely, for he knew about his homeliness, his bald head, and the decayed incisors in the middle of his face. Nor did the cologne with which he sprayed himself do much to compensate for the impression of insipidity and insignificance. His self-observation was interrupted by the doorman who reported, with a wink in his voice, that the chic person had arrived. The secretary turned around, straightened his necktie, and piped, "Show her in!"

Jana had wrapped her honor in a low-cut black satin dress. Around her neck she wore a golden chain from which dangled a mysterious agate. She was wearing a pair of morocco gloves and a hat that gave her a princely appearance. She had purposely left her coat in the cloakroom so she could display her shoulders, neck, and arms. She entered the secretary's office as if she were going to an intimate tryst, which was actually the case. She stopped in the doorway and, haughtily surveying the room, said, "It's the thirtieth of December, Mr. Oppenheim. It is twelve o'clock, as agreed."

"You are dependable, Mrs. Rosenbach. I feel honored to be visited by you." After a leaden pause he added, "Also, I am anxious to find out what you have brought me."

Jana slipped off her gloves and answered as unemotionally as she could, "Not the money, Mr. Oppenheim. I'm sorry, but untoward circumstances have frustrated my intention of repaying you the debt."

Oppenheim walked to the door, locked it, put the key in his desk drawer, and cooed, "That was to be expected, you charming person."

"No, Mr. Oppenheim. That was not to be expected. The war has turned everything upside down, including our bank account, which is why I am asking you to request a six months' extension from Baron Gutmann."

Now the little man sat down in an armchair, lit a cigarette, and said, "I am prepared to lay this sum out for you, you black angel. The baron doesn't stand for any nonsense in financial matters, and he never grants extensions."

Jana turned pale and asked, "What does that mean, sir?"

"That you should undress, madam."

It may be assumed that Jana had foreseen this, and more than that, she must have expected it. Her clothes, the fragrances with which she surrounded herself, and the manner of her appearance virtually provoked the secretary's boldness. The only question is whether she had actually intended to lie on her back for her husband's debt of honor. I certainly do not believe that she had. I never knew her, and yet she has my unqualified sympathy. Living witnesses maintain that Jana did not even let that man touch her. I am prepared to trust them. If she had loved Leo, many things would probably have happened differently, for out of love one may do anything; love rescinds laws. It is untrammeled and immoral in the truest sense of the word. Love is above morality, or one might say that it is the quintessence of all morality, and that anything that serves it is permissible. But Jana did not love Leo. She certainly would not have surrendered her body for money, not even for six thousand crowns. That is why I am willing to swear that my incomparable grandmother did not for a moment consider climbing into bed with the repulsive Mr. Oppenheim. But then why that finery, the astonishing get-up, the ornamentation with which she entered the voluptuary's den? The answer is obvious: because she somehow knew that he wanted to but couldn't. With a woman's sure instinct she had sensed that she would leave that office untouched if she provoked the man to the utmost, if, in absurd fashion, she treated him like a stud and attributed to him a potency that he did not possess.

That is why Jana replied with the boldness of a courtesan that she would be glad to disrobe in front of him provided he did the same. She unbuttoned her dress, zestfully and unhurriedly, and at the same time she whispered words that utterly confounded the flabby mollusc: "Denude yourself too, my mysterious Hercules! Show me your strong arms, your thighs of steel, and your hard rod, which shoots up like a snake's tongue when your eyes feel my body, my neck, the curves of my breasts, my belly, and my buttocks. I want to bare myself before you and open up like a water lily in the morning light. Why are you so far away from me? Why do you keep so stubbornly covered up? Don't you want to dip into my sesame? Are you afraid of my cunt, of the honey of my blossom? I can't wait to see your marble body and tight skin. I am standing before you na-ked. I'm waiting. I want to be taken by you. Now. This instant. Why are you hesitating?"

Jana achieved her aim. If she had put up any resistance or begged for mercy, Oppenheim would have become a man. He had expected a slave. Instead there stood before him a queen, and the secretary collapsed. He rose from his armchair trembling and said softly, "Put your clothes on again, Mrs. Rosenbach!"

A few thousand years have passed since we lived in holes in the ground and in trees. Compared to the millions of years of prehistory, that is a trifle. The cannibalistic drives in us are still considerably more powerful than the ethical brakes that Moses tried to instill in us with his thou shalts and thou shalt nots. There is no denying that we are a horde of cannibals, and yet we flatter ourselves that we have reached the peak of development. The philosophers of the eighteenth century jubilantly proclaimed that the age of enlightenment had dawned. The scientists of the nineteenth century trumpeted that they were about to unlock the last secrets of nature. The starry-eyed idealists of our age have even proclaimed the dawn of a classless society, an era of the peaceful coexistence of nations. Today even the stupidest people have noticed that such hopes are infantile, but the fans of progress behave all the more fanatically. The more hopeless their illusions, the more self-righteously they proclaim their triumph, though this does not mean that they do not harbor secret doubts. On the contrary. They are wracked by doubts, for most of them are rather intelligent, and notice the glaring contradiction between their formulas and reality. The more maliciously they sneer at God and eternity, the more they are fascinated by irrationality. The more disdainfully they jeer at ghosts, parapsychology, and miracles of every kind, the more susceptible they are to the most dubious oracles and prophesies.

The modern heathens who celebrated the wedding of Malva Rosenbach and Henry B. Kamin in early January 1915 tried very hard to endow that event with future significance. As rationalists they should really have known that the future is written neither in the stars nor in mysterious signs, but they interpreted everything that happened on that day as being pregnant with meaning, and some remarkable things did happen. At the very beginning of the ceremony a raging snowstorm blew the kitchen window open. A gust of wind rushed through the apartment, and the seven candles in the menorah were blown out. The rabbi reacted with irritation. He interrupted his prayers and bit his lower lip. The wedding guests blanched. Leo asked how such a strange occurrence ought to be interpreted. The bridegroom sat down for a moment to catch his breath, but when Jana asked him how he would explain this *mene, mene tekel upharsin*, this version of the handwriting on the wall, he answered peevishly, "As a Marxist and adherent of the exact sciences, I can say that there is a mutual relationship between the wintry weather and the resultant draft that caused the seven candles to be extinguished. There are no other connections."

The candles of the seven-branched candelabrum were relit and the wedding slowly got going again. The rabbi pointed out that by virtue of his position he had to give the young couple his blessing, though he knew exactly how unloved Jehovah was in that house. While he did notice a gleam in the eyes of the bride and the groom, this was more likely to be a flicker of lust than a glow of the faith that was the most necessary of all the glorious things bestowed upon us by the Almighty. At that point there was a second incident, one that threatened to disrupt the celebration even more severely. In the middle of the rabbi's sermon the parakeet mounted his mate with impetuous passion, but to everyone's astonishment the female denied herself. Until that day she had displayed exceptional affection when she copulated with her companion, but now she was hostile and cold. The gilded cage on the piano became the center of the celebration, one rich in symbolism. The wedding guests, including Malva's cousins, all of them fugitives from the battle areas of the East, exchanged meaningful glances. As always the smart-alecky Steffi played the role of the family pessimist. With a wrinkled brow she watched the strange spectacle and then proclaimed in the voice of a grouchy Cassandra, "The birds' feathers are flying; this means four childless years."

She happened to be right. Four years actually had to pass before I came into the world. But the rabbi did not like anyone to poach on his preserves. It was his opinion that divine providence was inscrutable, and if anyone was entitled to fathom it, then it was he and no one else. So he stared sternly at his fingernails and went on in an even more irritable, schoolmarmish tone than before. "In ancient Rome there were idolaters called *haruspices*. They were presumptuous enough to interpret human fate on the basis of the behavior of birds. If they had known Jehovah, they would have realized that He does not wish to be demystified. The future cannot be foretold, for each time heaven decides anew what will happen. Jehovah is great and unpredictable. He is above all rules and laws. He and not a soulless feathered animal decides whether this young couple will have children and when. Anyone who prophesies, sins against the Lord. Thus I do not wish to prophesy. I can only offer you my good wishes. Whether they will come true depends on Him and on yourselves. I pray to our heavenly father to bestow His grace upon you, to unite you in love, and let harmony reign between your hearts. In the language of our ancestors I call out to you *Shalom aleichem*. Peace be with you! I hope that . . ."

He was unable to finish his speech, for the doorbell rang. For the third time the wedding was interrupted, and no one showed any desire to go out into the cold hallway. Hence this disagreeable duty once again fell upon the master of the house. Both he and the other wedding guests suspected that the third and most disastrous incident was impending. And so it was. Master butcher Hawlitschek, who was almost twice Leo's size, had arrived, and with him his illegitimate daughter-in-law, who was wearing widow's weeds and could not stop sobbing. Up to that moment the wedding had been going badly, and the two intruders were the last thing in the world that the court photographer needed. "What do you want from me?" he asked gruffly.

The master butcher stood there as motionless and rigid as a corpse. "The photograph you took of my Tony."

The blood rushed to Leo's head and he screamed, "The very idea, Mr. Hawlitschek! It's Saturday evening . . ."

The menacing butcher spoke so softly that shivers ran down the spines of the wedding guests. "It's war, and in wartime there's no Saturday or Sunday . . ."

My grandfather hit the ceiling and roared, "You can see that I'm marrying off my daughter, can't you? That doesn't happen every day."

Hawlitschek stepped quite close to Leo and snarled, "And

I'm burying my only son. That don't happen every day neither. You see, he's been sacrificed, Mr. Rosenbach. He's had to kick the bucket for the emperor, and all we've got left of him is the picture that you made."

With these words his daughter-in-law began to emit muffled moans and wiped hot tears from her eyes with her black crepe. Now the atmosphere had really been poisoned. Most of the guests left. Henry was perturbed and said to Malva, "You know me. You know that I believe neither in God nor in the devil, but I've lost all desire to get married."

Leo Rosenbach, my grandfather, died of a broken heart. Because his wife did not love him. Because his brother had ruined him. And because his daughter—so it seemed to him after the abortive wedding—was bringing misfortune upon him. Good Lord! Who brings good fortune upon himself when he gets married? Leo ought to have known that, for then he would not have grieved himself to death. But he didn't know it.

When his hour came, two people stood at his deathbed. Jana trembled as though she were standing before her judge. She held Leo's hand and implored him, "Forgive me! Do not leave us!"

Leo's lungs were consumed by pneumonia, his voice was weak, and his eyes were feverish. "I've always loved you, Jana. From the first day to the last."

Jana felt guilty and begged, "Stay a while longer! What shall we do without you?"

Leo did not answer. He looked at Malva, who was desperately fingering her rings, and whispered, "You must complete your studies, my child. That is my last wish."

Malva sobbed. The finality of these words seemed unbearable to her. "I won't let you say such things, papa. You will live. Say that you're going to live!"

Leo no longer heard what they were saying to him. He

stared into the distance and whispered with his last strength, "My distinguished service cross, Jana. On the dresser over there!"

Jana now hoped that her husband might weather the crisis, and so she replied with a smile, "Distinguished service crosses are only put on the chests of dying people. But you, Leo, are going to live."

"Do you hear me, Jana? The cross. On my chest!" Jana obeyed, but she said imploringly, "It isn't time yet, Leo. I beg of you."

Leo raised his right index finger and pointed at the camera, which was attached to its tripod, ready for historic moments. "A picture, Jana. Me and Malva . . ."

Jana did as he instructed. She adjusted the tripod and whispered, "It's dark in here, Leo."

That revived the court photographer, and he commanded, "Aperture setting five point six, exposure time a sixteenth of a second. Open the curtain!"

Jana opened the curtain and set the camera. Suddenly she moaned, "I can't do it!"

But Leo's last concern was with the technical details, and he repeated, "Five point six and a sixteenth of a second! Malva shall pray for me."

"What shall I pray, papa?"

"For God to forgive me that I economized on coal. Our house was always cold."

Now there no longer was any doubt that the end was near. The women sobbed. Jana took the shutter release in her hand and said in a stifled voice, "God will forgive us, Leo."

The court photographer raised his head for the last time and said in a barely understandable slur, "And pray for the emperor . . . that the war . . ."

Jana pressed the release. Leo's voice failed in mid-sentence. His chin dropped and he sank back on the pillow. A small light that had flickered on a low flame for a lifetime was extinguished.

November 20, 1915. I have not opened this diary since July of last year. In the meantime I have become a woman and bear a new name. So does the war, for it has become a world war. Papa has died. Of natural causes, thank God, and the German troops have used mustard gas on the western front. It is so horrible that I'm ashamed of looking in the mirror. These are our allies. The poisonous vapors are stored in steel barrels. When the wind is favorable—that's what they unblushingly call it—the Germans open the gas taps. At five in the morning, when the cocks crow. Thick yellow smoke rises from our trenches. I write "our" trenches, because I'm part of it. I share the guilt. I've done nothing to prevent that. The thick yellow smoke approaches the French lines. The northeast wind helps spread the cloud over the ground like a carpet. The effect on the other side is devastating; most soldiers die instantly. Some are able to flee, but even they have breathed in the vapors. After a few minutes their faces turn black. They cough up blood and croak. We are exterminating the French like vermin. Because we are a civilized nation, so it is said, and the others are barbarians. We also bombarded the cathedral of Reims. In the name of civilization. With our zeppelin we bombed Paris. To save German morality from southern immorality! Providence is on our side. So is right, for the French postulate liberty, equality, and fraternity—a mockery of the monarchist principle. That must be punished. With cannons, fire bombs, and poison gas. Rush the Russians! Long live civilization! Wrench the French! Henry is right: We are guilty because we participate. Today I understand the omens of our wedding day. Heaven loathes us because we are blind. God chastises us because we celebrate festivals instead of doing our human duty. We are standing on the top of Mt. Ararat. The deluge is raging around us. The world is drowning, but we are marrying. We dance and laugh as if we were living in the deepest peace. This war is lost; mankind has lost it. Endless trains rattle across the Danube bridge. They come from the eastern front. From the Vistula, from Masuria, from the Bug River, where

237

we are winning one victory after another; at least that's what the newspapers say. Thousands of maimed men lie, sit, and stand in the wagons. Their heads are bandaged. Only their eyes stare out and curse us because we don't know what we are doing. We eat, drink, and multiply while mustard-brown fumes of poison gas are destroying hecatombs of sons, brothers, and lovers . . . We cannot talk our way out of that. We sit in box seats and look on. I have incurred particular guilt. I have kept Henry from stemming the tide. I impeded him when he wanted to obey his conscience and go over there. Now I have him all to myself, but he is no longer the man I chose. He fritters away his days at the university and his nights in my bed. Every Monday he has to report to the police. He is lucky that they don't intern him. As a potential spy, an enemy alien, a subject of the czar of Russia. He is allowed to run around freely because he was able to prove that he is a revolutionary. Sentenced to death in absentia, an ally of Austria against the despot of St. Petersburg. What an honor! An ally of Emperor Franz Joseph, Kaiser Wilhelm, the Sultan of Constantinople, and the steel tubs full of mustard gas. He wanted to resist the war fever, but I threatened to jump in the river . . . I blackmailed him, and love made him stay. I do love him so, but I hate him because he allowed himself to be blackmailed by me. He is no longer the god I was praying to. In him I idolized the unbending Baltyr, the brave Daschynski, and the mad Henner. To me he was the embodiment of all my ideals, but what has he become? I love him as I did on the first day, when he stood in front of our door and said he was a cloud in pants. I love him as I did on that summer afternoon when he painted my belly and abducted me to the garden of delights. But then came our wedding with all its false notes. There was the matter of the mustard gas, and I no longer smile. I must do something, otherwise our passion will go to the dogs. But what?

In the summer of 1916 the Austrian chief of staff, Conrad von Hoetzendorf, was in a bad bind. He requested

German troops for the fight against the Russians in Volhynia and Galicia, for he no longer had any reserves with whom to stop the march of the old Moscow trooper Aleksei Brusilov. Austria was on the verge of disaster. Italy and Rumania had abandoned their neutrality—perfidiously, according to the official reports—and sided with the western powers. Germany, true unto death, came to Austria's aid, but demanded in return that the entire eastern front be placed under German command. Around that time General Ludendorff wrote in one of his ungainly letters:

> There is no end to the *Schweinerei* with the Austrians. Their troops are falling apart, as the infernal events of the last few days demonstrated once more. Now my attention is instinctively drawn to the Poles. The Poles are good soldiers. If Austria breaks down, we simply have to get ourselves other forces. Let us turn Poland into a grand duchy [that's the only form of government he could think of] and then form a Polish army under German leadership!

This was the astonishing scheme of a Prussian military mind: Polish cannon fodder for the thinned ranks of the German-Austrian coalition. So a Polish state was to come into being in exchange for Polish blood—at least a Polish grand duchy, but under German hegemony. For more than a hundred years Poland had been obliterated, divided up among Prussia, Austria, and Russia. This country existed neither on the map nor in official linguistic usage. The Polacks, as people were kind enough to call them, were forcibly Germanized or Russianized, but lo and behold! Suddenly the eyes of the Prussian commander-in-chief fell tenderly on Poland, for, as he deigned to put it, Poles are good soldiers. What he didn't say was that in 1915 alone Germany had lost 881,922 men on the western front—despite the use of mustard gas, despite the bombardment of Reims cathedral, despite the shelling of Paris. Evidently there was no end to the *Schweinerei* as far as *German* soldiers were concerned, too. They had the impudence to die in the fire of the French and British counterattacks, and so a blood transfusion was needed. The Poles were promised a grand duchy by the grace of Prussia—a "little freedom," as it was called in Warsaw—and by way of thanks they were supposed to let themselves be slaughtered—for Ludendorff, Hoetzendorf, and all the blue-blooded members of the master race from Berlin and Vienna, who had never learned anything but how to reckon without the host. True, the German leaders knew that the Poles were good soldiers, but they forgot an important factor in strategic calculations: that they are inclined to risk their lives only under very special conditions. During the preceding hundred years they had made six revolutions. Six times tens of thousands of them were mowed down, hanged, or put before a firing squad—but not because they enjoyed dying. On the contrary. Because they enjoyed living—in Poland, as free people in an independent fatherland.

This was the very reason why a number of Polish politicians assembled in Vienna around that time—secretly, as may be imagined—in order to discuss what could be done to thwart the designs of Ludendorff and his associates. Thus it happened that one cool fall morning Malva met a man on Ringstrasse who seemed familiar to her. They stopped, stared at each other in surprise, and waited for the other to say something. Suddenly the man whispered, "We know each other, don't we?"

The blood rushed to Malva's head and she replied as softly, "My mother still has a pledge from you, if I'm not mistaken. An amulet."

"Miss Rosenbach, am I right?"

"I am married and have a different name now. I never stopped thinking of you . . ."

An awkward pause ensued. Then Daschynski suddenly asked, "And your mother? Is she still thinking of me too?"

Malva gave him an ambiguous smile. "She has aged, poor dear. My father is dead. I moved out of the house and she is alone . . ."

The man looked around nervously, as if he were afraid of being shadowed. Then he whispered, "I'm leaving in three hours. May I invite you to have tea with me?"

Since their wedding Malva and Henry had been living in a furnished room near the university. It smelled of sauerkraut and moth flakes and was good only for making love. During the day Malva worked as an assistant at the Mohrenapotheke on Wipplingerstrasse. Henry was in medical school and earned some money by giving English lessons.

When Henry came home that evening, his wife seemed changed. Somewhat overexcitedly she informed him that she had to go to Galicia at the end of the month. When Henry said that she would be crazy to go to the immediate combat zone and asked what business she had in Galicia, she replied mysteriously that she had an assignment and would be back in a few days. Henry thought he had misunderstood and wanted to know what that assignment was, and even more important, who was behind it. At first Malva wouldn't tell him. Then she made Henry promise that he would keep it to himself. She said a certain Daschynski had asked her to take twenty thousand leaflets to the Tarnow area, a village called Iwonicz, and give them to a confidential agent there. Henry could not believe his ears, and asked gruffly, "Who is Daschynski?"

"A socialist leader from Stanislav."

"That much I know. Where do you know him from?"

"I know him, and that's that."

"Do you have anything to do with him?"

"Don't ask so many questions. That isn't important."

Henry smelled danger and hissed, "When *I* wanted to go away, also on an assignment, you threatened to kill yourself!"

Malva was enjoying the situation. As she cheerfully continued playing her game, she felt that her beloved was wavering. She was on the right track, then, and raising her eyes mysteriously, answered, "Two years have passed since then. Both of us have changed. You especially . . ."

That was a low blow, well aimed and perfidious. Henry felt that his cover was blown—and furthermore, that he was in immediate danger. He therefore tried to shift the discussion onto another track. "I want to know who this Daschynski is."

"I told you. A Polish socialist."

"That is known. He is a misleader of the people. From the Pilsudski group. A nationalist who cares more about his fatherland than about the liberation of the proletariat."

"They are equally important to me."

"By lying about this fatherland one incites the nations. Two million fallen soldiers are rotting on the battlefields of Europe—in the Masurian swamps, before Verdun, in the ruins of Belgian cities, by the banks of the Isonzo."

"Then you don't want a free Poland, Henry?"

"I want a free world; can't you understand that? I believe in the international working class. I loathe the accursed flags for the sake of which the blockheads of all countries are driven to their deaths!"

"And what do you prefer, a free Poland or an enslaved one?"

"You blather like Daschynski. What is he to you, anyway? Have you slept with him?"

"And what are *you* blathering about? You claim that you want a free world. What are you doing about it?"

"Not enough, because I'm sitting in your cage. Because I dance like a monkey to your hurdy-gurdy. When I wanted to do something, you blackmailed me."

"You were glad to have me blackmail you, Henry. You've become harmless. Aren't you aware of this? A toothless tiger . . ."

That was their first lovers' quarrel. It seemed to be about Daschynski, but it really involved more than that, and Henry sensed it. Malva had hit a bull's-eye, hurt his vanity, and questioned the seriousness of his convictions. In this she had gone too far. Her last remark was no longer a criticism but a degradation. Henry reacted like a wounded animal. His pupils shrank to small yellow points and his lips became thin and twisted. He was still keeping himself in check, but he was snorting and groaning. He pressed his fists together, gritted his teeth, took a deep breath, and lunged at her like a wildcat. With his left hand he grabbed her by the crown of her hair and bent her head backward, with his right he slapped her face. Again and again, until finally she collapsed and sank feebly to the floor. She struck her temple on an enamel jug and blood flowed from her forehead. This woke Henry from his maniacal fury. A mist cleared from his eyes, and he was horrified to see what he had done. He dropped to his knees, laid his hand on Malva's hair, and began to cry. At first he whimpered softly, but then a spasm loosened in his chest. The Bolshevik of steel, the athlete and center forward, the fighter in the class struggle without a god or a fatherland burst into tears. He bent over the marble-white face of his wife, covered it with kisses, and implored her, "Forgive me, Malva, I beg of you!" He raised his eyes heavenward, and from deep inside him rose words from his distant childhood: "Got, groisser Got, lo mir davenen!" He spoke to his Lord whom he had reviled for twenty years: "Oh God, great God, let us pray!" Then a miracle happened. Malva opened her eyes and then her mouth. She seemed to smile, and Henry thanked the Almighty with words that he thought he had forgotten long ago: "Adonoi, hu ha-elohim," the Lord, he is God.

October 20, 1917. He beat me. In the face. I ought to leave him, because I promised myself that I would not endure any degradation. I swore that I would never let a man beat me. Now it has happened, and I can't leave him. I provoked him. I reproached him with having become harmless, a tiger without teeth. Yet it's my own fault. It was I who kept him back. I threatened to kill myself if he went to Russia. And now I am disappointed.

243

Does he have to be a hero—a Baltyr or a Bogrow—who is shot at dawn? Those were girlish dreams. Life is different. It consists of compromises, even if compromises lead to hell. If I were true to my principles, I'd pack my bags and leave. But I love him. He is more important to me than my principles.

Malva was one of the first female students at the University of Vienna and the first female pharmacist's assistant in Austria. The war and the acute shortage of men made it possible for women to be admitted to academic professions.

I hardly believe that Dr. Korwill was a champion of women's emancipation. On the contrary. He was merely a shrewd businessman and calculated that a charming saleswoman could be a lure in his pharmacy, which promptly turned out to be so. During the third year of the war the Mohrenapotheke on Wipplingerstrasse quintupled its business. The competition was boiling with envy. With increasing frequency advertisements appeared in professional journals for young female pharmacists. However, none could be found, for in those days the prejudice still prevailed that women were inferior in intelligence, that the female brain was twenty percent smaller than the male, and that a girl was destined to become a mother, a cook, or, if she was lucky, a courtesan. That is why almost every means possible was used to keep female students from enrolling at the universities, which for a long time remained bastions of male vanity.

In the lecture halls a barracks mentality prevailed. The students' language was predominantly risqué, and the absence of women encouraged an atmosphere of off-color double entendres, even among the professors. Significantly, however, the misogyny went hand in hand with a sophisticated gallantry, and one could almost be sure that the most zealous philanderers, appreciatively called *Poussierstengel,* appeared in the dining hall or in the men's room as grim anti-feminists. Concealed behind this dual game were a primitive professional jealousy and a distinct fear of the sexual superiority of women. Thus the behavior of the lords of Creation was determined, plain and simple, by fear of impotence. When Dr. Korwill hired the enchanting Malva, his intentions were purely mercenary in nature. Besides, he simply was after her, and he missed no opportunity to engage her in risqué conversations.

One afternoon Malva was standing at the dispensing table. She was preparing a medication and did not notice that the boss was approaching. Suddenly she felt his breath on her neck and heard him ask, "Who is this prescription for, Miss Rosenbach?"

"You know, don't you, that I'm married and use my husband's name."

The pharmacist ignored this and continued, "Am I right in assuming that the prescription is for our court counselor?"

"For *your* court counselor, not mine."

"*Adonis vernalis* as always, right?"

Malva smiled disparagingly and replied, "The court counselor doesn't have it in his head but farther down."

"Which means, Miss Rosenbach?"

"*Cortex frangulae*, doctor. He has chronic constipation."

"It's my impression that you have something against him."

"I'm preparing his medicine. That's all I can do for this person."

"He has complained about your brusque treatment of him."

"What he needs, doctor, are anthraquinone derivatives."

"The court counselor wishes to be serviced in keeping with his social standing."

"Then he should behave in accordance with his social standing. He has the plebeian habit of not keeping his hands in check."

"But Miss Rosenbach, you're not a nun, are you?"

"I'm Mrs. Kaminski, and I don't like being pawed by the court counselor." Malva looked her superior in the eye and added, "He's old enough to be my grandfather."

Dr. Korwill understood the allusion. He glanced at the mirror on the wall and aggressively twirled his moustache. Then he chirped as seductively as he knew how, "Do you think that I look my age?"

Malva went on working and replied drily, "I really don't care how old you are, doctor."

"Does that mean—do you mean to say that you find me kind of attractive?"

"Your son was here a while ago. He asked me to tell you that he had to see his tailor."

The evasive answers of the young woman could be interpreted in various ways. When she said that she didn't like to be pawed by the court counselor—so reasoned the pharmacist—this could mean that the suggestive behavior of another suitor might please her. She also said that she didn't care how old her boss was. That might mean that his years didn't bother her. Be that as it may, Dr. Korwill interpreted the words of his assistant in his favor. He now came so close to her that there was no thought of escaping and whispered in her ear, "I think we are going out tonight."

Malva did not let this upset her. She carefully poured two liquids into a glass, shook it over the flame of a Bunsen burner, and replied ironically, "Oh, so you two are going out. Where, I wonder?"

Now the boss put his arm around her hip and cooed, "You misunderstood, Miss Rosenbach. You and I are going out tonight."

"I hardly think so, doctor."

"Why not, my sweet child?"

"Because your wife wouldn't like it."

That was too much for the pharmacist. He proceeded to the attack, grabbed Malva, and tried to take her in his arms. He failed, however, because Malva instinctively knew how to bring lecherous superiors back to their senses. At the moment of greatest danger she dropped the glass, and it broke into a thousand pieces. A yellow liquid oozed out onto the parquet floor and a pungent smell spread through the room. The doctor cared more about his property than his lust, and so he dropped his arms and piped, "Be careful with my inventory! And be nice to your boss!"

To which Malva replied derisively, "Mrs. Korwill wouldn't like it."

"What do we care about Mrs. Korwill? Let her go to the devil."

The assistant reached for the wall telephone and asked mischievously, "Shall I tell her that?"

Convinced that Malva wouldn't go that far, the pharmacist said nonchalantly, "But of course. Just give her a ring!"

Malva didn't wait to be told twice. She rang the number and said slowly and distinctly, "This is Malva Kaminski. Is this Mrs. Korwill? Yes? Your husband asked me to tell you . . ."

The boss lost patience. He wrested the receiver from his assistant, put it down, and gasped, "Miss Rosenbach, you're fired!"

With these words he went to the coat stand, took his coat, and hurried off. He had already reached the door when Malva called out to him, "And what about my salary? You owe me for three months!"

"You can stick it. You are summarily dismissed. Goodbye."

November 15, 1917. A German proverb says that lies have short legs. That isn't true. Lies have long lives, and especially myths. The older they get, the longer their legs are and the more probable it is that they will become part of history without being challenged. Our trip to Iwonicz is such a myth. Everybody knows how it really was, but no one considers it appropriate to call a spade a spade. Henry says the party sent us and that he simply went without hesitating, though he knew what we were risking. He reports that it was a daredevil enterprise. To travel to Galicia, to the immediate war zone, in the middle of the war—that was foolhardy. Iwonicz was twelve miles from the front—that's what he says, though it was thirty—one could hear the artillery fire hit its targets, and pillars of fire lit up the sky. We rolled through an ocean of destroyed villages, burned-down farms, and decaying dead bodies. Slush and morass as far as the eye could see. To this extent, and by way of an exception, Henry's report is true. We really did sit huddled together on the horsecart. Paralyzed from the cold and soaked to the bone, we rumbled through the hell of a collapsing world. In the forests the wolves were howling. Swarms of ravens were circling over charred ruins, and Henry claims that if we had not had that assignment from the party to take those fifty thousand leaflets to Iwonicz— there weren't fifty but twenty thousand, and besides, we were pursuing very private business—we would have returned to Vienna. That's a lie, but he doesn't care and goes on fibbing that chickening out was out of the question. He says that we rolled through the immediate war zone and crashed through dozens of road blocks with our leaflets. In reality there were three, and nothing happened to us. Henry exaggerates everything. Neither he nor I kept the leaflets hidden. The coachman sat on them without knowing it. So we risked someone else's life too. That was dastardly, but it leaves Henry cold. He tells about the coachman, an old warrior who laughed about his suicidal journeys through the front lines. He is supposed to have been a typical Pole, a man who fears neither death nor the devil. A nameless hero, a wonderful person with whom one can build a new world. Of course he was *not* a wonderful person but a repulsive drunkard, filthy and lice-infested. A hopeless idiot who has never been sober but impressed Henry because he knew so many proletarian curses and always stank of schnapps. From this my dreamer concluded that he was a socialist. That's a laugh! He was a cipher, and just as corrupt as all Poles. For a bottle of booze he drove us through the minefields of the German-Russian war zone. We had brought along ten liters of grain alcohol, for in Galicia money had lost all its value. When the Russians were there, people paid in rubles. Then the Germans had come and they paid in Reichsmark. But soon conditions were changing so constantly that people calculated only in alcohol, for it is well known that from alcohol you can make schnapps, and for schnapps a Pole will give you anything—though Henry denies it. Nevertheless, he had ordered me to pinch ten liters of alcohol from old Korwill. For the wages he owed me. Henry was always suspicious, and thought I had a lover in Galicia. Ridiculous; I don't want a lover. Henry is enough for me, though he swindles like a Turk, fibs our life into shape, and makes a heroic epic out of it. In reality, the journey to Iwonicz was a hoarding expedition. We did take the leaflets there on the side, but we also carried on quite ordinary black-market activities. There is nothing wrong with that, but one should have the courage to acknowledge it. After all, in Vienna we're starving. We get a hundred and fifty grams of meat a week. And a hundred grams of fat that is usually rancid, and one has to be grateful to get it at all. People have to stand in line for hours for their ration. If you don't use your elbows, you leave empty-handed, and everyone needs some trick to survive. Everybody must find someone who does him a favor for the appropriate quid pro quo. Everybody learns to grease palms, to cheat, and to flimflam. A whole people practices the art of profiteering, and anyone who does not participate is crushed. Well, then. We went to Iwonicz with ten liters of alcohol and came back home with half a pig. Everyone profited. They all filled their stomachs again. For a month we had ham, sausages, salted meat, and pâtés. Even grandmother participated, although she is a pious Jew and had never before tasted pork. That's reality, but Henry insists on his version. He tells everything so colorfully and in such detail that I'm beginning to believe his fairy tales myself. Yes, we did take twenty thousand leaflets to their destination. It is also true that we had an assignment from the party; but Daschynski's socialists and Henry B. Kamin's Bolsheviks were as different as night and day. To me this is unimportant. I am not interested in political nuances. The main thing is that we have enough to eat, for our food supply is going from bad to worse.

On December 15, 1917, Uncle Henner, followed by his son Nathan, walked out the iron gate of the Villach fortress. He lifted his eyes heavenward and whispered, "Praised be Jesus Christ!" He owed his release to divine providence as well as to the magnanimous support of his brother Leo. A third person was also involved, to be sure. His name was Ulyanov, and he had recently seized power in Petersburg under the name Vladimir Ilyich Lenin. Henner, however, was not aware of this, for he never read a newspaper. Nor did he know that Leo had put his entire fortune on the table—as we know, not entirely of his free will—in order to stand bail for him. Lenin, for his part, had made peace with Russia's enemies, including Austria, whose exhausted emperor was so pleased that he immediately released half of all prisoners. Henner was one of the first to benefit from this amnesty. Since he had committed no crime, and bail in the amount of many thousands of crowns had been posted for him, he was released under the terms of the general imperial pardon, which meant that the bail was forfeited and became the property of the dual monarchy. This should have pleased everyone: Henner was free, the emperor received ransom, and Lenin was in control of all Russia. World history continued on its course, and after a three-years' hiatus Henner was able to resume his pilgrimage where it had been interrupted on the first day of the war. The two men set out for Vienna. Their possessions consisted of a fiddle, a black wooden cross, and the belief that they were under the protection of the Virgin Mary.

Shortly before noon on December 18 the two turned into Freytaggasse. A minute later they rang the doorbell on which it now said "Jana Rosenbach, Widow of the Court Photographer Leo Rosenbach." The court photographer's widow opened and could not believe her eyes. "I'm hallucinating!"

Henner made a deep bow and said in a transfigured baritone, "You are as beautiful as you were ten years ago, Jana. You haven't changed."

"Where have you come from, for God's sake, and why so late?"

"We languished in jail for three years, a thousand days. All that's left of us is our souls. Our bodies have disintegrated."

"What's going on? Won't you come in?"

"For a thousand days I thought of your eyes, Jana. I trembled that they might lose their gleam . . ."

The two men stepped into the apartment, looked around in embarrassment, and could not utter a word. Everything had changed. Finally Jana broke the silence and said sadly, "As you can see, I've become an old woman."

"I feared your lips would shrivel up."

"Leo is dead, Henner. Your brother is no longer alive. He left me. Forever and ever, because I wasn't good to him."

"But you've stayed young, Jana. You're still the woman of my dreams."

"Malva is married. She too left me, and lives downtown. Our house is empty."

"I know that you trust me. You've always trusted me. I'm innocent, Jana."

"Let's not talk about it anymore, Henner!"

"They wanted to make a spy out of me, those blockheads. Yet we pray for Austria every day. Every morning when we wake up. Every evening before we fall asleep."

"You are barefoot, Henner. Why aren't you wearing shoes? And what's the meaning of this cross in your hand?"

"I was already standing under the gallows, my child. They had already put the noose around my neck. I said the Lord's Prayer and bade my son farewell, but the cross protected me. At the very last moment."

"Leo put up bail for you, Henner. Did you know that? For the first time since our wedding there was money in the house. He gave it away. For you. He paid them his last groschen. Because we believed in you."

"*You* believe in me, Jana. I know it. I feel it. I felt it under the gallows. But not Leo. Leo despised me. Always. And besides, he was jealous because you loved *me* and not *him*."

"Quiet, Henner! The dead can hear us."

"What I say is the truth."

"Why are you wearing these ugly rags, Henner?"

The inventor raised the cross above his head and heavy tears ran down his cheeks. "I'm doing penance, Jana. I have to do penance because I have laden my heart with guilt . . . I went to see His Holiness the Pope in Rome. Now I've come to Vienna to speak with the emperor."

Jana's eyes flashed like summer lightning. "Oh? You want to speak with the emperor? How convenient! Tell him that we've had enough of his war. It's been four years, and an end is not in sight. If he doesn't put a stop to it, *we* will, and things here will be as they are in Russia."

"My audience with His Majesty will deal with other problems."

"There are no other problems. The whole world is drowning in blood. It can't go on like this!"

"My invention is important for our total strategy. Decisive for air reconnaissance. With the aid of color photography we shall be able to identify every dung beetle behind the enemy lines. If the emperor gives me the concession and the necessary funds, the war will be over in a few weeks."

"Tell me the truth, Henner! For once in your life. Are you there or are you still daydreaming?"

"I'm not daydreaming, sweetheart. I never daydreamed. The only thing I lack is money. That's all. We come from the dungeons of Villach. We don't even have the wherewithal for a piece of bread. We haven't eaten in three days."

"I'm not that much better off. What do you want from me?"

"Not a thing. All I need is the imperial concession. Everything else is finished. In my head."

"Are you going to Schönbrunn in this getup?"

"I am one of the greatest inventors of this century."

"*You* know that, Henner. The emperor doesn't. If you appear in Schönbrunn in this getup, you'll be arrested."

"Ridiculous. The emperor needs me more than I need him. And besides, I'm the victim of a miscarriage of justice. Through no fault of my own I've lost a thousand days of my life. I deserve restitution for that."

"And where are you living now?"

"Until I get the concession, in the third-class waiting room at the West Station."

Now Jana was seized with pity. The old passion awakened in her heart and she said, "Then stay with me, for heaven's sake! We'll find something to eat. As far as clothes are concerned, I haven't touched Leo's wardrobe. After all, he was your brother. What's his is yours, right?"

Henner rushed up to his sister-in-law and clasped her in his arms. He was trembling all over, and whispered in her ear, "You won't regret it, my angel. I am one step from completion. It's a matter of days. What am I saying—of hours. God's son will stand by us, I swear it to you. We shall be rich as never before."

"Heaven grant that you're right, Henner. I believe in you whether you are telling the truth or making it all up. I have always believed in you, though out of love and not prudence."

Since his trip to Iwonicz Henry had made himself believe that he was at the center of world history. As he had done earlier, he enveloped himself in the aura of an unyielding fighter. He again played the uncompromising old warrior whose life was dedicated solely to socialism. He played the part so well that even Malva became a believer, though she must have noticed that he was uttering platitudes and avoiding genuine discussions. She noticed that her husband was doing an about-face, but she could not shake the feeling that his reversal should have been accomplished *before* the revolution. Henry had not forgotten his Bolshevik past, but he remembered it only when the councils of workers and soldiers were already in control in Russia and it might have seemed promising to jump on the bandwagon in time to join the victorious faction. Such thoughts went around in Malva's head, but she did not dare utter them. She only noticed with some apprehension that Henry engaged in peculiar skirmishes and indulged in schoolboy pranks, as though he were amassing proof of his revolutionary activities. He built his own barricades and engaged in private battles against self-chosen exponents of the dying world, displaying a bizarre diligence. One cold February morning he entered the Mohrenapotheke on Wipplingerstrasse and told the manager that he had to speak with Dr. Korwill.

The owner appeared and asked what he could do for him. Pretending to be a patient, Henry answered, "A strophanthin preparation, please."

Dr. Korwill replied with deep regret, "You should know that strophanthin preparations have toxic side effects. Therefore they cannot be dispensed without a prescription."

"I'm a medical man myself," replied Henry with a forced smile, "and know all about it. However, it's a matter of . . ."

"I understand," answered the pharmacist with an accomplice's wink, "we're colleagues."

Henry put his hand on his heart with a theatrical gesture and whispered, "The medicine is for me. I come from Russia."

"My goodness! How'd you manage to do that?"

Henry sat down on a stool in the corner and stared desperately into space as though he were trying to remember. "I was able to flee. At the risk of my life. Now I'm in Vienna, and I'm horrified to see that Austria too is making deals with Lenin."

"Austria will fight on till the final victory," growled Dr. Korwill. "Anyone who capitulates will be shot."

"This country is full of capitulators."

"We will win the war. Period."

"The civilized world has already lost it."

"I'm an Austrian officer, sir. Keep your tongue in check!"

"Have you heard the news?"

"The news is good."

"And do you know what's happening in Russia?"

"Russia is far away. It doesn't concern me."

"Watch out, doctor! The same thing will happen in Austria too."

"Do you think so?"

"I know so. Bolshevism is an epidemic disease for which there is no cure."

The proprietor began to boil. "You're not getting any strophanthin preparation, and that's that!"

"He expropriated the factories."

"Who?"

"Lenin. And distributed land among the masses. Blew up the churches, and *you* say the news is good."

"We'll smash our enemies. Including the Bolsheviks."

"Or the other way around, if you're not careful."

"A few more days and they'll drown in their muck."

"Right now they're being supported by you, as far as I know."

The pharmacist's eyes fairly bulged out of their sockets.

"How dare you, sir?" he gasped. The blood rushed to his head and he screamed, "Hold your tongue or I'll throw you out!"

Henry got up and walked to the door, but Dr. Korwill called him back. "Who's supporting those bandits?"

"Austria and Germany. Officially and without being ashamed of themselves. You are waging war against England and France but making peace with these highwaymen, these dregs of the lower classes."

"How many fronts are we supposed to fight on? Let's be glad that we're left in peace in the East at least."

"Oh, so you're being left in peace? They are expropriating you. They are taking away all your possessions. Everything is nationalized; the state is taking over everything that isn't nailed down. The railroads, the women, the steambaths . . . What's the matter with you, doctor?"

The proprietor had turned white as chalk. He held on to the counter and asked in a thin voice, "And what about the pharmacies?"

"Those too, of course."

At this the pharmacist screeched like a barn owl, "Never here! That is impossible here!"

"Watch your employees! They're only waiting to take revenge. Your pharmacy will be nationalized too; you'll see."

"I once had such a hussy, but I threw her out!"

"All the worse, doctor. She'll come back and take revenge."

The pharmacist breathed heavily and gasped, "What do you want from me, you monster?"

"A strophanthin preparation for my heart."

"I need one myself," gasped Dr. Korwill and staggered into the dispensing room where he collapsed and lay as if dead. Henry hurried after him, examined him briefly, and made this diagnosis for the employees who came rushing up: "A coronary sclerosis, gentlemen, with the formation of a blood clot in a coronary artery . . ."

One evening in April 1918 Uncle Henner decided to establish parapsychological contact with his dead brother Leo. He was at his wits' end. Business was worse than ever, for while Nathan was still playing the *Ave Maria* at the West Station, people no longer gave him money because they didn't have any themselves. Vienna was starving. The supply lines of the capital had broken down. Austria had reserves for no more than three weeks. Emperor Karl was too busy to receive the inventor of color photography in Schönbrunn, which made the Rosenbachs conclude that salvation was to be found only in the beyond.

The family assembled: Malva and Henry, who now lived in a furnished room on Florianigasse; the two cousins Helli and Steffi; the grandmother; and of course Jana, who helped Henner with all his preparations. It was a matter of using every resource to create an atmosphere in which a consultation of the deceased could take place. Even though those present were inclined to be skeptical about extrasensory phenomena, no one doubted that the participants in a séance had to be dressed in black. It also was self-evident that the living room had to be appropriately decorated for the invocation of the dead Leo. Trivial objects—for example, the parakeet—had to be removed, and unsuitable books were taken away.

Henner hung the cross which he had brought from Rome on the wall. For this purpose he hammered two steel pins into the wall and used a spirit level to determine whether they were lined up horizontally. All this took place in the atmosphere of mandatory exaltation that is part of such rituals. No one dared to speak until Malva suddenly broke the spell and whispered, "What purpose is served by your cross, Uncle Henner? After all, papa was a Jew."

To which the inventor responded with grim sarcasm, "Christ was a Jew too, and he let himself be nailed to the cross anyway."

This reply was so daring that those present were rendered speechless. Helli silently ironed her black silk blouse. Steffi seemed more sullen than usual and laced her boots without so much as looking at Henner. The hero of the evening tried to lift the branches of the cross onto the two steel pins, and Jana examined herself in the wall mirror, for, as she had indicated, she wanted to look decent when Leo appeared. However, she harbored certain doubts about the success of the experiment and kept muttering, *"Matko boska, zlituj sie nad nami!"* Why she suddenly invoked the Virgin Mary, and in Polish to boot, remains a mystery, all the more so because she began to scream, "Don't imagine that a leopard can change his spots. You're all Jews, like it or not. Jehovah gave us life, and will take it back when the time comes."

These words were meant for Henner, but they did not upset him. He stepped back, squinted to examine his handiwork, and declared, "You see, when the cross is properly hung, it ionizes the air. But it has to hang right. This is an absolute prerequisite!"

Henry watched all these goings-on with amusement. Suddenly the devil started riding him and he asked Steffi why she was in such a foul mood. After all, everyone knew that evil women put ghosts to flight. To this Steffi haughtily replied, "Evil women and stupid Marxists." Still ironing her blouse, Helli suddenly asked, "What are we supposed to say when he comes?" Jana, who was powdering her nose, replied, "*We* won't say anything, but Henner will. This séance was his idea, so he must know what should happen next. His invention is at stake. If you say foolish things, papa will be offended and disappear again."

Henry remarked, "It will be hard for him to disappear, because he hasn't appeared yet." To which Jana replied irritably, "And he will have a tough time appearing if people make dumb jokes."

Helli did not seem to be listening to anything that was said, and blurted out, "I will ask him how much longer this war is going to last."

"You won't ask him that," hissed Jana. "You'll keep silent when Leo appears."

"I shall do as I please. The war is more important than anything else. More important than that ridiculous color photography with which all of us have had it up to here."

Jana threw her powder puff on her makeup table and screamed, "Keep quiet, Helli, or you'll have to leave the room!"

Feeling that she ought to reduce the tension, Malva asked, "What did you mean, Uncle Henner, when you said that the cross ionized?"

"That it smells of opium," said Henry derisively, "opiate for the masses."

"No, my dear Malva," said Henner, who had finished his work and was washing his hands. "At its outermost tips the cross creates a magnetic field, you understand? A concentration of static energy, and in it Leo's spirit will materialize. That is quite simple, but as I've said, it must hang properly, otherwise our experiment won't work."

Henry had shrugged his shoulders while listening to Henner's nonsense, and now he said with a sarcastic smile, "How do you know that our phantom will answer your questions correctly when he does not know a thing about color photography? Why, he doesn't even know whether it hasn't been invented long ago."

Henner painstakingly dried his fingers and replied, "Our phantom—that is, my brother of blessed memory—is in heaven. In contrast to you, Mr. Kamin, he does not doubt; he *knows*. He knows everything, for he is part of the heavenly hosts. We shall invoke him and he will come . . . We shall ask him and he will answer."

But Henry continued his provocation. "And what if he makes a fool of himself? Ghosts can make mistakes too, can't they? That would be still another of your failures."

At this point the grandmother threw her knitting on the floor. She had been listening in silence, but this was too much for her and she now joined the conversation. "The dead never make fools of themselves. They're finished with that. Leo was a serious person, and if you do invoke him—it's a sin, and one shouldn't do it—then behave properly, otherwise there will be a misfortune!"

Steffi felt that this was aimed at her, and she stung her grandmother like a wasp. "What do you mean, behave properly? You want to ask my dead uncle what Henner has to do to become rich at last. Uncle Leo, of all people, who never achieved anything in his life. He doesn't know the first thing about business, and in heaven he hasn't been able to learn anything because they don't need money there."

Henner had no intention of engaging in theoretical squabbles with Steffi. He took a candle from the bureau and lit it. Then he turned off the electric light and said solemnly, "In the name of the Father, the Son, and the Holy Ghost . . ."

Now there was an uncanny atmosphere in the room, and Jana whispered, "I think I feel something."

"What?" asked Malva.

"The air is becoming ionized, and I'm in the middle of a magnetic field. Take your seats around the table and get ready! We must concentrate. Concentrate very intensively. We can see a glow. A dim light is shining over the table . . ."

Shivers ran up and down Jana's spine. This spread to the others, including Henry, and Helli stammered nervously, "I'm chilly; I'm afraid."

Henner crossed himself and assumed command of the operation. "We close our eyes and touch the upper rim of the tabletop with our fingertips. The light is getting brighter. We can distinctly hear our heartbeat. We lift all our fingers except the thumb . . ."

The company followed his commands, for despite their doubts they hoped at least to catch a glimpse of the other world. Suddenly the grandmother felt that she was being tempted to participate in a godless enterprise, and muttered, "Leo will be offended by the cross. I'm warning you."

To which Steffi peevishly replied, "He, offended? He was half a heathen himself."

Jana was of a different opinion, however. "He wasn't pious, but in general he kept the commandments."

Henner felt that the connection with the beyond would soon be broken if this foolish talk continued, and so he cried in a hollow voice, "All those present touch the upper rim of the tabletop. It is quiet as in the eternities of the macrocosm. We are rushing through the endlessness of the galaxy. And now . . . we beg Leo Rosenbach of blessed memory to approach. In the name of the Father, the Son, and the Holy Ghost . . ."

Nothing happened. An uneasy silence ensued. Then

Henner cried for a second time, this time in a trembling and imploring voice, "Leo, my only brother. Forgive me all the sins I have committed against you. I have robbed you and cheated you, but we are of the same blood. Let me know by some sign whether or not you hear me . . ."

At that point a horrible noise roused the seven persons from their absorption. Something had crashed to the floor. Henry jumped up and turned on the light. Everyone sat there dazzled, and Helli cried, "The cross. It's kaput. Broken in three pieces!"

Jana stood up and said, her hands theatrically extended, "This is a sign, my dear Henner. Leo is angry with you."

Henry was also impressed by the strange occurrence, but he said mockingly, "Of course he is angry with all of you, because you believe this balderdash."

Henner lowered his eyes. Ignoring Henry's remark, he replied softly, "Leo was always angry with me. Angry and envious, because I can see in the dark and he couldn't. I can hear the angels sing and he couldn't. He is jealous of me beyond the grave."

Jana walked up to Henner. All arrogance had gone out of her. She put a consoling hand on his shoulder and said, "He is angry, or rather, sad, because you deny that you are a Jew."

The grandmother also rose from the table. She walked to the door and said sternly, "No one around here listens to me. But I did warn you!"

The newspapers of the Austro-Hungarian monarchy were censored to the point of indecipherability. It was impossible to learn from them anything about the state of the war. Since the beginning of the war they had printed nothing but reports of victory. Advances were all one heard about; no one ever talked about retreats. In theory the emperor's armies had already reached Polynesia. Anyone who had taken the trouble to add up the casualties on the other side—that is, those listed as dead in the communiqués of the Austrian general staff—would have become convinced that Russia, Serbia, Italy, and Rumania had been depopulated and had disappeared from the map long ago. For that reason serious-minded people gave up reading the domestic press and procured the newspapers of neutral foreign countries. These were, of course, *verboten*, but they were traded on the black market, where they cost almost as much as a pair of leather boots.

One day Henry managed to obtain a copy of the *Neue Zürcher Zeitung*. He took it home and perused it from the first to the last letter. That way he learned, among other things, that the Austrian government, through the good offices of Switzerland, was seeking ways of making a separate peace. He also read that a mass strike started in Wiener Neustadt had spread to Brünn, Budapest, Graz, and Prague, and that the strikers demanded immediate peace without annexations. The newspaper also said that during the last year of the war alone 58,467 German soldiers had fallen . . . and that a certain Doctor Halblützel, a pharmacist in Zurich, was looking for someone to replace his chief pharmacist, who was on border patrol. This news electrified both Henry and Malva. There was finally a chance, the shadow of a chance or at least the reflection of a glimmer of hope, to escape the threatening end of the world and get to a safe place. To be sure, it was not an opportunity for both of them but only for fair Malva, if she was lucky.

They composed a clever letter of application and were canny enough to enclose a photo that showed Malva from her most enchanting side. They did not say that she was expecting a child; for one thing, they were not absolutely sure, and for another, they wanted to reach their goal at any price. The photo worked wonders. Six weeks later the couple stood at a track of the Vienna West Station and bade each other farewell. They laughed and joked, for they were afraid of tears. Cleaning his glasses, Henry said casually, "They say that in Switzerland there are more cows than people."

"I shall write to you," replied Malva. "You'll get a letter from me every day."

"And there are supposed to be a thousand bees for every cow. You are going to paradise, Malva."

"How on earth shall I live without you, Henry?"

"You'll get used to it. In every kitchen there are two pipes. From one flows milk, from the other honey."

"What is going to become of our child, Henry?"

"He will become a trumpeter, of course. Our child will be a son, and trumpet playing is a male profession."

"Not a son, Henry, but a daughter. On the mother's side of my family there are only girls."

"My father has eleven sons."

"You're a silly fool, Henry. Why should our child become a trumpeter?"

"He is going to stand on Mount Everest and wait for the world revolution to break out."

"And then?"

"He'll blow the *Internationale*."

"And what will he do if it doesn't break out?"

"Then he'll take up another instrument."

"What will he live on?"

"On air and love, like his parents. Is that so bad?"

Malva nervously looked at the station clock. There were only a few minutes left before the departure of her train, and she sighed, "We won't see each other for a long time. Do you want me to stay?"

Henry felt his mouth become dry, and he changed the subject. "If you cheat on me, you'll get a goiter."

"I'll never cheat on you."

"Woe to you if you're lying. I'll kill you."

"We are mad. Both of us. I'm leaving for Zurich today, you for Warsaw tomorrow. Does it have to be like this?"

"Thirty million Poles are waiting for me."

"I know. Fifteen million of these are women. Tell me to stay!"

"At the Warsaw citadel, at the place where they were going to execute me, I shall run up the red flag."

"Are you sure they're expecting you? Perhaps they've forgotten you. Or don't even need you."

"You are beautiful, Malva. You are so beautiful that the mere thought of you makes my knees shake."

"I went to Iwonicz with you, Henry. I've seen some of your thirty million Poles. What do you think they really want?"

"They want wings. To detach themselves from the earth. To build whole cities of dream castles . . ."

"And swill their fill at the expense of the proletarian revolution. You'll get the surprise of your life."

"The war is coming to an end. A new Poland will blossom, and the two of you will join me in Warsaw."

"Or you'll join us in Zurich."

"You'll be welcomed by a military band. You and your son."

"It will be a daughter."

"It'll be a son, and he'll fly like his father."

"And land on his face. Just like his father, who talks crazy and mopes around. And whom I can't live without . . ."

At this point they were interrupted by a croaking voice, official and unfeeling, that cut them to the quick. "All aboard, ladies and gentlemen. The express train is leaving for Salzburg, Innsbruck, Feldkirch, and Zurich!"

That was it. Their reprieve was over. Henry squeezed out one more sentence. It was intended to be comforting, but it sounded thin and wooden. "When our boy is born, the war will be over!"

When he is born . . . And what if he isn't? That was too much for Malva. The comedy had lasted too long. For days both of them had been trying to mask their fears, to be brave, to tell themselves that over there, on the other bank, was the straw at which they could clutch. But now they had to separate, and God only knew whether they would ever be in each other's arms again. Malva broke down. She sobbed desperately and uncontrollably. She dug all ten fingers into the shoulders of her beloved, and for the first time the words that she had so long suppressed escaped from her: "I don't want to go, Henry. I'd rather starve here. Why aren't you holding me back?"

Why indeed? Did he want to be rid of her? Was he planning to plunge into fresh adventures? The revolution? Mysterious women? Back to America? All that is certain is that Malva did finally board the train, wracked by tears and in despair. She looked back once more. There Henry stood, trying to smile. His lips twitched and his eyes were moist. The train started moving, and he hid his face in both hands. Why? Is it shameful to cry? Evidently it is. For a Bolshevik it is unseemly to cry. Tears are an expression of weakness, and Bolsheviks must be strong. So says the code of honor of the proletarian revolution. A man who cries has feelings, and a man with feelings is an impediment in the class struggle, a menace to the party. The ideal soldier has neither a brain nor a heart. His face is of stone and his eyes are of steel. Together with Marxism and Leninism, a prototype of "the new man" has come into being—the man of marble who gazes into the future with pinched lips. The grimly determined hero of labor who remains unmoved even if the world collapses on him. He knows neither elation nor depression and looks like the statue of a warrior. He is neither likable nor hateful but a cold-blooded animal, a fossil of the species man, which is becoming extinct, a robot of the impending ice age. Such a robot was now standing at the track. Shaken by tears, he tried to pretend that this farewell was easy for him. Malva stood by the window and saw through her husband. The train rumbled out of the station. Henry became smaller and smaller, but his tears flashed in the morning sun. They were a comfort to Malva, for behind those hands was a human being who was crying.

Poor Uncle Henner had only one way out. With a heavy heart he decided to call on the chief rabbi of Vienna, who, significantly, was named Schreckmann. Rabbi Frightman

265

lived in a bare apartment in the attic of an apartment house that stank of cat droppings and mothballs. A plain iron railing enclosed the staircase, and Henner had the uneasy feeling that he was climbing into the beyond. He caught sight of gray ghosts flitting through the hallways, pallid figures that appeared like will-o'-the-wisps and immediately disappeared again. Everywhere doors seemed to open a crack, and chalky faces peered out. They examined him suspiciously, and several times he was on the point of turning back, but where? Where was he to flee when there was no retreat? After all, he had burned all his bridges behind him. Intentionally? Unintentionally? He didn't know. Finally he arrived, breathing heavily. After hesitating uneasily he pulled the bell, but it was an eternity before someone came shuffling along and opened the door. A man with waxen features. Stern and forbidding, haughty as Torquemada, the Inquisitor General of Castille. An angel of death with long, spidery fingers and thin lips. His beard was the color of rust. His voice sounded hollow, and as though continuing a conversation that had just been interrupted he asked, "*Nu*, my friend? What now?"

The two didn't know each other. They had never met, yet that man seemed to know what was wrong with Henner. That he had lost all hope. That a leaden uneasiness was choking him. That no one believed in him anymore, not even himself.

The chief rabbi read Henner's eyes and knew everything. He sighed. "*Nu*, my friend? What now?"

That was precisely Henner's torment: that he didn't know what would happen next. Schreckmann invited him to come in. Into his apartment, in which there were only two chairs and a clothes stand. Henner did so. After an awkward pause the eccentric ordered, "Sit down, my friend, and speak the truth!"

How did he know that Henner was a liar? That he hadn't spoken a true word in his life? Schreckmann sat down opposite him. He saw through Henner until the latter felt an icy shiver run down his spine. "What do you have in this case, you unfortunate person?"

"Nothing special . . . Nothing at all, really."

"Thou shalt not lie, you foolish creature!"

"I am ashamed . . ."

"God be praised. If you are ashamed, you are saved. What did you bring me? Out with the truth!"

"The remnants of my sin . . ."

"Call the sin by its name! Without beating about the bush. Straight out, as our ancestors did."

"It is . . . I can't say it . . . It is a cross."

The angel of death turned pale. "With a cross you go to see the chief rabbi of Vienna? What is that supposed to mean?"

"I invoked the ghost of my dead brother. That's when the cross fell from the wall and broke to pieces."

"How did you invoke him? With what words?"

"Simply the way one usually invokes the dead."

"I ask you with what words you invoked him."

"I cannot remember, Mr. Schreckmann."

"One more lie and I'll throw you out. Tell me the words!"

"I called, 'In the name of the Father, the Son, and the Holy Ghost.' That is all."

"Oh, so that is all. A mere trifle. And what do you want in my house?"

"God's grace, if that is possible. I want to return, Mr. Schreckmann. Return."

"What do you mean by that, my friend? To us or to the others?"

"To Jehovah, Mr. Chief Rabbi. To the living God, so he can give me a new heart and a clear mind . . ."

Schreckmann got up and walked over to the window. Solemnly and stiffly. He stared out and whispered, "Anything is possible. Even a return to the Almighty, but I advise you against it. You have committed ninety-nine mistakes. Don't make the hundredth one!"

"This is what *you* tell me, the chief rabbi of Vienna?"

"The Lord himself would counsel you against it, you fool, for he loves you. He loves all his children, and those who have turned out badly most of all."

"That's why I am longing for him, Mr. Schreckmann."

"Do you know, my friend, what that involves? Do you know the price of belonging to the chosen people?"

"I don't want to know. I want to go home to the God of the Jews. That's all I want."

Schreckmann turned around and looked daggers at the crestfallen Henner. He raised his hands heavenward and thundered, "It is a distinction to profess one's loyalty to Jehovah. It is not given to everyone to be his servant. But God honors us by chastising us."

"I am ready, Mr. Schreckmann."

"In the Book of Job it is written: 'See how happy is the man whom God reproves. Do not reject the discipline of the Almighty. He injures, but He binds up; He wounds, but His hands heal. In famine He will redeem you from death, in war from the sword. You will have no fear when destruction comes.' "

"I have no fear, chief rabbi."

"That redounds to your honor, my friend. But if you are a wise Jew, you will remain a Christian. It is better for your health."

"The cross fell from the wall. That is a sign. God wants me to return."

Schreckmann grinned maliciously. "God does not meddle in your affairs. God doesn't want anything. If you had done a better job hammering the nails into the wall, the cross would still be there."

Henner felt offended. Cautiously he played his trump card. "I am what they call an inventor. I am on the eve of a historic breakthrough."

"But you don't know how to drive in nails."

"I want to place my success on the altar of Jehovah."

"Take it to the competition, my friend! It pays more and the risk is less."

Now Henner fell on his knees and implored, wringing his hands. "Why do you mock me, chief rabbi? After all, I am not asking for anything bad. I am dreaming of a roof to protect me. I want to return to the bosom of my people."

"What you desire is foolish. You don't know what awaits you."

"All hope is foolish, Mr. Schreckmann. It was also foolish to leave Egypt, because no one knew what awaited him. But on the other side of the desert was the Promised Land . . ."

The chief rabbi sensed that Henner was speaking from the depth of his heart. He put his hands on his hair, closed his eyes, and said, "I shall inflict terror on you, said Jehovah to the Jews, consumption and a high fever."

"I am looking forward to it."

"Your eyes will be extinguished and your soul will waste away."

"I deserve it."

"You will sow your seeds in vain, for your foes will consume them."

"I have sinned and must atone for it."

"You will be slain and tormented. Those who hate you will rule over you, and you will flee when no one chases you."

"I am a son of the people of Israel. An apostate, but flesh of its flesh. I want to share its fate."

Schreckmann now believed the words of his supplicant. He sat down and bade Henner do the same. For the first time his expression relaxed. A smile flitted over it, and he said in an almost conciliatory tone of voice, "If it *has* to be, I can't oppose it, my friend. But I cannot circumcise you, because you are already circumcised. Nor can I make a Jew out of you, because you were born a Jew. All I can do is warn you, my friend, and this I have done."

In the fall of 1918 a journey by train from Vienna to Warsaw took approximately five days and five nights. It was not certain whether the destination would be reached. The windows were boarded up and the carriages were jampacked with Austrian soldiers and Polish black marketeers. Gone were the days when a train trip still promised pleasant experiences. The starving passengers sat silently on their paltry luggage. The pungent odor of disinfectant and urine, sweaty feet and a Russian tobacco called *makhorka* made the journey a hellish torment. Conversations were avoided, and when anyone looked around, it was only to make sure that everything was still there. Sometimes the train stopped in an open field and sometimes at a wretched whistlestop. That gave people an opportunity to relieve themselves, fill a bottle with water, or simply find out where they were.

Henry was daydreaming when the train stopped. Polish sounds came from the outside, so there was no doubt that they were in Poland, where the destitution was even more oppressive than in the rest of Europe. What kept Henry going was the prospect of going to Warsaw at the risk of neither the gallows nor exile. Warsaw, Warszawa—the scene of his first adventures, youthful feats, and madcap daredeviltry . . . Hearing his mother tongue for the first time in years, he was gripped by emotion. He felt as if some mysterious force were pulling him back to the house where he was born, to his family, to his friends, to the wellsprings of his happiness. While Henry loathed sentimental attachment to one's homeland in all its manifestations, he now felt homesick. He remembered the time when he had strolled from Three Cross Square via Nowy Swiat to the Cracow suburb. In his mind's eye he saw himself on Castle Square in front of the King Sigismund column. He looked down to the green bank of the Vistula and across to the black smokestacks of Praga. What was the name of that song? *A jego kolor jest czerwony.* Bullets whistled past him and the sound of horses' hoofs came rumbling over. Blood flows over the pavement, and he raises the flag over the roofs of Piwna Street, *bo na nim*

270

robotnicz krew: for its color is red from the blood of the proletarians. Over there a girl is standing. She is slender as a reed. Her eyes are green. She beats the drum for the attack. Wanda, flaxen-haired Wanda from the workers' district Wola. Where are you? I long for you. Give me your hand and we'll stroll on. To St. John's cathedral. To the heart of the city, where there was once a winecellar. It was called Fugger's, and it is still so called if it has not been destroyed. At Fugger's I am supposed to meet Anka. On October 15 at noon. That is madness. How can one make such an appointment? The world is going to pieces. In the East civil war is raging. Trotsky captures Kazan. Dora Kaplan shoots at Lenin. The social revolutionaries rise up against the Soviet power. In the West the German front collapses. The Kaiser bombards Paris. Ypres falls to the Americans, but Henry makes a date with his youngest sister. At Fugger's for coffee and cake . . . She is his favorite sister. The confidante of the eleven brothers, who have broken off all relationships with their old man. Because he did not ransom them that time, the old skinflint. Because he let them be sent to Siberia. To the lead mines of Verkhoyansk, from which no one has yet returned. He trembles when he thinks of it. That is why he did not send a cable to his father but to Anka: "Meeting Monday noon at Fugger's. Embraces, Hershele."

Henry was cogitating, dreaming, hallucinating. It was dark in the carriage. Then the door opened, light came in, and a conductor appeared. He turned to Henry and said in a marked Viennese accent, "If you want to go to Warsaw, Herr Baron, you've got to change in Kattowitz!"

Henry awoke from his somnolence. "In Kattowitz, you say? But that isn't in the timetable."

The conductor shook with laughter. "The war isn't in the timetable either, Herr Baron, and it's still taking place. If you knew what was happening that's not in the timetable, you'd be hopping mad."

At that point the conversation was joined by a man who

271

had hitherto not attracted anyone's attention. He was wearing a gray officer's tunic and dark glasses that lent him an air of great reserve and dignity. "You are still green and foolish. If I were you, I would go to the moon. To the Pleiades, if need be, but not to Warsaw!" Henry felt disconcerted; this man was voicing his own fears. He answered hesitantly. "For years I've been dreaming of returning to a free Poland. Why shouldn't I go to Warsaw?"

The stranger twisted his mouth into a weary smile. "Because you won't find there what you're looking for. You are under a misconception, young man."

"How do you know what I'm looking for?" replied Henry peevishly.

The blind man ignored these words. "Take my advice and go to Palestine!"

Henry responded irritably. "Why don't *you* go to Palestine?"

The blind man clumsily filled his pipe and said after a pause, "Because I'm not a Jew. If I were one, I'd go there, and immediately."

A hostile silence ensued. The mysterious man took Henry for a Jew even though he spoke faultless German and his appearance suggested he was American. The conductor said with an undertone of malice, "If the Polacks had their way, they'd kill all the Jews. Isn't that right?"

Henry got hot under the collar. "You seem to know exactly what the Poles want. Are you one yourself?"

In place of the conductor the answer was given by a man who was sitting by the door woolgathering with his eyes half closed. He was wearing a fur jacket and knee-length kulak boots. "*Ja jestem Polak, prosze pantstwo.* I can confirm what the conductor said. If there's anything that keeps us Poles together, it's hatred of the Jews."

The blind man tried to reduce the tension and said, "There probably are Poles of this type as well as others, right?"

Henry mounted a counterattack. "There are Poles of this

272

type as well as others. There are speculators and down-and-outers, exploiters and starvelings, no matter whether they are Jews or Christians. And above all, there are scoundrels who incite the weak against one another so they can dominate them more easily."

Whereupon the man with the dark glasses said, "I hear that you believe in Lenin. It is now the fashion to pray to him. But beware, young man! Even Lenin has to speak the rabble's language, and one day he, too, will shoot the Jews . . ."

Henry kept himself in check and asked, "What makes you think that I believe in Lenin? You behave as if you were a clairvoyant."

The blind man lit his pipe and took some puffs. "I lost my eyesight on the Isonzo. In this holy war for God, emperor, and fatherland. No, I'm not a clairvoyant, but my vision now is clearer than it was before."

Henry was ashamed of his impertinent remark. He pulled a bottle of schnapps out of his vest pocket, unscrewed it, filled the aluminum cover, and handed it to his strange traveling companion. "I am sorry, sir! Have a drink and forget what I said!"

The blind man downed the schnapps and replied, "I'm not angry with you, young man. I simply advise you to turn back, for no one is waiting for you here. Go in the opposite direction! Look for a station where someone is waiting for you!"

Henry was about to say something, but the man with the kulak boots interrupted him: "*Wierzysz w Lenina, prawda?* You believe in Lenin and his whole Jew riffraff. It's high time you told us whether you're a Jew. If you are, make yourself scarce and get out of here, or we'll throw you out."

The blood rushed to Henry's face and he countered, "If you've never received a walloping from a Jew, come here! I've handled bigger people than you."

The man was half a head taller than Henry, but he got scared. He had never before met a Jew who risked a brawl so fearlessly, and so he grumbled, "Maybe you can handle *me, koszerna swinio,* you kosher swine. But why don't you take on all of us?"

Henry's voice broke. "All of us, you say? Are you speaking for the whole compartment?"

"Oh yes. I speak in the name of thirty million Poles. In the name of the whole Catholic people, if you know what that is."

Now Henry staked his *Weltanschauung,* his faith in reason, and his youthful trust in man. "I assume that you are the only one who believes such nonsense here. Or am I mistaken?"

There was deathly silence. Only the rattling of the wheels was audible. No one cared to express himself, neither the Poles nor the Austrians. At that moment Henry realized that his ideals were soap bubbles. That he could count on no one. He was alone. The conductor broke the silence and said jovially, "It's an hour to Kattowitz, Herr Baron. Seems to me you should jump off now if you value your life."

The eyes of his traveling companions gave Henry to understand that there was no other solution. He got up, took his luggage in his hands, and was escorted out of the compartment by the conductor. He unlocked the carriage door and whispered words that he had not uttered since his childhood: *"Avinu sheh bashamayim!"* He was invoking God in heaven. Not from fear but from despair. He jumped off, hit the ground, rolled over several times, and came to rest in the middle of a fallow field. *Avinu sheh bashamayim!* Every bone in his body hurt, but Henry soon pulled himself together. Moaning and groaning he got to his feet and started walking. Toward evening he reached a small provincial town. There he went to the post office and sent the following telegram to Warsaw: "Visit postponed indefinitely. Letter follows. Hershele."

23

.~.~.~.

NOVEMBER 1, 1918. I'M IN SWITZERLAND. IF HENRY
were with me I'd be jubilant, but he's at the other
end of the world. Here it is so indescribably beautiful
that my heart aches. Over the lake hangs a melancholy
haze through which one guesses the Alps, the silvery tips
of the snow-capped mountains. Weeping willows hang
into the water. Near the shore swim swans the color of
mother-of-pearl. I'm sitting on a bench, writing in my
diary, and longing for him. Over there stands an old
man who's feeding the pigeons. I don't know whether
I'm alive or dead. This is the Garden of Eden. A gentle
beyond of peace and quiet. My train arrived at the Zurich
railroad station on time. I got off and wondered what
the first thing I'd see would be—an oracle, so to speak.
It was a man who was selling little sausages with rolls
and mustard. Inside his little cart he had chocolate and
oranges. I thought I was dreaming. Such delicacies
haven't existed in Vienna for a long time. And then I
went to the hotel. It's called Victoria—an ugly name—
and is located directly behind the railroad station. It looks
like an enormous raspberry cake. At the desk I was given
a respectful greeting, and the proprietor called me
"madam." I was taken to an elegant room with silk tapestries, flowers on the table, and a basket of colorful
fruit. I have a double bed with fresh sheets. Tears came
to my eyes because I have to sleep alone here. God, if
he only knew how hard it is without him. When I crossed
the border at Buchs, something stirred in my belly. Quite
distinctly for the first time. Our child, who is roaming

the world alone with its mother. The trees are yellow, some even red as rust. Wonder where he is now, my only beloved. I can't enjoy myself, even though here I can have everything my heart desires. After washing up I left the hotel and took an exciting stroll through the Bahnhofstrasse, the main artery of Zurich. This is where all the banks, all the jewelers, all the luxury shops of the city are located. Everything seemed unreal to me. In the shopwindows there were wonderful things that I didn't even know existed. After all, I don't come from the provinces but from Vienna, a world-class city. But Vienna is finished. The war has consumed entire countries and entire peoples. Switzerland is an island. A museum for those who have survived the end of the world. They will make a pilgrimage here. With wooden crutches and clattering prostheses. To gape at what once existed on this earth, all the wonders they have lost. Through their own fault. This continent has bled and burned to death. The soldiers have died winning. But here, wedged in between the arch-enemies, lives a miniature nation that plays at peace. People here speak four different languages and don't kill one another. It is Sunday. All the shops are closed. Tomorrow morning I shall start. I have stage fright. I tremble at the thought that people might notice I'm expecting a child. At the hotel I undressed and stood in front of the mirror naked. If one doesn't know, everything looks normal. But I can see that my pelvis is broader and my breasts are firmer than usual. Now I'm curious to see whether the pharmacist will notice. Wonder whether he is as dry as his letter and as florid as his handwriting. I've already been to the Rennweg and looked at the shop. From the outside, of course, because today everything is locked up. There was one thing that astonished me. On the door there was a different name: Obermüller. I'd never heard that. Who knows what all this means. Well, we'll see. All that is unimportant. The only thing that counts in my life is he. Always he alone. Is he still in Warsaw or back in Vienna? What about the thirty million Poles that have been waiting for him? How did they receive him? Badly, I hope. I pray to heaven that he will soon shed his illusions and come to me. Or rather, to us, for more and more frequently something stirs under my heart. Where am I? That's what I ask myself again and again. In a forest of rabbits. Everyday life seems totally unheroic. The Swiss have good noses and little eyes that always express surprise. I would bet that no one here would be willing to die for an ideal. People lead their little lives and feed pigeons on the lake shore. The question is whether this is the purpose of existence. Whether it would not be more fascinating to climb up to heaven and create a new world. But more and more often I ask myself whether there is a higher purpose at all. If only I could at least believe in God— but I can't. God has been shipwrecked; otherwise he would not permit his world to be destroyed and people to exterminate one another. All great purposes are ship-wrecked. One after the other. Without a higher purpose not a single soldier would have gone off to war, but now they are all caught in the barbed wire—Frenchmen, Englishmen, Germans, Russians, and Italians. They are all moldering in rubble fields, and with them the ideals for which they marched off. I loathe great goals. Henry will reply that *his* ideals are better. That they are the quintessence of human dreams and of the longings of all nations and epochs, that they have long ago ceased to be ideals but are reality on one-sixth of the globe— in Russia, where the force of gravity has been suspended and the impossible has become possible. Henry is an Orlando Furioso. I would like to believe him, but inside me a voice whispers that even the Russian trees don't grow into the sky. What will become of us, my one and only beloved? Surely I can't expect him to sit by the lake and feed the pigeons. But there are other solutions, some-where in the middle between the exalted ideals and the life of a mole. For me there is an attainable dream: love. I can feel Henry beside me. In my arms. Soul to soul. Skin to skin. Deep in my body. Is that not enough for him? I'm tired. I'll write more tomorrow . . .

24

Y ANKEL KAMINSKI WAS NOW OVER SEVENTY, AND AS PIG-
headed as ever. He was a rich man; he owned numerous houses, several textile factories, and the famous theater
in downtown Warsaw. His wife still drew ovations when
she stepped out on the stage. His five daughters made a
splash because they were intelligent and exceptionally witty.
But the patriarch was down in the dumps. Nothing could
cheer him up, because he had no news of his sons. He had
cast them out and told everyone that he had no male off-
spring. He strictly forbade people to mention their names
or remind him of them in any way. He had broken off all
contact with his favorite colleague, Hersh Blumentopf, because he could not bear to hear his first name. He was the
worthy procreator of eleven unworthy sons, who had disowned him as inexorably as he had disowned them. Yankel
waited for some sign of life, but in vain. Rumors circulated
about their fate, their successes and failures, but he knew
nothing for certain and would not have known now if it
had not been for Anka, his youngest daughter, who was
secretly in touch with her eleven brothers and was already
beginning to continue their political activities.

On that November day something monstrous happened.
Chaim Lewin, Yankel's faithful chief clerk, waked his boss
from his afternoon nap, which in theory was tantamount
to a capital offense. Lewin knew that nothing short of a
natural catastrophe or the outbreak of revolution would
justify such a criminal act, so he carried his shoes in his

hands, tiptoed to the holy of holies in his stocking feet, and knocked so gently that for a time the old man kept on snoring peacefully. Lewin repeated his punishable act several times and each time a bit more bravely, until finally the whole house was shaking and the flower-like Rahel jumped up from her sofa in fright. Yankel woke up and roared, "What's happening, *do jasnej cholery?*"

From the anteroom came a contrite whisper: "A telegram, *panie* Kaminski."

The old man breathlessly pulled on his pants and screamed through the door, "Lewin, I'm going to chop you to pieces!"

Today, however, the chief clerk refused to be intimidated, for he knew how revolutionary his news was. He now whispered so loudly that the watchdog in the neighboring house began to bark: "A telegram from Mr. Hershele, *panie* Kaminski, or rather, two . . ."

Yankel felt the floor shake under his feet. A telegram from Hershele, his favorite son! On the one hand, Yankel's heart was bursting with happiness, but on the other he could not let anyone notice it. Furthermore, this Lewin was taking liberties for which a man was summarily shot in peacetime. So Yankel screeched, "Where's the telegram, you *schmuck?* Give it to me and get out of here, otherwise I'll tear you to pieces!"

"I don't got no telegram, *panie* Kaminski, and because I don't I can't give you none."

The patriarch was about to faint. That was too much for a seventy-year-old Jew. He fairly tore the hinges off his bedroom door, grabbed the chief clerk by both shoulders, shook him like an apple tree, and yelled, "Where do you think we are, you schlemiel? In Russia or where? An underling disturbs the sleep of his boss and turns the world upside down like the Bolsheviks. You say a telegram has come. A wire that you don't have and from a man I don't know. How do you know who it's from if it don't exist?"

Chaim Lewin scratched his neck in embarrassment. The

sum really didn't seem to come out even, and he said with his head lowered, "There's a telegram all right, *panie* Kaminski. There's even two. They came, but not to us . . ."

"Rather?"

"To one of your daughters, if you don't mind. And without a date."

"So you were with one of my daughters?"

Old Lewin blushed and replied submissively, "God forbid, *panie* Kaminski. I heard it from your servant Fela, who was cleaning up Miss Anka's room. And that's when . . ."

"Keep it short, Chaim Lewin! What's in the two telegrams?"

"One says that Mr. Hershele is coming to Warsaw . . ."

"And the other one?"

"That he's not coming to Warsaw."

"What, then? Are you trying to torture me?"

"Only the Almighty knows, *panie* Kaminski. There's no date on the telegram, and so I can't know what will be. Maybe he comes, maybe he don't come."

"I know that much, you *schlimazl.* And besides, I don't know any Hershele. If he wishes to see me, let him come and apologize."

"What for, *panie* Kaminski?"

"Another question and I'll kill you."

"I wasn't asking questions. I was just expressing my surprise. They shipped him off to Siberia. His brothers too. So where's the crime?"

"I'm telling you for the last time. If he wants to see me, he's got to apologize."

Fair Rahel had put on a wrapper and followed the two men's verbal battle with amusement. Now she walked up to Yankel and said with a smile, "He doesn't really want to see you, my dear. Otherwise he would not have telegraphed his sister but you."

Yankel turned toward the window, for now his eyes were filling with tears, and he answered hoarsely, "He does *too* want to see me, the fool!"

25

·~·~·~·

IT WAS A GLOOMY NOVEMBER DAY. THE WORLD LAY IN ruins, but Zurich was as intact as a thousand years ago. It was like a stage in a fairy tale—unreal, pastel-colored, and small. Over the houses hung patches of fog. Towers and bridges were reflected in the oil-green water. It was the start of a new week, bustling and cheerless. The city smelled of mold, rotten seaweed, and freshly painted railings.

Malva was feverish and raring to go. She was wearing her yellow cape and a broad-brimmed black felt hat that calmed her pounding heart and made her feel secure. She had left her hotel as early as half past seven and was hurrying toward the pharmacy. But suddenly she thought better of it and slowed her pace so as not to arrive at her new place of work too early. No one was to notice how excited she was and how much hope she had for this new position. So she strolled along the water across the Schipfe up to the Lindenhof. From there she was able to survey the entire expanse of the gingerbread paradise. She was firmly resolved that this was where she was going to stay, and here she would give birth to her child. She was not attracted to the East at all, nor to any ideals. All she wanted was to prove herself and be successful in her profession. Here she wanted only to lead a normal, unheroic life. To her Zurich was more than just another city in Europe. It was an alternative, a palpable bird in the hand as against all the unreal ones in the bush. Malva was under no illusions;

this bird was anything but a songbird. She understood that it was stifling and narrow here. But still, thousands had sought and found refuge here. The best people came to Zurich, the elite of the old world, for here they were free to think what they wanted, write, paint, compose whatever they felt like, and no uniformed cipher was permitted to keep them from doing so. These were facts, and yet she knew that it would be hard to lure Henry here. How was she to make this miniature city palatable to him? With what arguments, when he wanted to live for a better world, and if need be die for it? Switzerland was not a better world. It was well-nourished, self-satisfied, and clean, but not better. Everything was on a small scale—a toy state for business-minded Lilliputians who greedily and piously ran after the Golden Calf. There was no concealing that. Henry would come some day—because he loved Malva and was curious about the child. But soon enough he would reproach her with having clipped his wings. Or was she mistaken about that? Perhaps he was not really the highfalutin Don Quixote that he pretended to be. Who knew what was in his mind and heart today?

Such and similar thoughts were buzzing through her head when she reached her destination. There it was in big letters: RENNWEGAPOTHEKE. This was the golden straw with which she planned to pull herself ashore, the pharmacy of Dr. Halblützel, who needed a pharmacist and had circumvented numerous regulations to bring Malva from Austria, which was going under, to Switzerland, which had been spared by the war. Yesterday's wooden shutters had been removed, giving an unobstructed view of the interior, where two graying gentlemen were waiting on the first customers. Malva stood lost in thought for a good minute, but suddenly she roused herself, gritted her teeth, and entered. It was shortly after eight, but the pharmacy was already full of people politely waiting to be served. The pharmacists wore white smocks. One had a fencing scar running across his face, the other wore a signet ring. They waited on the public with reserve and condescending courtesy. Therefore they could not see that Malva had come in, though they did sense that something was happening on the other side of the desk. A natural phenomenon. So there she was: a Scheherezade in a yellow silk coat with pulsating eyes and bluish black hair. No one dared to look her straight in the face, but all were bewitched. Malva stood by the door and made the room iridescent. It was evident that she was not there to buy anything. She waited, and it became increasingly impossible to ignore her. She emanated a beguiling fragrance. Pearly white teeth gleamed between her lips and her eyes sprayed honey-colored pollen. She did not say a word, nor did she push forward, but she was so prodigiously present that the pharmacist forgot his principles and waited on her ahead of the others. "Good morning, what can I do for the young lady?"

"I would like to speak with Dr. Halblützel."

"Unfortunately that's impossible. But *I* am at your disposal."

"Is the doctor off today?"

"Yes, and permanently. He died of the Spanish influenza. You must have heard that half of Switzerland is bedridden and the other half in the grave."

Malva thought the ground was opening up beneath her. She turned white as chalk and stammered, "What am I to do now? Dr. Halblützel sent for me."

"He knew a pretty woman when he saw one, the old Casanova."

"He was looking for a pharmacist."

"Who isn't these days? Do you know one?"

Malva gave a slight, embarrassed cough. "May I introduce myself? I'm Malva Kaminski."

"And my name is Oskar Obermüller. That man over there is my brother Emil. We are Dr. Halblützel's successors."

"If I am rightly informed, you are looking for a pharmacist too."

"Urgently."

"Under what terms?"

"That depends on who applies."

"As I've already told you, *I* am applying."

Scarface was open-mouthed. "You? A girl of peaches and cream? You must be kidding."

"I am a graduate pharmacist."

"Oh, come off it! It's past April Fool's Day, and it isn't Twelfth Night yet."

Malva controlled herself. "I am a graduate pharmacist, and here is my diploma." With these words she put a cardboard tube on the table and pulled a sheepskin out of it, but Scarface wrinkled his nose. "No thanks, I'm not interested in your diploma."

Now his brother, the man with the signet ring, joined the conversation and said urbanely, "But *I* am interested in it, because I like you. I'll put you in the window as an attraction for our male customers."

The idea of such a charming lure now excited Scarface as well. "You must excuse us, but this is simply something new to us. We tend to be old-fashioned in such matters."

Malva replied disdainfully, "In what matters? Dummies?"

"I mean . . . female academicians. In our country only the men go to the university."

"But that's strange. Why is that?" mocked Malva, and put her diploma away again.

This question caught the two by surprise. Signetring gave a reply with which he tried to elicit the agreement of the impatiently waiting customers: "Because the exact sciences require exact minds. That's why!"

"And do you possess exact minds, gentlemen?"

"Yes, we have extremely exact minds, though you seem to doubt it. Let's see your diploma!"

"You said you weren't interested—because I'm a woman."

"Are you single?"

"Is that any of your business, Mr. Obermüller?"

Now she had gone a bit too far, and Scarface replied, "Our women haven't been to the university, but they know how to behave."

Malva began to get nervous, and parried. "I have the impression that it's just the opposite with your men. They've been to the university, but they have no manners."

Signetring had never experienced such insolence, and he cried, "You see, we care about good manners. At least here in Zurich we do."

"So do we. I'm from Vienna."

"Why didn't you stay there?"

Malva felt that they had reached the limit. From the words of the two pharmacists she could conclude that she would have no trouble finding work in Zurich. Therefore she said coolly, "I won't take up any more of your valuable time, gentlemen. Your customers are waiting to be served."

The exact minds were stumped. Signetring tried to straighten things out and said conciliatingly, "How much would the lady like to earn, if I may ask?"

"As much as a male colleague with the same qualifications. Not in the window, though, but at the dispensing table."

"Who do you think you are? We're not in Russia, you know."

"Not a franc more and not a franc less. It's a matter of fairness."

Signetring saw that they couldn't get anywhere with this woman, so he asked her in an altered tone of voice, "Tell me, you peculiar person. Didn't they teach you how to smile at the University of Vienna?"

"They did," smiled Malva stealthily, "but smiling was my minor subject."

This broke the ice. Scarface extended his right hand to Malva and growled, "See, all we have to do is talk with one another."

"Then tell me when to start here."

"Now."

26

SINCE IT WAS IMPOSSIBLE TO DETERMINE WHICH OF THE two telegrams was valid—as we have said, they were undated—whether or not Henry was coming to Warsaw, and whether there was any chance that he would be willing to visit the patriarch, Yankel swallowed at least some of his pride and went to the Silesian Station on that Monday, saying that he wanted to buy a box of cigars and a newspaper. He would never have admitted that he was picking up his favorite son, since for thirteen years he had grumbled that he had no sons and didn't want to have any. He asked his young wife to accompany him, and told Lewin to order a droshky. The whole house was informed, and so was half the city. It was shouted from the housetops that a prodigal son was about to arrive and that his father, the old fool, was going there to take him in his arms. It goes without saying that there was no one, or hardly anyone, who would have dared to call a spade a spade, because Yankel still was the unchallenged autocrat in his dominion. Anyone who aroused his ire had to be prepared to be crushed by him.

The express train from Kattowitz was scheduled to arrive at 11 A.M., but Pieczynski banged at the door at 9:30. He was the scruffiest coachman in the area, and howled through the stairwell, "My carriage is waiting outside, *panie* Kaminski."

Yankel had been standing in the hallway for twenty minutes. He was impatiently waiting for Rahel, who was late as always. When she finally appeared, she said with a smile, "You seem nervous, Yankele. What gives?" Replied Yankel, leading her to the droshky, "Me, nervous? So why should I be nervous? I'm not expecting anyone."

Rahel seemed to know more than he, and replied, "I know that you aren't expecting anyone. Then why do you insist that I go with you? Do you need my help, and if so, what can I do?"

The patriarch sensed that his wife was mocking him, and answered in embarrassment, "When I go to the station, I don't want to be alone, otherwise I get depressed. There's nothing that depresses me as much as the railroad."

Rahel continued her game and said craftily, "I can't stand the railroad either, my dear husband, but why do you go to the station, of all places, to buy cigars, and to the Silesian Station, which is even drearier than any other station in the world?"

The coachman didn't understand why they were beating about the bush, and so he turned around and said, "It's really none of my damn business, madam, but everybody knows that your husband is going to the station to pick up his son and not a box of cigars!"

"You take me where I order you to take me, and worry about your own fleas!"

Pieczynski was not about to let himself be intimidated and went on provoking Yankel. "The young *pan* Kaminski is coming from Vienna, and his old man is busting with impatience to see him."

"Keep quiet, you boor!"

"His conscience is bothering him because he cast him out and betrayed him."

"Hold your tongue or I'll kick your teeth in!"

"He sold young *pan* Hershele down the river, and the ten others too. Or isn't that right what I'm saying?"

"I'm going to beat you to a pulp, you pig's teat, and right here in the street."

"He was too stingy to pay the ransom, and let the Russkies send them to Siberia. To the lead mines of Verkhoyansk."

"You're telling the truth, you louse. I tanned his hide

with my own two hands because he was making a revolution, the snotnose, instead of doing his homework. And as for you, if you say another word I'm going to skin you alive."

Now Rahel intervened and calmed the potentate, who was about to go out of his mind. "Don't get excited, Yankele! He's become a doctor in the meantime. Got his doctorate at the University of Vienna. And he's twice as smart as the two of us taken together. You won't recognize him."

"How do you know what I will recognize and what not? How come, *do jasnej cholery*, that you know more than me, and what he has become, and that he's smarter than . . ."

"Because I can control myself and don't yell like you. People tell me things that they'd never tell you."

"A better world is what he wanted. Now he's got it. The Bolsheviks are at the Bug River, two hundred versts from here."

"They'll never get as far as Warsaw, Yankele."

"And I'm telling you they'll get as far as Honolulu. They'll bring their blessings to the whole world, and my former sons—you hear, my ex-sons—are going to march in the front rank."

"Your favorite son is living happily in Vienna and waiting for the war to end. He has a pretty wife, slippers on his feet, and a doctor's diploma in his pocket."

"But what is he doing, the schlemiel? He has to come to Warsaw to bring us communism. May lightning strike him out of a blue sky."

"Don't blaspheme! He's going to arrive in ten minutes, and you'll soften up like a yellow pear."

The patriarch wanted to go on bellyaching, but they were already rumbling up to the station. The coachman stopped and asked maliciously, "Shall I wait, *panie* Kaminski, or will you carry the cigars home yourself?"

Yankel considered attacking the lout, but concluded that he would only be making a fool of himself. Therefore he said nothing, only muttered to himself and took his wife to the hall. The tension was at its height. He ran up to the stationmaster and asked him whether the train from Vienna was on time. He was told that this information would cost three and a half zloty. Yankel paid him twenty and heard what his own eyes could have told him. The express train from Vienna was just coming in, and among the few dozen travelers who got off there was no Hershele Kaminski.

It is hard to guess what went on inside the old mule at that moment. All that is certain is that he rushed to the kiosk, bought a box of cigars, and returned to the droshky with Rahel. It is said that at that moment two tears shone in his eyes, that he gave the coachman a resounding slap in the face, and then said calmly, "Now you take me, my cigars, and this well-born lady home, *rozumiesz*, understand? And if you add your two cents' worth again, I'll kill you."

The Spanish influenza epidemic was abating. It had claimed more than twenty thousand lives and gained the pharmacists fabulous profits, though there was no remedy for that treacherous, still incurable disease. Normal life had returned. The Zurich pharmacists had to content themselves with normal profits again, but in the Rennweg-apotheke the exceptional situation continued. Every day the store was packed with people who were not always ailing, but were eager to gape at the dark-eyed naiad from up close. Malva displayed a surprising competence. She was courteous, nimble, and exemplary in every way. Messieurs Obermüller had acquired a hit, a drawing card that stimulated even more business than the infectious disease. Of course, they endeavored not to let the attractive pharmacist notice how profitable she was, but Malva caught on to the situation. She didn't attempt to exploit her success— she was too decent for that—but she displayed a nonchalance that her male colleagues could hardly afford.

One November morning she overheard a conversation between Scarface and the well-known Professor Rottmeister that enhanced her self-confidence. The professor was fascinated as he looked at Malva and purposely said in such a loud voice that everyone could hear, "Well, all sorts of things are going on here."

The pharmacist winked at the prominent customer and answered modestly, "Our pharmacy is doing pretty well, thank God, and it always has."

The professor was bent on flattering Malva, and responded, "I've been frequenting this store for over ten years, but I've never seen such crowds."

Scarface was afraid that his new employee might be eavesdropping, so he minimized the situation by sighing, "Oh, this grippe! You work and you toil, but you're never done!"

The professor knew better and corrected the pharmacist by saying that fortunately the epidemic had already abated. During the past months there had been only a few dozen new cases, and if the pharmacy continued to be so full, then this was of course due to the black-eyed Melusina. "You caught a goldfish there, Mr. Obermüller. You are to be congratulated on that, for it takes courage to hire a woman in this philistine city."

Signetring smiled and said softly, "We thank you kindly for the compliment, Herr Professor."

Up to now the flatterer had spoken loudly, but now he became clamorous and boisterous. "I can tell you in confidence that some of your fellow pharmacists have already become jealous and plan to hire your bird of paradise away from you."

Malva had heard everything, but she went on working as though she had not understood a word. This reassured the Obermüller brothers, but they had been warned and grew cautious. Shortly afterward Malva had to wait on a group of foreign diplomats, with whom she conversed in their mother tongue. While this increased the admiration of the customers, it also made the two proprietors more irritable, and they watched for an opportunity to take their brilliant employee down a peg. The opportunity came shortly before noon, when a foreigner entered and, unobserved by anyone, looked around in the store. He admired the ancient mortars that adorned the glass case behind the cash register and watched the goings-on with evident amusement. Malva was just trying to decipher an illegible prescription. The two proprietors came up and offered their help, but neither was able to demonstrate his acumen. Malva became nervous and looked around for help. The stranger cleared his throat and said, "Let me take a look at this prescription! I can decipher anything—if necessary, even Egyptian hieroglyphics."

That was an earthquake. A feverish fantasy. Now it had gripped Malva too—the Spanish flu with its typical manifestations, its mirages, illusions, hallucinations. She held onto the desk and thought she was fainting. In the corner of the pharmacy she glimpsed Henry, whom she knew to be in Warsaw and who had not sent her word in weeks. He was there, and she was seeing him here. That conflicted with the basic law of logic: An object cannot be in two different places at the same time. Anything that conflicts with logic is an illusion, and illusions are products of mental confusion. That was the proof: Malva was sick, the last victim of the epidemic. She stared horrified at the man who had offered to decipher the prescription. He smiled, and when she asked him who he was, he replied, "Never fear, madam! A cloud in pants."

She didn't believe her ears. That could only be he, for he had described himself thus when he had first come into her life. But that certainly was no proof. Perhaps she was hearing voices, like Joan of Arc. After all, there were acoustic delusions too. She had to make sure, so she went up to him, touched his neck, his face, and his hand and asked him for the second time, "Who are you? Do we know each other?"

To which the delusion responded, "My name is Kaminski. As far as I know, you are my wife. I love you."

Even this was no proof, but now Malva did not care a whit about the laws of logic. At worst, these were febrile visions or some other kind of parapsychological phenomenon—which seemed utterly unimportant to her at the moment. She didn't care about the customers either, and she rushed into the arms of the ghost. She sobbed, laughed, and whispered nonsense: "You are my beloved phantom, you false pretense. I know I'm only dreaming, but it's so wonderful. However did you fly here? On what cloud? On what whirlwind?"

Henry affectionately stroked her hair and said, "With Mr. Marconi's wireless telegraphy. I simply had myself transmitted. Through the air, like a telegram . . ."

Malva wasn't surprised at her phantom's nuttiness, and asked in a tearful voice, "How are the thirty million Poles?"

Henry preferred to skirt this issue, so he held Malva tight, kissed her on the mouth, and whispered, "I brought you kisses. Thirty million of them. One for each Pole."

"And the revolution?"

"I can't breathe without you, Malva. You are so beautiful."

Now the two embraced as if they were the only people on earth, and Signetring thought it time to intervene. "We're not at a carnival, Mrs. Kaminski. This is Switzerland."

Malva was much too happy to pay even the slightest attention to her boss. She asked Henry, "Now you are going to stay with . . . with us, aren't you?"

Henry glanced at her stomach and whispered in her ear, "How much longer?"

Malva was afraid of being found out. Up to now she had kept her pregnancy a secret. She hoped to be able to keep her job and earn money for as long as possible. Thus she did not reply but stealthily raised four fingers. Henry kissed her on both eyes, then asked suddenly, "Is kissing prohibited here?"

The pharmacist felt addressed, and replied angrily,

"What is forbidden and allowed here is decided by the Obermüller brothers. Who are you?"

Henry bowed, put his card on the desk, and answered, "Dr. Kaminski. I am your employee's spouse, and have official permission to kiss this lady whenever and wherever I feel like it."

On November 11, 1918, the First World War ended for mankind, and the illusion of his life for Uncle Henner. What happened on that day had all the earmarks of a cruel practical joke. My grandfather's brother experienced such a grotesque fiasco that his breakdown almost could not be taken seriously.

As he did every morning, Henner accompanied his son Nathan to the West Station, where the latter was to treat people to Schubert's *Ave Maria*. When, however, the news vendors appeared and hawked the news that peace had broken out, Henner ordered his son to play Beethoven's *Ode to Joy*. To be sure, Nathan was already over thirty and had long ago ceased to be a child prodigy, but his playing had now attained a mellowness that went straight to the heart of all his listeners. The idea of playing the *Ode to Joy* was a commercial stroke of genius and brought unprecedented success. Since it was unusually cold on that November morning, Henner was wearing one of his brother's enormous felt hats. In this hat he collected the alms that were given by the blissful throng. The receipts surpassed his wildest expectations. By noon they had over a thousand crowns, more than all the receipts of the many preceding years, and a fortune in the real sense of the word. With this kind of money one could buy a house or take a trip around the world if one felt like it. The impoverished uncle wanted to do neither. He was not of this world. He didn't know a thing about politics. He had a vague idea that there was a connection between the end of the war, the jubilant crowd, the *Ode to Joy*, and the unheard-of receipts, but he didn't understand what that connection was. For the first time in his life he bought a newspaper, for he wanted to know what the map would look like henceforth. Since up to then he had heard reports only of victory, he was under the illusion that Austria had won the war, the enemy had been smashed on all fronts, and the emperor was once again ruler over the entire earth. Henner's son was even more innocent than his father. He looked gloomily at the whooping crowd and did not understand why people were suddenly so happy.

In any case, the two denizens of a dream world decided to treat themelves to a ride home to Floridsdorf. They put their fortune in Nathan's violin case, boarded a train of the elevated railway, the Stadtbahn, and took two window seats. They enjoyed being rich, and the *meshugge* uncle glanced at the *Kronenzeitung,* which he had bought for all of five kreuzer. To his indescribable astonishment he read on the very first page that the Austro-Hungarian double eagle lay on the ground, that the emperor had abdicated, and that the world would never be the same. The war was lost, the monarchy was smashed, and Europe was a madhouse. Outside the raving rabble was dancing in the streets. Prepared for the worst, Henner read on and saw that this newspaper was full of bad tidings. He was just about to throw it away when his eye was caught by the Science and Technology section. He hoped to find some encouraging news here at least, but instead had to raise his eyebrows. His pupils widened, he turned white as chalk, and suddenly he uttered a cry, a terrible moan of animal despair. Then he collapsed and fell to the floor dead.

Two hours later, when the grandmother, Jana, and the two cousins Helli and Steffi were having lunch, the doorbell rang. Two men carried a stretcher into the living room. On it lay poor uncle Henner, and next to him stood his weeping son Nathan.

My dear mourners, esteemed son of the deceased. You are the smallest community of mourners that I have ever

had to address, but surely not the lowliest. Five of God's
children, so the Talmud says, are mankind, and five tears
from a pure heart are the ocean. The important thing
is not the number, but the grief. Henner Rosenbach was
a Steppenwolf, a lonely dreamer, a flickering will-o'-the-
wisp in the marsh of our time. He trekked through the
desert with one traveling companion, his taciturn but divinely gifted son Nathan, who accompanied him to his
last stop. Now we are mourning him and asking ourselves
who this man was. He called himself an inventor, and
he was one—in the original sense of the word "invent":
to come upon, to find. He wanted to find, but he did
not find; he sought. He was a lifelong seeker, a true son
of the people of Israel. Hardly ever in his seventy years
did he go to the synagogue. He was ashamed of his descent, which burdened him like a hereditary illness. He
even had himself baptized in hopes of finding at last what
he was seeking, but that too availed nothing. Shortly before his death he came to see me because he yearned to
return to his God. I did my duty. I attempted to get him
to change his mind and keep him from taking a step that
brings nothing but torment and recurrent afflictions. But
he would not be deterred. He insisted on becoming a
Jew, and I had a hard time explaining to him that one
cannot become a Jew if one already is one. He who comes
into the world as a God-seeker returns to eternity as a
God-seeker . . . And a further question suggests itself:
What was he searching for, that unfortunate man? He
said he was searching for the magic formula that would
enable him to imitate the palette of the Creator—color
photography. A dubious search indeed. The desire to
imitate the forms of the Almighty is already presumptuous, but to imitate the colors, the innermost secret of
the objects, the real soul of the world—that is a sin. More
than that. That is *the* sin. A typically Jewish arrogance
that ignores the Commandments and shamelessly eats
of the tree of knowledge. Yes, my five survivors. We are
a small but presumptuous people of sinners, curious,
thirsty for knowledge, and bent on getting to the bottom
of everything. We try to fathom the unfathomable. We

295

unriddle the last riddles of God, but what does the Infinite One do? He forgives us. He even makes us His Chosen People, for in us are combined all faults of the human race, and that is why we are more than just Jews. We are simply human beings. He has chosen us for our arrogance, our immoderation and our misdeeds, for He loves us for seeking Him. Henner Rosenbach was such a primally sinful, mortally sinful Jew who sought God by striving to become like God. This was his undoing. This is what burned his heart. He wanted to be the first to reveal God's secret, and two days ago, on the first day of peace, he had to find out that someone had beaten him to it. Henner Rosenbach sat in the Stadtbahn and read in the paper that a Frenchman, a Catholic named Lumière, had invented color photography long ago. A Frenchman and a Christian who, on top of it, was named Lumière, which means light. Who but someone by the name of Lumière should have unraveled the mysteries of light? Henner Rosenbach died of envy, of base jealousy, and we shall ask ourselves a third question: Will the Lord forgive him? Yes, He will, dear mourners. He will forgive him, for despite all his sins he was seeking God and not the devil . . .

On the way home from the Jewish cemetery Jana took Nathan, a broken man, aside and asked him what he was planning to do now.

Nathan was unable to utter a word, for he was sobbing. He had been swimming in tears since Henner had been gathered to his fathers. Jana put a consoling arm around his neck and said gently, "Thank God you've got your fiddle. Nothing can happen to you."

Nathan sighed and whispered, "I haven't got it."

Jana became suspicious and asked excitedly, "Where is it, for God's sake?"

"I lost it—no, left it. Including the case, and in it was more than a thousand crowns."

"How could that have happened, you poor child?"

"In the Stadtbahn. When my father died. That's when I died too, and I don't care about anything."

Jana touched her temples. Everything went black and she felt dizzy. Clinging to Nathan, she screamed, "But *you* are living, child. You must have something to live on. What are you going to do without your father?"

Nathan dried his tears with a large handkerchief and said, "Schreckmann has made me see the light. I shall return to my brethren. I am going to beg my way to the Holy Land."

After all we have heard thus far, it will astonish no one that Malva and Henry's baby came into the world in pain. These pains were so great that the obstetrician on duty—who, significantly, was named König—decided on a cesarean section. Thus it was an imperial-royal birth, a truly awe-inspiring event that took three days and three nights in all. It is also characteristic that the last act of the drama was staged under anesthesia, since in the two dynasties concerned, the Rosenbachs and the Kaminskis, scarcely any of the actors in any event were ever completely conscious.

At the special request of the mother, Henry was called in as an assistant, which was a first in the Zurich women's hospital. The sober-minded Swiss knew from experience what a tough time young fathers have surviving the birth of their first child. In this particular case, this preconceived notion turned out to be correct. When the operation was at its climax and the umbilical cord was cut off a healthy boy, Henry dropped the basket with the instruments and fell in a faint. It was the will of Jehovah, however, that father and child should survive the convulsive day. It was the fifteenth of January. Powdery snow covered the streets, and the sun glittered on the roofs. On that day Rosa Luxemburg and Karl Liebknecht were murdered in Germany. In the hall of mirrors at Versailles Castle the notorious peace treaty was being negotiated. Lord Rutherford transformed a nitrogen atom into an oxygen atom with the aid of radioactive radiation. Adolf Hitler registered as the fifth member of the Nazi party, and the horoscope for January 15 read: "Boys born on this day will become mountebanks, tramps, jesters, or magicians. They will fib their way through life as permanent victims of their own telling of tall tales, but at the end of their road they will find the truth."

One hour after giving birth Malva came out of her anesthesia. Her first question was not about the child but about the father: "How is my husband doing?"

Dr. König stood beside her bed smiling broadly. "All concerned are healthy. Even the father is still alive."

"And the girl?"

"Is a boy and has the record weight of eight pounds."

Malva felt so light that she seemed to be sailing through the air. At the same time she was unspeakably tired. Her limbs seemed leaden and she had a hard time collecting her thoughts. Finally she managed to say, "I thought I was dying."

"No wonder. The little rascal simply wouldn't come out. He liked it in your belly. We literally had to chisel him out."

Chisel out. These words made Malva weak and she asked with tears in her eyes, "Did something go wrong?"

The doctor had some fun keeping the pretty puerpera on tenterhooks and answered casually, "Nothing bad, my good woman. He has what is called a birth defect."

"You are keeping something from me, doctor. I want to know it. Without beating about the bush!"

The obstetrician pulled a violet hunk of life from the adjoining little pad. He lifted it up by its little head and showed it to Malva. "This fellow was born circumcised. From a scientific point of view, that's abnormal."

The relieved Malva smiled blissfully and said, "That doesn't matter to me, doctor . . ."

Dr. König put the little man back in his cradle and pontificated, "I've taken all sorts of strange things out of women, but this is a phenomenon. A total deviation from the norm."

Malva had been prepared for something terrible, but now she felt like shouting with joy. "You're trying to pull my leg, but it won't work. I couldn't be happier . . ."

The whimsical gynecologist continued being playful, however, and lectured her pedantically. "A thing like that happens in one case out of three million. Switzerland has a population of about four million. Half of these are women, who can't possibly be born circumcised, even if they'd like to be. That proves that this boy is a rarity. He belongs in a museum."

Once more the young mother became suspicious, and she asked uncertainly, "Tell me the truth! Can this have any bad aftereffects?

"What?"

"This birth defect."

Dr. König walked to the door, turned around once more, and replied jovially, "The scientific literature is silent on this subject, but I assume that with this malformation the boy is going to become a rabbi."

Malva worriedly closed her eyes and moaned, "Then it would be better for him to be in a museum!" But suddenly she awoke from her nightmare and cried, "Where's my husband?"

Dr. König cheerfully reassured her. "I gave him a coffeepot full of schnapps. This did the trick and roused him."

"And?"

"And then he went to the post office. To send a telegram."

27

"**P**ANIE KAMINSKI, A *SENSAZIE.*"

"What's going on, *do jasnej cholery?*"

"Miss Anka got a telegram."

"Chaim Lewin, I'm sleeping."

"A telegram from Zurich."

"I warned you, Chaim Lewin."

"From your son Hershele."

"In the first place, I haven't got a son, you *schmuck . . .*"

". . . and in the second place, *panie* Kaminski, he's become the *tata* of a circumcised *yid.*"

"Some feat!"

"Not a feat, *panie* Kaminski, but a record. The child weighs four kilos or eight pounds . . ."

Yankel could no longer conceal his excitement. He jumped up, put on his robe, and began to cry, "A circumcised *yid.* So how can he be circumcised? A *mentsh* is born a *mentsh,* and later he is circumcised so he can become a *yid.* But to be circumcised from the beginning is impossible. Did you hear that, Rahel? Your husband has become a grandfather. Seventy-two years old, and still able to have a grandson . . ."

Yankel's spouse was a famous actress. She had known for hours what had happened, but she pretended to be ignorant. "You've got a grandson, Yankele? At your age? That really is a sensation. Your favorite son, one of the sons you don't have, has become a father and you a grandfather. Now you ought to make up, it seems to me. It would be high time, wouldn't it?"

"Me, make up? I won't make up with him even if I drop dead!"

"But what?"

"It's *him* who's become a father. Let *him* make up if he wants to, but not me. Why me, *do jasnej cholery?*"

"One of you has to be the wiser one, Yankele. By the way, what's the child's name going to be?"

"How should I know what his name is going to be? Anka got the telegram, not me. Lewin read it, not me. Old Kaminski isn't told a word, because he's a piece of goat shit in his own house. Chaim Lewin, tell me my grandson's name or I'll throw you out the window!"

The chief clerk quivered like jelly and whispered, "The child's name is . . . I don't dare, *panie* Kaminski."

"What don't you dare, you *putz?* Tell me every word that's in the telegram."

"The telegram says that . . ."

"What?"

"That in honor of the proletarian revolution . . . I can't go on."

"You can, *do jasnej cholery!*"

"That in honor of the proletarian revolution the child will be named . . ."

"Chaim Lewin, go on!"

"Vladimir Ilyich, like the leader of the international communist movement."

Yankel gasped for air and shrieked, 'I'll stop that!"

The famous actress sensed that something outrageous was about to happen and asked soothingly, "What are you going to stop, Yankele?"

"That my son ruins me a second time, this *hultay*, this no-goodnik. He wants to chop up my business. My grandson is supposed to be named after that *gonif?* Vladimir Ilyich, like that red *barabantshtshik*, that drummer who's turning the world upside down? Oy, Hershele, Hershele. I'm going to rip off your balls, you *kolbeynik*, you rascally know-it-all, you *trayf* pig, you . . ."

"Yankele, my dear husband, are you *meshugge?*"

"Sure, Rahel, I'm *meshugge!*"

Yankel rushed to the wardrobe, flung the doors open, took out his winter coat, his fur hat, and the sacred checkbook without which he couldn't breathe, and roared, "I'll be back in a month or sooner. My grandson can have any name he pleases, even Jesus Christ if need be, but not Vladimir Ilyich. If necessary, I'll . . ."

"*Panie* Kaminski!"

"You got nothing to say, Chaim Lewin. You'll take my place while I'm gone, and make a profit, or else . . ."

In Jewish homes the circumcision takes place eight days after a birth; its purpose is to distinguish the sons of Israel from the philistines and the godless generally. The removal of his foreskin reminds the new member of the human race of his covenant with Jehovah. He should always feel on his most sensitive spot that he is different and has been chosen to stand Jehovah's tests steadfastly. Since, however, Malva and Henry's son was born circumcised, for technical reasons the circumcision could not take place, and this created a somewhat dubious situation. It might mean either that the new arrival was not fit to join the covenant with the Almighty, or that providence had decided to send him out into the world *ab initio* with God's hallmark. Thus the boy was destined to remain a heathen because he had to forego the ritual of circumcision—or, conversely, to become a Messiah, an anointed of the Lord, since he had, as it were, already been given his chosenness. It was with this ambiguity that the boy began his life. It was to become his destiny.

In general, the circumcision also involves the naming, and as we know, the latter has a particularly magical function. With the name the parents express their expectations, their secret desires, and their educational plans. Someone who names his daughter Eva wishes her to become an archetypal woman, a temptress, and a queen of love. Someone who names his son Benjamin, which means "son of

the right hand" or, in a figurative sense, "fortune's favorite," wishes him success with women and good luck in
games, business, and duels as well as victory over all his
adversaries. Henry and Malva chose the name Vladimir,
which means "ruler of the world," and in their modesty
they thought of Vladimir Ilyich Lenin, who had in the
course of a single revolutionary night become the sole ruler
of Russia, the dictator over one-sixth of the earth, and the
caesar between the Baltic Sea and the Sea of Japan.

Since, as we have indicated, a circumcision was out of
the question, it was decided to have only a modest naming
ceremony. Of course there was neither space nor money
enough for a proper celebration, but the couple made a
virtue of necessity and held the event in their attic apartment in the old part of Zurich. The invitation said that in
honor of the proletarian son and heir, a solemn naming
ceremony would take place over bread and wine, and that
it was planned to call the new human being Vladimir Ilyich.
About thirty people were expected to participate: the five
sisters from Warsaw and the ten brothers from New York,
Malva's grandmother, Jana and the cousins from Vienna,
as well as some unwashed intellectuals from all points of
the compass who indicated with their stubbly beards and
wire-rimmed glasses that they belonged to the same sect
as their host.

Only one person had not been invited: the patriarch.
When the food was brought out and the glasses were raised
to drink a toast to the child's health, those absent were remembered, but Yankel was not mentioned. Finally Henry
opened the ceremony with a short speech, but even he did
not remember the progenitor. "My dear *compagnons de route*
and comrades in arms. You have come from afar to admit
a new soldier to the ranks of the revolution. He will have
an easier time of it than we did, but also a harder one.
Easier because our red flags are today waving over one-
sixth of the globe and because we no longer are the ones
who are always beaten and defeated. Because our Russian

comrades have shown us how even the mightiest enemies can be brought to their knees. However, he will also have a harder time of it than we did, because abstract dreams have been replaced by concrete everyday problems. To us communism has always been only the beautiful end of an ugly journey. For him it will be the ugly beginning of a torturous road that will lead to a happy end. For this thorny path we must fortify him. For the long road through the darkness he will need a lamp to light his way, and this lamp is called Lenin. Our child shall bear his name, for he will be loved for this name by human beings and despised by barbarians. His name, then, shall be Vladimir Ilyich Kaminski!"

Following hearty applause, Henry's oldest brother, Ber, took the floor. He had become the editor of a socialist daily, the *New York Daily Worker*, and his speech had considerably less pathos than that of the preceding speaker. "I address myself especially to you, Hershele, for seven years have gone by since we said good-bye in New York harbor. Since then we have lost sight of each other and grown apart, or at least so it seems to me. We no longer are the men we used to be. The world has changed beyond recognition. Only you, my extravagant brother, are almost the same, which I deeply regret. You rejoice that the red flag is waving over one-sixth of the globe. We too rejoice at this, but we know that the banner of power, even if it is the banner of communism, can no longer be red. Our high-flying ideas have become constitutional ideas from the Gulf of Finland to the Chinese border. You ought to know that constitutional ideas are narrow and unimaginative. You want to turn your son into a soldier of the revolution, Hershele. Which revolution do you mean? The revolution of the people, of the working class, or of the party leaders? You see, these have become different things. The people want to continue the revolution, but the leaders want to throttle it, for now *they* have what they wanted. They have the power. To them revolution is something past, which belongs in a museum . . ."

The brother's words spread unease through the room, although no one knew what Ber was actually driving at. Henry was determined to make a row, correct these statements, and protest, but Ber was the oldest brother and no one dared to contradict him, and so he continued with his speech. "This little human being is to bear the name of Lenin. Fine, for after all, Lenin turned the old world upside down. Lenin led the proletarians of every country into the battle for a new life. He is the personification of liberation from all kinds of chains. Okay. That is indisputable, and so is the idea of honoring Lenin's name. But Hershele! Did you ask this baby whether he feels like bearing Lenin's name? That would really be advisable, for the name of Lenin is a mark of Cain, and you know very well that anyone who is so named no longer has a choice. Whether he wants to or not, he has to become a communist. A rebel. An outsider. More than that. An outcast, someone who is always hunted, ostracized, and outlawed. If that's what he wants, fine. That's his business. But what if he doesn't want it? Since when has good fortune been forced down people's throats? Look out the window of your apartment! You see the round cupola of the university and the pointed tower of a church. You have the choice between reason and faith, science and mysticism. You can decide freely between two worlds, and that is your good fortune. That is the opportunity offered you by Switzerland. But your son is not to have this chance. He must follow the path you force upon him. Is the fruit of the great upheaval that laborers are turned into forced laborers and children into forced recruits of the revolution? Surely that cannot be your intention, for . . ."

"Your time is up." With these words Henry interrupted his brother and began to lecture himself. "No one chooses his own name. There is and has never been such a thing. Your name is Ber, because that's what your *meshugge* father wanted. I'm called Hersh, because that was my *meshugge* father's will, and my son will be named Vladimir Ilyich. No one will change that . . ."

While the host was puffing himself up, the door opened. A little man entered with a fur hat on his head, a winter coat over his body, and galoshes over his shoes. He went right up to the cradle and looked fascinatedly at the little mite that was the object of the celebration and the heated exchange of words. After a while the old man bent over to Malva and whispered in her ear, "Who does this little person belong to?"

Malva suspected who the intruder was and whispered back, "And who are *you?*"

"I asked you who this little person belongs to."

"He belongs to me. Why?"

"Because I'm his grandfather and want to know what his name is."

One could have heard a pin drop. All eyes were on the intruder. They sensed that a storm was brewing, a threefold scandal, because the little man was none other than the cruel father, the brute who had delivered his eleven sons to the hangman, or at least had refused to ruin his business for their sake. Yankel Kaminski had the *chutzpa* to step into the lion's den and stick his nose into matters that were none of his business. For this he had chosen the most unpropitious moment imaginable. His oldest son, Ber, and his favorite son, Hershele, had come to blows, and about the most delicate subject of the twentieth century, the Russian revolution. He was the last person in the world who should have been aware that his sons were arguing about this. The attic apartment on Trittligasse resembled a powder keg. Irritation and hatred crackled through the rooms: the overbearing old man versus his uncompromising sons, the ten rationalists from New York against the true believer of Zurich, and the more conciliatory women against the self-righteous men.

All it would have taken to blow up the family celebration was one spark, but at that point a miracle occurred. One of the unwashed friends picked up the guitar that he had fortunately brought along. He struck a chord and started to sing an old folk song:

> And when the rabbi laughs,
> And when the rabbi laughs,
> All the little Hasidim laugh.

Whereupon everybody joined in the refrain:

> Ha ha, ha ha, ha haaa,
> Ha ha, ha ha, ha haaa,
> All the little Hasidim laugh.

It was obvious that Yankel Kaminski regarded himself as the rabbi of the illustrious company, and he intoned the second stanza of the song, lifting Malva from her chair and exuberantly swinging her around:

> And when the rabbi dances,
> And when the rabbi dances,
> All the little Hasidim dance,
> All the little Hasidim dance.

At one stroke humor and good spirits had returned to the attic apartment, and now the chorus of the thirty guests sang lustily:

> Hop hop, hop hop, hop hop,
> Hop hop, hop hop, hop hop,
> All the little Hasidim dance.

The guests danced too, even the toothless grandmother from Vienna, who was having fun again for the first time in many years. They sang, clapped their hands, and whirled round and round until the song was finished. An embarrassed silence fell, broken by the question that most agitated Yankel: "I'd like to know what his name's going to be."

To this Malva responded, winking at the old man, "And *I'd* like to know who you are. You come into my apartment. You don't take your hat off. You dance with me as if you were my bridegroom, but you never introduced yourself."

"I'm your father-in-law, you nightingale. But the reason

I came is to find out what my grandson's name is going to be."

Now Henry replied in a vague voice from which one could not tell whether there was still war or already a truce, "Your grandson's name will be Vladimir Ilyich Kaminski."

"I'm talking to a lady, not to you."

Malva gave Henry a propitiatory smile and said gently, "My son will be called whatever his father wants."

"And what does his mother want? Does she have nothing to say in this house?"

Malva understood the provocation and headed it off. "I want him to stay healthy and be popular with people . . ."

"With such a name?" said Yankel heatedly. "People are going to lock their houses when he comes."

Henry saw that it was time to act if he did not want to lose face. He went up to Yankel, grabbed him by the neck, and screamed, "*We* decide what our son's name is going to be, and not some capitalist from Warsaw!"

"The heir to a million-zloty business, my grandson, isn't going to be named Vladimir Ilyich! You'll never understand this, but thank God your wife is a more pleasant person than you . . ." With these words he pulled out his checkbook, opened it, and scribbled something. Handing a check to Malva, he said, "As a starting capital for the education of my grandson. Thirty thousand ought to be enough."

Malva blanched. She had never seen that much money, and looked uncertainly first at Henry and then at Yankel. "I don't understand . . ."

"For your son and my grandson Andrzej Kaminski."

Malva handed the check to her husband, who tore it up with a theatrical gesture visible to all present, and roared, "I don't know any Andrzej Kaminski, and I certainly won't let myself be bought. Take your lousy thirty thousand and leave us in peace!"

Yankel regretfully shrugged his shoulders. He pulled out his checkbook again and said: "I understand. Thirty thousand isn't enough. All right." Scribbling in his checkbook again, he continued, "Fifty thousand will certainly be enough for my grandson named Andrzej. This is my final offer!"

Henry was about to hustle the old mule out of the room, but Malva took him by the hand, stroked his shoulders, and whispered to him, "Henry, my dearest, are you going to sin against your own father? For a few miserable Swiss francs? On account of a name that's only a name? Heart is what matters, not a title!"

Henry looked around like someone waking from a fourteen-year dream. His brothers smiled at him as though they wanted to encourage him to do the natural thing, and so did his sisters. He walked up to the old man, put his arms around the *meshugge* patriarch, kissed him on both cheeks, and said in a tearful voice, "You miserable scum, you usurer. For the hundredth time you are committing an outrage against me. You will go under with your whole goddamn class, your drafts and your checks and your banknotes . . ."

"And?" smiled Yankel.

"Nothing. I love you."

28

THIS, PERSEVERING READER, IS THE END OF MY STORY, AND you will ask me if it is all true. I find it hard to give you a conclusive answer; after all, I wasn't there. It all happened before I was born. What I know, I know from hearsay. For years I searched for the components of my genetic makeup. Since I have a boundless curiosity, I wanted to find out what kind of people contributed to the palette of my chromosomes. I asked the survivors—uncles, aunts, close and distant relatives of my clan, which is scattered all over the world—how the union between the Rosenbach and Kaminski families came about. It turned out that the average age of my informants was about ninety-one, and their memory was as reliable as one might expect. Besides, those I interviewed displayed a vanity that all but stunned me. They missed no opportunity to build up their own roles in the family chronicle and did their best to obliterate the parts of their antagonists; therefore, almost all the statements in this book should be treated with reservation. I would regret it if serious-minded contemporaries relied on my story in any way. I do not accept any sort of responsibility for historical dates, localities, and biographical details. After all, on the very first page of this book I quoted the inscription on the tombstone of the long-departed Rabbi Shloime Rosenbach from Czernowitz. Remember? "Truth is the most precious of all possessions, and should be used sparingly and with restraint." As I indicated, his descendants—and I am one of them—have striven to live faithfully by this maxim. We speak and write the truth only when we have no other choice. Therefore, treat my chronicle as a figment of the imagination and a crazy tissue of lies, and if you should nevertheless discover a scintilla of truth here or there, this is purely accidental. I beg you not to use it as a noose to put around my neck. With this I shall close, and wish you what Jews customarily wish each other when they part: Next year in Jerusalem!